"A touch of danger and suspense make the latest in Carr's Thunder Point series a powerful read."
—_RT Book Reviews_ on _The Hero_

"With her trademark mixture of humor, realistic conflict, and razor-sharp insights, Carr brings Thunder Point to vivid life."
—_Library Journal_ on _The Newcomer_

"No one can do small-town life like Carr."
—_RT Book Reviews_ on _The Wanderer_

"A delightfully funny novel."
—_Midwest Book Reviews_ on _The Wedding Party_

"Well-rounded characters, a plot rich in emotion and humor and one sweet romance make this a great read."
—_RT Book Reviews_ on _A Summer in Sonoma_

"An intensely satisfying read. By turns humorous and gut-wrenchingly emotional, it won't soon be forgotten."
—_RT Book Reviews_ on _Paradise Valley_

"Carr has hit her stride with this captivating series."
—_Library Journal_ on the Virgin River series

ROBYN CARR

four friends

ISBN-13: 978-0-7783-1854-5

Four Friends

Copyright © 2014 by Robyn Carr

Recycling programs
for this product may
not exist in your area.

For questions and comments about the quality of this book, please contact us at CustomerService@Harlequin.com.

www.MIRABooks.com

Printed in U.S.A.

To Dianne Moggy, my dear friend,
who always believed in me.

four friends

one

Gerri Gilbert answered the door in gray sweats with a tear in the knee, hem on one leg falling down and a gray T-shirt under her black hoodie. Her short, dark brown hair was spiking every which way from bed head. She held a cup of coffee in her hand; her eyes were slits and there was a snarl on her face. "You're five minutes early. Again. We've been over this. Can you please not be early? I value every minute in the morning."

Sonja Johanson put a finger to her lips, shushing Gerri. The sun was barely over the rooftops and she didn't want to wake the house. Sonja wore her salmon sweats, white T-shirt and salmon hoodie, her silky, shoulder-length mahogany hair pulled back in a neat clip.

She backed away from the door and pointed down the street. Gerri stepped outside for a better view. A big pile of clothing, books and what appeared to be miscellaneous junk was on the Jamisons' lawn. Right at that moment their friend Andy appeared in the doorway of her house and with an angry cry hurled the tower to a desktop computer atop the pile.

Andy disappeared into the house and Bryce Jamison backed out of the door wearing business attire that was not fresh, his shirtsleeves rolled up, his collar open, his tie hanging out of his pants pocket and he sported an even worse case of bed head than Gerri. He held a packed duffel bag. "You're fucking *crazy,* you know that?" he yelled into the house. He turned and stomped past the pile toward his car in the driveway.

"And you're fucking *through* here!" Andy screamed out the open door. Then she slammed it.

"I think Andy might be coming to the end of her rope," Sonja said gravely.

Gerri's response was a short burst of laughter. "Ya think?" she asked.

"Should we do something?" Sonja asked.

"Oh, hell no," Gerri said, pulling her front door closed. She put her coffee cup on the brick planter that bordered dead flowers and bent to stretch. "It's for them to work out. Or finish off."

"Should we ask her if she's walking?"

"She's not walking today," Gerri said. "Let's get this over with." Gerri started off down the street at a brisk pace.

Just steps behind her Sonja asked, "What do we say?"

"Say nothing. Do nothing."

"But…"

Gerri looked over her shoulder. "Nothing," she repeated.

Sonja came up beside her. "We should see if she's all right."

"We should give her time to finish throwing things,

if that's what she's doing. I'll check in with her before I leave for work."

Sonja tsked. "I tried to talk to her about the relationship quadrant of her house—it's all torn up and the feng shui is a disaster. She's all out of balance. Now look."

Gerri stopped in her tracks. She looked at Sonja. "That's exactly why you'd better stay away from there today. You know how she feels about all your woo-woo stuff. If you pull any of your feng shui, chakra or karma bullshit today, you're going to end up on top of that pile."

"But something could have been done about that!"

"For God's sake," Gerri said impatiently, walking again. "It was destiny."

Ahead of them, about half a block away, a small, lean woman came out of her house, also wearing sweats. She stopped to stretch on her front walk. She was still stretching as they passed and Gerri called, "Morning, BJ." But Sonja added, "Wanna walk with us today, BJ?"

"Thanks, but I need the run," she answered, waving them off.

When they had cleared the house Sonja said, "She's making an awful lot of bad karma, the way she acts."

"She wants to run," Gerri said. "Quit asking her. I'd run if my knees wouldn't collapse."

"But it's unfriendly," Sonja said.

"Some women don't want girlfriends," Gerri pointed out. "I think she's been clear, and not unfriendly. Just private."

"Don't you think that's pretty suspicious?"

"No, I think it's private. Are you going to talk the whole time? Because if you are, I might risk permanent paralysis and just run with BJ."

"Little grouchy this morning? I bet you had liquor instead of chamomile before bed last night."

"Shut up, Sonja," Gerri said.

The 6:00 a.m. power walking had been going on for almost two years; Sonja had initiated it. She was the health guru, the motivator, often the pain in Gerri's butt. It was Sonja's profession. She was a feng shui consultant and home organizer who did personal color charts and something she referred to as life reading, which was like a mini study of your past, present and goals with the objective of total balance and personal success. Additionally she was a vegetarian, novice herbalist, part-time yoga and meditation instructor and impossible perfectionist. Gerri had an entire shelf dedicated to books given to her by Sonja on everything from studying your body's pH to gliding through menopause on herbs—books stubbornly left unread.

Gerri and Andy had been neighbors and good friends for fifteen years, since before Andy threw out her first husband. They were both now in their late forties while Sonja had just scored the big four-oh. When Sonja arrived in the neighborhood a few years ago, Gerri and Andy welcomed her and immediately grew bored with her naturalist and metaphysical leanings. However— and it was a big however—when someone was sick or hurt or in trouble, it was always Sonja who came forth with anything from a massage to a casserole to transportation to, well, whatever was needed. When Gerri had been brought to her knees by a killer hemorrhoidectomy Sonja was there, drawing the sitz bath, making broth, administering pain meds and, of course, she was armed with the perfect, natural, gentle laxative.

Gerri had learned you just don't give the right laxative enough credit until you find yourself in that position.

Still, she could be tiresome as hell.

After three miles in just under forty-five minutes, Gerri sweating like a boxer and Sonja glistening attractively, they separated. Gerri entered her house noisily. "Everyone up?" she yelled into the house as she wandered into the kitchen.

Phil was sitting at the table with coffee, newspaper strewn around and his laptop open, going through email and checking the news. "They're up," he said. "More or less."

The Gilbert kids were thirteen, sixteen and nineteen. Boy, girl, boy. "You're supposed to make sure they're up, Phil."

"I did," he said without looking up. "I do every morning."

She trudged up the stairs and started throwing open doors. "Get up! Don't make me late!" Then she backtracked to her shower and wondered why the hell Phil couldn't accomplish one simple task—get the kids out of bed while she was out walking. Despite the fact she was planning to go in late today, it annoyed her. But lately everything annoyed her because she was doing the menopause drill and she was often testy.

She let the water run over her naked body, cool water to lower her body temperature. At the moment all she wanted in life was to feel level. Even. She'd always had a short fuse but lately she was positively electric and could burst into flame anywhere, anytime. She'd been trying on bathing suits one day and when she made her purchase, she'd flared up so bright she thought the clerk would call security to frisk her for stolen goods.

Talking to the mayor at a fund-raiser one night, great balls of perspiration had begun to run down her face. She'd started sleeping naked because of the night sweats and when Phil rolled over, found flesh instead of flannel and began to grope her, she'd mutter, "Don't even think about it."

When she was out of the shower, dry and cool, she had one of those reprieves that came regularly—she felt perfectly normal, sane and in control. Then came the inevitable guilt—she should be fined for ever snapping at Phil. She didn't know of a husband who pulled his weight as well as Phil. She knew of no family in Mill Valley in better balance, and that was as much because of Phil as Gerri. While Andy was throwing her husband's clothes on the lawn, Phil was doing his morning chore, trying to get the kids up. It wasn't his fault they pulled the covers over their heads, as teenagers did.

By the time she was putting the finishing touches on her face and hair, she was wilting again, her makeup melting off her face as fast as she put it on. She flipped on the little fan that was now an accessory in her bathroom.

When she got back to the kitchen, Phil had gone to work. Jed, her nineteen year old was racing for his car to get to class on time while Jessie and Matthew were arguing over whose turn it was to take out the trash. "Just get in the car," she said. "I'll take care of it myself." After dropping them off at their schools, she called her office. Gerri was the supervisor of case workers with Child Protective Services. She said she had a family situation to resolve and would be a little late. Then she drove back to the neighborhood, but parked in Andy's drive.

Andy didn't answer the doorbell, so Gerri knocked and then rattled the knob. "Come on, Andy," she yelled. A few long moments passed before she saw a shadow cross over the peep hole and the door opened slowly. Andy's curling, shoulder-length black hair was clipped up off her neck, a few tendrils escaping, and her face was a combination of ashen and blotchy from crying. Gerri glanced over her shoulder at the pile on the lawn and said, "Have a little tiff?"

Andy turned and walked back into the house, past the living room into a kitchen that was torn apart, under construction. That would be the relationship quadrant of the house. Andy sat in the breakfast nook where there was a cup of coffee. She rested an elbow on the table, her head in her hand and groaned. "Go ahead. Say it. Say I told you so."

"I'm not feeling that mean at the moment," Gerri said. She went into the disastrous kitchen, grabbed a coffee mug from the sink and quickly washed it. The cupboards had all been emptied of their contents and would soon be ripped off the walls, replaced with new. Gerri poured herself some coffee, then joined Andy at the table. "Must've been a good one."

"Same crap," Andy said. "Out all night, comes home smelling like a whore, lots of excuses about some account executive sitting too close to him at a marathon meeting and smelling him up. No phone call. And apparently they serve booze at those meetings…"

"Hmm," Gerri replied, sipping her coffee.

"There's a new twist this time. I spent most of the night hacking into his email account and read all the romantic little notes he's been sharing with some woman known only as Sugarpants."

"Sugarpants?" Gerri repeated, forcing herself not to laugh out loud. "Jesus, that's subtle."

"Erotic emails. Dates being set up. Steamy postmortems on the dates. Do you think if he'd hit me over the head with a naked woman I would have come to my senses sooner?"

"Well, you've suspected…"

"God, why didn't you stop me? I must have been out of my mind!"

Gerri just reached out and gave Andy's upper arm an affectionate stroke. As she recalled, Andy couldn't be stopped.

Andy had been the divorced mother of a fifteen-year-old son when she met Bryce a few years ago. He was younger by ten years, sexy and eager, possessing at least eight of the ten requirements to deliver instant happiness to a forty-four year old woman. He made her feel young, beautiful, desirable. Bryce was good with Noel—they were like a couple of kids together—one of the few men she'd dated who had taken to her son quickly, easily. He had a good job in pharmaceutical sales, though it required considerable travel. She fell in lust with him and for a while there was an orgasmic glow all around her.

Andy was far from straitlaced, but she wouldn't live with Bryce because of Noel, a touchy and vulnerable teenager. Plus, there was the matter of an ex-husband and his wife to contend with—Andy didn't want anyone making an argument for custody under those circumstances. And of course, she was in *love* with him, so she married him.

Bryce quickly emerged as immature, selfish, short-tempered, inconsiderate, in no way prepared to cohabit and, indeed, had no experience in cohabitation. He knew exactly how to treat a woman to get into her pants, how to send her to the moon night after night, but couldn't share the day-to-day workload or be accountable to a partner. He didn't like being questioned about where he'd been nor could he say for certain when he'd be home. The relationship with Noel deteriorated; Bryce became exasperated by the noise, mess and back talk associated with teenage boys. This had the effect of turning Andy, who was by nature a humorous and agreeable woman, into a demanding, suspicious, resentful nag. They were like water on a grease fire. Everything was always about those buttons—you push mine and I'll push yours.

Bliss hadn't lasted even a year for Andy, but she'd hung in there for three. She'd been talking about a separation and divorce for two years now and whenever she'd get close, two things stalled her out. One, Bryce knew how to turn on the charm when he wanted to and he could treat her to short periods of good behavior laced with hot sex. And, two, it just isn't easy to be forty-seven and acknowledge yourself as a woman who had twice failed at marriage.

"You're going to be late for work," Gerri said. "Let's pull it together."

Andy shook her head. "I called in divorced," she said. "I need a day or two. I have to get my bearings, pack up his stuff, call the lawyer, close the joint accounts."

"This is really it, then?"

"I was through a long time ago. There were just times I thought divorcing him might be more painful than living with him." She blinked and a tear rolled down her cheek. "I guess I'm beyond that now."

"You'll be all right," Gerri said gently, earnestly. "You were all right before—you'll be all right again."

"It's so hard," Andy said. "When you don't have anyone."

"Yeah, I know," Gerri agreed. "Yet it's harder when you have the wrong one."

You're not forty-nine and married twenty-four years without having helped a few friends through the big D. Each one had left a mark on Gerri's heart. Even the fairly simple, straightforward ones were gut-wrenching. To promise to love forever and find yourself pulled into that dark world of animosity and vengeance as you tore the promise apart broke the strongest men and women into pieces. And one of the roughest in Gerri's memory was Andy's divorce from her first husband, Rick.

They'd moved into this little bedroom community in Marin County at about the same time fifteen years before. Andy and Gerri had both been the mothers of four-year-old boys who'd become instant friends. Gerri had also had one-year-old Jessie balanced on her hip and a couple of years later there was a hot lusty night when birth control was the last thing she or Phil considered; that night produced Matthew, and a vasectomy for Phil. Andy, however, stopped with Noel, her only child.

Young, energetic working mothers in their early thirties with tight bodies, small happy children, virile husbands, great things looming in their futures, they became good friends immediately. Gerri was working a large slice of Marin County for Child Protective Services as a case worker and Phil, a bright young assistant district attorney, had to commute into San Francisco daily, on occasion staying overnight. Andy was a middle school teacher at the time, married to a teacher and coach from a local high school.

Andy's divorce came when Noel was ten. It was sudden—what seemed a balanced and content marriage went sour overnight. Rick was unhappy and distant, they were in counseling, then separated, the divorce was quickly final and, before anyone could blink, Rick was remarried to someone who'd been in the periphery of his life all along—the school nurse at his high school. Clearly he'd chosen his second wife before dispensing with his first.

Gerri and Phil, as happily married couples will do, had blistering fights over Andy and Rick's marital problems, each taking their gender's side; for a while it tore everyone apart. In the end Phil relented and they kept Andy, lost touch with Rick, seeing him only occasionally when he came back to the neighborhood to pick up Noel for the weekend. Andy's recovery was much more difficult. It was a couple of years before her bitterness eased enough to allow her to date. In the years since she had advanced herself to middle school principal.

Meanwhile, Gerri and Phil settled into a routine, if you can call it that when you have three kids in seven years and two demanding jobs doing the people's work, jobs that required commitment and a strong sense of justice. Neither of them punched a clock; both of them were tied to pagers in the old days and cell phones now, backing each other up as well as they could. Their lives could be chaotic—children in dangerous situations that had to be investigated or rescued by CPS or crimes against the people that fell into Phil's bull pen didn't happen on a nine-to-five schedule. If Gerri failed to do her job well, a child could be at serious risk and if

Phil slacked even a little, the bad guy got away. Phone calls from the police to either of them came at all hours.

Gerri would think back to the beginning with longing from time to time. A bright young social worker with a master's degree in clinical psychology marries a handsome young lawyer four years her senior, a man who's already being noticed by the district attorney and the attorney general—they were often referred to as the Power Couple. It was predicted that one of them would land in state politics; they were still fixtures at official state and political events and fund-raisers attended by movers and shakers. Their hours in their offices and in the field were long and hard, but in addition they managed to keep up with the kids—band, choir, PTA, neighborhood watch, gymnastics, ball games and track meets, concerts, and enough sleepovers and car pools to dull the brain of any card-carrying parent. They had to tag team these events—if Gerri had to table a case load to attend something for the kids, the next time Phil might have to push some trial work on a younger assistant D.A.

"Right after the last pancake breakfast of my high school career, I'm going to take a bottle of Johnnie Walker Blue into the garage, sit in my car and drink it right out of the bottle until I can't focus," Phil had said after one of his father-duty assignments.

That was one of many things that had held them together through twenty-four years of pressure—humor. Phil, when he wasn't mentally and emotionally tied to some case, could be very funny. And Gerri had a cynical wit that could make him laugh until he cried or farted. They had a remarkable partnership and friendship that was the envy of many. Their own personal appraisal was that they were busy, overworked, tired and somewhat dull—but they were doing a damn fine job nonetheless and had come to worship boredom as a great alternative to chaos.

Gerri had known from the beginning that Andy's second marriage wouldn't work. Bryce might've been thirty-four when they married, but he was not grown-up enough for family life. He had his business trips, his buddies he liked to run with, a long and ingrained history of never answering to anyone for any reason and a lot of women before Andy, the last being something Gerri had known would be a tough habit to break.

Selfishly, Gerri dreaded what she knew was coming with another divorce, another friend in recovery, and this was her closest friend. She consoled herself that it was like giving up cigarettes—once the pain of withdrawal was past, Andy would gradually reclaim her stable self. Still, she resented the hours it would eat up, listening to the transgressions of Bryce.

Feeling grateful for her anything but ordinary yet predictable life and her committed spouse, she called Phil's office. He was in court. His assistant said there was nothing on his calendar for lunch and Gerri, feeling like toasting her wonderful partnership and telling Phil how much she loved and appreciated him, called his cell phone. She knew it would be turned off for court. To his voice mail she said, "Hi. I'm coming into the city. I thought you might like to grab a quick lunch with me. No kids. I'm flying solo. My cell is on."

The morning was almost gone and Andy was done crying. She was working on a list—things to do to scrape Bryce Jamison out of her life. Number one was to call Noel and explain. Noel was in his first year of community college and split his time between his mom's, his dad's and a couple of friends who had an apartment near the campus, thus he had missed the fireworks early this morning. But he'd witnessed plenty and Andy knew that was the reason he spent less than the majority of his time at her house. The most humiliating part was the knowledge that he reported back to his father and stepmother. Well, maybe that would change now; maybe he'd hang around more.

Empty the closet and drawers into boxes, she added. Call lawyer. Copy tax returns. Print out bank statements and close accounts. Cancel credit cards. As an afterthought she wrote, "Call gyn clinic, get screened."

The doorbell rang and immediately she heard the sound of a key in the lock. Bob. She had forgotten about Bob. She looked around the dismantled kitchen and wondered how that was possible. Bob was the carpenter who was renovating the kitchen and he would have expected her to be at work as usual. He was slow and careful and had other jobs, so it took him longer, but the inconvenience was reflected in his price. Among Andy's many regrets right now was that she'd decided to redo the kitchen. She wasn't sure she could afford it now, without a husband.

Bob was whistling as he walked into the kitchen, carrying his toolbox and accompanied by his Lab, Beau. When he saw her sitting at the table, he shouted out in surprise, jumped back and grabbed at the front of his shirt. For a second he looked as if he might have a heart attack. Beau jumped, as well, but then he wandered over to Andy, tail wagging.

"Lord above," Bob said in a shaky voice.

"Sorry, Bob," Andy replied, giving Beau a pat. "I'm home today. It never occurred to me to call and warn you."

He took a breath. "Whew," he said, obviously willing his heart to slow. Then he bent a little, peering at her. "Not feeling so good?" he asked.

"I'm okay. Personal family business that needs taking care of. Help yourself to coffee if you like."

He straightened. "Thanks so much." He resumed his whistling and hefted his toolbox onto the kitchen counter. He retrieved a crowbar and began prying the baseboards off the walls and lower cupboards. He stopped whistling and asked, "You expecting the Goodwill truck today?"

Andy laughed in spite of herself. "No, Bob. I had a huge fight with my husband and threw his stuff on the lawn. I'll have to go clean it up."

"Hmm," he said, turning back to his work. He didn't ask any more questions.

After a bit, Andy refilled her coffee cup, which put her in his space for a moment. She leaned against the torn-up cabinet and asked, "Married, Bob?"

"Hmm. In a way," he said.

Again she couldn't help but laugh. "Well, gee whiz, you and my husband have something in common. He's married in a way, too."

Bob straightened and faced her. There was a sympathetic curve to his lips. He was a few years older than her; he had a sweet face, engaging smile and twinkling eyes. He might be considered a tad overweight, but Andy thought he looked a lot like a college football coach, or maybe a farmer—large and solid. Robust and cheerful. One of the reasons she'd hired him for the job, besides glowing recommendations, was his delightful disposition. She had trusted him to be alone in her house the moment she met him and after spending many hours together during the measuring, selecting and purchasing for the renovation, they almost qualified as friends, though she knew very little about him. He seemed the kind of man who'd give comfort well. She pictured him with a happy grandchild on his knee. "I've been separated for a long time," he told her.

"Oh," she said. "I'm sorry."

"Nah, it's okay. It's been years now. My wife moved out and neither of us has bothered with a divorce."

"Oh. What if one of you wants to get married?"

"Nah, I doubt it. Well, if she wanted a divorce, I'd be happy to split the cost with her, no problem. So you see, legally I'm married, but not really."

"Children?" she asked.

"Unfortunately, no. It was a brief marriage, an uncomplicated split."

Andy held her cup up to her lips. "I guess you must be over the worst of it by now."

"Oh, yes," he said, applying the crowbar to the baseboard and with a hearty pull, separating it from the bottom of the cupboard.

"Well," she said, pushing herself off the counter. "I have things to do."

"Mrs. Jamison?" he asked. "I'm having a Dumpster delivered in two days for the scraps and trash. The new cabinets are in the shop, the tile is ready for me to pick up and I'll keep moving here as much as possible. If you'd like, I'd be happy to work weekends on the kitchen."

"Bob, you work anytime it's convenient for you—just

let me know when so I'm not trying to throw a costume party when your saw's running, all right? Leave me a note or message on my voice mail saying when you'll be here next. The quicker the better, huh?"

"I have a couple of hours in the evenings," he offered.

She shrugged. "Fine with me."

"It'll go a little faster that way."

"I don't have anything to do but go to work every day and get a divorce," she said.

His face looked pained. "Oh, Mrs. Jamison, I'm sorry to hear that."

"Actually, I think it might be a positive change. Bob, would you mind calling me Andy? Please?"

"Sure. Anything you want." Then he tilted his head and smiled. "Short for Andrea?"

"No. Short for Anastasia. My father is Greek. Know what it means?"

"Can't say I do."

"One who will rise again," she said.

He gave a friendly nod. "And of course, you will."

She took a deep breath and sighed heavily. "I just hope it's not again and again and again."

Gerri spent a couple of hours in her Mill Valley office. She only did the occasional home visit now. As a supervisor her job was administrative, overseeing other case workers and their files in addition to a million other things from paperwork to hiring and firing. She'd spent many a night and weekend working at home and in the field, still had to be on call for emergencies with families at risk, so taking the rare long lunch was definitely not an issue with the director. She headed for San Francisco. She could use just an hour with Phil. She'd get an update on city dramas and politics, tell him about her morning with Andy. When she was troubled about anything, she turned to Phil, her best friend. No one could give her a reality check and reassure her like he could, and she was able to do the same for him.

When she stepped into the elevator in Phil's office building, she saw that his administrative assistant, Kelly, was standing there, looking at her feet. "Hey," Gerri said. "How's it going?"

Kelly looked up and the second their eyes connected, hers welled up. She couldn't respond or even say hello; she hit the button on the elevator to let her off on the next floor, not where either of them was going. "Sorry," she said in a shaky voice, bolting past Gerri, headed for the ladies' room.

Gerri was paralyzed by confusion for a moment, but then, given Kelly had been with Phil for twelve years and they were friends, she put her hand in the path of the closing door, forcing it open again, and followed her. Whatever was wrong, she hoped her husband hadn't been an ass. That would be hard to defend.

Kelly was in her late thirties, plump and lovely with ivory skin and coal-black hair like Snow White, the mother of a nine-year-old daughter. Her work was hard, her hours long, but she was devoted to Phil, and she saved his bacon daily. She made everything he did look even better than it should; she covered for him, cleaned up his messes, ran his schedule, fielded his calls, everything. They jokingly called her the Office Wife.

By the time Gerri got into the restroom, she could hear soft crying in one of the closed stalls but there was no one else there. She went directly to that stall.

"Come on, Kelly," she said. "Come out. Talk to me. We're alone."

It took a minute before the door opened slowly and she was faced with Kelly, who was looking down in shame, her cheeks damp and her nose red. "I'm sorry," she said. "I kind of fell apart. I'll be fine now."

"That's okay," Gerri said, gently rubbing her upper arms. "You don't have to apologize to me for having an emotional moment. Can I help?"

"I don't think so," she said, shaking her head. "It's just marital…stuff."

"Oh, I wouldn't know anything about that," Gerri said with a soft laugh. "I'm not going to grill you, Kelly. I don't want to pry. But if you want to tell me what's wrong, I'll listen. And you know I'm on your side."

She gave a sniff and raised her eyes. "That's just it, I have no idea what's wrong," she said. "It's John. We've been struggling lately. I don't know what to think. He's become so different. Distant."

"Now why would you say that?" Gerri asked, her mind flipping to this woman's husband, a quiet and kind man who seemed very much in sync with his wife, his family.

"I can't find him a lot," she said with pleading, watery eyes. "He has a lot of lame excuses about where he's been. He's distracted, like he's depressed or something. And he's dressing up for work more often—he's a programmer, he doesn't have to wear a starched shirt and tie. And he's not interested in… He's not romantic. I keep asking him what's wrong, but he keeps saying 'nothing.' And we can't agree on anything! I haven't said the right thing in months!"

Oh, no, Gerri thought. *I can't have two cheating*

husbands in one day. "That doesn't sound like John. You've been married how long?"

"Twelve years," Kelly said.

"Oh, Kelly, there might be something bothering him that you haven't considered. Work? Family pressures? Money? Stress about his age, trying to keep things together for your daughter's future? Are you sure he's not worried about a medical problem?"

"Nothing has changed in the checkbook and we can usually talk about those things."

"How about your hours? I know you put in a lot of hours for Phil."

"That's the same, too. He hasn't complained about my hours or asked me when I'm taking time off. I don't know what to do."

"Have you suggested some counseling? To help you figure things out? Get back on track?"

"He doesn't want to go," she said, shaking her head miserably.

"They never want to, Kelly," Gerri said with a sympathetic laugh. "I'll email you the names of some real good marriage counselors. I'll include men—sometimes that goes down better with the husband. Tell him if he wants to be happy again, this is a must. Push a little, Kelly. And if he won't go with you, go alone. You have a good benefits package."

"I suppose," she sniffled.

"Believe me," Gerri said. "At least get some support for yourself. Hopefully for the two of you."

"Is that what you did?"

"What I did?" Gerri echoed.

"Made Phil go to counseling?" she asked.

"Don't tell anyone," Gerri said with a small laugh.

"I wouldn't want to bruise his macho image, but Phil has succumbed to counseling once or twice. He hated it, but he went. And I think he cleaned up his act just to get out of it."

"I can see that. You two seem to be real happy now."

Happy now? Gerri thought. "We've had our struggles. Everyone does. But there's help out there, you know." She took Kelly into her arms for a hug.

"I think I admire you more than anyone," Kelly said.

"Aww, come on..."

"Being able to forgive him for something like that... That took such courage, such commitment." Kelly's chin was hooked over Gerri's shoulder, their arms tight around each other, and Gerri could see her own eyes in the bathroom mirror. They were huge. Her mouth was set; she ground her teeth. Suddenly she thought she looked much older than she had that morning. "I'd forgive John an affair, if he just wanted to be forgiven, to be together again, like we were. God, I miss him so much! I know most women say they'd never forgive that, but I would."

Gerri had to concentrate to keep from stiffening, to keep herself from either squeezing Kelly to death or throwing her against the stall doors in a fit of denial. Kelly knew everything about Phil. In some ways, she knew him better than Gerri did. He definitely checked in with Kelly more than Gerri; Kelly had to know him like a wife, a buddy, a best friend and a mother to do what she did for him.

"Some things are very hard to get beyond," Gerri said softly. "But anything is possible."

Kelly pulled out of Gerri's embrace and, smiling gratefully, said, "But you did it because you're strong and wise. You amaze me. You could have just gotten mad and thrown him out—and both of you would have lost each other forever. But you're so good together."

Gerri tilted her head and smiled, a completely contrived smile. Her gut was in a vise. "You like him too much," she said. "I should be jealous. You know more about him than I do."

"Not hardly." Kelly laughed. "Seriously, you're a role model for me. If you can put yourselves back together, better than ever, after another woman, then I can at least try harder to understand what's wrong before I give up on John."

There it was, the smoking gun. Another woman. Kelly knew Phil had had an affair, something Gerri had never once suspected. Her mind raced. *When? How? Not Phil,* she thought. He was a complete partner! He bitched about it, sure. What he wanted was to devote himself to his work, which was important work, and come home to tranquility and order. That wasn't happening at their house, which was full of kids, strife, challenge, noise, confusion. There was always something. He complained, true, but he always came through. Not always grinning like an idiot, but neither did she.

She was no different. Her work was equally vital and she faced the same chaos at home. Being the woman on the team, however, it seemed to fall to her to attempt to pull it together, assign jobs, schedule events. To keep things running smoothly, she needed him and she didn't take him for granted any more than he did her. They'd made the kids together; there were obvious compromises involved in growing them up. As far as she could remember, they'd never failed to work together to get it done.

When? How?

She could remember a few rough patches, some periods of adjustment, but she could not remember noticing any of the obvious signs. She paid the bills—there were no unexpected withdrawals of cash, no charged jewelry, flowers, hotel rooms. He'd never been missing for long periods of time. There were no odd phone calls, even on his cell. He took every evening and weekend call within her hearing; he had a tendency to talk so loud she shushed him so she could hear the TV or read. He'd never come home too late to explain; he'd never smelled like another woman. Those nights he stayed in the city, she'd often called him late. He'd always answer, they'd talk for a long time—you don't do that if someone else is lying beside you. *Oh, God,* she thought. *This isn't happening to me. He can't have had an affair! When the hell did I leave him alone long enough for an affair? We were on our phones all the time, checking in, working out schedules....*

"Counseling," she said to Kelly, giving her arm a pat. "Now wash your face and get a grip."

"Thanks," she said. "Email me those names?"

"Of course," Gerri said. *He's going to fire her when he finds out about this.* "Do me a favor, will you please? I invited Phil to lunch, but I had an emergency come up just as I got here and I have to handle something immediately. I was going to swing by the office and tell him myself, but I have to get moving. Please tell him we saw each other in the elevator and I'm sorry, I have to stand him up."

"Oh, too bad," she said.

"I have to rush, Kelly. Oh, and Kelly—don't mention our talk to Phil. About…it's a very sensitive subject."

"Still?" Kelly asked as if surprised.

"I'm sure he'd like to keep all that private stuff from the rest of the office."

She laughed. "Well, the gossip died off a long time ago—years ago."

Years ago? Years ago? Years ago? *Where* was *I?*

"Still," Gerri said. "It is. At least for us."

"I understand," Kelly said.

"Good luck," Gerri said, giving her one last squeeze. Then she almost ran out of the ladies' room to the elevator, to the ground floor, to the parking garage, to the Golden Gate Bridge. She was in a trance of disbelief. The first thing she did was think of the many explanations he might come up with to make this all go away. *Bullshit,* he would say. *When was that supposed to have happened?* he would ask. *That's impossible! If there was talk about something like that, I didn't know about it! I was always too goddamn busy with games and meets and concerts and meetings to fit in an affair! Where did you get something as nuts as this?*

But it was a long drive back to Mill Valley and by the time she got there, she knew. It was true. He'd had an affair. His assistant had known about it as had others in the office. And she had *not.* Not even a whiff. He had pulled it off.

She didn't go back to her office, she took the afternoon off and went home. She spent the entire time until the kids came home in the office she shared with Phil. They had a big home, one of the largest on the street. Their office and the master bedroom were on the ground floor, four bedrooms on the second floor, one for each kid and a guest room.

The office was nicely divided with a built-in desk running along three walls in a U-shape. They shared a computer, but each had their own laptops, as well, and bookshelves to the ceiling, plus two large walk-in closets—one for each of them that held their filing cabinets and shelves for supplies.

Gerri knew Phil's password and opened his email. But if she knew his password, he wouldn't save anything she could see, yet she looked through all the saved files, all the old emails. Nothing, of course there was nothing. And he certainly wouldn't keep personal, incriminating files in the prosecutor's office—it was a political job, constantly under scrutiny.

She spent a little time looking through hard files he brought home, but in no time at all she knew she wouldn't find anything. There wouldn't be any evidence.

Yet she knew. She knew.

two

Sonja had a meditation group in the morning at the community rec center and right after that she spent a couple of hours at the health food co-op, but when she got back home in the early afternoon, she noticed that the kitchen carpenter's truck was backed up to Andy's open garage, and Andy's car was there, as well. The pile of Bryce's things was gone from the front yard. She couldn't restrain herself any longer and she went into the house through the opened garage, guided by the sound of an electric screwdriver. When the noise paused she said, "Knock, knock."

The carpenter turned away from the shelf he was removing. "Hello," he said.

"Hi. Bob, isn't it?"

"That's right."

"Is Andy here, by chance?"

"She's around here somewhere," he said.

"Whew, this is messy work, isn't it?" she said to him.

"I'm afraid it gets to be a real messy ordeal," he confirmed, going back to his job.

Sonja wandered through the kitchen and into the

house. She called out to Andy and Andy yelled, "Back here."

In the master bedroom, Andy was folding clothes into a cardboard box. "Oh, boy," Sonja said. "This doesn't look good."

"Depends on your point of view," Andy answered. "It's probably long overdue."

"You're moving him out?"

"I'm packing up his clothes. He didn't bring much into the relationship. Bryce has always lived kind of loose—few attachments." She gave a sigh and folded a pair of jeans into the box. "I should have considered that."

"Does he have things like furniture?"

"Boy things—a big-screen TV, motorcycle, sound system, computer. Basics."

"How are you holding up?"

"Hanging in there. Noel is coming over later. I'll explain to him, but he won't be surprised." She looked back into the box. "Or disappointed."

"Oh, Andy, I hate that this is happening…"

"Like I said, it's overdue. If I'd had a brain, I wouldn't have gotten into it to start with."

"So what got you into it?" Sonja asked.

She shrugged. "I think it was his basic equipment. Handsome, young, funny, endowed." She looked up from her work. "I was just so lonely by the time he came along. You know?"

Sonja shook her head sadly. "I'm going to go home and make you something for dinner, something healthy and fortifying. Plus, a plateful of chocolate cookies. Well, they'll be carob without sugar, but it'll get you over the hump, and carob is so soothing to the digestive tract. I'll round up some tea that'll calm you so you can think clearly and feel your body's messages...."

"Thanks, I appreciate the thought, but my body is sending me the message that it wants a greasy burger and a pint of Ben & Jerry's, with a gin chaser. Or two."

"Oh, I know that's what you think you need," Sonja admonished. "But that'll just dull the senses and prolong the recovery. Trust me. And tomorrow morning, if it's okay with you, I'd like to burn some sage and waft the essence through the house with feathers. To clear away his presence."

"Shouldn't you wait until he picks up his stuff?" Andy asked.

"I'll do it again, after. Would you like something to equalize you? I could give you a massage and balance your chakras."

"No one's touching my chakras today, Sonja. Not even you."

"I have some cleansing herbs, if you'd like to do a body cleansing. It can give you such a fresh feeling."

"Doesn't that sound terrific? The shits for twenty-four hours? No, thanks. What I'd really like to do is get his stuff out of my space." Andy glanced at her watch. "I have a doctor's appointment in two hours, then Noel will be over."

Sonja's face took on a startled expression. "Are you feeling sick?"

"No. Just a precaution," she said. "It turns out Bryce hasn't been faithful."

"Oh, God! Oh, Andy! I'll whip up a herbal drink for you!"

"Due respect, Sonja, but if Bryce left me any souvenirs that drink will probably have to be made up of antibiotics."

Sonja actually got tears in her eyes. "I just hate him," she hissed.

"Good," Andy said. "That makes me feel way better than herbs. Let's all just hate him for a while."

Sonja opened her arms. "Let me hug you," she said.

Andy dropped the clothing into the box and let herself be drawn into Sonja's arms. There was something about the way she held her that almost brought tears to Andy's eyes. Sonja's remedies and hocus-pocus bored her to sleep, but she had a nurturing spirit underneath it all that was wholly genuine and, in fact, healing. She was small, soft and strong, gentle and comforting. Before letting go, Sonja whispered, "Is there anything I can do for you right now?"

Andy pulled back and smiled. "Nothing. Just let me finish all this. It will help, believe me."

"I'll be home this afternoon. Call me if you think of anything at all. If I can drive you to the doctor so you won't be alone, I'd be happy to."

Andy laughed softly. "Believe me, I know the drill. This is my second cheating husband and I was single a long time in between. I practically have a standing appointment."

Sonja said goodbye to Bob as she left through the kitchen. It crossed her mind that the disaster in there was very bad for relationships, it being the rear right of the house. She had suggested to Andy that they find somewhere else to stay during renovations, but Andy blew her off.

Ordinarily an afternoon with no classes or appointments for her consulting would make Sonja anxious—it meant she wasn't getting the word out through referrals from people whose lives had been enhanced, and that wasn't a good feeling. But today, she needed the time for herself. Even though she hadn't liked Bryce, she grieved for the marriage. It would upset the balance in the neighborhood. She thought about her friends. Their husbands didn't have a great deal in common, but on those occasions they socialized as couples, the men found plenty to talk about. They would stand around in a little clot, holding a drink or beer, talk seriously about their work or politics, tell some off-color jokes, pick at their wives behind their backs like men do— pure, simple pleasure for them.

Sonja met George when she was twenty-eight, he thirty-eight. They dated for two years before marrying and would soon celebrate their tenth anniversary. She hadn't had many relationships before George and she knew why. She was considered eccentric. But George being mature worked out so well—he was calm, consistent. He might not fully appreciate all her zealous care, but she was keeping him healthy and his home life serene. He didn't like to argue; he liked stability and predictability, and she liked that he liked that. She could work with that.

She prepared a small meat loaf for him that was more loaf than meat because his cholesterol was up. She lit a few candles around the house and put on one of her soothing CDs, the kind you would hear in the background at the spa. The effect was very calming. George was a financial planner and his work was fraught with tension as he dealt with clients' futures and moved people's money around. She had time for a warm soak in the tub and a brief meditation so that when he walked through the door she'd smell delicious and be perfectly centered.

When he came in she smiled at him, then her eyes dropped to his shirt. "Oh, George, what did you spill?"

"I don't know," he said, looking down. He brushed at the spot.

"Don't worry, I can get it out. Can I fix you a special tea? I have just the thing if you've had a hard day."

"No, thanks, Sonja. My day calls for a Scotch."

She clucked and shook her head. "If you must. I'll have dinner in just a little while—I have to run a meal over to Andy. She's under the weather."

"She is?" he asked, lifting his eyebrows.

"I'll tell you about it over dinner. Just be a minute."

She took two containers on a tray across the street to Andy's. When she saw Noel's car in the drive she knew she'd just hand them off; she didn't want to interrupt them. When Andy opened the door, the unmistakable aroma of greasy pizza drifted through and Sonja frowned, then forced a smile. "Trust me," Sonja said as she passed the tray. "This is better for you."

Andy said thank-you and Sonja went back to her own kitchen. She caught George fixing a second Scotch and chose not to comment.

Once they were settled with their meals—hers was a pasta and greens salad with beans, his was the loaf-meat and vegetables—she said, "Bryce and Andy have split up. They're getting divorced."

"Oh?" he said, looking up from his fork briefly. "Too bad."

"It was really dramatic. When Gerri and I went walking this morning, she was throwing his belongings out the front door onto the lawn, and they were screaming obscenities at each other."

George smiled. "Is that so?"

"It's not funny, George. She has to be tested for venereal diseases. Apparently he hasn't been faithful."

George made a face. "Really—I don't need to know that."

"Some people have pretty complicated, tragic relationships."

"I guess that's true," he answered. He pushed his plate away.

"You haven't eaten much. You're not upset, are you?"

"No," he said. "I had a late lunch."

"Not something bad for your cholesterol, I hope."

"Of course not, Sonja. I had a plate of grass. It was scrumptious."

She smiled patiently. "Oh, you had something bad, I can tell. Well, that's why I go to so much trouble to make sure you eat well in the evening. No matter how you carry on, I know you appreciate that I look after you as well as I can."

"Indeed I do. I just wish that occasionally you could look after me with a spice or two. I'd love to taste my food briefly before it passes through my body."

"And I'd like you to last," she said. "Because I love you so."

"You sure you don't want me to last so you have someone to control into old age?" he returned, lifting a graying brow.

"George! What a thing to say! Just when one of my best friends is going through a terrible divorce!"

"And getting tested for venereal diseases," he added. "You'd better rush her over some grains and herbs."

Sonja laughed at him. "You love to do that, don't you? Pick at my remedies. Well, I guess I'm smart enough to know that I don't have what she needs for something like that—it's prescription only. I am going over there first thing tomorrow to burn some sage and smudge the air with Indian feathers just to clear out the negative presence."

He stood from the table and shook his head. "I'd be disappointed if you didn't."

Gerri ordered a pizza for the kids. Once that was devoured, they headed for their evening pastimes—family-room TV, computers, phones, homework, usually in that order.

Gerri fixed herself a drink instead of dinner, wondering briefly if Sonja had a herb for homicidal tendencies. She was going to confront Phil, of course. She'd been with the man a long time. She thought there was nothing she didn't know about him. *I've been getting fart marks out of his underwear for almost twenty-five years for God's sake.*

Though it was still biting cold in the March night, she bundled up and went out onto the deck, under the starlight. At least she wasn't hot. She'd been trying to size up her emotions all day long and still didn't have a handle on whether she was enraged, confused, hurt or completely off base. She went over every day of their marriage—the births of the children, the fights, the really hard times. There was the year she lost both her parents, one after the other, to cancer—it was a blur. She'd been vacant, wandering around in a complete daze, but Phil had picked up the slack; he was completely there for her. No one could have comforted her better. Could he have done that and still had someone else in his life? Someone he went to and said, "You can't believe how bad things are at home...."

She saw Phil enter through the kitchen, toss his briefcase and laptop on the breakfast bar and wander through the house, looking for her. It was the first thing he did every night unless she was standing in the kitchen.

Eventually he found his way to the deck just as she was exhaling a long stream of cigarette smoke. Her first cigarette in twelve years. He stood in the doorway, noted the drink and cigarette and said, "Jesus Christ, did someone die?"

"You had an affair," she said evenly.

He took a panicked step toward her, his face in a frozen state of shock, and after making a partial recovery said, "I'd better get a drink and a jacket." He turned to go back into the house.

So. He had. If he hadn't he would have said, *"What? What the hell are you talking about?"* And all she could think was that the son of a bitch was still good-looking, maybe better looking than he had been at twenty-eight. Fifty-three now, still sporting a full head of that thick rich brown hair, now delicately threaded with gray at the temples. His face was just mildly lined but not so much from age as from the sun on the golf course. Then there were those teeth, beautiful and strong. He was not yet seeing the periodontist but she was. Up till today, she'd been happy for him about that. And he'd managed to stay fit, maybe the slightest paunch, graying chest hair, but he was tall and solid. Strong. She hated him so much.

He came back outside with his own drink, wearing

his weekend jacket over his shirt and loosened tie. "Lay it on me, Gerri. What's going on?"

"You had an affair. I just found out."

"And where'd you hear that?"

"Never mind. Just tell me. And start with the truth because you don't know how much I know."

He took a deep breath and a drink from his glass. Then he said, "I had an affair. Years ago. I'm sorry. It's been completely in the past for a long, long time. I'm sorry," he said again. "It wasn't your fault—it was my fault. My failing, my inadequacy. You can't imagine how much I regret it."

"You had an *affair,*" she said again, blown away by his admission. "I need you to tell me about it. The truth about it. When it started, who it was, when it ended. And most important, *why!*"

He leaned back in his chair. "The why might be impossible—I've asked myself a hundred times. Years ago, *years* ago, there was an attractive woman in the office. We worked together briefly and hit it off right away—she was very personable, funny. I did the one thing I thought I'd never do— Not only was it straying from my marriage, which I'd never even been tempted to do, but also it was a coworker, the potential for major-league sexual harassment. Defying all common sense, I made a pass. She responded to me. We had a couple of lunches, met for a drink a few times. She was single, lived alone and I made the mistake of going to her place one late afternoon and got carried away, knowing it was wrong, feeling like shit with guilt, but it got started. It ended almost six years ago. Nothing like that ever happened before, and it will never happen again."

Gerri did a quick mental calculation. Six years ago,

while he was having an affair, the kids had been seven, ten and thirteen. She remembered that year and the preceding year—soccer, band, one starting middle school. Her mother had died of uterine cancer nine years ago, her father quickly following of prostate cancer. That had been a horrible time, but by six years ago things had leveled out emotionally. As far as she could remember, there wasn't anything particularly noteworthy going on. They hadn't had a standoff about him buying a sailboat; none of the kids were sick or in trouble; she hadn't yet been having the menopausal symptoms that rocked her stable world.

"When did it start?" she demanded.

He hung his head briefly. "Seven years ago. It was on and off for a couple of years. Not steady, but on and off."

"A couple of *years?*" she asked, horrified.

"On and off, Gerri," he said. "I'd see her, then tell her I just couldn't do that and wouldn't see her again for months, then slip back, break it off, slip back. And so on."

"Oh, for God's sake! *Slipped?* Can't you come up with anything more intelligent than *slipped?*"

"No," he said. "I honestly can't. I never drank too much, my job was secure, my case load wasn't any worse or high pressure than usual, we weren't in any kind of huge crisis that I can remember, you and I were getting along just fine…."

She felt the sting of tears in her eyes and it made her furious. "Then *why?*" Her voice cracked.

"I don't know. She wanted me. Someone desirable actually wanted me. You and I were fine, but there were always so many complications keeping us from… I guess I was thinking like an eighteen-year-old. But really, there should be a statute of limitations on shit like this— I screwed up, I haven't screwed up since and you can be damn sure it won't happen again. And it was a long, long time ago."

"Who is she?"

"No," he said without hesitation. "She's gone. It's over. We haven't had any contact in over five years and there's nothing to be gained."

"I might have to see her," Gerri said.

"No," he answered again. "I don't know where she is, what her life is like, but I've messed up my life enough. There's no point in messing up hers, as well. Gerri, I realize what happened is unforgivable in your eyes, but I'm here because I want to be your husband and want to be with my family. That's the bottom line. That's all I want. Whether it's perfect or at times difficult, that's my choice, not something I have to rely on willpower for. There was never any question about loving you."

"God, you can't really have done this," she said. "You had an affair for two years, and I never knew. Never even smelled it in the wind...."

"I wasn't with her often. I'm busy—you know that. And I never once missed a family thing to be with another woman, I swear to God. I never let it interfere with my family, my marriage or my job," he said.

"Well." She laughed humorlessly. "What magnificent control. Tell me, was the sex at least fantastic?"

"Irrelevant," he said, bolstering himself with a deep drink.

"Not to me, it's not!"

"Gerri, the worst sex I ever had was fantastic. Men and women probably look at that differently."

"You know they know in the prosecutor's office."

He sipped again. Maybe nervously. "I realize there was some gossip, but I only leveled with one person—my boss. When it was over, I told the D.A. I'd been involved with someone in the office. I find it hard to believe he shared that with the troops. He has a lot of faults, but he learned how to keep confidences years ago."

"Why'd you tell him, then?"

"I told myself it was because we serve at the discretion of the people—because if there was ever an accusation of any kind, I couldn't let him be blindsided. But in the years since I realized that it helped to end it for good—confessing. Because I knew what I'd done was wrong and I was consumed by guilt. I think it was like standing up at a meeting and saying 'Hi, my name is Phil and I cheated on my wife.' He told me that behavior could not be tolerated and if I valued my job, it had to stop." Phil chuckled. "Imagine that from him, huh? Son of a bitch has a revolving door for a zipper." He took another drink. "I could have done the same thing here, with you—confessed, let you hit me over the head with a baseball bat until you were convinced I could be a better husband, but I couldn't risk losing you."

Tears rolled down her cheeks and she stamped out the cigarette. "My God, Phil. I think my insides are festering. I'll be peeing blood by morning."

He leaned toward her. He reached for her hands, but she wouldn't let him connect. "Listen, I did the wrong thing, not you. I hoped you'd never be hurt by it, I hoped I'd make it right over time by being a good partner, a good father. None of it was your fault and I'll pay the price—but don't let it eat you up. No reason both of us should carry the load."

And yet in her mind there were so many things she couldn't quite place in the context of the affair. She remembered that during sex one night he said, "Didn't you used to move your hips?" and she had laughed, thinking he was so funny. Was that when he realized he needed a woman with some passion? He'd remarked that he loved her coming to bed naked these days and she'd firmly told him not to get any ideas. They were too tired at night, too rushed in the mornings, had too many kids around the house on the weekends and never, absolutely never got away alone. And then there was the fact that she was hot-flashing her brains out and her vagina felt like sandpaper. The things people don't tell you about menopause… But five years ago, seven years ago, she hadn't had any of those symptoms. She had been so content.

He had asked her if she wanted to get away for a weekend, if only to the city. Just the two of them. When was that? He hadn't asked in a long time and she had never suggested it. They hadn't escaped—there were always too many family and work obligations. She asked herself if she had driven him to *her* by being so unlike a mistress, and that made her want to kill him on the spot.

"I never had an affair," she said.

"I know," he said.

"No! You don't know! You don't know any more than I knew about yours, but I'm telling you, I had just as many kids, just as little sex, just as much pressure and I never had an affair!"

"Gerri—"

"Phil, I don't think I can live with you now, knowing."

"Let's not do that," he said calmly. "Let's work

through it if we can, go to counseling if you want to, do whatever it takes. But let's not throw in the towel now, after almost twenty-five years and one terrible mistake that I'll do anything I can to make amends for."

She shook her head and wiped the moisture off her cheeks. "I don't know if I can do it," she said with a hiccup of emotion.

"After everything you've seen in families—the abuse, addiction, crime, neglect—Gerri, please keep your head. We can weather this. We love each other."

"We're not like those families." She sniffed. "You and I—we were always different. We always played as a team. Fuck you, you asshole, you played on another team!"

"All right, listen to me. If you decide you can't live with it, if you can't forgive me, we'll deal with that—but first, you have to give it a little time, some effort. You obviously just learned of this and you're hot as a pistol. If you feel the same way after we've tried to get beyond my crimes, we'll make a plan that's best for the family. But not the very day you find out. It's reactionary."

"Weren't you reactionary? Falling into bed with her like that? Not even sure why?"

"Absolutely," he said with a nod. "And trust me, the price was high, even without you knowing what I'd done. Give yourself a little time to think. Please."

"You've done some real stupid, lame-ass, highly punishable things in our marriage," she said. "I was with my dying mother and you were supposed to pick up the kids and bring them, but you lost track of time and left them standing around outside the school, waiting, while it was getting dark. And they were so little!" He nodded solemnly. She didn't add that she'd fired a hospital water jug at him when they'd finally shown up and despite the fact she'd left a nice purple bruise on his head, he'd held her close while she cried. For a long time. "I was about to go into labor with Matthew and you went on a fishing trip, because the mayor asked you to go, to represent the prosecutor's office." She'd been so angry with him for that. She was so afraid she'd have to have the baby all on her own. But Matthew waited for his father. "You drank too much at the neighborhood block party and peed in the clothes hamper in the middle of the night." A slight smile threatened his lips. "You don't deserve for me to think it over."

"I know. But I won't leave the house without telling the kids why."

"You're not *serious!*"

"I'm completely serious. It was my mistake, I'll fess up, take my medicine. I hope we don't come to that, Gerri. You know the best counselors in the business. Pick one out, set us up. If that doesn't help, at least we will have tried."

"See, right now you're just too goddamn calm," she said. "Like you've been ready for this day for a long time and had it all planned, what you were going to say, how you were going to play it. You lawyered up—you strategized it."

"You're partially right," he admitted. "I've had years to think about what I'd say if you found out, if you came at me. I decided a long time ago, I wasn't going to lie or make excuses." He shook his head. "I'm so sorry."

She wished he'd have spent that time coming up with a good story to refute what she'd heard—she didn't want to know what she knew. "Please don't sleep in my bed tonight."

He gave a resigned nod.

She rose to go to their room, but stopped before entering the house. Pulling her jacket tighter around herself, without looking at him, she asked, "Did you love her?"

"I loved you. Always."

"But *her?* Did you also love her?" She turned to look at him.

He stood up and faced her, his hands in his pockets. "I wasn't using her. She was a nice woman, I was fond of her. I was attracted to her and I cared about her. You know I'd have to have some feelings, that I'm not the kind of man who fucks around. But from the first time we were together, even before we were together, I told her I had a good marriage, that I loved my wife, that I didn't want a divorce. I feel as bad about what I did to her as what I've done to you."

"So. You loved her. In your way."

"I never weighed it, honey. I knew how much I loved you, but I wasn't thinking with the right head. I was all steamed up and driven. I wish I'd known how to stop that, but… Gerri, I wasn't done with my sex life. I was still interested. Responsive. I can't undo it. I can tell you one thing—I might've thought that's what I wanted at the time, but it didn't make me happy. It made me miserable."

She shook her head in equal parts disgust and pity, then turned and went to the bedroom. Wasn't done? She couldn't remember a time he'd let her know something was missing for him. The bigger ache came from knowing there hadn't been anything missing for her! She'd thought they had the perfect marriage, the perfect family.

If he'd been beside her in their bed, she would have kicked him every time she turned over. But having him on the family room couch left her feeling so alone, she cried. In every crisis of her life, she'd turned to Phil, and now *he* was the crisis in her life. She wanted him to feel more pain for her, yet if he'd come to their bed and tried to hold her through her tears, she would have torn his eyes out. If he apologized one more time, she might stab him in his sleep.

The next morning, she went for her walk and she wore sunglasses. Of course Sonja and Andy could tell something was wrong. "There's a dreadful situation at work I can't talk about yet," she said. "I'll tell you when it's okay to."

Andy called Bryce once she had his things packed up—it had only taken a couple of days. She got his voice mail and left him a detailed message: she was filing for divorce, would be canceling credit cards, closing the joint accounts and would have copies of the statements for him, a final accounting. She knew he had a company credit card he could use, but still she asked if he needed money.

He came for his things that very night. He told her, in a very subdued, boyish way, that he'd be fine financially. She knew in that instant that he was relieved to be free of her—she cramped his style. He was not the kind of man ready to have serious ties. She didn't bring up the house—there was already a divorce lien on its proceeds of sale from her first husband. It appeared Bryce was going to take his belongings and go away quietly, content to have the ball and chain removed from his life. There was something about the simplicity of it that hurt more than the screaming fights. He was so easily done. Finished. Why couldn't she have made the break long ago? She knew why—it was embarrassing to be so foolish, so wrong, at her age.

When Bryce came, he was with one of his closest friends, using his truck to load the big screen, sound system and speakers, boxes of clothes and books, toiletries and miscellany. Bryce rode away behind his possessions on his motorcycle and all the while Bob, working in the kitchen, managed to stay very busy and very quiet. It was completely over in an hour and Bryce would never be back. He hadn't even waved goodbye.

The trash was full of Sonja's concoctions, the entire house was filled with dust from Bob's construction in the kitchen plus the odor of burnt sage from Sonja's cleansing voodoo. Gerri, who was Andy's rock, was distracted by some heavy work problem and felt terrible about her lack of support, but Andy reassured her that she was getting along pretty well. She'd gone back to work the morning after the boy toys disappeared from her life.

While there was a part of her that wished for quiet and solitude in the evenings, there was another part grateful that Bob was in her kitchen, pleasantly working away as the sun set. She sat on her bed with the news on, there being no TV in the family room anymore, and took odd comfort in the humming, whistling and construction noise.

She wandered into the kitchen. "How's it going?" she asked him.

"Good," he said. The crowbar was being used to pry the old, chipped ceramic tiles off the floor. "Very good."

"I'm going to have a glass of wine," she said. "What can I give you?"

"Oh, I'm just fine with water."

"I didn't mean I was going to get you liquored up," she laughed. "I realize you use power tools. But how about a cola or something?"

He looked up from his work, smiling. He wiped a rag across his sweating bald head. "That would sure be nice, thanks."

She went for a glass in the laundry room where she kept the few dishes she needed since the kitchen cupboards had been torn out and carried away. The refrigerator was purring along in the garage now. She couldn't actually cook anything but she could get ice and keep things cold. As she looked inside she said, "Hey, have you eaten?"

"I have," he said. "Had something on my way over."

"How about Beau?" she asked, and as she did so, the yellow Lab lifted his head and looked at her with those sad eyes that suggested he hadn't been fed in days, lying eyes that made her laugh.

"Don't believe a word he says. I always take care of Beau first," Bob said.

She poured his cola, her white wine. She settled at the table in the nook, still undisturbed and covered with dust. "Could I ask you a personal question?"

He glanced over his shoulder. "Sure. If I get confused by it, I'll make up an answer."

"Funny," she said. "Why did you and your wife separate?"

"Oh, that," he chuckled. "It's real simple, actually. She left me. She's gay."

Andy actually choked on her first swallow of wine. "Gay?" she echoed.

He laughed. "Don't ask me the chronology of that, okay? I mean, since birth, I assume, but of course, I had no idea. We weren't exactly kids when we got married. I was over forty, she was over thirty. It was something she struggled with, spent a lot of time at church, trying to get the cure. I think she just wanted to be like everyone else—live an average life and have children. But that's really not the way to go."

"Holy shit, Bob," Andy said.

"Life's not easy if you're gay, even in San Francisco. If your family thinks you're just being difficult people keep trying to impress that all you have to do is concentrate and you'll stop being gay. It's a little more complicated than that."

"Well, I'll say," Andy said, taking a gulp. She wanted to know everything, right now. How'd that work? What made her choose him? How was sex? And the one she couldn't help, "You didn't have the first idea? Going in?"

"No," he said, shaking his head. "That was stupid of me and wrong of her, I guess. But I understand. I think she was really trying. She had high hopes."

"Oh, man," she said, overwhelmed. "I gotta know— How long did it last?"

"The time we were together? A couple of years from the time we met. She's such a sweet girl. We were good friends first, then decided to get married. I admit, when she first told me she just couldn't pretend to be straight anymore, I was mad. But I couldn't stay mad at her, you know? Her life was more of a struggle than mine, so I learned a little tolerance. For a long time there I'd been worried she was sick or something, but finally she just told me the truth, she'd thought she could stop being a lesbian and could be married with children, but it just wasn't going to happen." He lifted his head and looked upward as if remembering. "She asked me if it would be okay if she left. And I said of course. What was I going to say? No?"

"But did it… Well, you know… Did it damage your masculinity?"

He laughed. "I didn't have that much experience with my masculinity," he said.

"But you were an older guy and—"

She stopped. *I'm having this conversation with my kitchen carpenter,* she thought, internally appalled. Yet she couldn't help it. His take on this was fascinating.

"Nah," was all he said.

"Did you ever hear from her again?" she asked.

"Oh, yes, all the time," he said. "Once or twice a year now, at least. She's with someone now, very happy. They've been together quite a while. They'd like to have a child together. In fact, I was offered the job, but I declined. They *both* like me," he said with a lovable, almost mischievous grin. "She's still just the nicest, sweetest girl. She always thinks to ask me how I am. And I'm the same as before."

"Wow," Andy said. *And I thought he was an ordinary workman with an ordinary life.* But there was something about him that, in all its simplicity, was deep. Thoughtful.

"Doesn't she want a divorce?" Andy heard herself ask.

"I think it's kind of irrelevant," he said.

"Well, how do you know? You might meet someone someday."

"Aw, I sort of doubt that. A little late in the game for me. But I have her phone number. If I called her and said something about that, there wouldn't be a problem. We had an agreement when she left—real simple and nonlegal, you know. The date of the split, the assets—which were as close to zero as you can get. I scrounged up a couple thousand dollars to help her get on her feet and she was so grateful for that. We're good."

"You gave her money, too?" Andy asked.

"Well, she had to have some walking-around money. It's not easy to start over, especially around here."

"Bob, I think you're pure gold."

"Me? Nah, anyone would've done that. Like I said, she's a real sweet girl. I'm just so glad to know she's okay." He looked at her closely. "Understand?"

All she could think was, *I want to be like you.* That pure. So undamaged even though he'd gone through a potentially devastating experience. "Sounds like you've completely forgiven her. For lying to you, for trying to have a straight life at your expense."

"Mrs....Andy, it didn't cost me anything to forgive her for that. I just assume everyone is doing the best they can. Besides, she's a good person." He looked at her and asked. "How are you getting along since...you know."

"Since the TV and motorcycle went away?" she asked with a laugh. "I'm still kind of numb, I guess, because I haven't had much of a reaction. My son was relieved—he hadn't been getting along with my husband too well the past couple of years. And I know this is going to sound kind of silly, but it's nice you're work-ing here. Makes me feel less alone."

"Yeah, that's the hard part. All of a sudden, alone. My wife, she might've been a lesbian, but she was, most of all, a great friend. We had a lot to talk about every day."

"Well, I'm used to being alone. Bryce traveled in his job so he was gone several nights a week, anyway. And when he was in town, he wasn't the homebody type—he was more the party-boy type. Thus the divorce."

"I'm awful sorry, Andy."

"Thanks," she said. She got herself a refill of wine. "I'm going back to my room to watch TV—holler if you need me. In fact, I'm going to invite Beau if that's all right?"

"He's probably got sawdust and stuff on him."

"I'll ask him to shake. Beau. Wanna watch some CNN for a while?" Beau got to his feet and wagged his tail. "That'll be nice," she said to Bob. "A guy I can trust on the bed, watching TV with me."

"You enjoy him. He can be a real good friend."

"You can come and find him when you're done. I'm not going to bed or anything. I'm only in the bedroom because it's quiet…and there's no TV in the family room."

Three hours later Bob knocked softly on the bedroom door, which stood ajar about an inch, and Andy sat up with a start. Beau was sitting upright on the bed, wag-ging and making a noise that was a combination whine and moan. "Come in," she called.

Bob gingerly pushed the door open and Beau bolted off the bed to go to him. "He make a good TV buddy?"

"He put me to sleep," she said. She stretched. "That was great."

"It's his best trick. See you tomorrow night."

"Thanks," she said. *That might be one of the kindest men I've ever known,* she thought. *Too bad he's...Bob.*

three

Gerri booked herself and Phil for three emergency sessions with a crisis counselor. She chose a woman she'd used through CPS, a woman she thought was very good even though her instincts said if her heart was in it, she'd have selected a man who could understand Phil. But she didn't want Phil to get understanding—she wanted his head on a pike. And at this point, Phil would've taken counseling from Gerri's mother had she been alive, he was that accommodating, that beaten down with guilt and remorse…and hope. He would do anything to make this go away.

She scheduled them for three evenings running, from two days following his apologetic admission. They told the kids they had meetings. She had no idea what he had to say at the prosecutor's office to leave work on time for a change. She secretly hoped he had to say, "I cheated on my wife and if I don't go to counseling with her right now, I'm getting thrown out of the house." She wanted him to feel her pain. His claims of great guilt and remorse weren't doing much for her.

But he made it home on time to go with her. They

held it together pretty well during the session. Phil seemed to struggle but tried to answer the counselor's questions. Gerri thought, for a prosecutor, he'd make a lousy witness. Judges wouldn't accept answers like, "I don't know what I was thinking, what I was looking for," or, "There wasn't anything missing in my marriage that I was trying to make up for, I was just extremely tempted and I failed."

As was typical of marriage counseling, the real bloodletting and fireworks came later, after the session. Usually in the car on the way home, probably to the great entertainment of cars passing by.

"She's trying to get me to fight it out with you, take shots at your choice of sleepwear as the thing that drove me to it," Phil said.

"She's just saying it wasn't the affair, it's what was going on in our marriage," Gerri fired back.

"Bullshit! There wasn't anything going on in our marriage that hasn't been going on for over ten years! It was the same! It's always been a busy marriage, one full of pressure, stressful jobs, kids, horrible schedules, tight budgets. And you're not asking me if the marriage has been satisfactory lately. It's been the same!"

"If I asked, you'd say whatever you had to because now you're scared you're going to lose everything!"

"I was *always* afraid of losing everything! She's trying to get me to say I'm just a little boy who wanted to come my brains out!"

"Well, didn't you say as much? Isn't that what 'extremely tempted' means?" Gerri railed.

"I'm saying I don't know why! Seven years ago, for whatever reason, I didn't have much willpower, much restraint. I never once thought, 'Gerri's not putting out so this is okay.' I had accepted how we were."

"Accepted how we were? You're blaming me!"

"Jesus, I'm blaming us! I knew this was going to come back and bite me in the ass, but I couldn't help myself—I was tempted because it felt too goddamn good to have someone actually tempted by me! You and the counselor want to hear me claim you're a frigid wife, that I'm just an irresponsible asshole! Goddamn it, Gerri, I'm not a player. I have never been a player."

"You son of a bitch," she blustered at him. "Like it was my fault! Not wanting you enough!"

"Come on, don't go there," he said meanly. "You know as well as I do that for the past ten years, sex in our bed is rare at best. We'd have to get sex therapy to get up to once a month!"

"I know it's real rare for you to make any effort!"

"How many no, thank yous do you think a husband can get before he figures out that's not on the agenda?"

"Oh—so that's your story now? That I said 'no, thank you' too often and damaged your frail little libido? That I drove you to the other woman?"

"Listen, the most love I feel in that house is when you hand me my list of chores and praise me like a puppy for doing as I was told. Aw, Jesus, we don't need a therapist to help us say cruel things like this to each other! Christ!"

"Well, maybe if you'd fucking hold up your end, I wouldn't be so tired at the end of the day!"

"See what I mean? Why don't we just rent a cabin in the woods and fire insults and accusations at each other? It would be cheaper than a hundred bucks an hour! And it sure as hell isn't helping put us back together! You want to know all the ways you were a less-than-perfect wife? Wanna tell me all the ways I failed as a husband? Because I'm sure the list is long and ugly for both of us!"

When they got home, they separated in silence, holding back the rage in front of the kids. Given they were teenagers, they were mostly oblivious. Jessie asked Gerri, "You mad about something?"

"Just worn out from a problem at work, honey," she said. "Be patient with me."

"It's not, you know, that menopause thing?"

"No! It's not that menopause thing!"

By the end of the week, a mere five days after the affair came to light, Gerri told Phil, "It's time. I need to go to counseling alone, you need to find your own counselor, and we have to separate."

"You're giving up?"

"I don't know. If I can stop hating you, maybe we can work it out. But right now, I'm just in too much pain."

"Where do you expect me to go? Our finances can't withstand another residence."

"I don't care. Stay in the city, come out for dinner, visit on weekends, whatever. But I can't fight about it anymore. There's just no explanation for what you did and I can't get past the betrayal. You just have to give me some space and time."

"If that's what you want," he said. "But I still love you."

"Well, I don't love you right now. I want to, but I can't love a man who can do what you did without even knowing why. I don't know if I'll ever feel safe again."

"Fine," he said. "This weekend we'll tell the kids."

"I don't agree with that," she told him.

"We tell them what they're old enough to understand. That's what we do in this family. In fact, you wrote that rule. You're the social worker."

"I don't think they're old enough to understand," she said.

"Yes, they are. They're not old enough to sympathize and it's not in their experience, but they'll know what we're talking about. They'll know that what I did was wrong, that you being out of your mind angry is reasonable."

She shook her head and a large tear escaped. "Why did you do this to us, Phil?" she asked in a desperate whisper.

"I can't explain. I've had nightmares about this for over five years. If we're not stronger than one indiscretion, then I completely misjudged us. I thought, given all we've had to handle, both personally and professionally, if it came to this, we'd find a way. We've seen families through murder that didn't give up this fast."

"One *two-year* indiscretion!"

"Do you have any idea how many times, during those two years, I put my arms around you and held you? How many times you told me not to get any ideas? God, Gerri, I remember when the kids were little and we were both exhausted from work, the house was collapsing, everyone was screaming they needed something, and we still snuck away from them, locked ourselves in the bathroom and—" He shook his head. "I don't know when that stopped happening for us, but it stopped."

"Why didn't you say anything? Before it was too late?"

"I thought I had." He looked down for a long moment, then looked up again. "Never mind. It wasn't because of you. It was me. I should have found a way. But then, I didn't know it was going to be too late…"

There was a very small part of her, remembering those days so long ago, that wanted to say, *It was me, too, let's see if we can get it back.* But she said, "I'll tell Jessie if you'll tell the boys."

He gave a nod. "Sunday," he said. "Then I'll go to the city."

"You're going to drop it on them and leave them with me?"

"No, of course not. We'll tell them, separately. I'll stay through the evening and when the house quiets down, I'll head out. I'll handle as much of this as I can, but it's your decision for us to live apart and we don't do that to our kids without them knowing the reasons."

At five o'clock on Sunday, Phil knocked on Jed's bedroom door and said, "Hey, bud, I have to talk to you about something. Can you come with me?"

"Where?" he asked, getting up from his reclining position on the bed.

"We have to go somewhere away from the house so I can talk to you in private. Just come on, you'll have the details soon enough."

They walked a couple of short blocks to the neighborhood park. Phil sat on the top of a picnic table, his feet on the bench, elbows on his knees, head down. Jed stood in front of him. "Come on, man," Jed said impatiently. "What the hell's going on?"

"Your mom and I are having some problems," Phil said. He felt his eyes begin to water, his throat threaten to close. "Serious problems. Oh, Jesus, this is the hardest thing I've ever done."

"Come *on,* Dad! You getting divorced or something?"

"I hope not," Phil said, and watched his son deflate, as if all the air had just been sucked out of him. "It's my fault. I want to tell you why, and I need your help with Matt. He needs to know the facts, but he's kind of young to understand."

"You're shitting me," Jed said in a panicked breath. "Oh, man, you're shitting me."

"Several years ago—over five—I broke the oath. I cheated. I don't have an excuse—it was wrong. I never wanted to lose your mom, lose my family. I never wanted another woman, but I guess I was weaker than my hormones or something, because I cheated. Your mom just found out and she really wants to kill me right now. She'd like us to be able to work things out, but she'll need some time to decide if she can forgive me."

"What?" Jed asked, though he'd heard clearly. "What? You wouldn't do that to Mom."

"I hear ya, buddy. I never thought I'd be that stupid or that wrong, but I was. When she found out—and I still don't know how, though I have a few ideas—it just hurt her so bad, she got us right into counseling. We're going to keep going, but she's too angry to live with me right now." He reached out and put a strong hand on Jed's shoulder. "Doesn't mean I won't be around. I promise I'll be around plenty. I want to spend time with you guys, plus I have to hang close in case your mom wants to talk about it. Or yell at me about it some more," he added with a lame smile.

"Why?" Jed asked.

"Why what, son?"

"Why can't you work it out with you home? You guys fight all the time. You always work it out."

"We don't fight all the time," he said. "We argue about little shit sometimes. This is different."

"Well, did you say you're sorry?"

"Of course," Phil said. "I didn't just say it, Jed. I mean it. I've never been so sorry about anything. But there's all that trust—you count on it. You stake your lives on it, depend on it. And when the trust is broken, you can't just say sorry. You know? You have to pay penance. You have to work hard to put the trust back in the relationship."

"Oh, man, she isn't going to give in easy," Jed said, running a nervous hand through his short, spiky hair. "This is Mom we're talking about."

Phil wanted to laugh. At least smile. Boy, did they both know Gerri. She was brilliant, classy, strong and *stubborn*. There was that little male bonding thing going on with Jed and Phil was in a position to appreciate it more than his son knew. But he kept a straight face. "Here's what I want you to know. This is very important. I want you to know I'm willing to do anything for her forgiveness. Anything. I'll try to get her trust back, I swear. While we're working on that—if I'm not around the house and you need me for something, need to talk to me, you call my cell phone anytime. It'll be turned off for court, but I'll answer any other time—day or night. With me, bud?"

"Yeah. Yeah. You going off with some other woman?" Jed asked.

"No. Absolutely not. I love your mother, I don't even know where that woman is. I'll do whatever I can, son.

I'll try my best to get our marriage back. Our family. Jed, I'm so sorry."

"You mad at Mom for this? For saying she doesn't want to live with you?"

"Nah. But I'll be honest with you—this whole thing has caused us to say a lot of real nasty things to each other. We have things to get over. You're going to have to be mature. Patient. Give us a chance to work it out. This wouldn't be the best time to be the badass we both know you can be."

"When was this? When did you say?"

"Over five years ago," Phil said.

"Jesus. You haven't done that since, have you?"

Phil just shook his head.

"Well, then, what the fuck? "

"Listen, son, I didn't take the other woman out for a soda. I was intimate with her. That's the betrayal that sticks, that hurts. I'd love your mom to say, 'Oh, well, I hope you learned your lesson,' but it's not going to be that easy. And it's up to her. She's the one who was wronged, so give her a break. You understand, Jed?"

He thought for a long moment. Then he said, "I understand life around our house is going to suck *big*-time."

They talked awhile longer. Jed had questions that Phil answered a little differently than he had with his wife. He still couldn't say why, but he did relent that the woman was pretty, nice, smelled good, made herself available. Jed was nineteen and had been with his girlfriend, Tracy, for about a year. They'd had many father-son talks about Jed's responsibilities as a man. Phil knew the boy was sexually active and understood feelings of lust. He hoped he wouldn't follow in his father's footsteps and stray just because he was a little bored, a little needy or whatever the hell it was. "I thought I was a bigger man," Phil said. "I hope to God you learn from this. You have a problem with your girl, your wife, your frickin' *hormones,* you better find a way to communicate that. Find a better way to deal with things than I did."

"Man, you always seemed so perfect," Jed said. "But when you fuck up, you fuck up big."

If trying to tell her kids was horrible, preparing to tell Andy and Sonja was torture, and Gerri had no idea what she was going to say to her coworkers at CPS. She pinched the fat gathering below her waist and knew it was impossible to say she needed time to see her counselor twice a week for anorexia. On Monday morning when she was to meet her friends for their walk, Sonja was at her door five minutes early. Gerri came out with her coffee cup and led her to Andy's. When Andy opened the door Gerri said, "Got the coffeepot on?"

"Sure."

"I have to tell you both something. Let's go inside. We'll walk tomorrow."

When they were seated at Andy's sawdust-covered table, Gerri went through the chronology of events, from the encounter with Kelly in the elevator to the confrontation with Phil, the three disastrous counseling sessions and brutal arguments that followed. And then she described telling the kids he was sleeping elsewhere for the time being and why.

"Couldn't you have come up with some story?" Andy asked, horrified.

"Believe me, I wanted to," Gerri said. "Don't tell him

I said this, but Phil was right—they're not preschoolers, they have to know why. My husband had an affair and I'm too angry to live with him right now."

"How'd it go?" Andy asked.

"As bad as possible. Jed was silent and brooding, disillusioned, actually more angry with me than Phil, but Jessie fell apart. She sobbed almost uncontrollably. And Matt shrugged and asked something like, "How long will this take?" And then he asked if it was all right to go pitch a few balls with a couple of friends. Baseball season's starting. At dinner, it was quiet as a tomb except for questions about their routine—rides, takeout orders for dinner, chores. Matt asked if there was going to be child support—they know about those problems from friends—moms who are suddenly unable to pay for school trips, that sort of thing. Then before the plates were cleared, Jessie lost it, threw a glass across the room and screamed at us both, asking how we could do this to her. She's sixteen so it's all about her. When the house was finally under control and quiet, Phil and I had another fight in the garage as he was leaving with his suitcase."

"What did you fight about?" Sonja asked.

She laughed weakly. "Our routine. Child support."

"What's up with the routine? The child support?"

"He's going to stay in the city. He'll come out to Mill Valley as much as possible, when he's not working till nine or ten. If he's not around as much, can't car pool, he also can't be expected to drive all the way out here just to bring home dinner or help with homework. It'll be a major adjustment. Before, if I was going to be late, he was on time and vice versa. And he said he'd take care of the bills, but I've been paying the bills for over twenty years—he just gets his cash out of the instant teller or my purse. Now he's going to have his check payrolled to him rather than direct deposited and give *me* money. He needs money to pay for a place to stay. Oh, forget about it," she said, waving her hand. "It's just logistics. We don't know who does what. We always used to know who does what."

They'd also fought about him leaving, though she asked him to leave, so they fought about the fact that he made her make him. And she cried half the night again.

"I can't believe it," Andy said, resting her head in her hand. "I never even imagined this possible."

"Me, either," Gerri said. "I never knew anything was wrong with us."

"But it was five years ago," Andy said. "You sure you want to separate over something that's been over that long? Five years doesn't give you some peace of mind?"

"I can't just forget about it," Gerri said. "He said he tried but couldn't get my attention. I'll tell you one thing he never tried, though. He never said, 'I'm tempted by a pretty woman at work and I need us to have more sex.' He never came clean with me. Instead, he got involved, knowing the risk. Apparently we were worth the risk. I just can't go through that again."

There was a little lie in Gerri's memory. She couldn't exactly remember Phil romancing her, letting her know he was feeling needy. But she could remember their sex life dwindling, all but disappearing and not being sorry. It was so gradual she couldn't put a time marker on it. She remembered when Andy met Bryce and was flushed and floating because of all the erotic sex and Gerri had just laughed at the absurdity of it. "Better you than me," Gerri had said. "I don't think I could handle the stress at this point in my life. And God knows, I can't spare the sleep."

There was one truth—she hadn't realized it was just her. She thought it was both of them, their libidos beaten down by everything else. And, she didn't think he minded, either. She thought he'd gone as dry as she had. She did remember times he snuggled her, pressed up against her, tried fondling. Most of the time she said, "Aww, Phil…" Honestly, she couldn't remember when they'd last had sex. Months ago. And she had no memory of whether they were doing it more or less than that seven years ago.

But then along came a woman—a small, young blonde with fluffy hair in Gerri's imagination—to awaken him. Stir him. What was so unfair in that image was that Gerri couldn't possibly compete—not with her stretch-marked stomach, saggy boobs, torn sweats, her tired eyes, her menopausal mood swings.

What she did have, from the day they met to the day before she heard about the affair, was the ability to communicate with him about anything and everything else. Their professional lives had so much more in common, they used each other for sounding boards all the time. When it came to family, they shored each other up, at least one of them always being there for the kids. And they were unfailingly there for each other, whether it was a work problem or personal crisis, obsessively interested in each other's lives. They worked together like synchronized swimmers to keep everything running as smoothly as possible. And they didn't just have meaningful conversations sometimes—it was all the time.

And on those evenings they were both at home and

could relax with a glass of wine or sit in front of a fire on cold winter nights, their time wasn't consumed by passion or even that unhurried, gentle love she remembered from younger days. It was companionship that filled the hours—conversation, laughter, empathy, advice for each other. Maybe a movie or quiet time when they both read. Companionship. Partnership. Perfect symbiosis.

She didn't know when or how the lovemaking disappeared. She had always thought it was normal for the sex drive to relax, to become better friends than lovers. She thought his libido was exactly like hers—no longer urgent. It simply went to sleep. When she thought about growing older with him, she never thought of sex being a part of their lives. Their lives were so good, their relationship so strong, it never once occurred to her they needed anything more, except maybe time.

Honestly, if he'd said, 'I need a good, hard, sweaty roll in the hay before I lose my mind,' she would have laughed at him.

They argued, yes. But they had laughed a lot, too. Their chemistry was good. She kept telling herself the marriage had such value, such depth, it just couldn't have been all about sex. Sex was something they could've fixed. She wasn't sure how but something could have been done.

Their first week of separation was difficult at best. The kids were angry and quieter than usual until they had regular short flare-ups, outbursts that had nothing and yet everything to do with their parents living apart. Gerri watched them carefully, fully aware that few people understood how closely depression and anger were linked. Jed was absent a lot, typical for a nineteen-year-old in college with a steady girl, but when he was around he held his tongue, a feat for him. Matt, on the other hand, acted as if nothing had happened; his conversation was all about baseball.

Jessie was in the worst shape, snotty and disrespectful, sneering sarcastically when answering her mother, muttering under her breath. "You probably didn't notice there weren't any chips or Cokes since you're hardly ever here." And "Why do I always have to stay home just because you and Daddy have this thing going on?" Once in a while Gerri heard what sounded suspiciously like the b-word directed at her. She was so awful that Gerri wanted to smack her. But then Jessie got out the photo albums, looking through the family pictures as if someone had died. As if trying to remember how they'd been before this.

A second week passed, Gerri seeing her counselor twice a week, whole sessions during which she did little talking and a great deal of crying. She slept poorly and wondered often if Phil was finding comfort somewhere else, angry because she wasn't finding comfort anywhere. Angrier still because she had no desire to seek out any other form of comfort. It wasn't that she was bored with Phil sexually, there just wasn't so much as a spark in her. *How long can I do this before I say uncle?* she wondered. *Is it better with you as a cheater than without you as a partner?*

Then Gerri looked through the photo albums herself, left on the coffee table by Jessie. She studied their faces, hers and Phil's, twenty years ago, fifteen, ten, five. Two years ago. He was a good-looking man who had seasoned with age and experience. She looked at herself in the pictures very critically, but she had photographed well. She had probably never qualified as beautiful, but she was handsome—five-nine, slender, long neck, high cheekbones, engaging smile. She knew she was fortunate. Tall, slim women tended to look decent in everything from shorts and jeans to cocktail dresses. She marveled at the frequency of so many shots being captured while she smiled into the camera and Phil gazed at her. And in every goddamn one of them—from twenty years ago to two, even through the time it was happening for him with someone else, they looked happy and loving. How was that possible?

Gerri soldiered on. Walking in the early morning, driving kids to school, going to work, coming home in the evening to manage her home and family, sometimes finding Phil there using the computer in his home office after having spent time with the kids. Then she'd lie in bed at night feeling so robbed, so alone, every expectation shattered.

Sonja was having a really hard time with Gerri and Phil's separation. She was trained to intuitively know when intimates were in trouble. A hundred seminars and retreats had helped her to develop these skills. She tried not to say anything when she noticed small things, like a person's chakra auras or the balance in their homes being out of whack, but truthfully, except for the usual disruption of a busy household, she had always judged the Gilberts to have the stuff of a solid, unbreakable family. This troubled her because she loved Gerri; she should have paid closer attention.

She refused to offer to clear the presence of Phil out of the house with sage and feathers. She hoped this was just an altercation that would mend. She didn't offer healthy meals or special herbal drinks because while Andy would become annoyed and throw her offerings in the trash, Gerri was just testy enough to shake her till her teeth rattled. So she remained positive, urging Gerri to listen to her body's messages and use her instincts in getting through the rough patch with a goal of emerging stronger, better. And Gerri snarled at her.

Then she came home from a yoga class to find George was home early. She found his car in the garage and she went into the house and called out to him. He was in their bedroom, packing.

"George," she said, surprised. "Do you have to leave town?"

He turned slowly. Gravely. "No, Sonja. I'm leaving. I've rented a place. I'm sorry, Sonja. I'm moving out. I just can't do this anymore."

"Do? This?"

"The candles. The tinkling music. The little waterfalls. The bland meals. The way-out-there philosophies on destinies being altered by where people put the goddamn red candle. I just want a normal life."

"No," she said, shaking her head, laughing nervously. "You're just teasing me again…"

He took a breath. "This is no joke. I can't take it. I feel like a fucking Chia Pet, constantly fed and groomed. I don't want you in charge of my sleep patterns, my cholesterol. I take goddamn pills for my cholesterol. It's not necessary for me to eat grass. My home life is intolerable. Seriously, Sonja—if you want to do this for a living, have at it. Knock yourself out. But I'm through."

"But where will you go? What will you do?"

"What will I do? Spill food on my shirt and let the dry cleaner get it out. We haven't had an adult conversation in years. It's all you telling me what to eat, what to wear, scolding if I want a drink, going on and on about my fucking chakras. I managed fine never knowing I had chakras!"

"But we have sex at least twice a week," she said, remembering everything Gerri had said about her deteriorating sex life with Phil.

"We have sex *exactly* twice a week. Tuesday night and Saturday morning. And you want the truth? I couldn't care less. Sex isn't the problem, and frankly, it never was. Not even before I met you. But I can't be in this kind of relationship. It's loony. I want to come home and turn on the football or baseball game, eat bloody red meat on a TV tray, spill on my shirt, fall asleep on the couch, wake up tired and hungover once in a while."

"George—"

"You'll be taken care of, don't worry. I'm sure your heart's in the right place, but if I come home to candlelight and spa music one more time, I'm going to snap. We're not right for each other, Sonja. We're not. I don't want you to make me last so that every day of my life feels like an eternity. I'm miserable."

"But you'll be alone! No one will care about you!"

He thought about that for a moment and said, "I know." Then he zipped his bag, hefted it and walked out of the room. He turned at the door. "If you need me, just call my cell. I won't abandon you, but I have to stop this now. Before I go totally crazy."

"But, George," she cried, running to him, grabbing his shirtsleeve. "You want me to change? I can make changes! We'll compromise!"

He just looked at her. "Sonja, you can't change this.

And you haven't heard a thing I've said in ten years. You need to just carry on, be yourself and let me go."

And then he left.

Gerri walked out of her house at the crack of dawn, holding her coffee cup. Andy emerged from across the street at about the same time. Sonja had not been early; Gerri made a mental note to thank her for that. Sonja was go, go, go all the time; she seemed to see it as her mission to keep her friends in shape, moving all the time. Gerri and Andy met in the middle of the street. "Where's little Mary Sunshine?" Andy asked.

"Sleeping in?" Gerri asked with a short laugh.

BJ came out of her house down the street and the women waved at each other. BJ began stretching for her run while the other women wandered up Sonja's walk.

"We could sit on the planter box, finish our coffee," Andy suggested.

"Yeah, but I'd rather get this over with," Gerri said.

"You doing okay?" Andy asked.

"Ach," she said with a noncommittal shrug. "I think I'm doing what all women in this position do. Half the time I want him killed, half the time I just want him back."

"Bryce must be a real loser," Andy said. "I'm pretty miserable, but I don't want him back. I just want the kitchen finished and some energetic young stud to come over a least a couple of times a week, then leave quietly."

"You're disgusting."

Andy laughed at her. "Really? You're just bitter. Not that I blame you, but I hope you can work this out. I love Phil. I know he has to be punished, but I love him. If I didn't love you more, I'd take him off your hands."

They approached the door. "He watches himself brush his big, beautiful teeth, splatters all over the mirror and everywhere. He snores like a locomotive and farts in his sleep. He blows his nose in the shower and poops three times a day."

"Oh, he's regular, that's good. That's one of the things I'll be looking for in a man," Andy said with a laugh. Then she knocked on Sonja's door.

"Knowing what you know, you could not have a man like Phil."

"Sister, if I could get a man down to one infidelity per twenty-five-year marriage, I'd think I was queen of the universe." Andy knocked again.

"I'm not ready to laugh about this yet," Gerri informed her. "Where the hell is she? She's usually pacing outside my door at least five minutes early. Hit the bell."

"I don't want to wake George. He doesn't get up before six."

"I wonder how he gets away with that, being married to the hyper one. Ring it, anyway." When there was still no answer, Gerri pounded on the door. "What the heck," she muttered. "Andy, see if you can see in the garage windows, see if there's a car in there."

Andy handed off her coffee cup and jogged to the front of the garage. She had to jump up and down to get her eyes up to the windows in the garage door. Then she stopped and turned toward Gerri. "Just her car," she said. "You think they went out for a whole night somewhere?"

"She would've scheduled that with us three weeks in advance," Gerri said. Then she pounded again and yelled, "Hey, Sonja! Sonja, come on!"

"They're not home," Andy said.

"She would've called. You know her—she'd pull herself off the operating table and call to say she's running a little late because of major surgery." She pounded and yelled again.

"You'd better get in there," a voice said from behind them. They turned to find BJ standing on the front walk. BJ shrugged. "She's never missed a morning. She'd never be a no-show. She's relentless."

Andy and Gerri exchanged looks, knowing how true that statement was, wondering for only a split second how BJ, who didn't know them at all, would read the situation so accurately. So quickly.

"Don't you women have keys to each other's houses? Because something's gotta be wrong. If she's not in there, maybe she is in the hospital. But you'd better find out."

"What could be wrong?" Gerri asked herself as much as the others.

BJ shrugged. "I don't know. But she's wound a little tight."

Again, Gerri and Andy exchanged glances. Then Andy bolted across the street to get the key to Sonja's house that she kept in her desk. She ran back across the street, leaving her front door standing open.

Gerri opened the door slowly, peeking in. The house was still. Quiet and dark, all the blinds drawn. She stuck her head in and called, softly, "Sonja? George?" Then turning she said, "I don't think anyone is home."

Suddenly BJ was there, brushing past them and striding purposefully into the house. She paused in the great room, looked right and then left, then headed down the hall toward the bedrooms. Gerri and Andy followed a bit more slowly, unsure if searching the house was the right thing to do, even under these circumstances. Then BJ yelled, "In here!"

Whatever visions Gerri and Andy might've had as they raced to the master bedroom, nothing could have prepared them for what they found. Sonja sat on the floor between the bed and the bureau, her back against the wall. She wasn't wearing her usual perfect, colorful walking togs but rather a skimpy little outfit, the type she'd wear to her yoga class. BJ was kneeling in front of her, then backed away as the other women came closer, letting them in. Sonja's hair was limp and stringy, her face red and damp as if she was sweating, her eyes glassy. Her breath was rapid and shallow; she was hyperventilating. She almost smiled when she saw her friends, but instead, put one of her hands out toward them, showing nails gnawed down so severely they were nipped into the skin, pink and sore. "I bit them all off," she said weakly.

"Sonja! What's the matter?" Gerri asked. "Are you sick?"

"I'm okay," she said. "I just need to move pretty soon. I have to get up," she said, yet made no effort to rise.

"Maybe she had a seizure or something," Andy said.

"Ask her if she took anything," BJ said from behind them.

"Sonja, did you take something? Medicine? Maybe a whole bunch of your magic herbs?"

She shook her head, remaining against the wall.

"Where's George, Sonja? Has he gone to work?"

"George," she said, shaking her head. "Poor George."

"Sonja, what? What about George?" Gerri demanded.

"Get her to the hospital," BJ said from behind them. "She's having some kind of psychotic break."

Gerri turned and looked at BJ. She was shocked that BJ would catch this before her, with her master's in psych. But looking back at Sonja, it was obvious. Everything was all wrong—she wouldn't have put on yoga clothes to walk in the morning, but she did have an afternoon class three days a week. She might've been like this since yesterday. But where was George? And the torn-up nails, the sweating face and greasy hair...

Instead of asking any more questions, she said to Andy, "Get your car. Pull into her drive. Let's go."

"Maybe an ambulance?" Andy asked.

"Get the car. Right now!" Then to BJ she said, "Help me here," and they each took one arm and slowly lifted Sonja to her feet, urging her to walk. "You're going to be okay now," she murmured to Sonja, leading her out of the house. "It's going to be okay—just come with me."

BJ left them to take their friend to the hospital. Gerri sat in the back with a Sonja she couldn't even recognize. She asked her questions all the way to the hospital, but didn't get any answers. Sonja would sigh softly or whisper, "Poor George," or just shake her head and turn unfocused eyes toward Gerri.

It took quite a lot of confusing explanations at the emergency room before they put Sonja in an exam room. Gerri called her house and Jed answered. "Listen, I didn't walk this morning, I'm—"

"I know, Mom," he said. "Some lady came to the door and said you had to rush Sonja to the hospital. But she didn't say what was wrong. What's wrong?"

"We don't know, she hasn't seen the doctor yet. It's like she's drugged or something. I have to find George.

Get my address book out of the kitchen drawer and see if his cell number is there. Look under Johanson. I know I don't have it in my phone."

"Sure," he said. "Want me to get Jessie and Matt to school? I can be late for class."

"Please. I should stay here until—"

"Here it is," Jed interrupted, reciting the numbers.

"Thanks, honey. You're in charge. I don't know when I'll be back, but I won't go anywhere else without calling your cell or leaving a note at home."

"Want me to run your purse and phone by the emergency room?"

"Could you? That would help."

It was a long, tense hour before George entered the E.R. and went directly to the nurses' station. He produced his insurance information, asked questions, answered, nodded solemnly. Gerri crept closer to listen, but it didn't take long for the nurse to pull George away from the desk just as a doctor was exiting Sonja's exam room. Gerri would have liked to sidle up to them and eavesdrop, but the doctor was speaking in low, private tones, so she shrank back.

"Mom?"

She turned to see Jed standing there, holding her purse. "Oh, honey," she said. "This is so good of you."

He shrugged it off. "You know anything yet? Like what's wrong with her?"

"No, we—" She stopped talking as George approached them, his head down. She turned her attention on him, touching his arm. "George, what's wrong? What happened to her?"

He took a breath. "It's a little complicated. The doctor has called for a psych consult. They're going to be keeping her for a while. I'll go see her in a minute. They've given her something to calm her down, but—"

"Calm her down? She was almost catatonic!"

"Not on the inside," he said. "Her brain was on over-drive. She needs medication."

"She won't like that. Maybe they should tell her it's herbs. George, where were you? Aren't you usually home in the mornings?"

"Yeah, well that's the complicated part. Sonja and I have separated. I left our home yesterday. It must have come as more of a shock than I anticipated."

"What?"

"I imagine we'll divorce, Gerri. Don't worry—I'll take care of her. It was never my intention to abandon her. I just can't live in that loony bin any longer."

Gerri got in his face. "You *left* her?" She felt Andy and Jed each grab hold of one of her arms, keeping her back before she launched on him physically. "Did you talk it over with her first? Air your...your... Did she *know*?"

"Oh, I talked, but Sonja never listened. Do you have any idea what it's like, living in a temple? I thought I had prostatitis, I was peeing so much—but it was just all the goddamn fountains and waterfalls in the house. The candles, the meditation music, the herb-infested meals that tasted like lawn clippings..."

"She did all that for *you!*"

"I'm sure she thought so, but I asked her not to. There's more stimulation on a mountaintop monastery in Tibet," he said. "Really, I did my best. Sonja's kind of nuts."

Gerri was straining against the hold Andy and Jed had on her. "You know she can't take that sort of thing!

You should have given her a list to work from or a date to deal with! You can't just leave her! She's too fragile for that!"

"Mom," Jed said, pulling on her arm. "Jeez, Mom. There are people…"

"I have to make arrangements for her," George said. "Maybe we'll talk later." And he turned away from them.

"Jesus, Mom!" Jed admonished. "Calm down. People are watching."

Gerri turned abruptly and sat down on one of the chairs against the wall. Her cheeks were flushed. She threaded her fingers into the short hair on top of her head, kneading a little wildly. How could George know so little about his own wife? Didn't he realize Sonja clung to all that stuff to keep her steady? She had to have her bag of tricks to get through the days. It was her life raft. And organization, planning, they were her religion. She couldn't cope with a shock like suddenly losing her husband, her marriage.

And then Gerri realized it was *she* who couldn't cope with that. Her reaction to George was more about Gerri feeling her own marriage was gone, suddenly and without warning. Just as Sonja relied on all her woo-woo stuff, Gerri had always relied on Phil, on their marriage. "God," she said. "I'll apologize. I was emotional. Scared."

She took a few deep breaths and put her hand on her son's knee. "Go on to school, honey," she said. "I'm not leaving till I see her."

"Maybe I should hang around in case you…you know…"

"Nah, I'm fine. I'm not going to lose it. If I go berserk, I'm sure they can give me something."

"You sure?" Jed asked. "I mean, you've been a little rocky lately."

A huff of laughter escaped her. "Ya think?" she asked. Not only was her life falling apart, the whole neighborhood was hitting the skids. "It's been a rocky few weeks. But we'll be okay."

"Okay, then. Andy, keep an eye on her." Then he leaned over and gave his mother a kiss, something he never did in public and was loath to do in private.

"Whew," was all Gerri could say, leaning back in her chair to wait.

Two hours later, the nurse let them in to see Sonja. She was lying back in the bed with her eyes closed, her arms relaxed at her sides. They stood there for a second, looking down at her. She looked fifteen, lying there. Small and vulnerable, weak and pale. Not their perky Sonja. While her energy and zeal drove them both crazy, this image was far more unsettling.

Sonja opened her eyes, saw them, but didn't move a muscle. Gerri picked up one of her limp hands and said, "Oh, honey."

A tear gathered and ran slowly down Sonja's temple into her hair. She whispered something and Gerri leaned closer to hear. She whispered again. "He said I made him feel like a Chia Pet."

four

Gerri and Andy left Sonja in the late morning, went home and then to their respective jobs. Sonja was going to spend at least a night, maybe two in the hospital, but she was becoming more lucid by the minute, back in reality again. Still, a break like hers was going to require supervision at the least, medication and psychiatric follow-up at the most.

Paperwork had been piling up on Gerri's desk, with the distractions and crises in her personal life, and she called Jed's cell phone to ask if he could get the kids home from school so she could stay late to tackle some of it. She was more than a little conscious that if she didn't have her oldest son stepping in to help so agreeably right now, she'd be completely lost. She also took note that he was coddling her, trying to warm her up, get her more reasonable toward his father, as though all this inconvenience was her doing, not Phil's.

By the time she got home, it was nearly eight. Phil's car was in the drive and when she walked in, the first thing she saw was his briefcase and laptop on the table in the nook. Then he walked into the kitchen from the family room.

"What are you doing here? Did the kids call you?" she asked.

"Jed called, said you had a really bad day," he said. "Is Sonja all right?"

"She scared me pretty good, but I guess she'll be okay. You got the story?"

"I did," he said. "Kind of feels like the whole neighborhood is coming apart at the seams. You okay?"

"I've been better," she said, going straight to the refrigerator. "Kids eat?"

"Jed took care of that. He got takeout—their choice. I reimbursed him and gave him an extra forty bucks in case he has to do that again. Listen, it's not working out, me staying in the city. I'm going to find something around here, closer to home, in case there's some emergency. I don't want to be so far away through the dark hours, when the goblins come out."

She felt a smile threaten. The goblins, they called them—the problems kids had. The last-minute school assignment that was already late, a fight with a girlfriend or boyfriend, a ride that didn't show up to bring them home, a disaster of any flavor. "Is that in their DNA?" she asked Phil. "Our children have never had any problem in their lives before ten o'clock at night." She pulled out a bottle of cold white wine.

"Probably your DNA. You used to stay up late, get yourself all worked up over some problem with a co-worker or family at risk and poke me at about three in the morning to work it out with you."

"I'll take the blame for that one," she said. "Are you leaving right away?"

He eyed the wine and said hopefully, "I don't have to."

"Good," she said. She grabbed two wineglasses out of the cupboard and headed for the door. "Hang out here for them if you can. If they ask, tell them I'm home, but had an errand. I shouldn't be long."

"Andy's?" he wanted to know.

"Actually, no. A neighbor I barely know helped us with Sonja today. It's reasonable to say that if she hadn't stepped in, we might have left Sonja alone there, out of her head, for days. I think I should say thank-you, maybe try to get to know her better. If you have to go…"

"I can wait around awhile."

"Because if you have to go, just let me tell the kids I'm home and where I'll be. They stay alone all the time—they'll be fine."

"I'll wait for you," he said. "You sure you're okay?"

"Work's piling up," she said. "You just can't get separated, go to counseling, have medical emergencies and all that without some fallout." She was about to leave, then turned back. "Are you going to counseling?"

"I am," he said with a nod. He went to the table in the nook, opened his laptop and sat down. If he was staying, he'd get a little work done, she assumed.

"Getting anything out of it?" she asked.

"I'd rather have needles in my eyes," he said. "I'd rather have another vasectomy. I'd trade two sessions for a colonoscopy."

She smiled. "Those sound like good alternatives. I'll think about that." Once outside in the cold night she thought, *that's what I need—I need that Phil back.* But he was damaged now and not the same in her eyes. She had never thought they were so different, but apparently they were. He was vulnerable to sex, she was vulnerable to a mere sixty seconds of understanding, support. Humor. Friendship.

She walked down the street to BJ's house and knocked on the door. A young girl's voice asked, "Who's there?"

"It's Mrs…it's Gerri, from down the street."

"Hang on," she said.

In a moment a series of locks slid and BJ opened the door. She cocked her head, frowning, and Gerri lifted the wine in one hand, the glasses in the other. "I thought I'd thank you properly."

BJ held the door open for her and over her shoulder said to a young boy and girl, "Can you go do homework in your rooms, please?"

They picked up books and papers from the dining table and exited quickly, quietly. "Wow," Gerri said. "That was impressive. What do you have on them to make them obey like that?"

BJ almost smiled. "They're good kids. Listen, you didn't have to—"

"I thought you'd want to know about Sonja," Gerri said. She put the wine and glasses on the table, reached into her coat pocket and pulled out a corkscrew. She went after the cork.

"I've been wondering about her," BJ said. "Um…I very rarely drink alcohol."

"Have a little sip of this, it's good stuff. Unless you're in recovery or something?"

"Just not much of a drinker. How is she?" BJ asked.

"Very unstable, but leveled out at the moment, thanks to drugs. They're keeping her at least overnight to decide if she needs psychiatric intervention, medication, counseling, whatever. It turns out her husband left her yesterday. She went into a tailspin. Meltdown. You don't know this about Sonja," Gerri said, pouring, making sure BJ's was just a small amount, a taste. "She's the neighborhood health nut. She has a little business—she consults on all kinds of stuff—from feng shui to something she calls life patterning. She sells inner peace and tranquility, but she's really always searching, always trying to find the answers. Herbs, exercise, meditation, holistic cures. She thought she had everything figured out. And yet—never saw it coming—he walked out on her without warning. She went down like a torpedo."

"Wow. I thought she was just another suburban princess."

"Yeah, that's how she looks. Very superficial. But she's the best person I know. She'd do anything for anyone. A few years ago, when she was still new on the block, I had a hemorrhoidectomy that just wiped me out. The pain was indescribable. My husband ran for his life, my best friend got weak in the knees and almost passed out just looking at me, but Sonja was there, giving me every kind of comfort she could pull out of her hat. Without her I don't know what I would have done, and we were practically strangers. She removed the packing from my…" She stopped and shot BJ a look to find her smiling. BJ took a sip from her glass. "Well, suffice it to say, if not for Sonja, I wouldn't have had a bowel movement in the past three years. She's weird, but sincere. She believes all that shit." Gerri sipped. "If it wasn't for you today, we wouldn't have rescued her. We would have left, waited for her to call."

"I just thought the situation was strange. I've been watching you three for almost a year. She'd drive me crazy."

"Yeah, she drives us crazy," Gerri smiled. "Still… it is what it is."

"You mind if I ask what you do? I know you work."

"I work for Child Protective Services. Psychologist. I was a case worker for years and now, a supervisor."

"No kidding? You've seen some stuff, then."

"I'd venture to say I'm pretty desensitized. Life's rough out there."

"And you couldn't see something was all screwed up with Sonja?" BJ asked, confused.

"I would have in a second," Gerri said, defending herself. "But man, you got it right away." She clinked BJ's glass. "What do you do?"

"Nothing much. I work for my brother, an electrician with his own small business. I answer the phones, schedule for him and his guys, invoice. It's not a big job, but it's flexible and gets me by. I can cover the kids' schedules."

"Divorced?" Gerri asked.

BJ looked down. "Their father is dead."

"Oh, I'm so sorry."

"Thank you," she said quietly, not making eye contact. Then she lifted her eyes and said, "I haven't had a glass of wine in so long. You're right. I think it's very good. I don't know anything about wine, but I like it. This was nice of you."

"It was the least I could do."

"Listen, I know I haven't been exactly…well, outgoing."

"Hey, don't apologize. I figured you for on the private side, which is fine. Maybe if I knock once in a great while, you'll let me in. No obligation, of course. You should know—not that it matters to you—but the three of us, the power walkers, we're all separated from our husbands. Within three weeks of each other. It's brutal. I'm not here to dump, but just so you know. My husband's trying to carry his part of the load, but I'm relying on my son Jed. He's nineteen."

BJ took a sip. "I'm sorry about that," she said.

"Well, these things happen." Something told her BJ didn't want the details. She picked up the cork, shoved it back in the bottle and stood. "This is for you. Thanks for sharing it. I'll let you get back to your evening."

"It was nice of you to drop by," BJ said, standing also. "I hope Sonja's going to be all right."

"She'll be all right, we'll look after her. Do you have my number, in case you ever need anything?"

"Need anything?" BJ asked.

"We're a bunch of women without men around," Gerri said. "At least I have a nineteen-year-old around much of the time. Yours are still so young. I'm right down the street. You never know when something might happen in the middle of the night—a fright or something. Emergencies, I mean. I'm not recruiting you for the neighborhood bake sale, I swear," she added, smiling. "But I am on a first name basis with a lot of Mill Valley cops—CPS work and all."

BJ went to the kitchen and got a pad of paper. "Wanna write it down for me?"

Gerri did so, then turned away from the table to go home. "Want mine?" BJ asked. "Even though I'm not much good in emergencies."

Gerri went back to the table. "Looked to me like you're great in emergencies. I wanted to be sure to say, I'm grateful that you got involved this morning. I suspect it was a very big step for you. It's pretty easy to tell, you aren't quite ready to get too involved." BJ handed her a scrap of paper with a phone number. It said BJ above it, no last name. "Thanks for everything."

"You're welcome. Thanks for dropping by. For the wine."

Gerri was all the way home before she realized she'd left the wineglasses on the table, two of her nicest. Well, there would come a time to get them. If she was any judge of BJ, she'd make it a point to return them so she'd have no ties. This was a woman nervous about attachments.

Phil was still at his laptop in the kitchen. "That was pretty quick," he said, closing it up.

"Nice woman, but not really interested in finding chums around here," she said, taking off her coat. She was suddenly so tired.

"I'll take off. Unless you need me."

"You can have the couch, if you want it."

"Thanks, but I have court in the morning. I'll have to be pretty," he said, grinning. He shrugged into his jacket and picked up the laptop and briefcase.

"What are you working on?"

"Armed robbery. SOB fired on a cop. It shouldn't be complicated—it's a slam dunk. We'll have a plea agreement before trial. He's going away."

"Ew. Cop's okay?"

"Yeah, he missed." Phil moved toward the door and Gerri followed him. She walked him out to his car through the garage. He put his stuff on the hood and turned toward her. "I'm really sorry about Sonja."

"You don't like Sonja that much," she reminded him.

"Well, I don't dislike her, either. It just makes me uncomfortable when she closes her eyes all spooky and reads my aura. Maybe I'm just paranoid, afraid she's going to see some black squiggly thing that's gonna kill me."

She laughed. "Thanks for checking on things."

"You had a rough day," he said. Then he pulled her against him and for just a moment, held her.

It was what she needed, to feel him against her in the quiet of the night. It felt so good to have his strength wrapped around her; it had been three weeks since she'd felt the confident power in his arms. Then she pulled back. "I can't," she said in a whisper. "This is the hardest part to let go of, you, like this. My friend. My partner."

"You don't have to let go of it."

"But everything is different now," she said.

"It's not for me. Come here," he said, pulling her back. He put his arms around her again and her mind flashed back. *Do you know how many times I put my arms around you to hold you? And how many times you told me not to get any ideas? God, Gerri!* She allowed herself to be held for a luxurious moment, wondering if it was a mistake to indulge in him, even this safely, this briefly.

"Do you remember when I met you?" he asked softly. "You were my witness in a child molest case that was shaky. The second I met you, you scared the hell out of me."

"No, I didn't," she said.

"Oh-ho," he chuckled. "I knew immediately, you would never be uncomplicated, quiet. Manageable. You were on fire. I wasn't sure putting you on the stand was a good idea."

She pulled back slightly. "How'd I work out?" she asked.

"You were brilliant. I had to have you." He pulled her back toward him. "How are we doing here? We making any progress?"

"We're not screaming at each other, but I have a lot of issues."

"Any chance we can work on some of those issues under the same roof?" he asked. "I hate not living with you. And the kids need us to be together."

"Don't ask me to take responsibility for that."

"I understand," he said.

She pulled out of his arms and took a step away from him. "I wonder if you do understand, Phil. The kids—they want us together again, no matter what the cost is to me. They want me to look the other way, get over it. They're not hating you for what you did to our marriage, they're mad at me for taking offense that you had another woman in your life for two years. I knew this would be hard, but I never knew that, no matter which way I turned, it would end up being my fault."

"It's not."

"It is," she said, suddenly hurting all over again. "It's my fault I can't live with you because of it, my fault I found out, my fault I got mad about it.… You spent *two years* boinking some woman from the office, but three weeks is too long for me to be upset about it! What is it with mothers, huh? Why is everything in the whole goddamn world always the mother's fault?"

"You don't think they're just a little pissed at both of us?"

"No, I don't. I think you're coming off looking like

a good guy who made a little mistake and I look like a stubborn, angry, unforgiving demon."

"Aw, Jesus, Gerri—come on, let's not do this. For a minute there we were actually friends."

"There it is again. It's like I'm doing it to you."

"What if I let you hook electrodes to my balls and just fire away until you think I've paid? How about that? Huh?" he asked, giving in to his own anger.

She smiled at him and started walking backward. "Tempting, Phil. But I'm just going to try to resolve my problems with the situation. Thanks for helping me out tonight. Talk to you later," she said. Then she hit the electric garage door button and closed him out.

He'd never get it. It wasn't just the other woman. It was him *needing* the other woman. It made her feel not good enough. It bit so deep, she ached with it.

If it was true that men married their mothers, Gerri would be proud. Muriel Gilbert was on her short list of most admired women.

Phil had two younger brothers, both married. One lived back east, one in San Diego. Muriel and Stan Gilbert kept a small condo in Scottsdale, but they spent much of their time in other locales. They made use of time shares they'd had for years and owned modest investment properties in Boulder, Maui and San Miguel, Mexico, that they leased to vacationers when they weren't using them. That, and homesteading with each of their sons for weeks at a time.

Having been married as long as she had, Gerri had heard a million stories about the worst mothers-in-law on the planet, but hers was the best. Muriel had embraced Gerri as a daughter the second they met and proved to be a fantastic grandmother who was devoted but didn't get in the way too much. She was very careful to follow second to Gerri's mother after the births and never pressured them for visits, for time. They started out as friends, for which Gerri had been so grateful. But then Gerri's own mother died and had it not been for Muriel, she wouldn't have gotten through it. Muriel came immediately, skipping her summer in Maui, and stayed on, getting Gerri and the family past that horrendous period, and then came back when Gerri's father was dying, and again, helped them pull things together. But the time after all that was probably the most significant. Muriel stepped in as the mother Gerri had lost. Friendship yielded to kinship and Gerri adored and respected her.

Muriel and Stan were spending the spring in Mexico and they called every weekend to talk to the kids. Gerri knew it was only a matter of time before someone slipped, mentioned that Mom and Dad weren't living together at the moment. Gerri was pretty sure Phil hadn't dealt with his family on this issue—all his energy seemed focused on making it go away. So she called Mexico.

"I have some news that's going to startle you, so be sure you're sitting down."

"I'm sitting," Muriel said. "What is it?"

"Phil and I have separated. We have some problems."

Gerri heard a whoosh of air on the line, probably the sound of Muriel sitting down. "Merciful heavens," she said weakly. "What on *earth*?"

Gerri took a breath. "The kids know the bare facts, so it's only reasonable that you do. I just learned that years ago he had an affair, one that lasted two years.

He admits it, he's sorry, he'll do absolutely anything to atone, but honestly, Muriel… Well, it was me. I asked him to sleep somewhere else for the time being. While we both get a little counseling. That's the best I can do."

"An affair?" she asked in a breath. *"Phil?"*

"That was my exact reaction."

"Of all my sons… Oh, hell, of all the *men* I know, I would've judged Phil to be the last!"

"I know. Please," Gerri said earnestly, "please don't blame me."

"Oh, for God's sake, of course not! Listen to me, Geraldine—humans have lapses in judgment and when they do, it's their own burden. I hope you're not taking this on. As if there was any way you could've headed this off!"

"Maybe if I'd been more…amorous."

"Right," Muriel said with a snort. "And you'd have been too damn tired to work, carpool the kids and see everyone fed and clothed. Then he'd have to have found another woman for that! The stupid fool! He made a mistake! Sooner or later you'll have to let it be *his* mistake. Lord, I think I might kill him."

Gerri felt her eyes well up. "Thank you, Muriel," she said softly.

"Don't thank me for making sense. I just hope he finds a way to win you back because if he loses you, he will have lost the best thing that ever happened to him. And don't make it too easy for him."

"Believe me—"

"All the same, think carefully," Muriel said. "I know he's not perfect and now I know he's also not that intelligent, but do think this through. It will be hard for you to find a man who's truly your equal and while I don't know anyone more capable, life alone can be dreary. And sad. Very sad. Punish him as much as you need to, but dear girl, don't be hasty." Then she took a breath and muttered, "The ignorant fool!"

"It's already pretty dreary," Gerri said. "Muriel, thank you for not blaming me. Thank you for not saying I should just get over it, since it was years ago."

"All I have to say to you, darling, is thank you for letting the stupid fool live. I hate him at the moment, but he's still my son. No longer my favorite son, but I think I'll probably go on loving him even though he apparently doesn't have a brain in his head."

"Oh, Muriel, I do love you."

"Do you need me? Should I come?"

"No. I think we should try to carry on this way for now. He's spending some time around here, in close touch every day if not always present, and he's doing everything he can. We should let things simmer awhile. I have things to figure out and I can't be distracted. But thank you."

"If you need me, you have only to call. I'll come at once."

Gerri laughed into the phone. "That would serve him right," she said. "His mother and his wife on his case."

"Yes. I can't think of anything more likely to make him wish he were dead."

Bob was already at work in Andy's kitchen when she got home from school at five o'clock. She positively sparkled when she saw him. "Hey," she said brightly. "You're getting an early start!"

"I'm laying down the ceramic tonight. You're going

to have to stay off it for twenty-four hours. It could slide the grout."

"Okay. Did you have dinner?"

"I grabbed something on the way over," he said.

"I'm starting to think you're afraid I might poison you." She laughed. "I offer every night, but you've always already eaten."

He stood straight and grinned, patting his firm, round stomach and treating her to that hypnotic grin of his. "Look at me, Andy. You think I've missed many meals?"

"You look healthy," she said.

"That's not what the doctor says."

"What? Is your doctor worried about you?"

"Everything seems to be holding, but he's convinced I'm overweight and headed for a coronary. That's why I try to stay away from him. I feel fine most of the time."

"Most of the time?" she asked, suddenly stricken with worry.

"Doing the work I do, my back and knees kick up sometimes. I'm fine. My age, you get aches and pains."

"Do you mind if I ask—just how old are you?"

"Fifty-three. Getting up there."

"Well, you're just a few years older than me," she said, opening her takeout carton on the dusty table.

"Not possible," he said, getting down on his knees again. "You look like a young girl."

"I'm a forty-seven-year-old girl. Can I get a glass of wine before I'm closed out of the kitchen?"

"Sure. You have plenty of time. But it's going to go real fast now. After the tile, there's not much to do. Just the appliances, countertops, baseboards, touch up. Do you still like the new cabinets?"

"Gorgeous," she said. "What am I going to do with myself in the evenings when you and Beau aren't here?"

"Oh, I'm sure you have plenty to do without someone making noise and messing up your house."

She'd have to try to remember. This routine had given her so much comfort that she dreaded the kitchen renovation being finished. At first she thought it was just having someone around the house, but soon she noticed it was more than that, it was the quality time they spent together. Bob was there almost every day and she spent at least an hour just talking with him. Then she'd take Beau to her bedroom to lie beside her on the bed and she'd catch up on the day's paperwork or just relax. Sometimes Beau would curl up next to her and she'd nod off; sometimes he'd roll over on his back and she'd idly scratch his belly while she watched TV. She hadn't had a dog since she was a child. She realized more attention should be given to the serenity that came with scratching a big old dog's belly.

An hour of conversation every day for four weeks, at least. That was quite a lot of talking. She knew so much about him, had told him so much about herself. She knew he lived in the guesthouse behind his sister and brother-in-law's very large home. Their grown kids and grandkids were frequent visitors. It was like living with family while having his own place. He tried not to impose on them and helped them out whenever he could; they seemed to enjoy him being there. He felt no real urgency to move and certainly didn't have the income to afford real estate in Mill Valley.

Sometimes their conversations were quite personal. She told him about her marriages and their failures, about trying to raise a son without the regular presence of his father. She even told him she probably got involved with her second husband because she was vulnerable to a good looking, virile young guy—and then she tried to apologize for being so indiscreet.

But he brushed that off. "That's just normal. Biological. Don't be embarrassed by that," he said.

He told her about the few relationships he'd had, none of them intense. He felt he'd been a single man his entire adulthood, even though he'd been married once. "But I've always been very shy around girls," he said. "Never did develop a good line, a smooth move. I was destined to be a bachelor."

"That's hard to believe," Andy said. "You're a good-looking man and—"

He laughed at her. "Andy, please. I'm just an old bald guy with a little too much flesh on the bone."

But she didn't see him that way. He was a large man with big strong arms and hands. He might be a little thick around the middle, but it did nothing to detract from his appearance. He had the most beautiful smile and his eyes always glittered when he talked, as if he was happy to his core. He had nothing in common with the type of man she had found herself attracted to over the years—she always went for guys who could be models. But none had ever soothed her so deeply with their voice. She hadn't expected it from someone shy and quiet like Bob, but as she got to know him, she noticed he had a sexy voice, deep and rich. As for hair? Pfft. He didn't have much but that didn't make him unattractive. She especially liked his thick, dark expressive eyebrows and the tiny cleft in his chin.

They talked about how they chose their careers. Andy had majored in education, thinking she could fall back on her teaching degree after she'd done something fun, like work for an airline for a few years, travel and play and see the world. But then, during her student-teaching term she fell in love with the students and found enormous satisfaction in helping them learn.

Bob took almost an opposite turn. She should have guessed by his diction, his dialogue, he was an educated man. He had a degree in philosophy that was entirely useless to making a living. He'd planned to go on, get an advanced degree, teach. But then he began helping with home repairs, renovations, started working with wood, building and installing custom cabinetry. He discovered working with his hands filled his days with a quiet contentment he'd never felt before. It wasn't a high-powered career, it didn't pay all that much, but there was simply nothing else he'd rather be doing. He worked for a custom builder in addition to taking on some of his own jobs and the two added up to a lot of time and adequate income, but he wasn't exactly climbing the ladder of success. He was a working man.

"I guess I'm just a classic underachiever," Bob said with a laugh.

"Why would you say that? Look at the amazing work you do!"

"Well, I'm not striving for anything, really. Except to do what I do as well as I can. I'm self-indulgent. It feels good. I should challenge myself more, I guess. Did I tell you my wife has a PhD? In theology of all things. I guess that's why she tried so hard to fit into the straight world."

They had talked about their childhoods, their neighbors, their culinary likes and dislikes. Andy couldn't think of any subject that hadn't been covered, and the thought of him not working in her kitchen every day left her feeling more bereft than Bryce's leaving had.

"Really, I'll hate it when you're not here. Having you to talk to has been like therapy," she confessed.

"Probably not real good therapy," he said, laughing. "You should get a second opinion."

"It's been more than satisfactory as far as I'm concerned," she said, eating a little more of her chicken Caesar salad. "I don't think I ever had such meaningful conversations with my husbands."

"That's too bad," he said. "Men and women have such different perspectives, they should explore it more."

"You had good conversations with your wife, didn't you?"

"Oh, yes," he said. "That was the hardest thing to give up. If we'd never been married, the friendship could've remained very close, I think. But we had that history, you know. I wanted a partner who was also a wife, she wanted a friend who wouldn't presume that much. She had to move on. I had to let go."

Andy sipped her wine. "How's your sister's stomach?" she asked.

He sat back on his heels. "It turns out to be her gallbladder, and it's coming out in a couple of weeks. That'll fix her up. How's your neighbor Sonja?"

"Well, she's improving. But she'll never be the same, which is a challenge for me. On one hand, I'm so relieved not to put up with all her goofy stuff—from those herbal drinks to the way she insisted things had to be placed around the house. But on the other hand, she's gone into a decline—so disappointed that all her theories failed, she's not herself at all. She used to be peppy and obnoxiously positive, now she's like the rest of us, tired, ratty, worn down, feels like she failed."

"Oh, no," he said. "Isn't there any compromise in her mind? Like maybe all that stuff didn't work for her husband, but that doesn't mean it's all wrong."

"It's more personal than that," Andy explained. "It's not just that it didn't work on him, it obviously didn't work for her—because she couldn't see this coming. Now she thinks she doesn't know her stuff, doesn't have any intuitive power, can't head off a domestic disaster."

"Hmm. Someone needs to remind her that marital disharmony involves two people, even if one of them is intuitive."

Oh, how I need him in my life, Andy thought as she sipped her wine. "Dear God," she said. "What am I going to do without you? I'm thinking of renovating the entire house, even though I don't have a dime."

He laughed. "I admit, I haven't looked forward to a job as much as I look forward to this one. You turned out to be one of my most favorite people."

Phil Gilbert's secretary buzzed him; his mother was holding on line one.

"You utter fool!" she said, before he could get his entire cheery greeting out.

He let his head fall to his desk, but he kept the phone to his ear. "I thought this might happen eventually," he said, slowly lifting his head. "How are you, Mother?"

"Incredibly disillusioned."

"I hope you're not going to ask me what I was thinking…."

"Why bother? If you had a clever answer for that,

you'd be sleeping in your own bed! Are you going to be able to patch this up?"

"I'm doing everything I can, Mother. Really, there's nothing you can do to make me sorrier."

"More's the pity. That's a challenge I think I'm up to! Phillip, what are you doing to rectify this situation?"

"I'm doing everything she asks of me, Mother. Gerri's in the driver's seat."

"Take a leave. Take her to Tahiti or Alaska or Rome. Do something demonstrative and flashy. Buy her—"

"Mother," he said, cutting her off. "Mom, that isn't what Gerri wants from me right now. I can't win her back by throwing money at this. Believe me."

"You have to *do* something! What exactly are you doing?"

"I'm not going to explain the details of our attempts at reconciliation to you. If Gerri wants to do that, fine. But I'm doing everything I can and you'll have to be satisfied with that."

"Hogwash. Have you bought her jewelry? Flowers? Lingerie?"

"Mother, stop it. You know my wife and you apparently know all about our situation. If I bought her jewelry, she'd pawn it, she'd feed me the flowers and hang me with the nightie. Now back off before you make it worse."

"That hardly seems possible, Phillip. Who was it? Tell me that."

"Not on your life," he said.

Twenty minutes later, having spent the entire conversation refusing to discuss either his sins or his strategy for atonement, he told his mother he loved her and hung up the phone. He sat still for a moment. He'd been wrong. His mother could make him sorrier. He tried to remember Gerri's deep breathing techniques from those long ago Lamaze classes.

Well, certain things had to be faced, Muriel Gilbert being one. Obviously if he didn't tell those who needed to be told, Gerri would. Although it filled him with dread, he buzzed his administrative assistant. "A minute please, Kelly?"

She came into his office, carrying a notebook.

"Close the door, please," he said.

She did so and settled herself in the chair directly facing his desk.

"I apologize—this is overdue. There's a situation you should be aware of. I don't consider it confidential, but I would appreciate your discretion," he said.

"Sure. Yes," she said, pen poised to take notes. This kind of briefing was routine for her.

"Gerri and I have separated. I'm not living at home, but I can be reached on my cell phone."

She looked up, startled. Her usually rosy cheeks lost all color. "No," she said in a breath.

"It's been a few weeks, to be accurate. She just learned there was an indiscretion on my part many years ago. She needs some time to come to terms with that. We're in counseling. I'm optimistic."

"But I just saw her! We talked about—" Kelly stopped. "Oh, God," she said. "Oh, *no!*"

"That's all," he said. "It'll undoubtedly get out, but I haven't told anyone else. I'm hoping this gets resolved before there's a lot of conjecture."

"Oh, God," she said again. "How did this happen? I thought the two of you— Oh, God!" She took a few deep breaths. "How did she find out?"

"I'm not really sure," he said. "But she did. I had de-cided a long time ago that if I was confronted with it, I wouldn't lie. I guess it was bound to happen eventually. She's a frequent visitor in these offices."

Kelly scooted to the edge of her chair. "Phil. Boss. Listen, it could've been me. Oh, my God, if it was me, I'll just kill myself."

"I really don't think we need any collateral dam-age...."

"But I'd like to explain. Please."

"It doesn't matter," he said. "The important thing is that you know what's going on. It puts my schedule at some confusion sometimes because—"

"No, please. I have to explain. It was a while ago— I'm not sure exactly when," she said. "Gerri caught me crying in the elevator and followed me to the bathroom. I'd been having some trouble at home, with John. She was her usual self, counseled me, laughed with me. Really, over the years, the things she's said in passing made me think she knew everything... I mean, even I didn't know everything, but I was pretty sure something was going on with you and... Well, over time she'd said things like she was ready to leave you for being such a typical man, being led around by your—"

Kelly stopped and cleared her throat. "That she'd come this close to throwing you out, that some things seemed unforgivable, but with the right kind of infor-mation and help... Oh, Jesus, I thought she knew! And I praised her for her strength and wisdom, putting her marriage back together after something as difficult as another woman!"

Phil clasped his hands on top of his desk. "It was an honest mistake," he said.

"No, it wasn't," she responded, shaking her head. "I'm trusted with sensitive information all the time, officially and unofficially. I never say things I'm not sure about…"

"I know that, Kelly."

"She caught me in an emotional moment. It had even crossed my mind that maybe John had someone… Oh, God, I thought we might be kindred spirits, both having gone through the same thing. I did this to you. To your marriage."

"You didn't do anything wrong," he said. "Can we put this to bed, please?"

"I should resign. If you can't trust my judgment…"

"Don't be ridiculous. I could never replace you."

"I could call her! I could tell her I'd just been listening to idle gossip! That I had no evidence of any—"

"Kelly," he said somewhat sternly. "I admitted to the affair. And you weren't just listening to idle gossip. Although we never discussed it, you were taking my calls, making my appointments, delivering messages for me when something came up that prevented me from keeping an appointment. And there's the matter that she's kept in contact with you…"

"But you never allowed me to pass on a message or change of address! You never—"

"It's out," he said. "I was past it long ago but Gerri can't get over it yet. Can I count on you to keep this under your hat from now on? I think that's the best either of us should expect from each other."

She sniffed and lifted her chin. "I'll write a letter of resignation."

"I don't want you to do that. I won't accept it. You're not only very important to me personally, but extremely important to the District Attorney's office. Your mistake is understandable. In fact, the mistake was mine. I apologize that you were ever involved."

"Would it help for me to call her? Apologize? Tell her that—"

"I wouldn't recommend it. She's explosive. Really pissed. She's not angry at you as far as I know, but another mention of the situation might have her planting small bombs around government buildings."

"Oh, God."

"We're all going to have to take this one day at a time. There will be a period of adjustment. It might get worse before it gets better. If you could manage not to say anything more about it, that might be best."

"Sir, I just can't tell you how—"

"Kelly, you can't start calling me sir. I'm not angry with you. In fact, I'm relieved to know it was you and not a lot of office talk. We'll have to move on now."

"But if you end up divorced or something…"

"I'm not thinking that way. And if I know Gerri, neither is she. She's putting all her energy into figuring out what it's going to take for me to earn back my place in her life, and as soon as she lays it on me, we'll get it done. It's starting to sound like it could be really bloody, but hey—I'm a big man. Although some of her suggestions have been barbaric. Now really, that's all the time I have for this." He looked back at the paperwork on his desk.

"I just wish there was something I could do…"

"Hunker down," he said without looking up. "We're going to ride it out. Hope for the best."

"Yes, sir," she said, rising slowly. When she got to

the door she turned, "Sorry, boss, I almost forgot. Clay wants to see you at your first opportunity."

"Call his office," Phil said, picking up a pen and scribbling something in the file on his desk. "Tell him I'll be up in twenty minutes."

Almost half an hour later Phil exited the elevator to the executive suite of the district attorney, Clayton Sturgess. He made the trek to the top floor of the building almost every day and on some occasions, several times a day. The executive assistant told him to go right in.

Clay was standing in front of his windows, hands in his pockets, gazing out at the Golden Gate Bridge. He turned slowly toward Phil. "How do you like that view?"

"I've always liked that view."

"Well, it's going to be yours soon. It's time, Phil. I'm not going to run again. I'm leaving for private practice and you're the heir apparent. They want you to run, of course."

What should have been the best news in his career, hit Phil in the pit of his stomach like a boulder. He tried not to let anything resembling panic show on his face. "I'll have to talk to Gerri. The kids."

"Fait accompli," Clay said, waving it off. "You've been slated for this job for at least ten years. Tell her you're finally running. She'll be thrilled."

Phil thought if one more thing appeared to be going right for him in the middle of Gerri's breakdown, she might actually dig up some electrodes. He thought about explaining that the opportunity he'd always wanted couldn't have come at a worse time, but instead, he said, "Private practice?"

"A transitional phase. I have my eye on the attorney

general position. Public office tends to get into your blood." He picked up a folder. "The committee for my reelection would like to meet with you as early as next week. You have the option of putting your own people in place, but I can vouch for these folks. At least hear what they have to say."

"Really, Clay, I haven't made my decision yet."

"Meet with them, anyway. You have some time before you make the commitment, but I can't see you turning your nose up at this. You're ready, the prosecutor's office is ready, the mayor will endorse you. It has your scent all over it."

Phil took the folder. "Thanks, Clay. It's an honor to be asked."

Sonja was released from the hospital after two days. She was given a prescription for an antidepressant and a schedule of appointments for counseling, but her breakdown caused a one-hundred-eighty-degree turn in her behavior. She was lethargic and morose and it was hard for Gerri and Andy to know if it was the antidepressant slowing her down, if the medication just wasn't working yet or if it was simply how a woman feels when her husband walks out on her.

George had taken Sonja to the psychologist for daily appointments the first week and three visits in her second week, but she was still extremely sluggish and hard to motivate.

Gerri and Andy met in the street in front of Sonja's house at 6:00 a.m., each holding their coffee cups. For the past couple of days they'd been rousting Sonja out of bed to walk with them. If they didn't, they feared she might lie there until she got bedsores.

"Ready?" Gerri asked.

"Are you sure this is the right thing to do? It makes me uncomfortable," Andy said.

"We have to. She has to get up, get moving, get some exercise, work off the side effects of the antidepressant, or of George—who knows which. Give her another week, she'll start making her way back. Besides—" Gerri grinned "—think of it as tit for tat."

They went to Sonja's door, unlocked it and entered. The house was different now after just two weeks. It was no longer like walking into a pristine health spa— light, airy and calm with gurgling waterfalls, aroma therapies from spices and herbs to lavender. Now it was musty and dark, blinds drawn, dishes stacked in the sink, shoes kicked off anywhere, clothes tossed over chairs or sofas. In the bedroom, dirty clothes were left on the floor where they'd been dropped, and there was Sonja, a lump in the rumpled bed that looked suspiciously as though it hadn't been made in forever.

"Jeez, it's starting to look like my house," Gerri said. She opened the blinds in the bedroom, though it was just beginning to get light outside. She pulled back the covers and tugged on Sonja's arm. "Come on, La-La. Time to walk."

"Humph," Sonja said, limp. "I think I'll have a day off."

"No days off while the happy drug is moving through your veins. You have to get up. It's time to walk! Come on! You'll feel better, I promise!"

Sonja achieved a sitting position, skinny legs dangling, head down, her snarly hair canopying her face.

Andy was digging around on the floor for some sweats and a T-shirt. She found some wrinkled clothes and held them out to Gerri. They were the pretty salmon-colored sweats, but were definitely not clean.

Gerri reached for the sweatpants and Sonja flopped backward on the bed. "Humph," she muttered. "Maybe later, huh?"

Gerri squatted and began working Sonja's feet into the sweats. She started to laugh in spite of herself. "Oh, man, there was a time I would've paid to see this. Come on, my little La-La lamb, up you come. Don't make me slap you."

"You wouldn't slap me," she muttered, slowly pulling herself upright. Then she just stood there, the sweats around her ankles.

Gerri gave her a second, then resigned, she stooped, grabbed the waist of the sweats and pulled them up, tying them around Sonja's middle. She pulled the night-shirt over Sonja's head and watched as her arms just flopped back to her sides. "I could use a little help here, Sonja," Gerri said. Sonja slowly opened her eyes into mean little slits.

Gerri laughed at her. "Want a bra? Or are you free-boobin' it today?"

"Bra," Sonja said miserably.

Andy handed Gerri a sports bra plucked out of the pile of dirty clothes and Gerri handed it to Sonja. "Get with the program, Sonja. You know I can't get you in this thing."

Sonja took it, put it over her head and wiggled her arms through the holes, pulling it down tight over her small breasts. Next were the T-shirt and shoes. Then Gerri grabbed Sonja's hand and said, "Come on. Let's get this over with."

On the way through the living room, Gerri grabbed a

sweatshirt off the back of the sofa and held it for Sonja to shrug into. Then they went out the front door.

Standing in the street at the end of Sonja's sidewalk was BJ. "Morning," she said. "I thought maybe I'd walk with you today. If that's all right."

"Well, this is a nice surprise," Gerri said. "Isn't this a nice surprise, Sonja?"

"Leave her alone," Sonja said meanly. "She *needs* her *run*."

BJ surprised them by laughing. "Getting a little feisty, aren't ya, girlfriend? Well, you wait, I'll have you running right alongside me before you know it."

five

Andy had meetings after school and was late getting home. She didn't bother stopping for a take-out dinner. When she walked into her kitchen from the garage, she saw Bob sitting at the new breakfast bar. He stood immediately, grinning. He wasn't wearing his overalls, but a knit shirt and jeans, all spruced up. He threw his chest out, lifted his chin. When he did that, Andy thought he looked so confident and in charge, patriarchal. With that pose, he looked as if he should be standing in a photo behind a wife and seven sons, the proud leader of a strong clan.

Andy looked around. Blond oak cabinets, granite countertops, gleaming ceramic floor, shiny appliances, new stainless-steel sink, freshly painted trim. It was flawless and stunning. She shook her head, looked down at her feet and sniffed. A couple of tears spilled from her eyes and she gave a hiccup of emotion.

"Oh, you don't like it," he said, deflating in disappointment.

She lifted her head, the tracks of tears glistening on

her cheeks. "It's beautiful," she said. "It's more beautiful than I imagined it could be."

"I hardly ever do a good enough job to make someone cry."

"I don't want it to be finished," she said.

"But it took two weeks longer than my estimate," he said. "The sooner the better, you said. I should probably give you a discount."

Beau was sitting right in front of the kitchen sink, alert, wagging his tail expectantly. Andy walked toward him and reached into the jar of dog cookies she'd been keeping for weeks. Whenever she came home, he got a cookie and a pat. Then he'd lie back down, content, polite.

"I just don't know what I'll do without you," she sniffed. "I couldn't have gotten through the past month if you hadn't been here almost every day."

He gave her a sweet smile. "Come over here and sit down," he said. "Let's talk this through."

She sat across from him at the breakfast bar. There in front of him was his final invoice, the balance due, her house key sitting on top of it, and it nearly made her crumble. He reached his hands across the short space and took both of hers. His fingers were thick, his nails clean and trim, calluses on his fingers and palms. It was the first time they'd actually touched and she loved the feel of his hands.

He gave hers a little squeeze. "You did get through it, Andy. You're going to be fine. You rise again and again, remember?"

"Because of you," she said. "You helped with everything."

He shook his head. "Nah, that's not true. You've been

through a rough time. You're a little vulnerable, that's all. Just talking about things probably helped—it usually does. But you're young, beautiful, you have good friends, that son of yours—he seems like a fine boy. I can't help thinking what a comfort it must be to have a son—you'll never be alone."

"I'm not young, Bob. Or beautiful…" She sniffed.

He laughed. "I guess it all depends on where you're standing. That's how you seem to me. Really, if you'll just think about it, you have every reason to be happy, have a nice life."

She grabbed a tissue off the gleaming new counter. But then she immediately took his hand again, not wanting to let go.

"What is it now? You've always been so positive," he said. "In the worst of it, you haven't been this emotional. I don't even remember you getting upset when the TV and stereo went away."

She chuckled through her tears and shrugged. "Because I was never so happy to see anything go away in my life!"

"There you go," he said. "You're about to start a whole new life." He grinned. "With a whole new kitchen!"

"Why'd I have to do the kitchen?" she said. "I live alone. Noel's hardly ever here and I sure don't cook for myself. I don't even like to cook very much."

"But don't you just have the slickest counter, the prettiest wallpaper to look at while you're eating your takeout?" He laughed and pulled his hands back. "I've enjoyed it, too, Andy. We were lucky—we had a good working relationship. Doing this kitchen was pure joy for me."

"It was?" she asked.

"It was indeed. I don't know when I've had so much fun. But I have a favor to ask. Would it be all right to come back on the weekend, when it's nice and sunny in the kitchen, and get a few pictures of the finished job? It's for the book I showed you, the one I use to show potential clients." He lifted his chin and looked around. "I'm especially proud of this one. I owe it to you—you let me have my way about some things I've wanted to do for a while now."

She glanced over her shoulder. He'd talked her into the wine rack right in the breakfast bar, the paint trim around the wallpaper, the black granite with the blond wood, the smoky glass in the cupboard doors, scalloped trim underneath. She looked back at him. "It's awesome." She stood and went to the cupboard for two wineglasses. "We're going to toast it," she said. She pulled a bottle of wine out of the new rack. "Pinot Noir okay with you?"

"Fantastic," he said.

She removed the cork, poured them each a small amount and watched as Bob swirled, sniffed, tasted, gave a nod. She poured them a little more and lifted her glass. "To your amazing talent," she said, composed once again.

"To your trust, patience and money," he replied with a laugh, touching her glass.

"Money!" she said. "I have to write you a check."

"After the wine, Andy. Nothing better than enjoying a job well done."

"You really put your heart into it, Bob. And cleaned up so nicely."

"I'm afraid the rest of the house is probably a disaster from all the construction dust. It's the nature of the beast."

"I'll give it a good cleaning on Saturday. Why don't you come over on Sunday? Hey, how about dinner on Sunday, after your pictures are taken?"

"That's awful nice, Andy, but I probably shouldn't."

"Why not?"

"You don't like to cook for one thing."

"I'll make an exception for a really good carpenter. Noel might be here, too—of course, I have to schedule an appointment with him."

"Kids," he said laughing. "It's a real busy time of life. All right—what the heck. But only if you promise not to get all weepy on me again. I can't stand to see you sad about anything."

"I promise," she said, smiling. She reached for her purse and got out her checkbook. She wrote a check, tore it out and pushed her purse aside. Bob's hand was out to accept the payment, but she put it on the counter and slid it away. "No," she said. "First tell me one more time about growing up on that farm up north. About your dad and your sisters."

So he told her another story about his dynamic father, the strength in their family, a man of great humor and understanding—probably what had helped her form that image of Bob as the head of a clan of fun, hardworking, life-loving people. When he got to the part where his father died too young—only sixty-four—for a moment Andy identified with Sonja, feeding her husband grass and herbs, lighting candles around him to keep him balanced and healthy and safe for as many years as possible.

The thing about Bob was, even when he got to that

part where he lost his father, he could tell it pleasantly, as though that was also an important passage in his life. His memories of the man were stronger than his grief at the loss.

She picked up the wine bottle to pour, but he put a hand over the top of his glass. "I have to go, Andy. Connie is just home from the hospital after her gall-bladder surgery."

"Oh," she said. "She probably needs your help."

"No," he smiled. "She's all taken care of, but I'd like to visit with her for a little while. I like to make her laugh and watch her grab her fat middle and groan."

"That's evil."

"I know," he said. "It's a side of me I just can't control." He reached for the check, folded it and slipped it in his pocket. "What time on Sunday? I'd like to come before it's too late—I want to get pictures while it's light in here."

"Is five too late?"

"That should be perfect. I'll see you then. Come on, Beau. Time to go."

The dog got up and went directly to the back door, wagging his tail and looking over his shoulder at Bob. *I might just have to get a dog,* Andy thought.

"Thank you," he said. "See you Sunday."

When he was gone, she leaned her forehead against the door and felt the sting of tears again. *What in the hell is the matter with me,* she wondered. *I'm out of my mind!*

Noel and Jed had been inseparable in grade school, played on the same sports teams in middle school, were good buddies who drifted in different directions in high school. While they developed individual interests, they always remained close even when they didn't spend a lot of time together. After graduation they attended the same community college—each of their mothers had decided they needed a year to mature before going to a large university—but they didn't have any of the same classes. Jed leaned toward pre-law while Noel was more interested in the arts. Plus, Jed had Tracy—girlfriends took up time.

When they were little they looked as if they could have been brothers, a couple of skinny, freckled blond boys, but as they developed their own personalities, so did they come into unique appearances. Noel was a healthy, strong five-nine with clear, slightly olive skin, dark eyes and dark, curly hair like Andy's. Jed took after his father. He was tall and lean, just over six feet reaching for Phil's six-two, with thick, sandy-brown hair.

Despite the fact that they moved in different circles, they remained trusted confidants and the best of friends.

It was a rare Saturday night that neither had any commitments. Noel was trying to spend a little more time at his mother's house since Bryce had left and Jed's girlfriend was at some chick thing, leaving him on his own. Noel had called Jed to catch up and when they realized it was a free evening, they met at the park a few blocks from their houses at 10:00 p.m. They sat at a picnic table in the dark under a big tree. They could hear the noise from a raucous volleyball game on a brightly lit sand court not too far away.

Noel fired up a joint, inhaled it greedily and passed it to Jed. He held in the smoke for a moment and then let it out. "So…he around at all? Your dad?"

Jed took a healthy hit, held it. "Yeah," he said. "I

guess they have some kind of deal about who's picking up Matt and Jess, unless one of 'em calls and tells me to do it. It happened right here, man. He was sitting right here when he told me."

"How'd he do it?" Noel asked.

"Straight to the point. He cheated on my mom and she went out of her mind. Booted him out."

Noel sucked on the joint, passed it back. "You think they're gonna split?"

Jed took his hit. "They are split, man. It's just up in the air if they stay split. I know I'm supposed to feel sorry for my mom—I mean she got the bad end, right? But my dad... Christ, he almost cried telling me. I almost hugged him, y'know?"

Noel laughed, accepted the joint. "Is this good shit or what?"

"Very good shit. I'm gettin' high. Startin' to think about Tracy already."

Noel giggled. "I've got another one. By the time we finish it, you won't be thinking at all...."

"So...you okay with Bryce leaving?"

"Okay?" he asked. "Okay? Aw, shit, he couldn't leave fast enough to make me happy. Problem is, my mom thinks I should be at home all the time now."

"You talk to her yet? Tell her what's going on with you?"

"You know I haven't. She'll tell my dad. And Glenda, the stepwitch. It's over when that happens."

"You don't know that for sure," Jed said. "I mean, I didn't freak out when you told me you were gay, did I?"

"Yeah, but you're different. It's not like you could do anything about it. But my dad? Oh, he's gonna do something terrible."

Jed turned toward Noel. "Hey, man, to quote Geraldine Gilbert, the world-famous psychologist, 'it is what it is.'"

Noel had started wondering what was wrong with him when he was thirteen. When he was sixteen he fell for a guy in his theater class and realized he'd known since way before he was thirteen, he just couldn't put a name to it. He'd told Jed when they were both seniors. Jed wasn't the perfectly evolved high school senior; the news caused him to jump back about six feet in shock and probably fear. His best friend, gay? That just wasn't right.

But Noel and Jed had grown up in a part of the world where being gay wasn't exactly breaking news. Plus Jed had a mom who dealt with difficult issues on a daily basis and while being gay in itself might not be a case for a social worker, coming out was rough, and could lead to all kinds of issues that ended up in case files. Jed's dad worked with a few gay guys in the prosecutor's office and what homophobic attitudes Jed might have expressed when he was younger were pretty much worked out of him by the time he hit junior high.

But Noel's dad, Rick, the football coach, was a classic homophobe. He made frequent bigoted remarks about fairies, limp-wristers, queers. Not around the high school where he taught and coached, because that could get him in trouble, but at home he laid it on pretty thick. He liked physical, athletic, masculine guys who seemed to leave no doubt—but of course, Noel could enlighten him, it wasn't always obvious and some of those guys were actually gay. Noel had girls all over him all the time—way more girls than Jed had ever had around. His dad found that impressive.

Noel had a couple of gay friends who shared an apartment and he spent a lot of time there where he felt most comfortable, free to be himself. He had managed, with some difficulty, to keep his parents from meeting his friends because they would know at once—they weren't hiding their sexual orientation the way he was.

Jed and Noel talked for a while about the complications of their lives, their parents' lives. They were about halfway through their second joint when they heard a deep male voice. "Evening, gentlemen."

They both jumped in surprise. Jed quickly tossed the joint and it landed on the grass just a few feet away. There before them was a cop on a bike—park police. Riding up within seconds was his backup officer. "Go ahead and put your hands on your heads, all right?" the first one asked pleasantly.

"Aw, c'mon, go bother someone else," Noel said.

"Shut up, man," Jed warned him. "Just shut up."

Great! Jed thought. It wasn't as if it was his first joint, but he wasn't a frequent user, and he'd never been caught before. Not only did his girlfriend, Tracy, disapprove, but his dad had told him a long time ago that if he ever got picked up for anything that could embarrass him in his job, he should just assume Daddy wasn't going to step in and try to cover for him. Jed was on his own—he'd have to face the music and his father wasn't going to make any excuses or reel in any favors. *Figures it would have to be drugs.* Jed was more likely to have a few beers—and he never drove under the influence. Oh, no, his driving violations were all totally sober—his mother always pointed out he could be an idiot without the assistance of pot or beer.

The cops patted them down. Jed had been seen tossing the joint, which the first officer picked up. Noel, however, had a small baggie of marijuana and some rolling papers on him—that made the situation a little more serious. It wasn't quite enough for felony possession, and he didn't have the paraphernalia to be dealing, but he could actually go to jail if the police decided to take things to the extreme. If they didn't like Noel's mouthiness or were in bad moods, they could hook him up and call for a prisoner pickup. Jed had learned these things as a prosecutor's son.

In the end, they were issued tickets. Nineteen-year-olds didn't have a call placed to their parents. They'd have to appear in court, deal with the mood of the judge, at least pay fines, maybe get stuck with community service. Who knew what the end result would be? Noel didn't have to go home and tell his mom and dad what happened in the park, and he hadn't been exposed as gay, so his big secret was still safe. But Jed knew his dad was going to hear about this. If someone in the court system didn't pick it up and tip Phil Gilbert, then the press might. They were all over the prosecutor's office, looking for stuff to embarrass them. If the press could, they'd try to find a case where Phil came down hard against a person for a pot possession, then would claim he'd watched his own son walk away with a pat on the butt.

The officers left them with their tickets. "Hey. Sorry, man," Noel said.

"Not your fault. I was smoking when they came up."

"Yeah, but I never told you I had a bunch of stuff."

"I don't care about that. That's your stuff. But I gotta go. I have to think about what to do. What to say."

"Don't say anything," Noel said. "We go pay a fine—"

"You don't understand," Jed said, shaking his head. "At our house you can't keep a lid on this kind of thing."

"Lid." Noel laughed. They called a few ounces of cannabis a lid. "Funny."

Jed wasn't feeling high or giddy at the moment. His parents had split, both of them were leaning on him for help, Tracy wasn't going to like this, it wasn't going to be nice. "I gotta get home." He grabbed Noel's upper arm. "Try not to lip off at the judge. Trust me—that's the way to six weeks in a soup kitchen."

"Soup," Noel said, laughing. "I'm kinda hungry."

"Aw, Jesus," Jed said. "I'll see you later."

Jed plunged his hands in his pockets and headed for home. If he remembered, Jessie was out with friends, and Matt was somewhere overnight. When he was leaving a little before ten, his mother was nodding off in front of the TV in the family room with a stack of reports in her lap.

When he snuck into the house, those pages had slipped onto the sofa beside her and she was leaning her head against her hand, sound asleep.

He went to the kitchen to forage for food, conscious that he was moving slowly, making noise. It wasn't long before he heard her snort, shift. "Jed?" she called out.

"Yeah, Ma."

"You're home?"

He laughed. "Nah, I'm still out."

"Hmm," she responded, not moving from the sofa.

Jed started building a sandwich very methodically. Between layers he stuffed handfuls of potato chips into his mouth. He heard the sound of a noisy car, the laughter of boys. The front door opened with a crash, and he heard scuffling, more laughing, and the sound of rapidly departing footfalls, the racing of a motor, the squealing of tires. Then his mother screamed, "Jed!"

He moved toward the foyer of their house and what he saw made no sense. His mother was crouched in front of Jessie, who was sitting on the floor slumped against the wall, apparently passed out. "Jessie, come on, Jessie," his mother was saying, patting her cheeks.

"Hmm?" Jessie asked sleepily.

"Jessie? Whew, are you drunk?"

"Oops," Jessie said. Then she hiccupped and giggled without ever opening her eyes.

Gerri looked over her shoulder and up at Jed, who was towering over them, staring stupidly.

"Help me out here, will you?" Gerri asked, pulling at Jessie, who was completely limp.

Jed leaned over, but lost his balance and instead wobbled backward a couple of feet. Gerri frowned at him. "Can you help me here?" she asked. "I have to get her upstairs to her bedroom, check her over, make sure she's all right."

"Call Dad," Jed said.

"Just help me!"

"I can't, Ma. I'm stoned."

Her mouth hung open for a second. Then she slowly looked between her two oldest kids, muttered a disgusted curse and dashed for the phone in the kitchen, moving pretty fast for an almost fifty-year-old who'd been asleep on the couch for an hour. She dialed Andy's number. "Help. I've got my hands full—one kid's drunk, one's higher than a kite."

"The high one was with my high one," Andy said.

"If you can leave yours, I need help with Jessie. I've got a potentially terrible situation." She hung up and rushed back to her daughter who was vomiting in the front hall. The smell of secondhand beer filled the air. Gerri found herself thinking, at least it was beer, probably enough to create this disaster. There could also be drugs, the type of which she didn't even want to think about yet.

Jessie wiped her mouth with a trembling hand. "Oh, Mom," she said, starting to cry. She only cried for a second before she added to the catastrophe by retching again.

Gerri ran to the laundry room for a few towels, then back to the foyer to find Jed on his hands and knees, trying to communicate with Jessie. By the time Gerri had covered the mess in towels, Andy was in the doorway and Jed skulked away to the kitchen.

Gerri looked up at Andy with imploring eyes. "She was dropped off by a gang of boys," she said, her voice low. "Her blouse is buttoned funny."

Andy took just a second to absorb the meaning of Gerri's words, then took charge, squatting in front of Jessie. "Okay, chickie," she said. "We're just going to take off your icky clothes, honey." She began unbuttoning and helping her out of her blouse, leaving her in her jeans and bra. Then Gerri and Andy, one on each side, pulled Jessie to her feet and helped her up the stairs. The first stop was the bathroom where Jessie vomited again. They finally got her to the bedroom where Andy pulled back the bedcovers. Before sitting her down, they peeled off her sloppy, hundred-and-fifty-dollar jeans.

"Should we stand her in the shower?" Andy asked.

"I don't think so. Just the clothes off—I don't know

what happened to her tonight. I don't want to destroy any…evidence," Gerri said.

Andy froze. Then, shaking her head with worry, stooped to removed Jessie's boots and jeans so Gerri could ease her into bed. Before covering her, Gerri looked closely at her legs, including the insides of her thighs.

"Jessie?" Gerri asked, leaning over her. "Jessie, can you tell me what happened tonight?"

"Beer," she said with a drunken whimper.

"Did anyone hurt you? Who were you with? Who brought you home?"

"Drew," she said. "Oh, God!" She leaned over the side of the bed, retching. But she was down to just miserable gagging, her stomach empty by now and Gerri was quick with the trash can. Jessie lay back down on her pillows, moaning.

"Call Phil," Andy said immediately.

"No. I don't want Phil right now."

"Think of him as a legal consultant," she said. "If you need to know how to treat this situation, he'll know."

"I know. I'm a social worker."

"And he prosecutes crimes. If there was a crime against your daughter, he can help you now more than I can. Besides, you know he has to be told. I'll stay with her. Go call him. And on your way to the phone, whack Jed in the head."

Gerri glanced at the clock. It was late, per typical. She went to the kitchen to find Jed standing at the counter, eating. She shook her head in disgust. She hoped that all three kids weren't picking tonight to act out. She called Matt's cell phone and it went straight to voice mail. Against all good judgment, she dialed the number of the friend where Matt was spending the night. There was no answer. Her heart was pounding and her thoughts were racing as she left a terse message. "This is Gerri Gilbert. Matt is supposed to be spending the night there tonight. When you get this message, please call me and let me know that he's there, safe, no matter what time it is."

Then she called Phil. She called the phone in his small, one-room, rented flat near his office in San Francisco rather than his cell phone. It was Saturday night and she wanted to know where he was when she needed him.

He answered on the second ring. "How fast can you get here?" she asked. "I'm in way over my head."

"What's going on?" he asked. She'd heard him say this into the phone hundreds of times when he took calls from detectives at the scene of a crime, or from his office late at night.

"Jed's high on something, Jessie is drunk and puking and Matt doesn't seem to be where he's supposed to be."

"High? Drunk? Not where— Jesus, what's going on?"

"I'm not sure yet—but my big issue right now is that Jessie is completely wasted and was dropped off by a group of boys who just dumped her in the house and then ran. I don't know if I should shower her off or if something bad happened to her while she was…"

Phil didn't miss a beat. "No shower. Remove the clothes, bag them but don't wash them. Keep her comfortable. Is Jed in any danger?"

"Jed?" she said, turning to him. "What did you take?"

"I didn't take anything, Ma. Just smoked a little dope. Sorry."

Gerri went back to the phone. "Pot," she answered. "And there's no answer where Matt's spending the night."

"I'll have my cell on if anything develops. Sit tight. I'm on my way."

She hung up and highly resented the feeling of relief it had given her to connect with Phil and have him on his way. After all, he wasn't really hers anymore. He was secondhand—like buying back a suit from the consignment store. It was new when you first got it, then you sold it through consignment and someone else used it for a while, then put it back on the market. Someone had been in it for a couple of years then offered it back to her.

By the time Phil made it to Mill Valley, the situation had settled somewhat. Jessie was lucid though still intoxicated. She insisted nothing terrible had happened to her. However, she was supposed to have been out on a date with a senior named Drew, but they had hooked up with three other boys so it was Jessie getting drunk with four boys. Not a safe equation in Gerri's book. Jed had come down from his high. He sat on the sofa in the family room and didn't make eye contact with anyone. A call had come from the household where Matt was spending the night—they'd gone out for pizza and everyone was home safe.

Andy headed home as soon as Phil arrived, and Gerri got to work cleaning up messes in the foyer, bedroom and kitchen. Phil sat first with his daughter, trying to get whatever information she could give in her state of inebriation. By the time he got to Jed, Gerri had the laundry running and had gone to the bedroom, leaving them alone.

Phil sat down beside his son. "You talk to your mom about what went on here tonight?" Phil asked.

"She didn't want to talk to me. She told me to just wait for you," Jed said. He put his hand in his pocket and pulled out a ticket. "I got cited."

Phil studied it for a moment, then looked at Jed. "Got anything to say?"

"Like?"

"Like *why?*"

"I was trying to chill out." Jed looked at Phil hard, his eyes narrowed. "I guess you thought you'd be the only one a little jammed up by this thing with you and Mom."

"No, actually I thought it would go hardest on you kids. But I didn't think you'd take dumbass chances like this. I thought we understood each other."

"Like you never had a joint," Jed said accusingly.

"We went over that. I was a kid once. But you knew the risks." Phil tossed the citation back at his son. "Says you were cited in the park. Right out in the open. Smooth."

Jed sat forward angrily. "Listen, I'm sorry and I'll handle it, okay? Kind of sounds like you really don't give a rat's ass if I have a joint, but you'd rather I not get *caught*."

"Oh, I give a rat's ass," Phil said. "I'd rather you not drink underage, too, but I know you do from time to time. So let's at least be safe, be careful. I can't control you, Jed, I can only give you advice. I hope that before too many more years go by you grow up. See it's not in your best interest to dabble in drugs or take stupid chances with the use of alcohol."

Jed got red in the face and when he spoke, he sneered. "I hope before too long you decide it's not in your best interest to leave me holding the goddamn bag around here!"

Phil kept his cool, but he sat taller and matched his son glare for glare. "If you weren't a little stoned and a whole lot stupid, I'd have you up against the wall right now. But I don't think much I say is going to get through that cement block you're using for a brain. Go to bed."

"Fine!" Jed stood and bolted up the stairs. When he got to his room he slammed the door for good measure.

Phil knew Jed was at the end of his rope. He took a breath and wearily dragged himself to his feet. He walked down the hall to what was once his bedroom and knocked on the door. Gerri called out for him to come in.

Gerri had changed into clean sweats and a T-shirt. She sat cross-legged on the bed. "Sounds like that went well," she said.

"Listen, Jessie had herself in a real bad place tonight—one girl and four boys in a car with a bunch of beer. I'm not convinced all's clear there. She denies anything happened but she was very drunk, so who knows? Those boys could've taken advantage of her. Can you get her in to see someone this week? If she crossed the line, she needs to be better prepared—and if the line was crossed while she was unable to give conscious consent, maybe something will turn up or maybe she'll tell a professional."

Gerri's spine straightened a little more with every word. "If you think that's possible, I can take her to the E.R. first thing in the morning, have them run a rape kit."

"You see any bruises, any suspicious marks, semen stains? You undressed her, got her down to her panties—you know what to look for."

"No. Nothing suspicious. That's why I didn't call the police."

"If she'd been raped, you'd have a strong suspicion. Probably they just got her drunk, got her to say and do some things she ordinarily wouldn't. But we should follow up."

"We?" Gerri asked with a sarcastic laugh.

"I'd be happy to take her," Phil said a little impatiently. "Don't you want to be the one to go? Wouldn't it be less humiliating for Jessie to go with her mother?"

She sighed and nodded. "What's Jed got to say?"

"Oh, it's my fault he got caught smoking a joint," Phil said. "I didn't push him too hard. We'll talk again tomorrow morning."

Gerri shook her head and let go with a little humorless laugh. She punched the bed. "All this, just so you could get laid."

"I don't feel like going a round with you, Gerri. My kids are hurting."

"*Your* kids?"

"They are still mine, aren't they?"

"Oh, yeah, but I'm living here with them. And with all the hurt in this house."

"That's your choice. You want the key to my place in the city? It's up to you. And for your information, I wasn't just looking to get laid. I was looking for a lot more than that, but I knew the whole time I wasn't going to find it."

"You *did* love her," she said, keeping her voice down.

"I loved *you!* But we weren't firing on all cylinders! It was probably more my fault than yours—we aren't ever going to know. Now I just want to get my kids through this, because I know for goddamn sure it isn't their fault! I'll be on the couch!"

"I didn't invite you to have the couch!"

"I didn't ask your permission!" he shot back. Then he pulled the door closed as he left.

Gerri sat. Of course, Phil deserved every nasty insult she could hurl at him because he'd had the affair. She'd been over all of this with her counselor, twice a week. It was impossible to reconcile in her mind because she'd been okay with their marriage and he had not, and she'd had absolutely no idea. If you don't know something's wrong, something's missing, just what the hell were you supposed to do about it? It was like having some vital nutrient missing from your diet and not being aware until you're in kidney failure.

She was equally responsible for their marriage, she knew that.

When she called, he came. Then and now. It was because he was committed and she understood that. If only he hadn't reached beyond their boundaries to quench his thirst—anything else would have been easy to forgive.

She wanted to find a way to forgive him, but it just didn't seem to be in her. She was still so confused, so angry. And she hated the way she felt.

Gerri had never had an easy time with sleep, even when there wasn't a huge crisis. She drifted off only when bone tired, but even exhausted, she couldn't relax if something major had her mind whirring. Her thoughts drifted between what might've happened to Jessie, what Jed was going through, scary images of thirteen-year-old Matt running wild and unattended on the mean streets of Mill Valley.... But there were no mean streets in Mill Valley—it was an upper-class suburb. So of course, she had to revisit the image she had of her husband boinking some twenty-five-year-old buxom blonde because his ratty, tired, menopausal old wife didn't have the energy or enthusiasm to get all frisky three times a week.

But when she called, he came. Even though he'd have to suffer through her verbal barbs and spikes.

It was almost three in the morning when, frustrated, she got out of bed and crept into the family room. The TV was still on, though the volume was turned down. Phil was snoring and he was curled up as much as possible on the sofa. He usually just sprawled, spread eagle in their bed. His arms were wrapped tightly around himself; it was a chilly April night, typical in the valley at this time of year. The Pacific night breezes were cold straight through May.

She looked down at him and the one thing that struck her was that she missed him so much it hurt. She had relied on him so heavily through all the years of their marriage and *needed* him. Tonight was a real wake-up. Any other Saturday night in history, they'd each have known exactly where the other was when Jed wandered in from the park, when Jessie came crashing in the front door.

But tonight Phil was living somewhere else when she needed him.

She'd give anything to go back—not seven years but just seven weeks. She had no idea what going back seven years could do to change things but if she could just go back seven weeks, she'd somehow manage to miss that elevator ride with Kelly, and they'd be as they were. Firing on enough cylinders for her peace of mind, at least.

She couldn't forgive him. Not yet. But she did cover him with an afghan before turning off the TV and going back to bed.

six

When Gerri opened her eyes on Sunday morning, for just a split second everything was right with the world. She could smell coffee; Phil was up, moving around in the kitchen, like any Sunday morning. Then it all came crashing back to her—he'd slept on the sofa, Jessie was passed out in her bed. The night before was a wide-awake nightmare.

She dragged herself out of bed, splashed water on her face, brushed her teeth and headed up the stairs to her daughter's room. The clock on the bedside table said it was just after 7:00 a.m. Gerri sat on the edge of the bed and reminded herself she'd conducted hundreds of interviews. She knew how to read eyes, facial expressions, body language, knew the weight of words. That this situation was personally traumatic might compromise her judgment slightly, but it didn't even touch some of the horrific family problems she'd been required to assess in her job.

She jostled Jessie. "Come on, honey. Wake up for me."

"Umph," Jessie grunted. "Can't I sleep? Please?"

"Sure you can. After you talk to me. Come on, it's important."

"What?" she whined, trying to pull the covers over her head.

Gerri pulled the covers back and Jessie pinched her eyes closed in agony. "Open your eyes. We have to talk."

Jessie opened one eye. "I'm sorry, okay? I won't do it again...." She tried pulling the covers again, but Gerri held them. *"What?"* Jessie demanded.

"I'll let you go back to sleep after you tell me what happened last night. Right now I'm too worried to wait."

"I drank some beer," she said. "I told you I won't do it again."

"It wasn't *some* beer," Gerri said. "It was enough beer to make you pass out, you were very sick and your clothes were on funny when you came in."

Jessie's eyes opened and stayed open. She was still for a moment, then scooted up in the bed. "What do you mean my clothes were on funny?"

"Your blouse was buttoned weird, like maybe it had been unbuttoned, then buttoned up by someone else. Someone who was dressing you."

Jessie's gaze instantly dropped.

Gerri put a finger under her chin and lifted it. "Were you sexually assaulted last night? After you'd had too much beer?"

"What?" Jessie asked, aghast, her eyes open wide.

"Did those boys take advantage of you? Hurt you?"

"Oh, God," Jessie said, running a hand through her hair, her eyes tearing up. "Oh, God, please just leave me alone...."

"I have two choices, Jessica. I can get some answers

or we can take you to the hospital, make sure you're not hurt. Make sure you haven't been raped. Were you molested? Anything?" Jessie just stared at her. "You were dropped off by four boys who ran after they dumped you in the house, passed out. You—"

"They *ran?*"

"As fast as they could. I got to the front door in time to see them getting into the car. I checked you over as well as I could, but I have to hear something from you. What do you remember?"

"Ohh," she moaned. "Oh, no…"

"Did someone undress you?"

"No," she said, shaking her head, looking down. "I undressed myself. On a dare."

"Start at the beginning. You were going out on a date with Drew."

"We were out and we ran into a couple of his friends who had a case of beer in the trunk. We drove out by the vineyards, parked, drank some beer and I got…I got stupid. I guess I had too much. Someone said if I took my shirt off, I could have another beer. I didn't feel like I was going to pass out, get sick. I felt fine. Silly, but fine."

"What happened next?" Gerri asked.

"Nothing, really. Someone said something about my father and someone else made me put my shirt back on and they said they were taking me home. I don't remember anything after getting back in the car."

"Are you sure nothing happened in the car? After that?"

Jessie's eyes narrowed. "One of them said, 'You know who her father is? Get her out of here.'"

"Are you sore anywhere? Could you have been hurt? Raped?"

"I didn't have sex," she said. "I would know."

"And how would you know, exactly?"

"Because I know when I've had sex," she said.

Gerri felt her stomach knot, but she was a trained professional. Her expression remained passive. "Are you sexually active? On the pill or anything?"

"It only happened a couple of times. A while ago. I wasn't planning on it happening with Drew. I don't like him that much. In case you were too busy to *notice,* I don't exactly have a *boyfriend* right now."

"You're sure about last night?" Gerri asked. "Because if anything bad happened we can still get help."

"Nothing worse than this," she said. "You checked me over? While I was asleep?"

"Oh, yes, absolutely," Gerri said with a nod. "I would have called the police if I'd seen one suspicious mark on you. You were incapacitated, not able to make a decision, to consent to anything for yourself."

"God, please just let me die right now. First you throw Daddy out, then you examine me while I'm asleep…."

"Passed out," Gerri corrected. She wanted to talk about the suggestion that she threw Phil out, but this morning was not about that. They could revisit that later—she'd explain that she asked him to leave while they went to counseling and he agreed to go. It was the best she could do.

"They ran because I was totally drunk and it was their beer," she said wearily. "I *hate* them. They're a bunch of losers."

"But you went with them," Gerri said.

"I didn't have anything better to do," she said with a shrug. "I don't feel so good."

"I can imagine," Gerri said, standing up from the bed and getting out of the way.

Jessie swallowed a couple of times, went pale, charged out of bed and made a beeline to the bathroom.

Gerri left her daughter's bedroom and went downstairs to the kitchen. Phil was sitting at the table with his laptop open and the Sunday *San Francisco Chronicle* spread out in front of him. Except for the fact that he was wearing last night's clothes, it was almost as if their lives weren't inside out. It was how Sunday mornings had looked for years. They were a couple of hardworking public servants with never enough time and both of them took advantage of Sunday mornings to catch up on news, get a little work done while the house was quiet. Often they'd sit at opposite ends of their long kitchen table, individual laptops purring, maybe some conversation about the news, a case, a project, the kids, the week's schedule. It was one of the things she had loved about them, that they were so alike, so in tune. And it had all been a trick—everything was all wrong when it had looked so right.

What she missed most wasn't the deep conversations, not the warm reassuring hugs, but the times they were simply together, quiet, like this. Just being in the same room with someone you depended on, working or reading or watching TV, knowing you could speak if you had something to say, but there was no pressure.

She poured herself a cup of coffee and sat across from him. "I woke Jessie and made her talk to me."

"How is she?" he asked, closing the lid on the laptop.

"I'm convinced she just got drunk and made a giant

fool of herself with a bunch of idiots. We're lucky they're just a bunch of idiots. She could have been in serious danger."

He hung his head and shook it briefly.

"Listen," she said. "I'm really not emotionally ready to think about reconciling, but I need a better plan. I can't keep track of these hoodlums alone."

"I have a line on a place in town," Phil said. "A guesthouse. It's expensive, but close. Available in a couple of weeks. I was hoping by then…" He didn't finish.

She ignored that. "How often are you seeing the counselor?"

"Once a week. Twice a week would cost me a spleen."

"What are you working on?"

"Working on?"

"You know. Are you getting anywhere? Discussing anything that might help me…understand?"

"We're looking at my feminine side."

"What?" she asked with a sudden burst of laughter.

"I don't want to have a feminine side, but this is what we're talking about. Apparently I have an overdeveloped masculine side, which I took as a compliment but the counselor didn't. I make too many assumptions. I compartmentalize. I can put problems from work in one corner while I deal with problems at home and vice versa. I'm not sensitive unless my own little male feelings are at stake." He sipped his coffee. "Can't you just torture me for a decade or so? I'm in such agony. He's a weird little prick and I think he hates me. I thought, being a guy…"

"You thought he'd understand you."

"I hoped, since I don't understand me."

"Couple of weeks until the guesthouse is ready, huh?"

"She wants it painted. The landlady."

"Can you tell her that's not necessary? Because really, I have to have some help around here."

"It's a little old lady. She likes me. I could try."

"Please. Try. I'm going to take Jessie to the doctor, anyway, and I'm going to ground her. Will you stick by me on that? It's the only way I know to keep her safe until I figure her out. If I clip her wings, she can't end up in a car that has a case of beer in the trunk."

"I'm with you. Can we ground her till she's twenty-six?"

Gerri smiled at him.

"She's so beautiful. So brilliant. Such a dimwit," Phil said.

"Sixteen," Gerri said. "It's half grown-up, half too stupid for words."

"Do you remember being like that? Because I was never like that."

"Were you like Jed?" she asked.

Phil instantly hung his head. "Oh, yeah. I was probably two of Jed. The dumbass. He was sitting in the park smoking dope with Noel—I guess he really thought that one through. He knows there are park police all over the neighborhood, just looking for dipshits like him."

"I need you around more. I just can't do it alone."

"I know, Gerri," he said. "No one could."

"Women do it all the time," she said. "But I can't. They're independent kids, we made them independent but they're used to having two of us to ride herd on them. No matter how long it takes for us to come to a decision about where we're going, we have to figure out how to help each other get them through these years. Last night was too close. Jed could've been using something worse. Jessie could have been hurt."

"You're the only one making a decision about where we're going, Gerri."

"Okay, let me put it this way—while we're separated, we still have to work together until they're out of the woods. Really, I'd like to just shove you in a hole right now, but I won't sacrifice my kids because I'm hurt and angry. Help me with them, Phil."

He took a breath. "You're calling the shots. Tell me what you need, that's all you have to do."

"I need you five minutes away when you're not in the city working. I need you to help me parent more."

"Done," he said. "I'll talk to the woman with the guesthouse today."

She just shook her head. "I've walked at least a hundred women through separation and divorce and suddenly I don't know how it's done."

"Wait," he said. "Divorce? You're not thinking that way already."

She was quiet for a moment. "What if we can't put things back together? It's been weeks and I'm still…" She bit her lip. "I just don't feel married anymore, Phil. At least I know I don't have the marriage I once had."

"Don't go there, Gerri. That's a whole different subject. I'm real clear on the anger, on your need for space and time to work through this, but I'm not ready to have a discussion about divorce."

"Maybe we should talk about it," she said. "I can't reassure you that it won't come to that. Maybe we should know where we both stand."

He picked up his coffee cup and took a slow sip. "I

don't recommend it," he said. "It puts a final stamp on things. If you start thinking that way, you're not really giving me—us—a chance. I'm willing to do anything, whatever you need, but when you bring divorce into the dialogue, I'm not letting you call the shots anymore."

She stiffened. "Just what are you saying?"

"I hate this, Gerri. I don't think living apart is getting us anywhere. I think we should be here together, talking rather than fighting, eating at the same table, sleeping in the same bed—believe me, I know how to do that without touching you. I think we should be trying—both of us. I should be trying to do whatever I can to reassure you I can be trusted again, but you should be trying to get past the rage because we're not going to know if we can make it until that's not part of the landscape anymore."

"I just can't live with you," she said.

"Fine, if that's what you need. But I think of this as a temporary separation while we work on our problems. I don't see it as a separation preceding divorce. When you start talking divorce, you put me in a whole different place."

"The lawyer place?" she asked sarcastically.

"The father place. The abandoned spouse place."

"*You* abandoned *me* for *her!*"

"No," he said calmly. "Not for one hour of one day. What I did was wrong, but let's stay clear on what I didn't do."

"And just what *didn't* you do?"

He stared at her hard, thinking. He shook his head. "I'm not even going to bother. You already know."

They sat in stony silence.

"I'm going for a walk," Gerri said.

* * *

Gerri walked a hard half hour, ending up in the same park where her son had been nabbed for smoking pot. She sat on the ground and leaned against a tree trunk. *And just what didn't you do, Phil?* The thought kept reverberating in her mind. It's why she'd had no idea there was another woman—Phil never let his commitments slip. And not just his obligations to the kids, but also to her. He never really put anyone ahead of her. So that's what he wanted from her—for her to see the marriage as a whole entity with one small imperfection.

But, what Gerri couldn't understand, what filled her with anger, was the idea that the marriage could be so strong and balanced yet he would still need another woman. In making a list of pros and cons, it wasn't difficult to admit, even through red-hot rage, that Phil was a good father. Not just good, but excellent. And he'd been a committed partner, through the worst crap. He'd been a rock through death, disaster and at least a couple of years of Gerri's hot-flashing, sweating and mood swings that jolted her unpredictably. As a provider, no question—he not only put in long hours and made a good living, but he pursued an honorable task, working on the side of justice. Given what she did for a living, that meant a great deal.

And wasn't she all those things, too? Yet she had never succumbed to the temptation to stray. She felt tears on her cheeks and at the same time found herself shaking her head in soundless laughter. Oh, she'd flirted. She'd even found the occasional man tempting. But she'd never run into a man who had more to offer than Phil, who was everything to her. *Everything.* Handsome, strong, brilliant, funny, devoted. But she was not everything to him.

"Bad morning?"

Gerri looked up to see BJ standing over her. She was wearing her running clothes, panting, drenched in sweat. Gerri wiped off her cheeks. "Marital problems suck."

"Yeah, I'll bet," BJ said. She sat down on the ground in front of Gerri, folding up her legs under her. "Need a shoulder to cry on?"

"Nah, not really. It's so typical I'm going to be reading about it in *Good Housekeeping* in a few months."

"That right?"

"He's at the house right now," Gerri said. "I called him— My teenagers went nuts last night, everyone got in trouble and I was in over my head. So he came. Stayed. Slept on the sofa. And this morning we were having a conversation about how to work together as parents even though we're not living in the same house and it started, the button pushing." She shrugged. "That's how it works. I've been through it a million times with friends and clients. I said something about the potential for our divorce and he warned me he wouldn't go along with that quietly. I felt threatened, he felt backed into a corner, etcetera." She sniffed and wiped her nose. "He had an affair," she said.

"Ouch," was BJ's singular comment.

"A long time ago, but still…"

"Still ouch."

"Yeah. The son of a bitch. I might've never known and we'd have gone on forever, just like we were. Until it happened again."

"So you're glad you know," BJ said.

"No. I'm not. I wish I didn't know. I'm starting to feel like I don't have the right to be this mad. I wish I could *catch* him, that's what I wish. In our bed, that's what I'd like. With the children watching. Something so egregious no one would even question my feelings, which are still so hot I can't get a rational thought through." She sniffed. "Even my best friend asked me if I couldn't get over it, since it was a long time ago. Get over it? If I let myself think about it, I want to kill him."

They sat for a quiet moment, then BJ said, "Instincts are the hidden genius. Maybe the worst thing you can do is question what you feel." Gerri's head came up and she looked at her. "Okay, the second worst," BJ said, smiling.

Gerri was suddenly aware that when BJ smiled, a slightly crooked smile, she was a pretty woman. "Jesus, BJ, this almost qualifies as reaching out."

"Maybe I'm coming out of my shell," she said. "Anyway, you were nice to me. It doesn't hurt to be nice back."

"It's appreciated," Gerri said. "First walking with us, now this."

"It got easier when I realized you guys don't have perfect lives."

"Right now we don't even have manageable lives. I'm teetering on the edge, Andy's getting her second divorce and Sonja's half crackers." Gerri looked around the park. "Every year, right before school starts, we have a big neighborhood party here. It's an amazing party— celebrating getting our freedom back after a summer of having kids home. Well, everyone celebrates but Andy, who's going back to school with all the little jerks. Were you here for the last one?"

"Barely. I had just moved in. I watched some of it from the house."

"Weren't ready to come out yet?"

"Not then, no. I was new to paradise. Not really up to being scrutinized by the elite of Mill Valley."

Gerri laughed in spite of herself. "You live in the same neighborhood."

"Just sort of. It's not my house. I don't even rent it as a matter of fact. A friend of my brother's is letting us house-sit for a while till I get on my feet. I'm here because my brother's business is close and he could give me work."

"No insurance? With your husband's death?"

"'Fraid not," she said. "We're very lucky, so don't get the idea I'm complaining. It's an awfully nice house to just let someone use. But then, they have a lot to spare, I gather. I'm a little out of place here. I should be living much smaller, cheaper."

"Probably we all should," Gerri said.

"Oh, I think you're where you're supposed to be. I'm from a pretty poor section of Fresno, barely scraping by. But you and the girls? A district attorney's wife, school principal and the wife of a successful financial planner? I think you fit pretty good."

"Who told you all that?" Gerri asked.

BJ shrugged. "I asked the owners about the neighbors before I moved in."

"But you asked me what I did for a living."

"Yeah, I know. Making conversation. You and your husband…I mean, you and the son of a bitch are neighborhood legends. High cotton." She grinned her crooked grin.

"Huh," Gerri said, astonished. "And I don't even know your last name."

"Smith," she said. "Honest to God, Barbara Jean Smith and if you ever call me Barbara Jean, we're all done talking."

Gerri laughed. "Well, how do you do," she said. "Big sneak."

BJ pulled herself to her feet. "I'm going to go shower, run the kids over to my brother's for a while and break into Sonja's house. I stopped by there yesterday. Since it wasn't a walking day for you and she's still in a fog, I tried to roust her out. She wouldn't come out, she's living in a cave. But that house—whew. It's starting to actually smell bad."

Gerri stood. "Seriously? It seemed okay on Friday when we got her up. I mean, it's a mess, but…"

"Yeah, but it's turning." BJ made a face. "I have a lot to pay forward—I'm going to see if I can help her clean up."

"When will you be over there? Maybe I'll come over, too."

"Don't sweat it," BJ said. "You have teenagers going nuts and a son of a bitch to threaten and nag. I can handle it."

"When?" Gerri asked with a laugh.

"Ten or so, I guess. But really—"

"I'll stick the SOB with the kids. He needs to be punished."

"Right." BJ laughed.

Gerri got to Sonja's house ahead of BJ. "What are you doing?" Gerri asked when Sonja answered the door.

"Nothing," Sonja shrugged, running a hand through her tangled hair.

"You must be doing something."

"Watching the shopping channel, that's all."

"The shopping channel? You? Well, I'm meeting BJ here," Gerri said. "We're going to help you straighten up the house. You've been too groggy to get to it, I guess."

"I don't want you to straighten up the house," Sonja said. "I don't want anyone to do anything."

"Come on, don't be like that. You've been there for me a hundred times."

"This is different," Sonja said.

"Yeah—it's you this time." Gerri brushed past her and walked into the house. For the second time she was a little embarrassed that BJ had been more observant, caught that something all wrong was taking place before Gerri. She wrinkled her nose. The house was starting to take on an odor. Or Sonja was. "I guess I've been a little caught up in my own drama," Gerri muttered. "Are you just so tired, Sonja? It doesn't look like you've cleaned up around here in a while. Or yourself, for that matter."

"It doesn't matter," Sonja said with a shrug, turning away and going to the family room sofa. She flopped down, staring at the TV.

Gerri observed the squalor all around—discarded socks, kicked off tennis shoes, scrunched up tissues, dirty coffee cups, a couple of plates, glasses, an apple core in a bowl with what looked like little spit out bites, all rotten. She walked over to the table and picked up the remote, turned off the TV.

"Hey!" Sonja said.

"Go take a shower," Gerri said firmly. "See if you

can find something clean to wear. Do something with your hair."

"Really, I don't feel like it."

"I know. I can tell. Do it, anyway."

"I don't—"

"Sonja, I'm tired of looking at you all a wreck, falling apart. If you don't do as I say, I'm going to get in the shower with you and scrub you up." Gerri shook her head. "It's not like you to go to pieces like this. Jeez, you're in worse shape than I am and I had to call my cheating husband home to help with the drunk and stoned teenagers. Come on, we're going to get you straightened out. Now cooperate. What George did was pretty crappy, but really—"

"I don't want to talk about it," Sonja said. "I have to talk about it three times a week with that counselor and I refuse to talk about it anymore."

"Then go take a shower."

Without another word, Sonja turned and headed for her bathroom. Gerri went to the kitchen and surveyed the mess. Sheesh, it looked as if a plate hadn't been washed, a surface cleared or floor swept since George departed. There was rotten fruit in a bowl surrounded by tiny flies, the loaf of bread on the counter was green, the tissue box empty and surrounded by used tissues, balled up. She heard the shower running and went to open the blinds and windows in the front room to air the place out. She wiped a hand along the fireplace mantel and looked at the dust on her fingers. Then she noticed there were a couple of imprints of dust-free spots. A round spot on the side table, a square spot on the mantel, an oval shape on another accent table. Nothing had been touched in the house, nothing cleaned or tidied, yet things had been moved?

Looking around carefully she saw little tufts of hair on the sofa, the floor, the coffee table. *Holy Jesus*. She picked one up and rubbed it between her thumb and forefinger. *Sonja's hair. What the hell?*

She went through the kitchen to the garage. Everything looked to be in order. The work bench was tidy, Sonja's car was immaculate, the lawn mower and yard tools stored neatly in the corner. And there were a few boxes, taped and stacked. There was nothing written on them and Gerri knew Sonja was an obsessive labeler. She pulled back the tape and opened the top box. "Oh. Oh," she said. She moved it off the stack and opened another. "Oh, God," she said. She didn't bother with the third and fourth.

When she got back to the kitchen, she noticed the answering machine light was blinking. She pressed Play. "You have fifty-seven new messages," the mechanical voice said. Gerri's lips silently repeated the number, stunned. The first message played. "Sonja, we missed you at your meditation class and the center's director said you hadn't called in. Let us know if you're going to have class on Friday..."

The second message was similar. "Sonja, hi, Patty James—Um, have you stopped teaching yoga on Monday, Wednesday and Friday mornings? No one got a message. Are you out of town? Call me."

Gerri listened to a few more and then heard: "Sonja, it's Bev Sorenson—I was just wondering how long you're going to be on leave of absence, I want to sign up for your next class." Gerri stopped the machine.

Sonja wasn't taking or returning calls; she'd dropped out. Fifty-seven messages? *Yikes.*

She phoned Andy. "I need you at Sonja's," she said.

"Everything all right?"

"No," Gerri said. "Can you come?"

"Be right there."

Gerri opened the cupboard just above the phone. There, neatly taped to the inside of the door was a list of phone numbers, beginning with George's cell phone number. "Good girl, Sonja," Gerri said.

George answered on the third ring. "Hi, it's Gerri Gilbert. I'm at your house—Sonja's house. Have you been here since you left?"

"Sure. I pick her up for her counseling appointments, why?"

"Didn't you notice what's going on here? What's happening to her?"

"Yeah, I noticed. She's very depressed. The doctor said—"

"George, did you look around the house? Did you notice *her?*"

"I noticed Sonja, yes, but I just waited inside the door for her to get her purse. I just can't stand hanging around there. And, there didn't seem to be anything I could do except make sure she attended counseling sessions. I hoped in time—"

"George," she said, cutting him off, exasperated. "She hasn't cleaned a thing since you left, including herself. She hasn't washed a dish, done a load of laundry, changed the sheets or showered. She packed up all her fountains, candles, chimes, books, relaxation DVDs and CDs—everything that *defines* her. She's filthy, sitting in front of the shopping channel, hardly eating. I've only taken a glance, but I think there's nothing but rotten food in the house. And who knows if she's sleeping too little or too much. She's sick, George. Really sick."

"Hello?" she heard Andy call from the front door.

"She sees the counselor three times a week and she's on medication," George said.

"Well, maybe it isn't working, and the counselor obviously hasn't picked up on these signals. We've been coming over here weekday mornings to get her walking a little bit—we get her up and dressed and out the door, but I don't see any evidence that she's brushing her teeth, combing her hair or anything. Is there a psychiatrist on her case?"

George gave her the name and phone number. Andy stood in the kitchen, watching Gerri on the phone. By the time Gerri had written down the psychiatrist's details, BJ was standing next to Andy, both opposite Gerri across the breakfast bar. "All right, George, thanks," she said. Then, "Sure, I'll let you know."

Gerri hung up and looked at the other two women. "Okay, we've got a problem. Sonja's in bad shape. She's dangerously depressed, filthy, lethargic and she got rid of all her woo-woo stuff. I'm calling her doctor and then I'm taking her to the hospital. She can't be left alone in this condition. She might be suicidal."

"Well, holy shit," Andy said. "You sure?"

"Of course not, but I'm not going to take any chances or one of these mornings we're going to come over here to get her out of bed and she's not going to wake up." She swallowed and pinched her eyes closed. "She's pulling out her hair," she said softly. She dialed a phone number, got a recording and scribbled down the emergency number.

"What should we do?" BJ asked.

Gerri whirled around, picked up a couple of pill bottles from the windowsill over the kitchen sink. "Count these," she said, handing them each a bottle.

"You don't think if we get her cleaned up, she'll feel better?" Andy asked.

"It's not that simple," Gerri said. "It's medical. She's way around the bend."

When she got the emergency answering service for the doctor, she knew exactly what to say for the quickest possible response. "Hi, I'm Gerry Gilbert, calling about Sonja Johanson. I'm a clinical psychologist and I'm her neighbor and friend. I'm here at her house and I believe she may be suicidal. I need to talk to the doctor immediately. It's an emergency."

After she hung up, she faced Andy and BJ. BJ held the bottle toward Gerri and said, "Fifty-eight of sixty."

"Sixty," Andy said, holding out her bottle. "She isn't taking them. What made her so groggy and sleepy?"

"Depression. Black, dangerous depression. Look, I'm sorry to leave you two with the mess—just see if you can throw out the garbage, maybe wash a load or two, get it presentable and make the smell go away." The phone rang and she picked it up, looking at the caller ID. "I like that—he's right on it."

It wasn't a he—Dr. Sydney Kalay was a woman. Gerri explained who she was and what she'd found and Dr. Kalay told Gerri to bring Sonja to the mental health clinic at the hospital as soon as she could get her ready. When she hung up, Andy and BJ were still standing by, waiting. "I'm taking her in. Oh, God," she said, running her hand through her short, cropped hair. "Oh, man, I hope she doesn't give me any trouble."

"You want help?" BJ asked.

"No, I want to do this alone. I've done it before, but never for a good friend. Jesus, how did I not notice? Is it because I'm such a miserable wreck at six in the morning? Crap!" She started toward the master bedroom, then she turned. "BJ, once again, if you hadn't said something, this could have been so much worse!"

BJ shrugged. "Just take care of her."

When Gerri got to the master bedroom, Sonja was sitting on the edge of her unmade bed wrapped in a towel, looking at her knees. Her hair was dripping onto her lap; she hadn't gotten all the soap out of her hair. "Okay, my little La-La," she crooned. "I'm going to help you with your hair. Come back to the bathroom."

"Oh, just never mind it," Sonja said. "I should probably just lie down for a while."

"No, honey," Gerri said, pulling her hand. "We have things to do. Come on."

She led Sonja to the bathroom and let her sit on the closed toilet lid while she brushed and dried her hair. Gerri could see bald, scabby spots here and there on Sonja's scalp, and before she could finish, tears were streaming down her cheeks. But Sonja, so catatonic, didn't notice.

As Sonja continued to sit passively, Gerri went in search of clean clothes. There was a big pile of dirty clothes right in the middle of the bedroom floor, but fortunately Gerri was able to dig out some clean underwear from a drawer, and she found a fresh smelling and comfortable sweat suit. It was probably the only reason they hadn't noticed how badly Sonja was falling apart—maybe she wasn't showering, but she was putting on clean clothes now and then. Once dressed, she stood Sonja in front of the mirror. "Want a little lip gloss or something?" Gerri asked.

"Naw, forget it," Sonja said. "I should probably—"

"We have to talk now," Gerri said. She sat Sonja back on the closed toilet seat and knelt on the bathroom floor in front of her. She held her hands. "Sonja, you've been feeling pretty awful for the past couple of weeks, haven't you?"

Sonja shrugged. "I'm fine," she said, looking down.

"You're not fine," Gerri said. "You're pretty sick right now. You haven't been taking your medicine, you've been pulling out your hair," she added, her voice cracking. She felt the tears well up in her eyes and her throat ached. "You need a little help to get back to your old self. I'm going to take you to see the doctor."

Sonja looked up. Her face contorted. "No," she said in a barely audible breath. "No, I go to the counselor. I go all the time...."

"I know, baby, I know. It isn't counseling you need right now. The doctor has to talk to you, check you over. You have a chemical imbalance, that's all. But we have to get it straightened out before it gets worse. I want you to come with me and I want you to let the doctor help you."

"No," she said, shaking her head, and her face twisted in a painful and miserable grimace as she squeezed Gerri's hands. "Please, no. Just let me be. I'll be okay, just let me be." And then her shoulders shook as she began to weep.

Gerri was frankly glad to see a little emotion, but hoped she wouldn't have to hog-tie Sonja. She shook her head and ran a gentle hand over her shiny clean hair. "No, honey. If I let you be now, it would just get worse. I want you to come with me. I want you to trust me. I'll stay with you until the doctor decides what's best. Okay?"

"No. No. No," she cried, great tears rolling down her cheeks. "No, please."

"It's going to be all right, Sonja. You have to trust me, come with me. The doctor is waiting for us." She wiped the tears off her friend's face. "You'll be safe. I'll make sure you're safe."

Gerri stood and pulled Sonja up. She put an arm around her shoulders and led her out of the bathroom, through the family room. She grabbed her purse off the counter and said, "We'll take Sonja's car. Sonja, where are your keys?"

BJ and Andy exchanged looks, standing back. Sonja didn't even acknowledge them. She was completely focused on either Gerri or the floor. Andy reached over to the hook mounted on the wall by the back door and handed Gerri the keys. Then she hugged Sonja. Sonja hugged her weakly.

"I'm sorry. I'm sorry. I'm sorry," Sonja said, crying.

"Nothing to be sorry about, honey," Andy said.

Gerri pulled Sonja out the door. "Let's go now. I'll take care of you—everything will be all right."

"Need help?" Andy asked.

"No, we'll be fine. I'll call when I can. I'll come back when I can."

Gerri put Sonja in the passenger seat and backed out of the garage. Then she held her hand all the way to the hospital, steering with the other hand. When they got to the hospital, they took the elevator up to the clinic where Dr. Kalay was meeting them. When they were out of the elevator, Gerri stopped and, with her hands on Sonja's upper arms, looked into her eyes. "Sonja, listen to me. I love you. I want you back in my life. You tell the doctor everything she wants to know. Tell her about eating, sleeping, how you've been feeling. I want you to get better. Sonja, promise me?"

Sonja nodded weakly and Gerri pulled her into her arms, holding her for a moment. "Please, baby—please tell the doctor."

When Gerri pushed open the clinic doors, the place was dark and deserted. They didn't have clinic hours on Sunday, of course. But an attractive and smiling Pakistani woman in a pair of khaki slacks and a lightweight sweater was standing in the dimly lit reception area, waiting.

"Ah, Sonja, hello," she said. "Not feeling so well at the moment? How can I help?" she asked, taking her out of Gerri's care, leading her away to an office.

Gerri sat in the waiting room, in the semidarkness. It was several long minutes before it occurred to her that Dr. Kalay could have met them in emergency where there was always a crowd, always fast movement and a lot of action, usually tough to find a bed. But the doctor had used a personal key to open up the mental-health clinic, saving Sonja the stress of all that. She must have done that because she took Gerri's description of the situation very seriously, and for that she was so grateful.

During the first hour, sitting in the quiet, dimly lit room, Gerri couldn't help but picture what the past two weeks must have been like for Sonja, the nightmare of not being able to cope, feel nothing but darkness and pain. She'd been completely self-destructive, possibly there were bad dreams or even hallucinations.

During her second hour of waiting, Gerri thought

about her husband, her kids. And her friends—all in such transition, all in danger of collapsing around her. Yet, she was not falling apart. Oh, she was crying too much, lonely too much, furious too much, but even with a twenty-five-year marriage on the ropes and three teenagers testing her sanity, she was somehow hanging on. *You can never tell about a person.* Gerri didn't think of herself as strong. Sonja, on the other hand, who seemed to know every trick—how to calm nerves, listen to her body's messages, alleviate depression, help sleep, stimulate herself, how to level out and maintain serenity—was coming apart. Sonja—who always seemed to have an answer, a cure—was losing it.

Two full hours and change passed before Dr. Kalay came into the darkened reception area. Her expression was serious. "Thank you for bringing your friend to the hospital," she said with just a slight accent. "Sonja is going to be admitted to Glendale Psychiatric for a little while. At least a couple of weeks, perhaps a month. You were right, of course. She's clinically depressed and needs treatment."

Gerri's eyes flashed. "Her husband walked out on her a couple of weeks ago."

"I know this. But of course, that's not the cause of her depression. A trigger, perhaps, but the cause is medical and we may or may not get to the bottom of that. You're a psychologist, you say?"

"I'm a social worker with CPS. But I have a master's in clinical psychology."

"Ah, well you're very smart and we're so lucky you noticed. But please don't suggest to Mr. Johanson that he caused his wife's depression." Then she reached out and put a hand over Gerri's. "I'd like you to go now.

I've given her a very heavy sedative and will have her transported as soon as arrangements with the insurance company are complete. It won't take long and I won't leave her in the meantime."

"But I didn't pack a bag for her. I didn't even bring her purse."

"Perfect," Dr. Kalay said. "She doesn't need anything and the purse would be taken away from her during admission, anyway. I'm going to suggest she not have visitors for about ten days, then we'll reassess, but you're welcome to call me to inquire about her progress any time you like."

"Is she going to be all right?" Gerri asked. She'd had clients admitted to psychiatric hospitals before, but this felt so personal, so emotional, it left her shaken.

"I'm optimistic. Sonja is forty and has been functional for many years. I believe once she benefits from medication and therapy, she'll be functional again."

"And happy?" Gerri asked. "Because she was always happy."

Dr. Kalay smiled kindly. "I'm counting on that. But please be patient. It's a process that takes some time. And so much is up to Sonja."

"I know," Gerri said in a breath, afraid she had seen Sonja giving up. "Did I tell you everything? About her packing up all her feng shui and meditation and natural food stuff? Her relaxation CDs? Her little fountains and—"

"Yes, Gerri. You told me."

"And that she hadn't bathed? That she was pulling… pulling out her hair?"

Dr. Kalay nodded, that soft smile still in place. "Can you please leave her in my hands now?"

"Yeah," she said, running her hand through her hair again. "But I did promise her I wouldn't leave her...."

Dr. Kalay shook her head patiently. "She's not aware of any promises right now, it's all right. You can go. I can take it from here. She's safe with me. Trust me."

"I asked her to trust *me*," Gerri said softly, hanging her head. She turned to go, but at the door she turned back. "Thank you. Please take good care of her."

"I'll do everything I can," the doctor said.

"Will you call her husband? I understand it's not really his fault, but I don't want to call him. I don't think I can talk to him."

"I've already spoken with him twice. The insurance, you know. He's aware. If it's any consolation to you, he's being extremely helpful."

"He'd better be. Because it might not be his fault, but she was fine before he—"

"It's so much harder to be objective when it's a loved one," Dr. Kalay said, cutting her off. "I know you understand how this often works. If not the separation, perhaps an accident, an illness, a death in the family, a financial crisis. There is so often a precipitating factor that is not the cause. I think I should get back to Sonja now."

"Yes. Of course, yes," Gerri said, though it was very hard to leave. She heard the lock on the clinic door slide into place behind her and it sounded so like the crashing closure of prison-cell doors.

Gerri drove back to Sonja's house and parked the car in the garage. She found Andy and BJ just finishing up and they'd done far more than surface clean—they had the place just about up to the old Sonja standards in record time. She filled them in while they worked together to fold a final load of laundry and run the vacuum around the master bedroom. She reassured them—Dr. Kalay was very kind, very sensitive, and Sonja was safe and could begin healing. In fact, Gerri was more convincing to them than she was to herself. Gerri kept having visions of Sonja sitting on the couch, blankly staring at the TV while biting off her nails and tugging on her hair for two long weeks while her friends assumed she was simply responding to new medication with grogginess, lethargy. It must have been such a lonely, frightening time for her.

Finally Gerri went home, emotionally depleted.

When she walked in the front door, she was met with complete silence. She walked farther into the house—no one seemed to be around. She went through the kitchen and found Phil in the office he'd only visited for the past several weeks. He was using the computer rather than his laptop. He swiveled his chair around to face her as she stood in the doorway. "Where is everyone?" she asked him.

"Jed's at Tracy's for a while. We talked for an hour this morning—he's repentant and maybe one degree smarter. Jessie was up for a while, had something to eat and went back to bed, and Matt's down the street playing ball with his friends. You get everything taken care of at Sonja's?"

"Not really," she said, shaking her head. "Oh, the house is clean now. Laundry done. But I had to take Sonja to the hospital. They're admitting her for a couple of weeks, maybe a month. She's…she's…" Gerri dropped her chin, looking down.

Phil stood and came toward her. "What happened?"

She lifted her eyes and a large tear spilled over. "She

cracked. Went completely over the edge when George…
God, Phil." She gasped with sobs that begged to be torn
free, that when facing the best friend she'd had in her
lifetime she could no longer rein in. "She was tearing
out big hunks of her *hair.*"

"Oh, honey," he said, pulling her into his arms.

She leaned against him and cried hard tears and he
pulled her back into the room and down onto his lap.
He held her and for a few minutes all she did was cry
against his shoulder, his arms around her, reminding
her so painfully that this was where she'd always found
safety and ballast. Because of that, she started to wres-
tle free. "I can't do this, I can't."

But he pulled her back. "It's okay, Gerri. It's okay
to do this. It doesn't commit you to anything to let me
comfort you a little."

"Oh, God," she said, crumbling against him. "Oh,
God, you'll just confuse me."

"Stop it," he said, holding her. "You were never confused about this. I come to you when things are bad, you
come to me. That's how it is with us, no matter what
else is happening."

"No," she said. "It's not the same as it was."

"Stop it," he said. "*This* is the same as it was. Honey,
I'm so sorry about your friend." She felt his hand stroking her back while she cried and she remembered. She
had always depended on him in her very worst moments. And he'd never let her down. Even when there
had been someone else.

But she forced that out of her mind and stayed right
where she was, burying her face into his neck, smelling
him, feeling him. And he did what he'd always known

how to do—made her feel that everything was going to be all right. Given her state, she decided the illusion was worth the risk.

seven

After spending most of the day at Sonja's house Andy had to rush around. She'd done her own housecleaning, but not her primping and cooking. She felt strangely nervous and the whole time she was showering, choosing clothes, fixing her makeup and hair, she had one thought. It's *just Bob*.

But it was also Beau. Surely he'd know it was okay to bring Beau. And while it hadn't been very long since she'd seen Bob, she was positively elated that he was coming back to take pictures and join her for dinner. They would tell stories and laugh and hopefully he'd be in no rush to leave.

She couldn't quite figure out what it was that had her so completely enchanted by him—he certainly wasn't her usual type of man. But, she hadn't had a real male friend in longer than she could remember. There was something about a man's perspective on things. Not just any man's perspective, but Bob's. He was so deeply honest and guileless. He seemed innocent, but he was not. He'd certainly shouldered some of life's harsher blows—he'd lost a woman he loved. Yet he was the most understanding and forgiving man she'd ever known. Conversations with him were soothing and warm and exactly what she needed. But there was something she couldn't put her finger on—spirit, maybe. Or soul. He was so right with himself. He was alone with only that one brief relationship to report and had every reason to be grumpy, bitter, but he actually appeared grateful he'd had his wife in his life. Anyone else would've been hurt and angry. Andy wanted to know how he did that. How did he turn his heartaches into blessings?

She was very careful with how she staged the evening. Casual place settings, plenty of light and no candles, hearty food for a hearty man. She didn't want him to get the wrong idea. She was absolutely going to make a play for him—but for his friendship, nothing more. This was Bob, just an ordinary guy and not some young stud. She wanted to keep him in her life because he made her feel so full when he was around, but it would be cruel to mislead him, have him question her motives. He must not feel seduced. If that happened, they'd have to talk it out, get their boundaries back and she knew she might lose him in the process.

But when she opened the door to him, she *hugged* him. She was so startled by her own reaction, she jumped back before he could return the hug. "Well," he said, grinning, "wasn't that nice."

"I'm sorry. I think I really missed having you around."

"Don't be sorry. Been a while since a pretty young girl hugged me."

"Bob." She laughed. "I'm not a young girl. I hate to admit it but I'm actually a middle-aged woman." She crouched down to give Beau a proper welcome, scratching behind his ears. "Oh, thank goodness, I was afraid you might not bring him."

"I thought about leaving him home. But then, he pouts when he's left behind and he does like it here. He's had dinner."

"I'd have been so disappointed if you hadn't brought him." She straightened. "Hurry up—take your pictures so we can just relax."

He came in, saw that the kitchen table—not the formal dining room table—was set for two. "Aw, you couldn't get an appointment with your boy?"

"Oh, I started out with a commitment from him, but his life went to hell in one night and he ran scared," Andy said.

Bob looked at her, lifted his eyebrows and waited.

"He was here last night, got together with his best friend and they smoked a couple of joints in the park. The police cited them and Noel came home stoned with a ticket in his pocket."

"Oh, boy," Bob said. "He's nineteen, right? Isn't it amazing that nineteen doesn't make them all that much smarter than seventeen?"

"Or fifteen," she said. "I made us a brisket." She looked over at Beau, sitting patiently in front of the sink, waiting for his biscuit. "Oh, did I forget something?" she asked, going to him.

Bob pulled a small digital camera out of his pocket and began snapping pictures quickly, from various angles. "You're spoiling him, and you're going to make him fat like me."

"You're not fat," she said. "You're perfect. Generous."

"*You're* generous." He laughed. "It smells pretty good in here."

"It is good. I know how to make about three things. And if you eat all your dinner, I bought dessert."

"Oh, Beau," he said, bending to the dog. "Andy likes to spoil us." Then he turned to Andy. "I'm sorry Noel isn't here. I'd looked forward to getting to know him a little. He seems like such a nice kid."

"He's a great kid. When I think about what I put him through, I shudder. And he's been so good. It was nice of him not to get completely screwed up."

"*You* put him through?" Bob said, still snapping his pictures.

"Well, it was the two of us for a long time after Rick left. Until Rick got himself resettled with the new wife. And a baby—they had a baby right away and another child right after that. Then later, I dated a lot—that can't be very easy on a young boy, although I was careful about it. No one spent the night if Noel was here. But then I brought Bryce into his life, and I think Bryce was less mature than my son. There were so many fights, mine and Bryce's, and Bryce's fights with Noel…the poor kid."

Bob slipped his camera into his pocket. "You taking the blame for that, Andy?"

"Well, he's my son," she said with a shrug. "It's my job to protect him, to do my best by him. You know."

"He's a nice kid, Andy. I'd say you did just fine."

"Except for the pot," she added.

"I smoked a little pot in college. I mean, I didn't want to—but it was Berkeley, it was the law." Then he grinned. "God that was a long time ago. Kind of makes me nostalgic."

"Don't get any ideas about getting high with my son," she teased.

"Oh, don't worry about that. I'm so dull, I don't have a vice left."

"How about alcohol? You hang on to that vice? Because I have cold beer and a nice bottle of red wine."

"I admit, I'm weak when it comes to a cold beer," he said.

"Let's take one out to the patio," she said. "The weather's so perfect. Chilled glass?"

"Bottle or can, Andy. I'm pretty low maintenance. By the way, this is awful special, you cooking. I must've done okay on the kitchen."

She pulled a couple of bottles out of the new fridge. "Yeah," she said, smiling to herself. "You did a good job on the kitchen."

They sat outside and talked about his growing up outside Santa Rosa on a farm, and her growing up south, in San Louis Obispo, an only child like Noel. Her mother passed when she was only twenty-five; that was especially hard. But her father was alive and well and in excellent health. Bob asked about Noel as a baby and young boy; she asked about his sisters—there were three, only one of whom stayed in California. They talked so long the brisket almost burned. The mashed potatoes were packaged, the vegetables frozen, the rolls from the bakery, but Bob seemed thrilled. He dug right in. Of course, Bob also seemed like the kind of guy who'd have been honored if she served him up a charred briquette.

She poured glasses of Cabernet to go with the red meat and sat. "I want to hear more about you and your wife," she said.

"There's not too much to tell, Andy. I think we were just friends. Literally."

"Were you in love with her?" she asked.

"Oh, yes," he said. "I adored her, still do. It was over ten years ago I met her, through a dating service, if you can believe that. My sister made me do it—in fact, she filled out the forms." He laughed and shook his head. "I guess she knew I'd never do anything under my own power. She was probably afraid of being stuck with me for life. So, I met Wendy and she was young, pretty, incredibly smart—and she liked me. All the blood rushed out of my head and didn't reoxygenate my brain for two years. I'll probably always love that girl. But, that's pretty much beside the point."

"Okay, this is probably the wine talking, but didn't you know, during sex?"

He didn't blush, didn't shy away. He was so straightforward, even on delicate subjects. "No. I mean, I could tell she wasn't loving it, but I didn't know much about women. I assumed I wasn't very good at it. I kept…" He frowned slightly. "Is it wrong for me to talk about this?" he asked her.

She shook her head. "No," she said. Something inside her needed to know.

"Well, I kept asking her to guide me, lead me, show me or tell me what felt good, but she just couldn't. I thought she was awfully shy, but later realized she wasn't shy at any other time. She went along with it, but it was obvious she didn't enjoy it at all."

During their conversation something changed for Andy. She noticed the little bit of slightly graying hair popping out of Bob's opened shirt and the sweet, faraway look in his eyes when he spoke, softly, about being willing to do anything to please his wife. Elbows braced on the table, hands clasped together, he gently opened and closed his fingers and she felt a shiver run through her. She found herself imagining those big, sweet arms around her, those large hands touching her, his wonderful voice asking her what she'd like. *I'm losing my mind. Maybe the wine is way more potent than usual,* she thought.

"Of course, after the facts were in, I understood. There wasn't anything I could do. It just wasn't meant to be. Sometimes I'm real disappointed about that. But I also know, it's no one's fault."

"At least you never blamed yourself," she said.

"I did for a while," he admitted. "I don't know that there's anything harder than wanting someone when she wants someone else. It's all about chemistry, I guess. We had the right chemistry for some things, but not for all things…."

Andy recognized the stirring within her. She was getting turned on by a fifty-three-year-old balding carpenter with the most beautiful hands, sparkling eyes, incredible smile and sweet face. *There is something seriously wrong with me—I'm just a sex-starved nutcase.* But the way his voice lulled her, his gentle spirit soothed her, she wanted to fold into his body like warm clay molded to him. She wanted to hear that soft, seductive voice talk her through lovemaking, tenderly asking how he could please her. *I am totally nuts,* she thought. *I adore him! He turns me on! And tomorrow I'm going to be beet-red all day long, just thinking about what I've been thinking about!*

"Bob, you shouldn't give up. I bet there's a woman

out there for you who's not a lesbian," she said "I mean, you're a sweet, attractive man."

He laughed at her. "You think so, huh? I don't mind—my life is pretty good. I like what I do. I have a great family."

"But really..."

"Tell me what it's like, dating," he said, surprising her. "I haven't done much of that. I know, I should have, but I never did."

"Well, it can be very disappointing," she said truthfully. "It's meeting someone, getting hopeful, checking them over and deciding if they meet the basic criteria, and then it's like trying to put a round peg in a square hole. You try them out at dinner, with your friends, with your family, in bed—always hoping this time it will work. If one of these things clicks, you might have someone you can..." Her voice drifted off.

"You can?" he prompted.

"Someone who fits you just right, someone you feel you belong with, trust. I don't mean just trust to be faithful, but someone you trust with your feelings. Someone who will always be there for you and have your well-being as a priority, while you have his well-being as a priority. Someone you never doubt. Someone you understand. I'd say true love, but it's more than that. It's one of those symbiotic relationships that makes no sense to anyone but the two of you. I thought I was getting close to it twice and I was wrong.... And I thought my best friend, Gerri, had it, then her marriage started to fall apart after almost twenty-five years."

"Aw, that's so sad."

"It turns out he had an affair."

Bob shook his head. "We're such fallible creatures."

"I think I have that syndrome—you know, they used to call it the Cinderella Syndrome, a totally bogus fantasy of being rescued by a handsome prince and living happily ever after."

"I don't know that it's so bogus. I bet it happens for some people."

"But you don't have that illusion, do you, Bob?"

"Well, I'm different," he said, smiling. "I've accepted myself the way I am—just not the kind of guy who's going to have a woman fall madly in love with him. I mean, even my wife, who I know loves me, chose me because I was safe. Harmless."

And kind and sweet and gentle and earnest, Andy thought. Suddenly she wanted to get up, walk him to the door, enjoy her kitchen and forget this insanity before someone came after her with a net!

"But, Andy, it's not exactly over for you," he said. "You're a beautiful young woman."

She laughed. "But, remember, I'm twice burned. Believing in someone and having them fail you completely is very painful. I think it's smarter for me to learn to live as you do—happy with my life as it is. It's not a bad life, after all."

"Wanting what you have versus getting what you want," he said.

"What did you say?" she asked.

"Wanting what you have versus getting what you want."

She was quiet a moment. "That's brilliant. Where did you get that?"

"I don't know. A long time ago, standing in the bookstore, I had an epiphany. There were books on how to get everything and books right next to them on learning to live simply with less. There were books on losing weight next to books on how to be fat and happy, and I thought no one knows anything. No one knows the answer—whether it's believing you can have it all or believing having it all would be too cumbersome. I realized being happy doesn't have anything to do with things. It's all a state of mind. You shouldn't ask me, Andy. I don't strive for anything. I think contentment is addictive."

"God," she said. *If only I could be content with what I have. That would give me such peace of mind.*

"Lao Tzu said, 'To know when you have enough is to be rich beyond all measure.'" He grinned. "Philosophy major."

"Whatever you have, Bob—I want some of it."

"Be careful what you wish for," he said, laughing.

They talked through dessert and coffee. "I should probably get going," Bob said.

"So soon?" she asked.

"Andy, I've been here four hours. But it sure was fun. Thank you."

"Do you have to go?" she asked in spite of herself.

"I start pretty early tomorrow morning," he said, standing. "Can I help with the cleanup?"

"No, absolutely not." She rose, too, but reluctantly. "I'll need something to do to wind down from the evening."

"Wind down?" He laughed. "Did I get you revved up? We didn't play football or anything." He reached across the table and took her hand. "Really, it was great."

"It was," she agreed. He called to Beau and walked

to the door. He turned and Andy spontaneously put her arms around him and laid her head on his chest.

Slowly, perhaps doubtfully, he let his arms close around her and she couldn't remember ever feeling so comfortable. So protected and nurtured. She felt his lips touch the top of her head in a small, friendly kiss and her heart leaped. She lifted her head and looked at him. "Stay a little while," she whispered. "Just sit on the couch with me for a little while."

He smiled at her, ran a rough finger over her cheek. "Feeling a little lonely?" he asked.

No, she almost said. Not lonely. Nothing as innocuous as that. But all she did was shrug and lead him into the living room, which was dark. She sat and pulled him down beside her, then put herself into his embrace again, her head on his shoulder. His arm was around her and he stroked her curly hair, combing it with his fingers. She smiled, seeing Beau sitting by the door, waiting patiently, watching them curiously.

She sighed, lifted her head to look at Bob. She let her eyes close and pressed her lips against his. He was passive at first, letting her do this, but finally he kissed back. Then he kissed deeper, moving over her mouth with skill and desire, forcing her lips open, letting her tongue into his mouth. She put her hands on his face, pulling him harder against her, feeling his arms tighten around her. They kissed for a long, wet, breathy time, devouring each other's mouths, invading and being invaded, sighing and moaning. At length they broke apart.

"Andy, what's happening here?" Bob asked.

"Whoa," she said. "I didn't think I'd do that. In fact, I was telling myself I shouldn't."

"Oh, Andy. I think maybe you're just feeling…you know…needy."

She shook her head. "I don't think so. It think it's *you*. You and me, anyway." She ran her hands over his chest and shoulders. "You're a very good kisser."

"I don't know how that's possible. I haven't done that much kissing."

She unbuttoned his shirt a little bit and pressed her lips against his chest. Then she went to his mouth again. "Stay," she whispered.

"Oh, I don't know, Andy," he said, shaking his head. "Maybe that's not such a good idea."

"Why?" she asked. "Union rules? I'm not a client anymore."

"I don't want you to be sorry. I mean, if you're feel-ing, you know, like you need a little attention, there's nothing wrong with feeling that—it's just nature. But—"

"Stay," she said. "Please."

"This is such a crazy idea."

"Please," she said again.

"Where do you want this to go?" he asked.

"To the bedroom," she said without hesitation.

"Oh, man, this isn't happening to me," he said, pinch-ing his eyes closed.

"Yes, it is. But I want it to happen to me, too—and pretty soon." She stood from the couch and took his hand, pulling him up.

"What about your son?" he asked.

"Gone for the night."

"Oh, man…"

She laughed slightly. "I'll be gentle with you," she said, teasing him.

"Oh, you don't have to do that," he assured her. "Listen, I don't have anything, like protection. I've never carried anything like protection."

"It's okay," she said. "We'll be fine."

The bedroom was dark. Andy kicked off her shoes and flopped on the bed, but Bob moved more slowly, taking her in his arms, holding her, kissing her, pressing against her. She felt his large hand cup her bottom and pull her against him and she groaned.

"You sure about this?" he asked.

"Oh, yes."

"Oh, man, I can't be doing this."

"Yes, you can," she said. "And do it a little faster, will you please?"

He carefully unbuttoned her blouse, removed her bra, unzipped her jeans and helped her slide them down. His hands moved so slowly all over her body, almost as if he didn't want to miss anything, and then his lips were on her, kissing her everywhere, from her cheek to her ear to her neck and shoulder. He kept whispering her name as his tongue moved from her neck to her nipples to her navel.

Andy started squirming and pulling at his clothes. "Let me," he said, and he undressed quickly. He wore goofy patterned boxers, which slid down to the floor and disappeared from Andy's sight. And there he was— what she could see of him in the dim light, compact and solid, a small patch of hair on his chest, and so much more. *Bryce thought he was blessed—hah!*

Bob lay back down beside her, carefully drawing her into his arms, pulling her close. She reached down, closing her hand around him and was amazed by his size, his apparent power. Then she felt his fingers glide smoothly over her tummy and down, down, into her.

"Want to tell me what you like? Show me how to make you feel good?" he asked.

"I'll speak up if you seem to need advice," she said breathlessly. "So far, you know exactly what to do."

He caressed, kissed, massaged and then his mouth moved lower, down her body, over her breasts, across her belly. He gently pulled her legs apart and started to lick her. She almost rose off the bed, it was so erotic, so wildly sensual. She spasmed, lifting her hips against his face, crying out, gripping the coverlet in both hands, completely and instantly out of control. Her whole body trembled in an orgasm that was fast, long and deep.

When she fell back onto the bed, he released her, rising over her with a laugh that was soft, lusty and sounding very pleased with himself. "Well, that worked pretty well," he said.

"Oh, my God," she whispered, touching his face with gentle fingers. "Oh, my God, I didn't expect that."

"Neither did I," he said. "That was wonderful, just wonderful." He brushed the hair away from her face. "Want to stop now? You all taken care of?"

She shook her head and spread her legs to take him in. It was his way, she realized, to move slowly, carefully, luxuriously—filling her and rocking with her in an easy, deep, rhythmic motion that felt so good, Andy thought she would lose her mind. It had been in her mind to return the favor, not have a second pleasure, but she was already headed that way. She was prepared for this to be over for him quickly, having had so little sex in his life, but it wasn't. He took her lips with his. He was so agile and despite his size, kept his weight off her. The pressure began to build in her again and she thrust back at him greedily, wantonly, and he moved to her pace, pumping his hips. She dug her heels into the mattress and pushed against him, and it happened again—she exploded into an orgasm so powerful, it sent electric waves through her whole body, leaving her in quivering, clenching spasms. Yet he hung on, and when she was starting to come down from the experience, he grabbed her bottom with his large hands and plunged into her, enjoying his own release. And then gently, so tenderly, held her against him, stroking her softly while she struggled to catch her breath.

"Oh, you big liar," she said. "You've obviously been having sex twice a day for years."

"Huh?"

"You could never have done that, lasted like that, if you were... Well, you know."

He smiled. "I concentrated on baseball stats," he said. "I couldn't let you down."

"Okay, then you watch too much porn."

"Andy, I don't watch that stuff." He laughed. "How do you feel? Okay?"

"What I feel is so much bigger than okay." He made a move as if he'd leave her body and she grabbed his butt. "Not yet," she said.

"My arms are going to start to tremble pretty soon."

"Hang in there for the trembling arms," she said. And then she laughed. "You're amazing."

"I can't be," he said. "It's just not possible."

"Bob, you're amazing. Incredible."

"Really?"

"If you're as inexperienced as you say, how do you know what you know?"

"Wasn't that pretty ordinary stuff?"

"Nope," she said, shaking her head. "You didn't take Viagra or something, did you?"

"How would I guess I might have use for something like that?"

"Well, you're no kid. I mean, aren't you getting to the age where things start to go a little...you know what I mean. Unreliable."

"Yeah, I think I'm getting to that age, or at least close. Funny, I always thought it was such a cheap trick that I still had erections but lost the hair. I didn't seem to have much use for erections. I could've used hair."

"Who needs hair." She laughed.

His arms, holding his weight, began to tremble.

"Okay," she said, releasing him. He rolled over on his back and she curled up to him. "Oh, God," she whispered. "I think the women you work for have all had their way with you."

He laughed. "This is a first. Believe me."

She shifted, propping her head in her hand. "Bob, I think I just took complete advantage of you."

"I didn't mind too much," he said. "Would you like me to go now?"

"Go? As in leave?"

"I don't want to wear out my welcome. I'm sorry, Andy, I have absolutely no idea the etiquette on...on..."

"On how to act after a spontaneous, spectacular roll in the hay? No, I don't want you to go. I want you to stay. Can you stay?"

"Are you sure?"

"I'm so sure."

"I should take Beau out. Can he borrow your back-yard? Can I give him a bowl of water?"

"Sure. Can you be back here pretty quick?"

He grinned. "You bet." And then he pulled on the goofy, patterned boxers and trudged barefoot out of the room. She watched his departure and smiled. He was just so cute.

Andy visited the bathroom, then pulled back the covers on her bed and crawled in. It wasn't long before Bob was back, slipping in beside her. She snuggled right up to him, sighed deeply and his softness, his calm breathing beside her rocked her to sleep.

Somewhere in the night, she felt his hands on her back, her bottom, her hips, stroking her, and she turned in his arms and gave herself to him. Again, he amazed her, took her to heights she hadn't experienced before. As she came back to earth, she said, "God bless those baseball stats." Then she curled up to him and went back to sleep.

The next thing she knew, he was leaning over her, kissing her on the cheek. She opened her eyes and saw that he was dressed. She glanced at the clock. It was 5:00 a.m. She started to get up. "Oh—I'll make you some coffee...."

"Stay in bed, Andy. I made you some coffee. I get a real early start at the shop."

"Hmm," she said, snuggling back in.

"Andy," he said. "Would you like me to call you sometime? Or would you like me to..." He didn't finish. She knew what he was going to ask—should I just go away and never bother you again?

"I want you to call me *today*," she said. "Promise?"

"Sure," he said, kissing her cheek. "Thank you."

"Believe me, Bob. The pleasure was all mine."

* * *

On Sunday afternoon, Gerri had let Phil help her through the upset of Sonja's hospitalization. They made pizza together for dinner before he went back to the city for a few more nights. The woman with the guesthouse had relented—he could move in the following weekend and leave it unpainted.

Once he'd gone and the house was again quiet, she summoned Jessie to her bedroom for another talk. Jessie had been in bed most of the day, recovering from her hangover, so this time they were able to talk about the separation without the snottiness and high drama. Gerri was so worn out from the events of the day, she was feeling quite calm. They sat together on Gerri's king-size bed, cross-legged, and talked for at least the twentieth time about women's health, about birth control, STDs, about when it seemed right to be sexually active and when it could be just stupid or dangerous. Of course, Jessie already had all the facts and understood them; Gerri had made sure of that.

Jessie told Gerri that she believed sex was only appropriate in a serious relationship. She'd had such a boyfriend earlier in the school year. But she confessed she had lacked the courage to go to a family-planning clinic, to face an adult and ask for birth control.

"Even with a social worker for a mother? Even with everything you know about how scary doing nothing can be?" Gerri asked, rather astonished as her daughter merely shrugged and looked into her lap.

Well, that was exactly typical of a young girl, Gerri thought. Teaching them to abstain didn't help them abstain, and teaching them to ask for birth control to prevent an unwanted pregnancy didn't drive them to the doctor's office. It was an incredibly brazen yet vulnerable time of life, so hard on the kids in so many ways. And it was so impossible for the parents to get a grip on what was going on with their kids.

There were many times in Gerri's role as a case worker that it became necessary to have a woman or juvenile examined by a doctor with due haste—injury, assault, molestation, the list was long and the reasons almost always unpleasant. To this end she had developed a close relationship with a woman practitioner at a family-planning clinic in Marin County—Joyce Arnold, M.D. For better than six years, Gerri had been seeing Joyce for her own medical exams, and they'd become friends. She knew she could call her, get Jessie in to see her at once.

"Okay, we'll go to the doctor together," Gerri said. "But our appointments will be completely separate and you'll be alone with Dr. Arnold. She's very nice, very modern and knowledgeable and you can talk to her about anything. *Everything.*"

"Is she going to have this whole STD conversation with me again? Because I'm kind of sick of being talked down to like that—I made sure there was a condom."

"Very likely," Gerri said. "One mistake should get you grounded or your TV privileges taken away, not dead. Doctors are pretty adamant about that, for good reason. Try to sit through it, let her talk—but ask for what you need and tell her anything you think she can help with. Your conversation with her will be confidential and she's a pro. Anytime you need a ride there, I can chauffeur without asking personal questions, I swear. It's a promise I make to you, Jess."

"Sure. Okay."

"Now, about me and Dad. The separation. Listen, I need you to try your best to understand this—I didn't throw him out. He could have refused to leave—he's a lawyer, he knows it's his right by law to live in his house. I asked him to give me some time alone. To give me space while I get some counseling. I asked him to get counseling, too, and he is. Jessie, please. I'm not a bad person. I'm not being mean to your dad. This is terrible enough without you thinking that."

"Yeah," Jessie said, looking down. "I know. It's just that…" She met Gerri's gaze. "It's just that this sucks. And I don't get the point. He's a screwup and wishes he wasn't. How is he different from other guys?"

Gerri actually felt a smile threaten her lips. It was pretty basic logic. Her teen daughter was so brilliant, such a dimwit. "He's not very different, but the situation is a little more serious than that to me. Honey, I'm the one, maybe the only one, having a hard time with what happened. I know you and Jed and maybe Matt all think I should be a big, tough girl and tell him to just be good from now on. But it's more personal than that for me. He was in someone else's body and I'm just not ready to invite him back into my body until—"

Jessie covered her ears. "Eww! Stop! I don't want to hear about this!"

Of course, Gerri thought. Parents only had sex when necessary. Grandparents *never* had sex. In Jessie's mind only teenagers and movie stars and rock stars and pro athletes had sex. Okay, maybe people had sex until they were thirty, provided they were neither overweight nor icky, but after that, at the first sign of flab or wrinkles, it was over.

"It's more personal to me than a little mistake I can

just overlook. But I didn't throw him out. He agreed to a separation and counseling. We both love you, want to be there for you through everything, and goddamn it, Jess, we're doing the best we can. Cut us some slack. We can't work on the marriage while you kids are going out of your minds."

"Yeah, okay," Jessie said. Then she shrugged. "Whatever."

"I'm so mad about what you did last night," Gerri told her.

"Yeah, I know."

"It could have been so dangerous. You were compromised by alcohol, you could've been assaulted. And I know there was drunk driving involved—those boys shouldn't have been driving. You're just damn lucky all around."

"It was more stupid than dangerous," Jessie said. "I mean, going with them—the driving part, you're probably right. One of them only had two beers, he said. But they're just a bunch of idiots and believe me, I'm not going to be out with them ever again."

"Correct. You're grounded. You won't be going out week nights at all and weekends will be an early curfew. And I will double-check where you're going. If you break curfew or lie to me, you'll be grounded for life."

"Yeah, fine," she said without argument. "I expected that. And, Mom? Get this thing with Daddy fixed up, huh? It sucks around here."

This thing with Daddy. If only it was just a little thing with Daddy.

On Monday morning Gerri spent a long time in front of the mirror. Only five years ago she thought of herself as a woman who was holding up damn well, a decent-looking woman for her age. She was tall and slim, had high cheekbones, a nice arch in her brows, straight white teeth and a wide smile. Not many women could wear their hair cut so short, but she had the perfect oval face for it. Phil always told her it was sexy as hell.

But now she was conscious of every flaw. Her eyelids had drooped, laugh lines put frames around her mouth and there was something she'd never even thought about—back fat. Where the hell had that come from? That roll above the back of her bra. She could wear a low-backed dress well into her forties, but no more. Her breasts sagged and she had too much flesh. But she wasn't sure when all this had happened. It had *been* happening. It just hadn't seemed that important.

She leaned toward the mirror and pulled back on her facial skin, considering a little surgery. Maybe just the eyes and jaw; perhaps the neck.

After Jessie had her appointment with Dr. Arnold, Gerri took to the examination table in a gown. "What's up with you?" Joyce asked. "It isn't time for your annual just yet."

"Menopause. I'm struggling. Hot flashes, the usual crap."

"You've been trying to make due with all the natural aids, trying to avoid hormone replacement," the doctor said, reading the chart.

"I've swallowed so many herbs, when I burp I taste grass. I worry," Gerri said. "My mother died of uterine cancer."

"I know. That doesn't necessarily make you high risk. Years ago, when women took estrogen without progesterone, we saw a lot more of that. Let's at least do a blood panel, get some hormone levels and—"

"My husband had an affair," Gerri blurted.

Joyce looked up from the chart, startled. "Because of *menopause?*" she asked.

"It was over five years ago, but still…"

Joyce put the chart aside. "Okay, so you have menopause issues in addition to this, correct?"

"Is it my looks? I'm looking so much older. I'm starting to age fast. I'm grumpy. Goddamn Phil isn't aging. Or he's aging well."

"It wasn't your looks five years ago and it's not your looks now," Joyce said, leaning toward her. "You're a fine-looking woman. Very attractive, very fit, very sharp. Please, struggle to remember, brains and wit are sexy."

"But I can't compete with those young city lawyers," Gerri said. "I've gotten the message it was a lot about sex. The sex in our marriage was waning a long while back, but I thought that was normal."

"It is for some people," Joyce said with a shrug. "It's not necessarily a given. A large number of my patients are sexually active well past fifty. And sixty. And…"

"But now I have a vagina like sandpaper and it hurts. I heat up about once an hour, leave the sheets damp. I'm uncomfortable, haven't felt sexy in years, and, yes, I've run out of natural remedies."

Joyce looked down, shook her head and moved back to her stool. She sat looking up at Gerri. "If you feel like telling me, how are you handling it? This thing with Phil."

"It's like it's my fault," Gerri said. "My fault he was driven to an affair, my fault I found out. If I hadn't found out, we'd be the same. Now we'll never be the same."

"You okay?"

"Hell, no. I'm so far from okay, I'm not sure which end is up."

"Need an antidepressant? I know you don't need a physical exam."

"I need someone to tell me what I should be doing," Gerri said angrily. "I asked him to move out, get counseling. I'm getting counseling—and it's not good counseling. I get better counseling from my next door neighbor." She shook her head. "I feel like I never met this counselor before and I've known her for eight years. We're not accomplishing anything. Well," she said, giving a sniff but managing to keep her eyes dry, "we're keeping the tissue industry in business." She took a breath. "Joyce—how do other women deal with this— I have to know."

"Oh, shit, in a million ways. Some work on getting their husband's back, some leave them, some shoot them in their sleep, some ignore it and carry on. I don't think you and Phil are going to be able to do any of those things."

"He's been gone for weeks, though he's around when I need him for the kids. The kids want him home, need him home. And I can't share a bathroom with him, I can't. I can't do his laundry—half the time I want to torch his clothes. I'm trying to get past the anger, if only for the kids, but I hate him for what he did to us."

"So—that waning sex drive. That okay with you?" Joyce asked.

"I never even noticed," Gerri said. "Well, I barely noticed."

"You talked about it? With Phil?"

"I didn't know there was anything to talk about.

We've always done a lot of talking, about everything, but that didn't come up, so I thought it wasn't an issue."

"And the menopause symptoms? Really getting to you, huh?"

"Oh, yeah. Some of my friends glide right through it, but I'm not. You know you're flashing when your bra is wet. When your scalp is wet and your hair goes flat. Throw in an extramarital affair and it's like the bottom's falling out."

"Let's try something—we'll get a blood panel, see where you are and try some bio-identical hormone replacement, used in the form of creams. We can start with a low dose, see if you get some relief. Some women have good results. And I'm going to give you a tube of cream with testosterone in it. You can apply it anywhere the sun don't shine—try the inside of your thighs every evening before bed—see if you begin to develop a libido. And in case you do and want to enjoy it, I'll fix you up with some lubricant that'll make you much more comfortable."

"Now? Right now I don't *want* to sleep with him!"

"Then you won't," the doctor said easily. "On the other hand, if you decide you do want to, he's still your husband. Right?"

"That could really screw up my potential divorce! I don't want to give him false hope!" *But,* Gerri thought, *the truth is, I don't want to give myself false hope!*

"Gerri, I'm going to be frank," Joyce said. "You don't have to give up sex yet. Remember how much fun it was in your younger days? A lot of women are still having fun at your age." She shrugged. "Some are lying back and thinking of England for a few minutes a couple of times a week, but some are having hot sex. Women in their fifties often rediscover that part of life. It's pretty common, in fact."

"I don't think I'm one of the hot-sex girls," Gerri said.

"Maybe not—that's not confirmed yet. After talking with my patients, I'm convinced the ones who don't use it, lose it. Seriously, women who used lubricant for intercourse in their forties because they had to are having fun with it in their fifties, sixties. Whatever the case may be, in a marriage, it helps if you can assess each other's needs."

"Honestly, I didn't know these needs existed."

"Yes, you did," Joyce said, straight out, pinning it on her one more time. "You did. You know you did."

"I *didn't*," Gerri said angrily.

Joyce took a breath. "I attended this seminar once. We had workbooks and completed little homework assignments before each weekly workshop. They were silly little things that I thought were such a waste of my valuable time. One assignment was to go to your closet and take out the one outfit you know looks terrible on you and get rid of it. And I thought, I don't have an outfit like that! And who cares? I wear scrubs most of the time. Obviously my reaction was common because the next sentence said, 'Yes, you do and you know it—go take it out of the closet and get rid of it.' So I went to my closet and pulled out this beige outfit that made me look sick and fat. I'd spent a lot of money on it and I was determined that eventually it would look as good on me as it had on the mannequin. But I threw it out, because even though I didn't want to admit it, I knew. In fact, I had always known."

She's right, Gerri thought. If she was truly honest

with herself, she did know Phil was still interested in having sex with her. He'd made overtures from time to time. Not often, not desperately, not like a man driven. Certainly not like a man about to put those moves on someone else. All she'd had to do was tell him she was too tired or too moody or too menopausal and he'd roll right over, be snoring in sixty seconds. Now and then she took pity on him and gave in, hoping he'd hurry up. She didn't want to think about what kind of passive, disinterested partner she'd been on those occasions.

She sighed. "So, a little hormonal help, lubricant and that's your prescription?"

"I'm going to examine you, run some tests for STDs just to be safe even though the affair was years ago and you have no symptoms. And, I think you should try to talk to him, see if you can zero in on what's worked well for you as a couple, what hasn't worked so well. Even in the closest marriages, it's hard for couples to discuss their more personal needs. Cravings. It might've been quite easy for you to avoid subjects like that, and never even know you were becoming less close."

"Every time we start a conversation, it ends in a fight."

"That so? Then one of you is dropping the bait. Could be him, trying to get you to take the rap, could be you, letting him know just how angry you are."

"Is that the best you can do? Because I already know that."

"And you already know that gynecologically, medically, biologically a sex drive is a powerful force in nature. It'll make your beloved pet turn on you and maul you because he's picked up the mating scent. It'll cause animals to fight to the death. It could cause a good man to wander, even if that's not what he wants to do. Good women, too, for that matter. You owe it to yourself to find out what you're dealing with."

"Look the other way, be understanding and forgiving?"

"I don't know Phil. Is he a good man? Or is he just another bastard who cheats whenever he gets the chance? Whenever there's an opportunity? Was he looking for sex, or was there more to the story?"

"There's nothing Phil can say to me that will convince me there was a good reason to have an affair," Gerri said.

"I imagine not. Can I tell you one more thing? Orgasms are very healthy. They're great mood stabilizers, tension relievers. If you can't find it in yourself to enjoy that aspect of marriage, you can still indulge in orgasms. There's more than one way to skin that cat."

Gerri sighed deeply. "I don't think I'm going to be cured by an orgasm."

"I didn't mean to suggest that. But the waning sex drive, the affair, the discomfort of menopause… Gerri, you're a counselor—see if you can find out what happened to you and your husband."

"I always thought he was ethical if nothing else. Moral. I'm not thinking that way right now, and it's painful. I don't feel like giving him a break."

Joyce grinned. "I didn't suggest you couldn't leave a bruise or two. I mean, he was a bad boy, right? Try not to hurt yourself in the process."

"Can this marriage be saved?" Gerri said sarcastically.

"*If* you walk away, be absolutely sure you're burying something that was dead."

eight

Sydney Kalay was filing some charts in the office she shared with two other psychiatrists at Glendale Psychiatric. Sonja walked into the office and the doctor looked up with a smile. "Well, it looks as if you're feeling much better today," she said. "Please, have a seat. Give me a moment."

Sonja sat in the chair that faced the desk. She noticed that Dr. Kalay had some chimes hanging in the corner of her office, a miniature waterfall on top of the filing cabinet. She made a face, seeing these artifacts that once meant so much to her.

The upscale private facility was only partially covered by insurance, but George was taking care of the rest. It didn't bother Sonja that George was stuck with the bill, yet it made her angry that without his benevolence she'd be in some state hospital, sharing a ward with eight other patients, eating food off a metal tray instead of china. Sonja had never made a good living, not even before George. She'd always dabbled in things that interested her, was satisfied to live at home with her parents until she married. She'd immersed herself in those things that fascinated her, soothed her—subjects reputed to bring health, light, peace, serenity and balance to one's life. Now she felt she'd been tricked, wasted her time.

Dr. Kalay sat behind the desk, folded her hands atop Sonja's chart and smiled. "This isn't a therapy session, Sonja—just a medical evaluation. So, you're looking good. So much better."

"I don't feel much better," she said with a shrug. "In fact, I think I feel even worse."

"Tell me about that," the doctor said. "What doesn't feel better?"

"I'm crying like an idiot in group sessions," Sonja said. "I hate crying in front of people. I didn't do that much crying before…"

"Crying about?"

"About failing George, failing at marriage, falling apart, going crazy in front of my friends, finding out I've just been deluding myself about everything…."

"Grieving," the doctor said. "It's painful but important work."

"And what was I doing before?" Sonja asked.

"*Not* grieving," she answered. "You couldn't grieve, so you shut down emotionally, mentally, refusing to feel."

"So—I did that to myself on purpose?"

"Of course not. You did it on instinct, because feeling was very painful for you. Your mind and nervous system took over to protect you. If we could look way back, we might find instances in your childhood that were so traumatic, your system perfected a way to take over, keep you safe from feelings that could be dangerous to you. On the other hand," she said with a shrug, "there might be a DNA pattern in your family tree—a history of depression or something similar—that provided a natural pathway to your mind's ability to drift into that state."

"My aunt committed suicide," Sonja said, looking down. "I never knew her, though."

"A possible link to a family history of depression, but not necessarily confirmed."

"My lymph nodes have been swollen," Sonja said. "Like I'm coming down with something."

"I read this in your chart. I don't think it's due to illness, Sonja. I'm pretty sure it's a reaction to your medication and I'd like to ride it out for a while. It might pass. If it doesn't, we'll try something else. However, you're responding to the medication in a very positive way."

"I never took drugs before, for anything. Everything has been natural."

"The drugs you're taking are also natural, not synthetic," the doctor said. "Everything in nature has great power. Homeopathic remedies can be very effective but they can also be lethal, depending on the dose, the combination, the prescriptionist…"

Sonja waved an impatient hand. "Medical doctors. Always the same drill."

"Oh, you might be wrong about that. That's often a correct assumption, but not always. For example, I visit a Chinese herbalist in San Francisco. She's been tremendous in helping with my allergies." She laughed. "She has many remedies—for everything from aging to liver cleansing. She looks like bloody hell herself, which makes one wonder. It can be a leap of faith, with natural herbalists, with physicians."

Sonja leaned forward. "Who?" she asked.

Dr. Kalay shook her head. "No," she said. "I wouldn't make a referral like that. We're really here about another matter. A relatively simple matter—clinical depression. By now you've learned you're hardly alone. In fact, I would consider you fortunate—you seem to be responding to medication, despite the lymph nodes. Have you any idea the number of patients who don't?"

"I'm catching on," Sonja said. "There are people in my group sessions who have been hospitalized several times."

"Does that worry you?"

"Of course!" she said. "I don't want to be a high-risk patient!"

"I'm not concerned about that," the doctor said. "Would you like to know why?"

"Yes, please."

"A combination of reasons. You haven't had a previous breakdown like that in your adult lifetime, unless you're holding back information that could be pertinent. There's no pattern. I don't see any kind of toxic use of natural remedies in the list of herbs, roots and plants you used in your diet. Your break from reality was terrifying and seemed endless to you. But, in the great scheme of things, it was relatively short, thanks to early intervention. And your response to medical treatment was immediate. You've been lucky and I'm optimistic. But it's going to be entirely up to you to continue making progress toward health and to do what's necessary to avoid relapses."

"Then why do I feel so bad? So hopeless?" Sonja asked, her eyes round, her expression beseeching.

"Because, Sonja, you're grieving so many things. It will pass but there seems to be a structure to grief."

"I know," she said. "We go over this at least three times a day in group. Denial, anger, bargaining, depression, acceptance…."

"But, Sonja, people don't always go through these stages in order. Many people skip a step or combine stages or even go through them so quickly it appears they haven't grieved at all—it's very individual."

"I heard that, yes. I still don't know what I did."

"Of course you do. Denial and depression. You don't like to show anger—the anger was buried. And there was no bargaining—your life was changed in an instant and there was nothing in your imagination that could change it back, nothing you could trade. Add to that—for whatever reason—your depression was complete and dangerous, almost like it had been sitting there, waiting. Fortunately, we have tools now. We can help."

"That means I still have steps to go through?" she asked.

"We don't know that," the doctor said. "People actually do skip steps in the progression. Or maybe the progression is just a rough map that isn't always carved in stone. All I ask of you right now is that you allow yourself, with the help of medication, to feel. And report the feelings in your group sessions. Your group leaders and counselor keep good notes."

"I hate that," Sonja said. "Them writing down things about how I'm doing and not knowing what they say."

"They say very encouraging things," Dr. Kalay said, smiling. "You're an A-plus student. Just keep moving ahead, you're doing so well. Not such a hard task, really."

Sonja was quiet a long moment. "I always thought I knew exactly what to do, exactly what was right. I studied. I took courses, attended seminars, worked so hard, practiced such discipline—and I didn't expect big things. I wasn't looking for miracles, just balance. Just a life that worked, physically and mentally. My husband and my friends, they considered me radical, but I wasn't. I was just—"

"A person who feared loss of control," the doctor inserted. "It's common for absolutely everyone, not just patients in a psychiatric facility."

Suddenly Sonja's eyes widened dramatically. "Oh, my God, *was* I trying to control George?"

"Perhaps," Dr. Kalay said with a shrug. "Or perhaps you were controlling your own life, of which George has been a significant part. That's why you go to therapy, Sonja. All you have to do is gain an understanding of your responses and you can choose alternate paths that work better for you."

"Wow," she said, sitting back. She thought for a moment and then said, "You have the chimes, the waterfall. You visit an herbalist. Why?"

Dr. Kalay smiled. "Comfort. Personal taste."

"Is your house filled with stuff like that?"

"I have a six foot tall waterfall in the courtyard outside my office at home—it's wonderful for me. I love the sound of cascading water. My husband has a very large statue of the Virgin Mary in his—he's Mexican, Catholic. We have very few beliefs in common, just the ancient ones that descend from his Aztec roots and my Islamic ancestors, none of which includes waterfalls or Blessed Virgins."

"Really," Sonja said, kind of wonderstruck, impressed that two people from such different worlds could accept each other like that.

Dr. Kalay leaned forward. "I'm sorry you have so many adjustments to make, so much hard emotional work to do, but I'm very proud of your progress. Just a couple of weeks and look how far you've come," she said, paging through the chart. "You're eating and sleeping better, responding in group. It's so much advancement in a short period of time. Even so, I want you to agree to stay longer—at least the full thirty days. I recommend that, but you realize you're here by your own will and can check out whenever you like. In order to commit you involuntarily, it would require a life-threatening situation and a court order. I'm so glad we didn't have to act on something as alarming as that."

"Thirty days?" she asked weakly, though she'd known from the beginning it could come to that. "I miss my house. My bed."

"I know," the doctor said. "I would, too."

"And it's very expensive here, isn't it? I talk to some of the others—some patients have been in other, less fancy hospitals. It's hard to get in here, hard to afford."

"Correct," the doctor said. "Your husband has good insurance and in addition has guaranteed payment for your stay, no matter how long. You're very fortunate."

"I suppose," she said. "That's kind of hard to swallow."

"Is it?" Dr. Kalay asked.

"Of course," Sonja said. "I really don't like George spending a lot of money on something like this."

"Are you concerned about his finances?"

"Concerned?" she asked with a short laugh. "Oh, God, not at all. George is actually rich, though you'd never know it. He lives pretty cheaply, but that's because he's hooked on investing. He has a lot more fun looking at a portfolio balance than spending money on something expensive, extravagant or entertaining. It's just that if this is good for me, something I need, I'd like to be able to afford it myself—and I can't."

Dr. Kalay folded her hands and smiled. "It's beyond most of us, Sonja. It would be very difficult for me, as well. But apparently it's not a burden for George. I don't think you have to take on that worry."

Sonja let out a laugh. "Oh, believe me, I'm not. I'm just sorry I'm not successful. I never learned how to be successful. That comes in handy, especially in emergencies."

"Absolutely," Dr. Kalay said. "But then, there are many definitions of success."

"Yeah, I get that. But George's is to throw money at his problems—and right now I'm the problem he's trying to make go away. He's just a sleazy, passive-aggressive cocksucker in a business suit and I *hate* him."

Dr. Kalay was shocked enough that it showed in her posture, her startled expression. But then the expression melted into a grin. Not the usual soft, patient, sensitive smile, but a large grin that showed her beautiful teeth. "Well, now," she said. "Perhaps we won't skip the anger stage, after all."

A few minor changes brought some stability to the Gilbert home. Phil was living closer and thus spending more time around the house. Jessie was grounded, so there was no panic about whether she'd be getting into mischief. Sonja was in the hospital and without Phil to wake the kids in the morning, Gerri was going into her office a little later. Even though it pushed Andy for time in the morning, they moved their power walk to six-thirty rather than six. Thirty minutes of extra sleep felt like all the difference.

"I hate to admit this," Gerri told Andy, "but I think the hormones are helping. I'm on the lowest dose, but rather than a hot flash an hour, it's more like two a day."

"And you feel more stable mood-wise?"

"I haven't opened fire on anyone in a couple of weeks," she said with a laugh. "Seriously, that might not be the hormones. I have Phil right down the street, much more available, and the kids are mysteriously well behaved. Besides, if you ask Phil, I've always been a loose cannon, mood-wise. He's been on something for twenty-five years, I swear to God. I mean, what's he got to be so pleasant about? Huh?"

"He's spending more time around the house?" Andy asked.

"Sort of. If I have to work late, he can usually get to the house by six or seven and when he's tied up, I'm there. He comes over a lot of evenings just to use the office rather than being stuck with his laptop. He comes for dinner sometimes, sometimes he brings food, gets in a little time with the kids. He can stay longer since he doesn't have to drive back to the city. And we haven't been fighting much. It's almost like living together, but not living together."

"How's the counseling going?" Andy asked.

"Top secret," Gerri said. "I quit. We can't let Phil know—he'll think he can quit. I'm not letting him off that easy."

"Why'd you quit?" Andy asked, surprised.

"She wouldn't stick to the issues," Gerri said with a shrug. "I needed to talk about my relationship with Phil, how things got derailed, and she wanted to go back to my childhood, my parents' type of discipline, earlier relationships—all kinds of stuff that don't apply."

"Are you sure they don't?"

"Well, maybe there's some stuff in there that could be looked at, but I've had a lot of counseling before now. It's a job requirement. Believe me, I'm all caught up on childhood traumas, grief and anger, etcetera. I have a husband problem. At least I had one seven years ago, whether I knew it or not. Things are almost normal at our house these days. I'm thinking of going out on a limb and asking him if he'd like to have an evening out, away from the house and kids. See if we can talk about the future without fighting."

"Sounds like there might be a reconciliation in the wind," Andy said.

"I love Phil. That's why the idea of another woman has been so hard. It's like there was a gap in our relationship that he had to fill with someone else, and I didn't know about it beforehand, when I had a chance to face up to it, do something about it. How am I supposed to handle that?"

"But you seem to have some ideas now. What it was, what was missing," Andy said. "He told you he was tempted, he didn't want to be done with his sex life, and you're the first to admit that it was a low priority with you."

"Yeah, but that's after the fact. The problem is, I didn't stand a chance. He never said it was something he needed us to work on. I mean, come on. I can be honest—yes, there were times he suggested sex and I made excuses, but he accepted them so easily, it was like it hadn't really been that important to him. Maybe I'm not the hot ticket I was when he married me, but I've always listened to what Phil had to say. We've always been able to figure things out, compromise. But instead of making himself heard, he went outside the marriage, screwed around. I'm not a fucking clairvoyant."

Staring straight ahead and walking fast, Gerri's voice became a little warbly. "I want him home so bad," she said. "But not until, not unless I can be sure he can level with me, be honest about his feelings. And faithful. My God. I have to believe he'll be faithful. Is that asking too much?"

"Of course not," Andy said. "Gerri, I just don't get the whole low-sex-drive thing. I love sex. I'd be very vulnerable if I had a partner who wasn't interested in making love. Am I just plain oversexed? Or is it because I don't have three kids and a job filled with emotionally draining social-services cases?"

"Hmm, those things suck a lot out of me, that's for sure. Doesn't leave me feeling very sexy." Then she grinned at Andy. "So, how are you holding up? Need me to buy you a box of batteries for the vibrator to get you through the dry spell?"

"As a matter of fact, no," Andy said.

"Ah," Gerri said. "Sounds like you upgraded to the plug-in model."

"I moved on to the warm, cuddly, kissing model," she said quietly.

Gerri stopped walking. "Huh?"

"I guess you haven't noticed," Andy said. "There's been a vehicle in front of my house some nights…."

"I haven't noticed," Gerri said. "Oh, Andy, what are you thinking? You know it's too soon after Bryce."

Andy resumed walking, leaving Gerri to catch up. "Probably, but I don't care. My life is different now than when Bryce first materialized. Back then I had a teenager at home, now I barely see him. And even though I know what you're going to say, this is different."

"Bullshit," Gerri said.

"Bingo. That's what I thought you'd say."

"It's too soon, you're too vulnerable. It's going to suck you in, lock you up. You know a rebound lover will eventually tear you up, break your heart and send you out looking again."

"No," Andy said.

"And you're going to cry and ask me why I didn't stop you before you got involved."

"You're wrong."

"I've known you for fifteen years and I love you like a sister. You're nearly perfect in my eyes, but for some reason you can't make it long without a man in your life. Even if it's the wrong man," Gerri said.

"That's crap. I didn't have a guy in my life after Rick, not for two years. A long two years by the way. And after the courtship, Bryce wasn't all that attentive. But this is different. I swear, it's something I've never experienced before."

They both stopped walking and just looked at each other. "I've heard that before. What the hell's so different this time?" Gerri asked.

"It's Bob," Andy said.

Andy thought the look that came over Gerri's face was priceless. Her hand went to her chest in a mock heart attack. She took several steps backward, her heel caught on the curb and she fell back onto the grass in a fake collapse. Andy stood over her, hands on her hips, looking down at her with a wry smile. "Very funny," she said. "That verged on impolite."

"Bob?" Gerri asked from a reclining position.

"Sweet, lovable, precious, highly-evolved-spirit Bob," Andy said with a grin.

"Bob, the carpenter?"

"Oh, stop it!" Andy said, marching away. "Shame on you," she called out over her shoulder.

Gerri scrambled to her feet and quickly caught up. "Bob?" she asked yet again.

"If you keep doing that I'm not telling you why."

"Okay, I'm done. *Why?*"

"Because he's the greatest man I've ever known. I spent so much time with him while he was working in the kitchen and I adore him. He's so sane, so giving. He has an understanding of humanity that goes beyond anything I've experienced. I had deeper, more meaningful conversations with Bob before I even hugged him than I've had with two husbands and at least five boyfriends. I'm completely hooked on the human being he is. He's just amazing."

"He's five-eight, overweight, bald, withdrawn and a carpenter. Not your usual type," Gerri said.

"He's so totally wonderful. You have no idea. Besides, don't you think he's kind of sexy? In his own way? I love his smile, his eyebrows. His hands…."

"Andy, I've known you a long time. Through those two husbands and five boyfriends. By the way it might've been five boyfriends, but there was a baker's dozen that didn't achieve boyfriend status. Never mind—all of them were very good-looking hard-bodies with impressive jobs and lots of sex appeal. Most were younger than you."

"Yeah," Andy said. "I had no idea what I was missing."

"Oh, God, you've lost your newly reclaimed virginity to *Bob?*"

"You're pissing me off. I adore Bob."

"I'm having an out-of-body experience," Gerri said. "This isn't happening. Am I going to have to take you to the clinic, too? What's going on here? Are you thinking that with someone like Bob you can play it safe? That he won't have all the same flaws the men before him had?"

"Oh, for God's sake, aren't you listening? It's not about his looks! But by the way, I find him awfully cute. I know he's not tall, handsome and muscular—it just isn't what got my attention. Could I have a little credit for a working brain here? Maybe I finally got smart, ever think of that?"

"You've always been smart," Gerri said. "You've also always been really...what's a polite word?"

"Horny?"

"I'm sure there are more polite words, but that one works. Holy shit, Andy. How old is Bob?"

"Fifty-three," she said with a shrug. "How old is Phil?"

Phil was the same age. "And all the parts are totally functional?" Gerri asked instead of answering the question.

"If you mean private parts, he's outperforming the two, the five and the baker's dozen."

"Whoa," Gerri said, speechless.

"You can't judge a book by its cover. And he's nuts about me."

"What does Noel say?"

"Noel met him in passing during the kitchen work, and I've invited him to dinner about four times in the past couple of weeks and he's been busy. But why should I worry about what Noel thinks? Does he run his personal life by me? I haven't met a girlfriend since senior prom and I know he's dating. There has to be more than one reason that apartment his friends have is more appealing than his own home. I'm not looking for Noel's approval anymore."

BJ came up alongside them, winding down from her run, all sweaty and looking slightly euphoric. "Hey. What's up?" she asked breathlessly.

"Well, plenty. I'm starting to like my wayward husband again, sort of, and Andy just confessed she's seeing Bob, the kitchen carpenter," Gerri said.

"Just how far do you run every day?" Andy asked.

"You know," Gerri interrupted. "*Seeing* him. *All* of him."

"I try to do four miles, but I'm happy with three," BJ said, ignoring Gerri. "It works for me. I think it's the endorphins. Listen, I'm supposed to get a painter to do some work on the house for the owners. You think Bob could do it?"

"Want me to ask him?"

"Yeah, please. That would be great."

"You're renting that place?" Andy asked.

"Not exactly," BJ said. "I'm kind of borrowing it. Till I can save a little money. Friends of the family." Then she looked at Gerri. "You didn't tell her?"

Gerri shrugged.

"The kids' father is dead and I'm kind of…not capable of a good income. But my brother, who is my employer right now, had friends with so much money they could actually spare one of their rental houses for a while. Eventually I'll have to find something else."

"Wow," Andy said. "Sure, I'll check with Bob. He's a good painter."

"Thanks. So, is Sonja doing okay?"

"She's doing well," Gerri said. "I'm going to visit her this week. That shrink, Dr. Kalay, has been terrific—gives me very positive updates when I call her." They'd come back to their block. "Well, ladies, I'm out of here. Have a good day."

Gerri walked to her front door. She shook her head and laughed silently. *Bob,* she thought. *We're all going a little nuts.*

It was not yet nine in the evening when Bob and Andy sat in her bed, each with a book. Beau was curled up on the end of the bed right between their feet. He wasn't allowed on any other furniture, but he was welcome on Andy's bed until he was politely asked to get down, then he curled up on the floor at the foot of the bed. Bob let his book drop to his lap and looked up at the ceiling with a heavy sigh.

"What is it?" Andy asked. "Everything all right?"

He looked at her with a smile. "I don't even recognize my life," he said. "I thought I had the perfect attitude to take me into old age in my sister's guesthouse, alone. Do you know what it's like to be here with you, like this, sitting in bed relaxing? Reading? Knowing in a little while we'll turn off the light and I'll get to lie beside you all night long? Andy, what are you doing with a guy like me? Are you crazy?"

She put her book aside and turned toward him, her shoulder on the pillow. "I feel so lucky to be with a guy like you. You turn me on like gangbusters."

He patted her thigh. "I'm afraid I'm going to wake

up in the psychiatric ward like your friend Sonja. The drugs will finally kick in and they'll break it to me that it was just a hallucination."

"She's coming home this week," Andy said. "You know what that means? It's almost a month you and I have been…you and I."

"Pretty remarkable." His face took on a startled look. "Is that like an anniversary of some kind or something?"

"Don't be silly." She laughed.

"You have to coach me, Andy. You know I'm not experienced with this sort of thing."

"That's what you keep saying," she said.

"There's something I feel like I have to do pretty soon, if you're agreeable."

"What's that?"

"Well, my sister. She didn't waste any time looking out her bedroom window and noticing that Beau and I are out all night, a lot of nights. I told her I have a girlfriend. Was that presumptuous?"

"No. You have a girlfriend," she confirmed.

"Now she's after me to bring you around to dinner or something."

"I'd love to meet your sister," Andy said.

He ran a hand over her curly hair. "She's gonna just die," he said. "I'll try to put her off a while."

"You don't have to do that. I'm not going to disappear on you."

"Seems like we should get together with Noel first," he said.

"Noel," she said, turning onto her back. "I told him I've been spending a lot of time with you, that I wanted him to have an evening with us, get to know you a little better, and he just brushes me off. He's way too busy for mother things."

Bob laughed. "I vaguely remember nineteen. Your family is the last thing on your mind. There are exciting things to do, lots of places to go. He'll turn up one of these days. I look forward to that."

There was a distant sound, a key in the front door lock, and Beau lifted his head, then jumped off the bed to go investigate. "Speak of the devil," Andy said, throwing back the covers and getting off the bed. She was wearing pajamas, but she grabbed her robe off the closet hook while Bob sat on the edge of the bed and pulled on his pants.

"Mom?" Noel called into the house. "Hey, Mom?"

"Just a minute," she yelled back. But before she could move, he stuck his head right in the bedroom door. Bob had his pants up but not buttoned or zipped and he was just pulling on his shirt. Andy was tying her robe closed.

"Mom?" Noel said. "Mom, there's a dog in the... Mom?" he said, clearly flabbergasted. "Jesus, Mom, what are you *doing?*"

She glanced over her shoulder at Bob who was stuffing his shirt into his pants as quickly as he could. "To tell the honest truth, we were reading in bed," Andy said. "You might've called."

"Aw, *Jesus,* Mom," he said, whirling out of the room.

"Bob, give us a minute, please."

"Sure," Bob said.

Andy followed Noel down the hall and into the family room. When she got there, she faced his back. "That wasn't very nice," she said. "First you barge in and then you act like an ass."

Noel whirled on her. "Are you out of your *mind?*" he asked in a whisper that was not nearly quiet enough. "What are you doing with that old guy?"

"What's the matter with you?" she asked angrily. "Who the hell raised you? You come barging in here and then say something as mean as that?"

He took a step toward her. "Jesus, he's just a fat old guy, Mom. What's up with *that?*"

"He's the most beautiful man I've ever *known!*" Andy said, stepping toward him. "If you'd even bothered to keep one date with me to get to know him better, you'd understand—he's the best man in the world."

"I think Bryce leaving made you completely nuts!"

"Bryce didn't leave—I *threw* him out. He was unfaithful, abusive and immature. Getting him out of here made me *sane!* For once I'm happy! Bob is the most wonderful, genuine, loving—"

"Andy," Bob said from behind her. "I think Beau and I will just go—give you and your son some time."

She turned. "No!" she said. "Please, don't go!" Then she turned to Noel. "Why are you here?" she asked, folding her arms over her chest.

He hung his head, suddenly a little embarrassed to face Bob. "I wanted to tell you—I got off with a fine for the pot, and I'm finishing up with a three-point-six at school."

She looked at her watch. "It's nine o'clock. Did you just get the news?"

"I just got the time to—"

"You know, I wouldn't do this to you. I know where that apartment is that you like to hang out inland. I wouldn't ever drop in on you like this, then humiliate you in front of your friends. I'm over twenty-one, Noel.

I'm self-supporting. From now on, try to accept an invitation from me if you can, and you're welcome anytime but for God's sake, call me before you use your key to walk in and then embarrass me in front of someone who—" She turned and glanced at Bob. "Someone who means very much to me."

Noel lifted his head and his eyes might've been a little glossy. "I just didn't expect anything like... Um, sorry, Bob."

"Hey," Bob said. "Not a problem. I think she's crazy, too—but, son, I didn't trick her, honest to God. Your mom is pretty smart."

"Yeah," Noel said. "So. Sorry, man," he said. Then he turned to Andy. "Look, sorry. I'm going to take off now. Before I piss you off any more."

"I want you back here," Andy said firmly. "Soon. Tomorrow. Or in two or three days, tops. I've been asking and you've been blowing me off for weeks. I want you to have dinner with us. It's not too much to ask, I don't think. Bob is going to be around for a long time, but I want you to make an effort to get to know him now. Before he's been here a year."

"Sure," Noel said, sticking his hands in his pockets and staring at his feet. "Sure."

He turned to go, then turned back abruptly and gave his mother a kiss on the cheek, then got out of the house quickly.

For a moment, Andy just stared after the path of his departure. Momentarily she felt Bob's hands squeezing her upper arms. He turned her around to face him and there were tears on her cheeks.

"Aw, honey," he said, pulling her closer. "He's just a kid."

She leaned against his chest and sobbed.

"Listen," he said, stroking her hair. "It's your duty as a parent to forget a lot of things, all right? You have to let it go. He'll start thinking and eventually…" He lifted her chin and looked into her eyes. "Let it go. Kids are dumb. It's a rite of passage. Besides—" he shrugged "—he caught us in our undies. He'll have to be fifty years old to really understand what a trip that is for us."

"He was cruel," she said with a sob. "I couldn't bear for you to be hurt."

"I don't hurt that easy, Andy. It's all right. I'm sure not going to hold it against him."

"I didn't raise him that way."

"Yeah, but he was unprepared for what he was going to see."

"He's walked in on me and Bryce practically swinging from the light fixtures," she said with a hiccup of emotion.

"Well, now, they sure wouldn't hold us," he said with a chuckle.

"We don't even need anything like that," she said, smiling through her tears. "I'm sorry, Bob. He had no right—"

"Aw, he's right. I'm just a fat old guy. The luckiest fat old guy in the state." He hugged her tight. "That was so nice, what you said about me."

She pulled back and looked up at him. "It's just the truth. You're the best thing that's ever happened to me."

He pulled her against him again, hugging her. "Andy, I'm a flexible guy but I hope you don't come to your senses. You're the best thing that ever happened to me, too. Now, is he the only one with a key?"

"Uh-huh. Well, there's Gerri, but she'd never…"

"Good. Let's get back to our undies. I'm so happy when we're in our skivvies."

She laughed. "How can you joke? That was kind of traumatic."

"No, it wasn't, not really. Hardly anyone would put you and me together, if you think about it. So, like you said a while ago, we're going to have to make sense to no one but us. That okay with you?"

She smiled. "Oh, yes. Very okay."

Gerri had arranged with Phil that he be at the house around dinnertime so she could work late. When she came into the kitchen, she saw his back as he sat in the dark out on the deck, feet up on the rail, a steaming cup of coffee on the table. He was the only person she knew who could drink coffee late in the evening and fall asleep, snoring like a tugboat within ten minutes. Caffeine didn't bother him. During law school he'd trained himself to take sleep when it was available and manage on little when the pressure was on.

She poured herself a small brandy. Sleep had never come easy for her, but the past couple of weeks she'd been resting pretty well thanks to hormonal intervention.

She took her brandy outside. "Feel like company?" she asked.

He turned toward her, sitting up. "Yeah. Sure."

"It's beautiful out here," she said. "There probably isn't any better time of the year." She nodded at the coffee. "That won't keep you up?"

He chuckled. "You've asked me that same question for twenty-five years. I have some work to do tonight."

"Are you working here? In the office?"

"Nah, it's just writing. I'll shove off in a minute."

"Is that place okay? The guesthouse?"

He shrugged. "Gets me by. The landlady is a stalker, the showerhead is for a woman—a short woman—and the bed could use a new mattress. Not as bad as our first apartment."

"I never asked, what kind of commitment did you make? As in lease?"

"Cash up front," he said. "I don't want to have a lease. I want to be flexible."

She smiled at him, took a sip of her brandy. "You sound like a man who wants to come home."

He laughed and shook his head. "You have no idea."

"You think a couple of months mends the tear?"

"Jesus, Gerri, I don't know. How are you feeling about things? Because since I got back to Mill Valley, you seem to be doing a lot better. Generally."

She swirled her drink and laughed. "Well, I have a secret. I guess you deserve to be in on it. Not a panacea for things like affairs—that comes harder. But a big help for things like hot flashes, insomnia and mood swings. I'm trying out some hormones."

His eyebrows shot up. "You were always pretty stubborn about taking the cure."

"It's a low dose, just to test it," she said. "And there's another thing—Jessie's on the pill now. It could do a lot for her PMS, which in combination with my menopause gets us pretty ugly at times. You're relatively safe from the women in your life."

"On the pill," he said, sounding melancholy.

"That's probably hard for a father to accept."

"I have one baby girl," he said. "I don't want anyone to touch her. Ever. And yet the thought of her going forever untouched makes me want to cry. I can't find a happy place. I wouldn't trade her for anything, but we should've had three boys. They get out of line, you just swat 'em and don't lose any sleep over it."

"We should've had one boy and one girl, but you lost your head."

He grinned at the memory. "I don't remember the other two feeling as good to make as Matt did. I'm sure that's why he's so good-natured."

"How's your counseling going?" she asked.

"I hate it, but it's probably the right thing to do. After I spend a few hours getting over the urge to just smack the little prick, I find myself thinking about things. But when I tell him that, he gets uppity and I want to hit him all over again."

"He's making you talk about feelings. You've never liked that."

"Yeah. But at least I recognize I have them. That's probably progress."

"Really?"

"Here's what men do," he said. "Men tend to feel their feelings and are driven by them, but they hardly ever think about them, talk about them, reveal them. It bores men to do that. Men like to move a lot faster than that—they want feelings to be peripheral and actions to dominate their lives. If a man feels pain, he quiets down, internalizes, sulks. If he feels anger, he throws something. If he feels lust, he fucks. It's basic and uncomplicated, which is what gets men in trouble. They don't want to understand their feelings, but the women in their lives would like to know why they do the things they do."

She frowned. "Then why aren't all men divorced?

They feel, they do, they move on to the next driving force."

"Because most men know how to play the game and the game has rules. Socialization. It's just like football," he finished with a helpless shrug. He took a sip of coffee.

"You might've ignored an important rule," she said softly.

He nodded. "Driven by feelings I couldn't understand or think about. That's why we're doing all this crap in counseling, to see if I can work on that."

"Wow," she said. "I think maybe the guy's good."

"Don't tell him," Phil said. "Really, he gets snotty. Omnipotent. And he hates me."

She leaned toward him. "Think we're gonna make it, Phil?"

He looked down for a moment, then raised his eyes and looked right at her. "I think there's too much right about what we have for us not to make it."

"Well, do you think we can get it back? Like it was?"

A heavy moment of silence hung in the air, so long that Gerri almost spoke. "I don't want it like it was," Phil said.

Her breath caught. She couldn't speak, which was almost a first. Oh, God, she thought—he's leaving me for real! She swallowed a couple of times before speaking. "But you said there's so much right about us...."

"I want it like it *should* be," he said. "I'm not sure that can happen."

"What are you talking about?" she asked.

He pushed back his chair and moved so he was sitting in front of her, facing her. He leaned forward and rested his elbows on his knees. "Everything we have together is about keeping this boat afloat. There's isn't a family in Marin that does it better than we do, and under more pressure than 95 percent of the people in five counties. I mean, two public servants with three kids? People don't have that many kids anymore, but we not only have 'em, we think we wanted to. And we don't just feed 'em and keep 'em warm, we get right into their lives and make sure they're growing up strong and smart. And we do that while succeeding profession-ally and being good friends. I've never had a friend like you. But obviously our marriage wasn't complete. There were things missing...."

"Sex," Gerri said. "We're going to talk about not having enough sex again—"

"No. Well, yes, we didn't have enough of that, but that's the other thing about men—they know how to take care of that, without even getting a woman in-volved. But what about time together when we don't talk about work or the kids or the house? How about once in a while being so into each other we don't even smell smoke until the house is almost burned to the ground? I want more of you than Andy gets. I want your mind, your heart and your body. I want your pragmatism, humor, good sense and *passion*."

"Phil, I'm not young anymore and neither are you. There's nothing I can do to turn back the clock, make it all seem brand-new."

"I don't want it brand-new—I've put in too much time for that and so have you. I want the woman I've loved for twenty-five years. I want us in the next stage—the richer, deeper, closer stage."

"It's not like I've been withholding," she said, almost pleading. "I've wanted more, too, but I never had an affair to—"

"Not because you're more decent than I am," he said resolutely. "Because there wasn't anything you needed. You didn't need it, Gerri. There wasn't an empty spot inside you. You weren't unconsciously searching for something to fill you up inside. I'm sorry. That sounded like I was blaming you and I wasn't. You didn't know, and that's entirely my fault. Hell, I'm not sure I knew. I might've been moving on instinct."

I knew. She almost said it. But instead, she shook her head. "It sounds like that same old thing again. That itch. Physical desire. Wanting to—"

"No," he said. "It's way more than that. It's intimacy. Not familiarity. Not comfort. Don't get me wrong, I love those things about us. That we can be naked in the bathroom and talk about the stock market. I love that when we're in trouble, we go to each other first. But I also remember a time we had to pull off the road because we were so worked up, turned on. I remember, even after the kids, that we locked the bedroom door and just held on to each other until we got sweaty. I remember when you'd jump in the shower with me and offer to wash my back…and you could never stick to business. You made me late for court a few times…"

"It pissed you off," she reminded him.

"I never liked being late for court, but I sure liked not being able to stop. There were times we made love that we got laughing so hard, we almost couldn't seal the deal. It was all about you and me—just you and me. So tight it was hard to tell where I left off and you began. And I don't remember the kids or the jobs or the chores ever getting short-changed."

She looked at him for a long time. She took a sip of her brandy and put the glass down. "You got all this from your counselor?"

"No, he's not getting credit, if there's credit to be had. I've spent two months trying to figure out why I'd cheat on the woman I love more than my life—make that five years and two months. It couldn't have been the sex. I don't even need much sex. It was everything that came before and after that. It wasn't that I needed to feel desire—I feel that for you all the time. It was what I felt coming back at me. Someone wanted *all* of me. Wanted me enough to take risks, break rules, get hurt."

"Oh, God," she said in sudden realization. "She loved you! You might've cared about her, but she *loved* you."

"I hurt her," he said softly. "I hurt two women just going after what I wanted, what I instinctively needed, and the result of having done that ripped me up."

"Oh, God," she said, for a moment thinking that was almost worse news than learning he had loved the other woman. *He wanted to be wanted.* "Phil…"

"I love you so much," he said. "You just have no idea how much."

"I don't know what to say." She felt a tear run down her cheek and he wiped it away with his thumb.

"Don't say anything," he said. "I want you back in my life so badly, I'll take any crumb. If we could go back to the way we were six months ago, I'd be grateful. Even if we could only go halfway back, I'd be thankful." He pulled both of her hands into his. "But, Gerri, if we can start over, really start over, build a marriage that really serves us, I swear I'll find a way to be more honest with you. Even if it means sitting in that little prick's office once a week for life."

A huff of laughter escaped her, as did another tear. He leaned toward her and kissed her cheek, kissing the tears away. She was very close to begging him. *Come back to my life, my home, my bed.*

Just as she opened her mouth, Phil spoke. "Maybe you were right about this—the separation—maybe it forced me to understand some of this stuff. Let's think about things a little while longer. Think about what you really want. Not just the things any woman in her right mind would settle for, but what you *really* want. What defines the perfect marriage to you? I'll go get a concussion from that showerhead and curvature of the spine from that mattress while we both weigh it all. It's hell, but if we can walk through this firestorm, who knows. Maybe we can still make this right."

"You know I love you, too," she said. "It was never about not loving you. I mean, I hated you, but I still loved you."

He grinned. "You just gave yourself away. *Hated.* Past tense. That gives me hope."

She walked him out through the garage and let him kiss her goodbye. He kissed her deeply. He put his hands on her waist and pulled her against him and kissed her in a way that made her wonder if she could fall in love all over again. *Intimacy,* she thought. The thing men are always accused of *not* wanting, *not* understanding. Maybe it was the thing men craved and had no idea how to meet the need.

Phil left and she locked the doors, turned off the lights and went to her room, where she sat on the bed in the dark for a good half hour. It wasn't fair that he had an affair and she was filled with regret. It just wasn't fair.

She washed her face and brushed her teeth. She snaked a hand under her nightie and smeared a little of the magic cream on her bare belly. And then her hand froze. She picked up the other tube, the one she hadn't yet bothered to use. She squeezed a little cream onto her finger and applied it to the inside of her thigh. Then she did it again, more cream, the other thigh, rubbing it into her skin. *We'll see, Phil. We'll see if I can meet you halfway.*

nine

Gerri took an afternoon off to pick up Sonja at Glendale Psychiatric because Sonja didn't want to see George at all. Ever. "So how are you going to manage your counseling appointments and all that without George?" Gerri asked on the ride home.

"I'm cleared to drive. And Dr. Kalay suggested we try someone else for counseling—someone who might notice if I'm unwashed and half-bald. But, just once a week. Then there's a group I'm going to. Honestly, I hate the thought of that. I hated those group sessions. Some of those people are seriously fucked up."

Gerri laughed in spite of herself. "This new vocabulary of yours is blowing my mind."

"I might've picked up some bad habits at the nuthouse."

"Any more I should be aware of?" Gerri asked.

"Let's just wait and see. You might catch me picking at invisible things floating in the air. I've completely stopped chewing my nails or pulling my hair out—that's an improvement, huh? I never took pharmaceuticals seriously enough."

"Sonja, forgive me, but you got funny. When did that happen?"

"I'm funny?" she asked. "Must be the drugs."

"So—you're going to see a new counselor and go to group."

"Yuck. That was the price of release. They probably have G-men following me around to be sure I keep the appointments. At least I don't have one of those house-arrest ankle bracelets."

"How do you handle that? I mean, if you find everyone in the group to be seriously messed up?"

"Dr. Kalay said if you can't be helped, then help. I'm sure I'm not qualified, but then they're not qualified to help me, either, so we're even."

Gerri pulled into Sonja's drive. "How about having dinner at my place tonight?"

"Would you be terribly hurt if I declined? Because I am so sick of eating with people. Sick of hearing everyone's toilet flush, shower run. And then there were those people who cried at night. It's a wonder anyone comes out of that place better than when they went in. They should be worse."

"I would've thought Glendale, being so highfalutin…"

"Yeah, well, you can dress up the zoo, but we're all the same animals in there. For a month all I've wanted is to have a little time alone. I spent one night in the bathroom with towels stuffed under the door and I thought they'd have me in a straitjacket for life—but I just wanted some time *alone*."

"I can understand that," Gerri said. "Why don't I get you some takeout? Or run you to the grocery store real quick? Because I never thought to stock your refrigerator."

"Nah, don't worry about it," she said, opening her car door. "It's what—a mile away? I think I can handle the store. I'll just unpack and go grab a couple of things."

"Let me drive you," Gerri said.

"No," Sonja said. "I'm fine to drive. I'm not groggy, not dizzy or disoriented, and I don't have any problems being around people. And I haven't forgotten how to use the bank card, so it's all just routine."

"What if you run into women from your old yoga and meditation classes? Won't they want to know where you've been?"

Sonja shrugged. "How about feng shui rehab? Think that'll cut it?" She got out of the car.

Gerri got out, too, laughing. "Let me get your suitcase," she said, opening the back door.

"I can manage. You probably have to get back to work or something."

"I'm working from home the rest of the day," Gerri said. "Let me walk you in, at least."

"Fine," Sonja said. "But then I know you have things to do. And I'm on a new schedule now. I sleep a little later. I won't be walking at 6:00 a.m."

"Oh, that's going to be very hard to accept," Gerri said, hefting the suitcase out of the back of the car. "After two years of you panting at my front door while I'm trying to pry my eyes open…."

Sonja stopped walking and turned toward Gerri. "I'm sorry about that. I shouldn't have pushed my agenda on you like that."

"Oh, get over it. You kept me in shape for two years. We're still walking, but we've pushed it back to six-thirty. Besides, I enjoyed giving you crap about being early every morning." Gerri reached around Sonja and unlocked the front door, then dangled the keys out to Sonja. Gerri walked in behind her.

"I think there's been some housekeeping here, while I was in the loony bin."

"We wanted to make sure it was clean for you. We weren't sure how long you'd be gone."

"I stayed voluntarily," she said. "I figured, why worry about George spending money, huh?"

"I hope that wasn't the only reason."

"No, the real reason was I was coming back into focus. Starting to feel like a human being again. Slowly. So goddamn slowly my joints actually ached."

Gerri stroked her upper arm, softly, fondly. Underneath that priggish Sonja all along was this precious wiseass. She wanted to crush her in her arms and cry. "Do you remember when I took you?"

"Not much. Most of it was a blur. Dr. Kalay said I was out of reality for a couple of weeks, but it felt like a couple of days at most. I remember leaving here with you, but barely. They shot me up pretty good. But at least I escaped electric shock. People were pretty whacked after that."

"Hmm, yeah—that's a rough treatment. Screws up memory real good. Can I help you unpack or something?"

"Just let me be, huh? I promise, I'm okay. Really, I would've stayed on, awful as it was, if it wasn't safe for me to come home. I want to see what it's like, getting rational and everything."

"Want me to help you unpack your woo-woo stuff in the garage?" Gerri asked.

Sonja's gaze dropped and it was the first time Gerri saw any sign of sadness or grief. "I think the best place for that stuff is in boxes," she said. "I'm still trying to cope with the fact that it was all a bunch of shit."

"You sure about that?" Gerri asked. "I mean, it seemed to make you happy."

"I'm sure I don't want that crutch right now. I want to take this straight, no ice, no mixer."

"What will you do with yourself?" Gerri asked. "I mean, if you don't work, what will you do? I don't want to worry about you being lonely, sitting in front of the TV."

"To tell the truth, I want to be a little lonely for a couple of days. I was thinking of reading a bunch of trashy novels late into the night in a quiet house, eating some bad things to see if my digestive tract is completely fucked up by too much healthy food and maybe digging up the backyard and planting flowers. Not mushrooms and herbs, but big audacious flowers. After the grocery store, I'm going to Costco to buy a few DVDs. I got hooked on movies at the booby hatch. Of course, they were very carefully selected movies—we wouldn't want to get any nutjobs worked up. Maybe I'll order some new television channels. And I don't know what after that. But that could keep me busy awhile." She smiled. "Hey," she said, "how's it going with you and Phil? You haven't divorced him or anything yet, have you?"

Gerri forced a smile. "It's going pretty well. We're still sleeping in different places, but I see him almost every day and we're getting along very well. Who knows? We might work this out. It's a rocky transition, but Phil and I have a lot of positive history."

"Good," Sonja said. "I like Phil. I think maybe he's the real deal."

Gerri's next smile was genuine and had more to do with Sonja than with Phil. "You think?"

"I've learned that some people are actually okay, despite a brief mental departure. His departure might've been insulting and pissed you off, but it couldn't have been worse than mine."

Gerri just shook her head. "Holy shit, you're better than ever."

"I doubt that, but…shucks."

"It's about time for us to have our evening out and start planning the end-of-summer block party. I thought this time we'd include BJ."

"BJ," she said, frowning, shaking her head. "Why do I think I like her?"

"Maybe because she saved your life—twice. Remember any of that?"

"No. BJ? Why would she care about me? All I remember of BJ is that she didn't want anything to do with us."

"All facade," Gerri said. "BJ's kind of private, but alert, compassionate, decent—a lot of things you'd appreciate. I think you brought her out of hiding. You needing someone to step in and respond. Andy and I were too preoccupied with our own crises. If it wasn't for your episode, we'd still just be waving to BJ every morning."

"No shit," Sonja said, and Gerri laughed again. Four years knowing this woman and she'd never heard her curse once. Now she spoke like a truck driver.

Gerri couldn't help herself. She drew Sonja to her and hugged her. "God, I'm so glad to have you back."

"Don't get too excited," Sonja said. "I'm not back yet. I'm just starting the climb. I have lots of work to do. I still don't remember who I was, don't know who I'm supposed to be. And I don't know that those whack jobs in group therapy are going to get me there, so be patient."

"I'll be patient," Gerri promised. "Whoever this is—I love her."

"That's nice," Sonja said. "Thank you."

Gerri and Andy had organized the first end-of-summer block party fourteen years ago. In a mood of discontent when school let out—Gerri because she'd have to deal with three kids all summer and Andy because she'd be out of work for three months. They sat down with a bottle of wine and planned an event to look forward to. Once the idea was hatched, they checked in with everyone on their block, assigning food, drink and recreational duties. The first year there had been about eight families present. They'd had the inevitable party crashers over time and the guest list grew and grew. Over the years it had expanded to include about six blocks, over a hundred households, and they'd moved it from their street to the park.

For the past four years Sonja had been involved in the planning and while she had objected to hot dogs, hamburgers and potato salad warming up in the sunshine, she'd been an organizational genius. She was willing to make all of the phone calls and keep all kinds of lists. With Sonja taking on so much, Gerri and Andy simply oversaw things. "I feel like we're using her," Andy had said. "But she does all this so willingly."

"Don't worry about it," Gerri had replied. "She loves being useful."

For the past few years their end-of-summer party had included kegs of cold beer, jugs of wine, live music. They rented a bouncy castle and a dunk tank for the kids, held competitions from three-legged races to egg and water-balloon relays and they even dressed participants in Velcro jumpsuits and hurled them against a giant dartboard. Gerri thought nothing had been funnier than watching her big-shot A.D.A. husband flying through the air to stick—*splat*—on a Velcro wall. The whole neighborhood looked forward to the event.

This year, things were going to be a little different. Sonja wasn't inclined to take on a big project and she didn't want to be held to a schedule, though she was willing to go out to dinner with them to help plan.

Gerri tried to draw BJ into the fold, but she had a million excuses. She didn't like leaving her kids, aged nine and eleven, and she imposed on her brother and sister-in-law all too often.

"Jessie will babysit. She'd do anything to get out of the house," Gerri said. BJ said she didn't have time to organize a big event. "Not a problem—it's been pretty much organized for over ten years." She didn't feel well enough acquainted to contact neighbors. "Just come to dinner. Check out the new Sonja." Gerri, who had promised never to hound BJ, kept trying. "When was the last time you had a nice dinner out with girlfriends?"

In spite of herself, BJ grinned her crooked grin. "It's been a long time since I thought of myself as someone with girlfriends." She finally gave in to Gerri's efforts to include her.

Leaving the house was quite an ordeal for BJ. She

was nervous as a cat, making sure Jessie had the number for the restaurant and BJ's brother's number. "My dad's at the house tonight, working in his office," Jessie said. "Don't worry, I can call him if I need anything. And really, I've done this before."

When she finally got in the front seat of Gerri's car, the last of the four women loaded up, Gerri said, "You have to be the only woman I know without a cell phone."

"I'm on a real tight budget," she replied.

"Really?" Sonja asked from the backseat. "Then you'll be happy to know, dinner is on George tonight."

"Well, that's awfully nice of George," Andy said. "Have you talked to him lately?"

"Oh, I hardly ever talk to George," she said. "In fact, I usually just hang up on him. I *hate* George."

"Then how do you know he's buying dinner?" Gerri asked.

"He's buying everything," Sonja said. "George is extremely generous these days. You know, since I'm crazy."

There was a little laughter in the car. "Sonja, you're about as crazy as I am," Andy said.

"Oh, darling—you, too? I'm so sorry!"

"You're not crazy!" Andy said. "You suffer from depression, which has pretty much flown away on the wings of your happy pills."

"Well, don't tell George that. He's under the impression he drove me insane."

"How long do you think you can play that card?" Andy asked. "Maybe you should hang on to your money."

"Don't worry about it," she said with a wave of her hand. "George doesn't want the details, he just likes to write checks. It's relieving his guilty conscience. I don't know why I should deprive him of the pleasure."

BJ turned in her seat. "Gee, I don't think I can let George buy my dinner under false pretenses like that."

"Oh, don't sweat it. George has more money than he knows what to do with. The cocksucker."

"Sonja!" Andy said with a laugh. "I don't know that it's right to take advantage of George like that."

"I'm not taking advantage of him. I'm sure he's keeping very careful records. Believe me, when we get to the official splitting of the sheets, all my expenses will be carefully deducted from my side of the chart. And there will still be plenty left." She grinned. "California law. No fault. Community property."

"No prenup, huh?" Andy said.

"Of *course* there was a prenup," Sonja said. "George is very careful, and he was already forty when we got married. It was 25 percent for under ten years, then an even split. We're due to celebrate our tenth anniversary the end of June. I don't think we're going to get to that final dissolution in time." She laughed.

"Sonja, are you holding out for the even split?" Andy asked.

"Of course not!" she said, sounding insincere. "But, sadly for George, you can't serve papers on a person in the nuthouse. Poor George. He was trying to make a break for it in March, to cut his losses. You'd think someone who can time the market would have a little more sense about when to get a divorce."

"Sonja, you are a devil," BJ said.

"And just when I'd been thinking I'd never learned how to handle money."

Gerri was strangely quiet, though no one noticed.

The others yammered on about whether Sonja was being unfair in judging George, was there any possibility they might reconcile down the road, maybe compromise, etcetera. Gerri tuned them out, thinking, *we're a car full of women who feel completely powerless against these men unless we figure out how to get even.* She wasn't sure about BJ—but there was something amiss there. Most widows talked about their departed spouse, and BJ never did. She wondered if there was something strange underneath the surface. But Andy had thrown Bryce out on the street, closed him out financially and immediately taken up with a replacement who was very unlikely for her. Gerri had moved Phil out of the house and although she wanted him back, she felt it was too soon—even he wasn't ready for that. And now Sonja was preparing to get her half of the pie.

It wasn't that she thought any of these actions were wholly inappropriate. Bryce had to go, Phil had to be out of her bed, Sonja was entitled. What bothered Gerri was that they all came at this because they were forced; they felt powerless. They had too few choices and wielded the only bludgeon available.

When she pulled into the restaurant parking lot she said, "We'll split the check, no arguments."

It was becoming a tradition—dinner at Lemange—a small, cozy, dark, inexpensive French bistro close to their neighborhood. It was also a mere formality—the four friends could have met over a glass of wine on Gerri's deck and had the party organized in no time, but starting things off right was important to them. The first planning session, always in late May, had to be held in a nice place, it had to be comfortable with delicious food and a good staff. They didn't want to feel rushed because they didn't have time to get together for dinner very often, and apparently for BJ, never at all. The planning session required hardly any planning at all. Knowing everyone's current preoccupations, Gerri took charge and announced that she and Andy would split the list of neighbors from last year, set a date, call everyone and simply ask if they could provide the very same things as the year before. "All I need from you, Sonja, is the list," Gerri said.

"I don't know where it is," Sonja said stubbornly.

"You have two weeks to find it, then we take your house by storm. Now," Gerri said, lifting her glass of wine, "to the end of summer."

"The kids aren't even out of school yet," BJ said, lifting a water glass in confusion.

"I know—but no way am I toasting that. You can't imagine what happens to my life in the summer. The kids are on the loose. They're bored. They're impossible to keep tabs on. It's a hotbed of mischief. To the end of summer."

"I never toast this," Andy said to BJ. "I love having the summer off school. In fact, I almost always drink a little too much at the end-of-summer picnic."

"I'm looking forward to summer," Sonja said.

"Gee, I feel kind of disloyal," BJ said, setting down her water.

"It's okay, BJ. The only one who ever toasts the end of summer before it starts is Gerri. She does it alone every spring. You don't have to join in," Sonja said.

"Here, here," Gerri said, alone.

The rest of the dinner gave way to tales of previous block parties, delicious food, laughter that even

BJ couldn't resist. Gerri and Andy shared the bottle of wine while Sonja, medicated, had water and BJ joined her. Everyone ate light to save room for heavy French desserts and rich, robust cappuccino. And all too soon, it was time to call it a night.

"I'm really glad you talked me into this," BJ said. "I should probably do things like this more often. It's just that I feel like I have such a load to carry with two kids and a job. I think I practice way too much self-denial."

"Get over that," Gerri said. "We have to keep ourselves sane, present company excluded in case George is listening."

"Very funny," Sonja said. "Bitches."

"Isn't it just like she's been possessed by a spirit?" Andy asked, dropping an arm around Sonja's shoulders. "She is woman, hear her roar."

They were all laughing as they walked out of the restaurant and it was as though a lot of things were suddenly in motion—happening all at once.

The young man who worked as a valet was watching the parking lot intensely, frowning. There was a man shouting in the parking lot and BJ was immediately pulling back on Gerri's arm. "Don't go near that," BJ said, a note of panic in her voice.

Gerri didn't even realize she'd already taken two steps toward the scene of a vicious argument between a belligerent young man and cowering young woman. As she took stock of the situation she could see it was completely one-sided and Gerri knew from the man's posture, it was taking a bad turn. He was tall, good-looking, early thirties, strong and broad. The woman was one of those waif-like, fluffy blondes—too thin, big breasted, tight pants slung below her flat waist. An underfed beauty, speaking so softly that she couldn't be heard at all above his bellowing.

"Don't you fucking pull that shit with me! I was around when you were doing that shit to Jack, remember! That fucking acting like you know what the fuck you're talking about when you don't know crap! I made a lot of money off that deal and you fucking *screwed* me in there with your big mouth! Right in front of them! Goddamn it, you're not going to do that to me like you did to him."

The man was in the woman's face, looming over her, screaming as she was backing away, shaking her head, trying to explain or apologize or escape. The man was completely out of control, bending over her threateningly, bouncing his closed fist in front of her face, turning almost purple with rage. Gerri looked over her shoulder at the valet. "Call the police," she said.

He shrugged. "He's just yelling. They're not going to come out for yelling."

"Gerri, don't," BJ said, pulling on her arm again. "Let's just get out of here. Don't look, don't watch. It's not our concern."

Gerri ignored her as she watched the scene for a moment. She pulled her cell phone out of her purse and punched in 911. When the emergency operator answered she knew exactly what to say. "I'm at Lemange restaurant, in the parking lot. There's a vicious verbal argument between a large man and a small woman and it looks like it's going to escalate. He's threatening her with a closed fist in her face and it could get physical at any moment."

Right then the man shoved the woman hard, causing her to take a couple of stumbling steps backward. She put her hand to the shoulder he'd just hit. "And it just got physical," Gerri reported. "He just shoved her, hard. She's no match for him—we need a unit to respond before he gets out of the parking lot, takes her home and beats the crap out of her."

"Please," BJ said. "*Please* don't do this. Let's go. Let's not get in their business."

Gerri ignored her. She gave her name to the police dispatcher. "Of course, I'll witness charges. Whoa, he just shoved her again. She's up against the car and he's still at her, screaming, threatening with a closed fist. This isn't going anywhere good. Yeah, yeah, I'll get the license plate in case they clear the parking lot."

"No, we can't do this," BJ said.

Gerri glanced at BJ and saw she'd gone pale, her eyes wide, her lips white. Gerri could see something about this had thrown BJ into a total state of panic. But she couldn't take care of everyone at once. She fished her keys out of her purse and handed them to Andy. "Take everyone home, I'm following through. I'll get home later, probably get a lift from a cop."

"You'll be okay?" Andy asked.

"Of course. I'm steps from the inside of the restaurant and I have this big kid right here to protect me. Just go. Get Sonja and BJ out of here."

Andy took the keys. "Come on," she said to the others. It wasn't as though this sort of thing happened with Gerri on a regular basis, but given her job Andy knew she was on a first name basis with a lot of the local cops. And she was determined, committed. She handled cases of abuse almost daily—this didn't frighten her in the least and even though she was off the clock, she couldn't turn her back on something like this even if she wanted to.

Gerri was barely aware of Andy leading Sonja and BJ away as she watched the man grab the woman's upper arm, pull her back, shake her and drag her toward the car door. She still had the dispatcher on the line. "He's shaking her and forcing her into the car. You might want to put a rush on this." And then she watched, stricken, as the woman banged her head on the roof of the car while getting in. The man took that opportunity to grab her by the hair and give her head another cruel bounce off the car roof. "Oh, God," Gerri said. The young valet started into the parking lot, now pushed too far, but Gerri grabbed him, pulling him to her side. "No," she said to the kid. "No, don't get into it. He's got you way outsized. Go inside—get help." Gerri turned back to her phone. "He's banging her head against the roof of the car," she said. "Where are the cops?"

Gerri took a couple of brazen steps into the lit parking lot, cell phone against her ear. The man slammed his passenger's door closed, shouting furiously at her through the closed window. But he was caught—he'd beat her in front of a witness and even if he got out of the parking lot, the police could be in pursuit as long as they had the description and plate number. As he rounded the front of the car he caught sight of Gerri.

"What are you looking at, bitch?"

She took another step, very conscious that she could quickly retreat to safety if necessary. "You," she said. "I'm watching you! I have the police on the line!"

He stopped where he was and snarled at her, baring his teeth, but then he whirled and got into the driver's seat. Gerri described the car and rattled off the license plate to the dispatcher, using the phonetic code on the letters.

"Ma'am, are you P.D.?" the dispatcher asked.

"CPS," she said. And then she watched the man scream at his companion, likely blaming her for making a scene, right before he pulled back a fist and let it fly into her face. He was so out of control, he continued his assault even through the threat of police. "He just punched her in the face," Gerri reported. "He started the car."

Gerri heard sirens in the near distance. "I think your cops are gonna make it," she said into the phone. And then she glanced in the direction of her departing vehicle, saw Andy driving, Sonja sitting in the front seat with eyes very wide and BJ in the back, her hands pressed over her face. They cleared the parking lot seconds before the police vehicle came flashing around the corner. The abusive man was too busy screaming and hitting the woman to get out of there. His rage had slowed him down.

The valet came out with a couple of waiters and Gerri pointed at them. "Stay back," she said. "The police are here and won't know who's who. Stay back."

Gerri stepped into the parking lot under the lights and flagged the police car, moving her hand in a circular motion, pointing. They stopped in front of her and with the phone still pressed to her ear, she indicated the car with the couple in it. It was too dark inside the car to see exactly what was happening, but the couple appeared to be still.

The squad car blocked the suspect's car and the officer got out, brandishing his weapon, his flashlight propped on top of the gun and shining it into the suspect's car. "Please step back into the restaurant, ma'am," he said. "Right now."

She backed away quickly. It hadn't for one second crossed her mind that the man could be armed, but it should have. Domestic disputes like this were frequently accompanied by panicked shots fired, people killed or wounded. She grabbed the sleeve of the valet, realizing the boy was about Jed's age, and pulled him and his reinforcements back against the restaurant door, out of the parking lot lights, into the darkness. But she didn't go inside because she was too invested in the situation. She wanted to watch as this asshole was apprehended. It took only seconds for the next cop car to make the parking lot, lights and siren flashing. He blocked the exit.

"I should'a stopped him," the young valet said.

"The best thing you can do now is give the police a report," Gerri said.

And almost immediately the abuser got out of the car, hands in the air, protesting loudly. "What?" he yelled. "What? I'm just trying to take my girl *home!*"

The police had him on his knees in seconds, cuffed and rendered helpless for the time being. The woman, however, remained in the car, sheathed in darkness.

Gerri stepped out of the doorway. "You better check the victim. He beat her," she called out.

"*She* hit *me!*" the cuffed man shouted back.

"She didn't," Gerri said calmly, clearly.

The police officer took charge. "Ma'am! I want you to stay back!" And like a good girl, she skittered back to the restaurant.

Ah, yes, she thought. She knew very well the police had procedures and wouldn't take risks. They brought the victim out of the car at gunpoint, as well, and when she exited the vehicle Gerri could see her nose was bleeding. At least they didn't cuff her, though they did pat her down. It wasn't unheard of for a battered woman to pull a gun on police and rescue her abuser—it was a complex and often irrational syndrome. But the young woman came out, hands up, crying, bleeding, and the second officer took her to the back of his vehicle.

Two more squad cars appeared, though the officers let the original two handle their suspects, standing by if needed. Gerri listened in fascination while the young man argued in a whimpering tone about never having hit, never having raised his voice, they were just having a discussion when she struck him and he merely defended himself.

Within ten minutes the young man and woman were seated in the backs of separate patrol cars, the restaurant manager was outside and patrons were pouring into the parking lot to see what was happening. It took Gerri less than fifteen minutes to give her statement to the police. Because there was an injury, paramedics were called but the victim was released to drive herself home or to the hospital because she refused medical treatment.

"Can you please give her this," Gerri said, passing a business card to a patrol officer. It had the number on it for victims of domestic abuse. She had no confidence whatsoever that the young woman would seek help, but at the very least her abuser was going to spend a night in jail. Gerri knew it was highly likely he would be picked up by his victim at daylight—such was the typical scenario.

"Any chance you have time to give a witness a lift home?" she asked one of the superfluous cops. "If not,

I can get myself a cab. I sent the party I was with home in my car while I stayed to give a statement."

In just an hour from start to finish, Gerri was being dropped off in front of her house. When she walked in, Phil was sitting in the family room and he stood and approached her. "Got in the thick of it, did you?" he asked.

"Well, what else could I do?" she replied, dropping her purse on the sofa. "I guess Andy told you what was happening?"

"I got the bare facts," he said. "They're waiting outside on the deck."

"Waiting?"

"For the debrief, I assume. And at least one of your girls is shaken up."

Gerri glanced out the window. "Yeah, that would be BJ, who Jessie's babysitting for. She kind of panicked at my getting involved."

"She must not know you all that well. I gave her a glass of wine. Then I left them the bottle."

"But you didn't sit out there with them? You're usually a lot friendlier than that."

"I'm keeping a low profile until I'm officially received in the neighborhood again," he said, smiling.

"You want to take off?"

"I don't think so," he said. "Think I'll get in line for the end of the story. If it's all the same to you."

"It wasn't that big a deal, Phil," she said. "I saw an ugly argument in the parking lot, had a hunch where it was headed, then saw him get physical while I had the dispatcher on the line. I had to wait around for all that to be taken care of, that's all."

"He hurt her?" Phil asked, frowning.

"Gave her a bloody nose and whacked her head on the roof of the car."

Phil winced and shook his head. "Scumbag."

"She refused medical and left in his car. She'll probably beat him to the jail to try to spring him."

He tilted his head toward their deck. "Take care of your girls out there. I'll hide in the office till it's all clear."

"Really, you don't have to—"

"I want to wait for you, Gerri. That okay?"

"Yeah," she said. "That's absolutely okay." Then she headed for the deck.

Her friends had a candle lit on the outside table and they were completely silent until she sat down. "Everything is all right," she said. "The police arrived seconds after you left and took him away. I don't know how much you saw—"

"He hit her," Sonja said. "I didn't want to leave until I saw you throw yourself on him and beat him senseless with your purse."

Gerri chuckled. "He was a little on the huge side. You okay?"

"Me?" Sonja asked. "Peaceful as a river. BJ's pretty unstable right now, though. I offered her one of my pills, but she decided on wine."

"You okay, BJ?" Gerri asked.

"Sorry," she said. "I didn't mean to get all weird on you like that. I have one or two real mean bastards in my personal history. I think I might've had a flashback or something."

"I wondered."

"I wanted you to do what you did, but, Gerri…"

She paused and swallowed. "You know how it'll end up, don't you?"

"Unfortunately I know the statistics. But I'm relentless. Know why? Every once in a while I get a case that works out. We get the kids and the woman out of there and they actually break loose. Like you obviously did."

"Yeah, but the price can be—"

"I know, kid. I know." Gerri ran her fingers through her short hair. "It just kills me when they're so young. I don't know how old he was but she was twenty-five. And so beautiful. They're not married, how about that? It's a boyfriend. We didn't have a conversation, but if I know anything, he's not the first boyfriend who's treated her like an animal. Listen, here's how it is— if she doesn't leave him, he's going to beat her again no matter what I do. If he's locked up, she has a window of opportunity to get away, though the odds are she won't take it. I'm pretty well educated on these issues and I understand how it happens, especially if the woman was raised on abuse. But I still can't figure out how they never seem to get to a point when it's enough. I mean, she's stunning. There must be a hundred good men who'd love to love her. It's baffling."

"Well, I could explain that, but if you don't mind…"

"I'm sorry, BJ," Gerri said. "You're obviously traumatized by that whole circus we witnessed. Maybe someday when you're feeling a little more in control and comfortable we'll have that conversation."

"That kind of thing happen to you a lot?" BJ asked, taking a sip of her wine.

"When I'm not working? Only once before, almost an identical scenario. It was ten or twelve years ago, if I remember. Another domestic in a parking lot, but I was alone. I had stopped off for groceries on the way home and it happened right in front of me. I didn't have a cell phone. I had to go back into the store. The manager and bag boy held them apart until the police could come." She leaned forward. "I see things professionally. I used to get in a lot of tight spots when I was doing more home visits. But it's what I do—it's not something I can turn on and off. You know?"

"Of course you can't," Andy said. "So—they took him away?"

"And one of the cops gave her a card with a phone number on it. If she's up to it, if she's had enough and isn't too terrified, she might call it."

"Did you get their names?" BJ asked.

"As a matter of fact, I did. I thought I should know, in case they need a witness. The police charged him."

"Do you ever, you know, run 'em up? Check out the record? Check and see how things come out?"

"I don't have access to police files, but I never have any trouble getting whatever information I need," Gerri said. "We're pretty well connected at CPS."

"Maybe you'll check," BJ said. "If you do, maybe you'll just tell us that he didn't kill her or anything."

"Listen, it wasn't nice, what happened tonight. But I don't think we have to worry that her life's in immediate danger. Long-term danger is more likely. She'll go to her mother's or sister's, he'll face battery charges, probably misdemeanor, make up with her, and this event will repeat itself several times before they either break up or something worse happens. It's true, it's a deadly game, but not every domestic ends that way, BJ."

"But you'll check?" she asked.

"Would it make you feel better?"

"It would. If I hadn't seen it, it wouldn't matter. But I saw it. And I tried to get you to walk away from it. So now…"

"Okay. It'll be all right, but I'll check and let you know."

"Thanks."

"I'm sorry," Gerri said. "It must have been so difficult."

"Tonight?" BJ asked.

"All of it."

"Yeah. But it's okay now." She smiled her crooked smile. "I got loose."

"Good for you," Gerri said. "You all okay now?" she asked, her gaze connecting with each of the women in turn.

"I want to be you when I grow up," Sonja said. "I want to be strong like you. You're invincible."

Gerri laughed. Remarkable, she'd been feeling so powerless about her personal situation, having completely forgotten that she'd been programmed to react in crises like the one she encountered. It was the crisis at home she wasn't trained to manage. "Maybe I've just turned into a crusty old broad," she said.

"You?" Andy said. "Anything but." Andy pushed back her chair. "You're just amazingly efficient and Sonja's right, you are very strong."

"We're all stronger than we realize. You girls ready to give it up? I'm shot."

Chairs scuffled back. Women stood. BJ touched her arm. "Listen, your husband. I tried like hell to hate him tonight, but it was hard. He seems like a pretty decent guy, first glance. He was real concerned about me. He could tell I was upset and he… He tried to be nice, you know? Got me a drink, told me to relax, reassured me that you knew exactly what you were doing."

"He's a very decent guy," Gerri said. "That puts a strain on me."

"Well, thanks for what you did," she said. "Before that happened, it was one of the nicest nights I've had in a long time. Maybe ever."

"Hey, we'll do it again real soon. I mean, what are the odds of trouble again, huh? Just send Jessie home, will you? And watch her out the front door till she gets here?"

When the door was closed on the women, Gerri went to the office she'd been sharing with Phil for fifteen years. He was focused on the computer screen. She walked up behind him, put her hands on his shoulders.

"I need some information right away. I need you to get it for me. I could go through channels, but I don't want to wait and it's important," she said.

"Tonight's event?" he asked.

"Sort of. I want you to find out if Barbara Jean Smith of Fresno is in the system."

He swiveled his chair around to face her. "Your new friend?"

"She overreacted tonight. It's obvious she's been the victim of abuse. Maybe there was a court case or something. I can wait till she lets it out, but if you don't mind."

"Sure," he said, turning back to the computer. "Age?"

"About thirty-five. Give it a three-year span."

All he had to do was log in to the prosecutor's office database. It would take quite a bit of searching, but Phil was accomplished at multitasking. While he got under way, she went to the chair at her end of the desk. "You okay with what happened tonight?" he asked.

"It was kind of routine, sad to say. The only things that got to me in a big way were BJ's and Sonja's reactions."

"Sonja do okay?"

"Too okay," she said. "She's had a complete personality change. It makes me wonder what's happening to her in private, when no one's around to see her react to this shift her life has taken. By the way, BJ confessed to me that she's having trouble hating you. You must have been very nice to her."

He turned in his chair. "Does everyone in the world know what I did?"

"I think so," she said. "I told my girlfriends. I haven't told them at work yet. They're too busy to care. They're oblivious."

He turned back to the computer, reapplying his reading glasses, clicking away. "You told my mother."

She laughed. "Has she been in touch?"

"She's making my life miserable…."

"Ahh…" There was a definite sound of satisfaction.

"She's threatening to visit."

"That would be nice," Gerri said, smiling to herself. "We haven't had a common enemy in years."

"It would finish me off."

"You said you'd do anything," she reminded him.

"I did," he said, scrolling through documents. "I was thinking public evisceration, castration, mutilation— not my mother."

"She adores you."

"Not lately," he said. He turned back to her, plucking off his specs. "She suggested I buy you some flashy jewelry, take you on a trip to the islands or something."

"Really? Why didn't you offer that?"

"Because I knew your idea of amends would be much closer to the soul—like moving me out. Telling my mother." She laughed at him and he turned back to the keyboard, the screen. "You're getting too much pleasure out of my comeuppance," he said.

"It has been interesting, I admit. Listen, I had to tell Muriel. One of the kids was going to slip. You understand that."

"I know better than to suggest constrictions, Gerri. You do what you do. I'll grovel. I think that's the recipe here."

"Oh, you make a fabulous victim," she said. "I'm sick of laughing about this. I'm still pissed off."

"Yeah, I know. You're—" He stopped talking and studied the computer screen. "Two hundred and nine arrests of women named Barbara Jean Something between the ages of thirty-three and thirty-six. Note to self. Our kids can't name any of our grandkids Barbara Jean." He scrolled through arrest documents slowly, reading the screen. Then he turned his chair away from the computer and pulled off his glasses. "I don't think you're ready for this."

"What?" Gerri asked, standing and moving away from her chair. She glanced over his shoulder and read the screen. "Dear God," she whispered.

There on the screen was BJ's picture. And a headline. Barbara Jean Smith Spraque Stands Trial for Husband's Murder.

ten

If there was one gift in the news about BJ, it was that Phil's office had not prosecuted her—it happened in a different county. He logged off the prosecutor's database and left the rest to Gerri. Once he was gone she got back on the computer, researching news articles about Barbara Jean Spraque—Smith was her maiden name. And she stayed at it until 2:00 a.m.

There were undoubtedly many more details to the story, but the gist was she'd been battered by her husband. Married at eighteen, a mother at twenty-three, she was hospitalized several times. Her husband went to jail on occasion, though never for long. He was charged multiple times with battery as well as other offenses. By the time BJ's children were four and six years of age, he'd been hitting, shoving and shaking them, as well, and she'd tried just about everything from orders of protection to shelters. And then on one dark and dangerous night shortly after he'd hit them all again, he started to party with a few of his friends…and lots of alcohol, pot and his favorite, cocaine. BJ put her children to bed, told them not to leave the room for any reason, and she served the drinks. She added small amounts of cocaine to her husband's drinks all night. Then, late that night, right about the time most of his friends had either moved on or passed out, she fixed his final cocktail. She scraped a large amount of coke into his drink. According to her own testimony, he was a big man and she was afraid it hadn't been enough. When he passed out, she loaded her children into the car and drove to her mother's house where she waited for her husband to find her and beat her senseless, or for the police to arrest her.

BJ's attorney pled her charges down to manslaughter, and she had served three years in a women's state penitentiary—Chowchilla. The timeline suggested she'd moved to Mill Valley right out of prison.

She was just reunited with her kids after three years of separation. *No wonder she's so private,* Gerri thought. She was skittish around people, no doubt afraid they'd find out. Gerri couldn't imagine what that might be like—constantly worrying the kids would pay again and again as neighbors, people around school, looked at them as the offspring of a murderer. And children could be so unbelievably cruel. If the news got out, it could be horrible. BJ had undoubtedly prepared herself to do a lot of moving around.

In over twenty-five years with CPS, this was only the second time Gerri had been faced with a situation this dramatic. Phil had been involved prosecuting similar cases a number of times. Gerri had supported him when it tore him up, prosecuting a woman for a crime she had to commit to stay alive, to keep her kids alive. To his credit, when moral if not legal innocence was implicit, he did whatever he could to keep the sentencing reasonable. But the law is the law. Killing is not justified unless you're in *immediate* danger.

They'd had their share of arguments about that, naturally. Gerri was convinced the perspective of the law and the prosecutor's office were based in testosterone. Of *course* men didn't kill sleeping men! They'd have a gun or a knife handy for that next attack and the self-defense would be indisputable. The thought of that couple in the parking lot came to her mind. What was a five-foot-three, one-hundred-pound woman supposed to do to defend herself against a six-foot-three, two-hundred-and-twenty-pound man? Unless she had some kind of special training, he'd take her weapon away from her and use it on her before she could even aim. *Special training, hah!* Gerri knew abused women couldn't sign up for marksman training or karate. In most cases, they were barely allowed to use the phone.

And yet it was the thing women and men alike always said they'd do if they couldn't escape the abuse— kill the son of a bitch. Gerri had always said she would. She wouldn't live under that kind of oppression. She'd go to prison to keep her children safe. Phil said if his daughter was in such a situation and couldn't get out, was hopelessly locked in and ruthlessly battered, he'd kill the son of a bitch. *Talk, talk, talk.* When truly faced with it, how many people actually *could?*

If Gerri was a betting woman, she'd lay odds that BJ had known exactly what was going to happen to her. She knew she'd be tried and convicted of something if not murder one. She knew she'd go to prison. And yet it must have seemed the only option left to her. Better Mommy in prison than everyone in the ground.

Gerri knew there would come a time when she would

ask her about that. She wouldn't tell even Andy what she'd learned, but she would eventually level with BJ. Gerri wanted to know how she could have been sure her children would be safe while she was locked up. How did she know she'd get them back? Who was on her side? Obviously she had her brother's support—but what had happened to the husband's family? The abuser's kin were notorious for denial, for going after the killer until the end of time. And that house—whose house was it really? Gerri could barely remember the original owners and didn't know if it had sold privately, without signs or open houses. Then Gerri realized the last renter had been a single mom who also kept to herself. *Hmm—a recovery house? Owned by some philanthropist?*

Too stirred up to sleep, she took a rather large brandy to bed. She turned on the TV but it didn't drown out her thoughts, all jumbled up in a mess that included BJ then and now, the couple in the parking lot, her job.

Inevitably, her thoughts moved to her own situation and her friends and their marriages—all in various states of flux. Andy and Bryce were over and it seemed like Sonja and George were headed that way, as well, for entirely different reasons.

She thought maybe she and Phil might salvage something, but she had a secret and desperate fear—that they'd get back together, sleep in the same bed, talk about the stock market while naked in the bathroom, attend the kids' college graduations and weddings as proud parents and then, after they'd done all the work, done all they could, they'd give up in exhaustion because getting it back wasn't possible. And starting over was just a romantic idea that couldn't be achieved.

* * *

With the end of school, the early morning walks had been suspended for the neighborhood women. Andy had no reason to rise at the crack of dawn, Sonja was sleeping in these days and occasionally Gerri got out there by herself, but she was slacking, taking great pleasure in the days she could languish in bed until seven or seven-thirty.

For Andy, the summer was shaping up differently than ever before. She usually planned a long visit with her father in San Luis Obsipo, but this summer she had hedged on such plans. She had such a nice routine with Bob. He had cut back on his evening work most nights so he could be with her, and she loved that he would do that. Almost every weekend they toured model homes and open houses. Bob was always looking for new ideas and Andy loved looking at houses, something she never indulged alone, since she wasn't in the market to buy. In her entire life, she'd never had a man interested in the same things until now. They went out to dinner at least once a week, sharing each other's favorite places, holding hands across the table. There were a couple of TV shows he liked and sitting beside him to watch them, rubbing Beau's belly with her bare feet, was more pleasurable than a trip to the islands. Bob was a big reader, about an hour or two every night, and the book he was working through always stayed on the table that was on what had become his side of the bed. And he spent the night often—three or four nights a week.

Noel had done as instructed—he came to dinner. He was still on the quiet side, maybe not entirely sure his mother was playing with a full deck, taken with this man who, even Andy could admit, was far different from the men she was usually attracted to. Maybe Noel wasn't as enchanted by Bob, although Andy thought Bob came off well—his usual affable and interesting self. Or maybe Noel was slightly embarrassed by his last encounter with Bob, which was simply rude. In any case, it wasn't a bad dinner. But it sure didn't reel Noel in. He left right after they ate.

Andy was already feeling the impulse. She wanted Bob all to herself. She wanted his overalls hanging across from her clothes in the closet, his shoes by the door. She hadn't breathed a word to anyone because she'd always been accused of *needing* a man, of moving too fast. In her private thoughts, she knew there was a kernel of truth in that. But this was different. She was feeling a strong need for *Bob.* Her plan was to gut it out until a respectable period of time had passed before asking him if he and Beau would consider a change of residence.

They returned from a Saturday evening at a local bistro and the message light was blinking on her home phone. "What's this?" she asked herself.

She put the phone on speaker and dialed in the code while Bob let Beau outside. Her ex-husband Rick's voice, panicked and angry, came blistering into the room. "Andy! You're not answering your cell! Call me the second you get home! We have a problem! Hurry up!" And right after that, a second, a third and a fourth similar command. She pulled her cell out of her purse and saw there were messages and texts and her ringer had been off.

"Oh, God," she muttered. "Noel. Noel." It was simply the only thing she and Rick had in common.

Bob looked at her from the back door. He had a look

of concern on his face, a very rare expression for him. "Call," he said.

Feeling afraid, feeling vulnerable, she left the phone on speaker when she called Rick. He came on the line all worked up. "Do you have any idea what's going on with your son?" he demanded loudly, sounding enraged.

"I talked to him twice today," she said. "I see him at least twice a week if not more. What—"

"He's *gay,* that's what! Your son is *gay!*"

"What?" she said. "What did you say?"

"He's *gay,* I said!"

"Did he tell you he was gay?" she asked, in a state of shock.

"Of course not! I went to that apartment where he likes to hang out and it's full of faggots. Fairies! And your son is right at home there!"

"Rick, he works a lot in theater arts—he has a lot of gay friends…."

"I confronted him!" he blustered. "He admits it! Said he was afraid to tell me." He laughed meanly. "Smart kid. He should've been afraid!"

"Wait," she said. "Wait a minute. You went there? Why?"

"I wanted to see what he was up to, what he was hiding. I'm not paying child support and college tuition if he's using drugs and that's what I thought was going on. He sure wasn't coming around here much. I wish it had been drugs, but it's not. He's a fag!" He coughed in disgust. "Obviously *you* had no idea where he was…."

"Of course, I knew where he was—I checked it out, saw that it was in a good complex, asked the apartment manager if she'd had any trouble there because my son liked to hang around there with friends. She said those boys were good boys. But Jesus, I didn't barge in. I wouldn't do that!"

"I blame this on you!" he stormed. "You and your weird boyfriends!"

"Wait a minute," she replied angrily. "If it's true, it has nothing to do with my boyfriends. They were all incredibly straight."

"Yeah, right. I always thought that Bryce guy was a little light in his loafers."

"Oh, bite me, Rick. How about you? Leaving him with a mother and no father for at least a couple of years while you ran off with the school nurse!" She put her hand up to her mouth. "Oh, God, what am I saying? If Noel is gay, it doesn't have anything to do with either of us. You can't *make* a person gay!"

"Yeah? Well, he sure didn't get it from *me!*"

"How do you know?" she asked. "If he is gay he was born gay!"

"Not possible! No way!"

"Yeah, that would be a tough pill to swallow, wouldn't it? Because all I have are all these big, hetero Greeks in my ancestry."

"Yeah, Greeks—they started this, right?"

"Oh, for God's sake! Don't you have a couple of gay uncles you've crossed off your Christmas card list? Get a grip! He didn't do this to you! Whatever is going on with Noel, it's not about *you!*"

"I'm through with him," Rick said. "He's all yours. I'll be damned if I'll have some queer around my kids!"

"Oh, you didn't do that," Andy said. "Please, Rick— you didn't do that to him!"

"When he straightens out, he's welcome back. Till

then, I'm not going to have his influence around the boys!"

"Rick, what have you done? If he's confused or scared you could've done terrible damage. For God's sake, Rick! If you're angry with me, don't take it out on Noel. He's just trying to grow up."

"Trying to grow up a fag! I'm not having him in my house! I'm not paying any more support while he's in college. I'm through with that!" He disconnected.

Andy just looked at the phone for a long time, numb. Shocked.

"That was awful," Bob said.

She looked at him. "What am I going to do?" she asked.

"You should call Noel. Tell him you heard from his father and you're sorry his father's so angry and worked up. And he should come talk to you because you're not going to act crazy like that. But you'd like to know what's going on with him and you want to know he's all right."

She stepped toward him. "Did you know?"

"Know?"

"Did you know my son was gay? Did you get that vibe from him?"

"No," he said, shaking his head. "Why would I? Because my wife was a lesbian? He seemed like just your average, regular kid to me. Listen, there aren't always a lot of signals. I'm proof of that, right?"

"I wasn't missing anything, was I?"

"Andy, what were you going to do if you were? Deprogram him? Come on, you know we don't control this part of life. I mean, mothers are incredibly influential, but really, you don't have that kind of power."

"Do you have any gay kids in your family?" she asked.

"I don't know. I might have a gay nephew back in Connecticut, but if he is, he hasn't come out. Why? What does that have to do with anything?"

"Are you comfortable around gay men?"

He shrugged. "Gee, they're so good with color..."

"This isn't funny!"

"It's also not a catastrophe, Andy. You don't really think your son got to thinking, Gee, let's see what I can do to make my life more difficult, more challenging. It's not an easy life, even around here. I mean, look what the boy just went through with his dad. Noel had to know that wasn't going to be easy. Cut the kid a break. We're all pretty much stuck with who we are."

She shook her head. "Why aren't you a father?" she asked softly.

"I got to the real thing too late in life," he said with a smile. "Call him. Tell him it's okay to come home. Tell him you're not upset. He'll be glad to get that message."

Gerri answered her front door and found Andy standing there, clutching a coffee mug in one hand and her cell phone in the other. It was very clear from her reddened eyes that she'd been crying. "Is your house a little on the quiet side?" Andy asked.

"Oh, God, what is it? Is it Bob?" Gerri asked, reaching out and pulling her inside.

"No, no. It's Noel. Please, could we talk? Do you have a lot of people around?"

"Just the opposite. Phil didn't come by tonight, he has a big case. Jessie's babysitting, Matt and one of his friends are playing video games in his room and Jed has a phone growing out of his ear. What's the matter?"

"Oh, you're not going to believe it. Or maybe you will, I don't know."

"Come on," she said. "Deck."

Gerri lit a couple of patio candles and through some tears, Andy explained the events of two nights earlier, the horrible phone conversation with Rick. "Now Noel won't return my calls or come over," Andy said. "I know Rick must have really upset him, but I've left messages asking him to please talk to me, let me see that he's okay, and I've promised I'm not going to react the way his father did. Oh, Gerri, he's scaring me to death. I'm going to have to go over there, to that apartment his friends have. I just don't want to make things worse."

"You don't think he'd do anything...desperate?" Gerri asked.

"I'm starting to wonder. I'm starting to fear it. The only thing that's stopped me from chasing him down is that I assume he's where he wants to be. That he's getting some sympathy and support or something. But why in the world would he be afraid of me?"

"Maybe he's not afraid of you. Maybe he's just totally upset about Rick. What an asshole—what was he thinking? Was it just the shock? Is that what happened?"

"I doubt it. I mean, I'm sure Rick was stunned, but it's also the way he is. It never once crossed my mind that we'd face something like this with our son and unleash that monster inside Rick. Oh, God," she said, tears spilling over. "I just can't imagine what Noel's going through."

The patio door opened noisily and Jed leaned outside. "Mom, I'm headed over to—" He stopped suddenly when he spied Andy wiping off her cheeks with a hand. "Oh-oh," he said, retreating, pulling the door closed.

"Jed," Andy called.

The door swung open slowly and he stood there, his eyes wide and his posture tense. *Now what?* was written all over his face.

"Jed, Noel's in trouble," Andy said, standing.

He inhaled sharply, stiffened and waited nervously.

"Jed, I just found out Noel is gay," Andy said, stepping tentatively toward him.

He let out his breath in a whoosh of relief. "Oh, that," he said, taking a stabilizing breath. "I thought maybe he mouthed off to the judge or something. But I did tell him to keep his stupid mouth shut or he'd get like years of community service. You know, he doesn't always think."

"Jed, I said he was gay," Andy tried again.

"Yeah, I know."

"You *know*?" Andy said, taking another small step.

"Well, he's like my best friend, you know. Even if we don't…well, I think we might have different drummers." Then he grinned. "I think his might be a majorette."

"This isn't funny," Andy said.

Jed shrugged. "Guess I've gotten used to it. Hey, don't blow a gasket. You'll get used to it."

"You're not… I mean, you're not upset? Your best friend? Gay?"

"Yeah, well I admit it kind of freaked me out at first. But I mean, come on—it's just Noel." Then he smiled and put his hands in his front pockets. "I don't think he's attracted to me or anything."

Andy backed up a step, sank into her chair and wept into her hands.

"Hey, sorry," Jed said, coming out on the deck. "I won't make jokes, okay? But just so you know, Noel doesn't get all pissed off about that. I think he secretly likes the jokes. Makes him feel like I'm playing on his team." Then he put up his hands, palms toward the women. "But, hey, I am not playing on that team, all right? I mean, I am totally straight, okay? So don't—"

Gerri was having trouble keeping a straight face. *Good old Jed,* she thought—so down to earth sometimes. If Andy hadn't been bawling her eyes out, she might've cracked a smile. But what she said was serious. "Jed, Noel's dad found out. After he humiliated him with every gay slur on the books, he told him never to show his face around him or his family again. At least not until he's straight."

"Man," Jed said, making a fist and striking the air with it. "He was afraid of that. Hey, no offense, Andy, but Rick thinks he's so fuckin' cool and, man, he's just retro. A real ass clown. Totally out of the loop. I don't know what his *deal* is!"

Andy looked up from her hands. "No offense taken," she sniffed. "Those are the kindest things you could say about that jackass." Then the tears came again. "Poor Noel."

"Don't worry too much. He totally expected it," Jed said.

Andy picked up her phone, displaying it to Jed. "He won't talk to me. Won't return my calls. I left messages saying I wasn't angry or upset or anything, but he won't even… I'm so worried. I don't know what to do."

"He's probably just stoned," Jed said with a shrug. "By the way, I think he does too much of that."

"I don't care. I just want to hear his voice. It's been *two days!*"

Jed shook his head and rolled his eyes. He pulled his phone out of his pocket and punched in a few numbers, backing away from the women a couple of steps. Then he said, "Hey, dick wad, you stoned again? Well, call your mother. She's over at my house crying because you won't call her. You got ten minutes, then I come over there and haul your scrawny ass home, you copy?" He listened for a moment. "Yeah, so? You're bummed. But you're not surprised, right? And you got it over with. So call your mother. You have nine minutes. Jeez, what are you thinking? You can't drop a bomb like that and then disappear! These women—they think you hung yourself in the shower or something! Call her!" Then he clicked off without saying goodbye. "He'll call," Jed said. "Or I'll go get him. Stupid shit. He should know better than to freak everyone out."

"Oh, Jed," Andy said, overwhelmed with gratitude.

"Yeah, no big deal. You don't need to tell him what I said about the weed. It's not like I haven't done a little of that." He glanced warily at his mother and said, "But I swore off it! I mean things are goofy enough around here. You know?"

"Sure," Andy said, sniffing back tears.

"I'm going to Tracy's, Mom. If Noel doesn't call in—" he glanced at his watch "—seven minutes, call me. I'll go get him. But he better call—I have *plans* with Tracy."

Andy just nodded and sniffed, so Jed left the deck. As he was about to make his getaway, Gerri stopped him. "What?" he asked.

"I just wanted to say, that was a nice thing you did."

"I told you, no big deal."

"You were fantastic."

"Well, there's something I don't hear every day."

"You're not fantastic every day," she said with a grin.

"That's the Geraldine I know and love," Jed said.

"It was a big deal," Gerri said. "And not getting all worked up about it, too—I think that helps more than you realize."

"Well, get this—I'm not worked up about it. I mean, whatever blows his skirt up, you know?" Then he grinned his best bad-boy grin.

"Jed." She laughed.

"I did like it better when you women were in charge, though," he said. "Ciao."

Sonja *hated* group therapy. She thought of the people in her group as total nutjobs or victims or they were so depressed they could barely lift their heads. Then there were a couple who fancied themselves cured and felt that gave them the right to be confrontational. She *hated* confrontation, and not just when directed at her, when aimed at anyone in her presence. Their moderator rarely stepped in to direct the dialogue—it was like he got great satisfaction out of watching them disturb each other. And he took copious notes, which also bothered her. Whenever she prepared to attend, she felt her anxiety rise. Her palms would get sweaty on the way to group and she'd be so exhausted coming home she'd struggle to stay awake behind the wheel. And she had to do it every Tuesday and Thursday evening for two whole hours.

Sonja made it a point to arrive a little early. She never wanted to be the last one to arrive. She hated walking into that room with eight chairs positioned in a circle, all filled but one. Hers. This evening she was the first to get there. The second to arrive was Martin, their barely postpubescent, zit-faced leader. He was a brand-new college graduate, but from looking at him it appeared he'd started college at twelve.

"Well, Sonja, hello," Martin said brightly.

"Hello," she said quietly.

"How's your week going?"

"Fine," she answered. It was not required that she be friendly, merely that she be present.

Soon everyone else filed in. Janelle, sixty, an unhappy housewife, very overweight and domineering; Carl, forties, skinny and nervous; Blythe, twenty, a tattooed biker chick coming down off cocaine and a little on the pissed-off side; Terrence, thirties, a bit chubby with a sallow complexion and dull eyes—medication just wasn't working for him and he missed a lot of sessions; Susan, who didn't seem to belong—she was cheerful and attractive and appeared balanced; and Paul, fifties, businesslike, efficient, direct and impatient. Sonja wanted to knock Paul's block off. They all said hello to each other as though they liked one another, a phenomenon that surprised Sonja completely because they weren't easy on each other. They took to their chairs—she was happy to have Blythe beside her, unhappy to have Paul directly across from her. The person beside you didn't seem to direct too many questions at you, the person across usually fired away.

"Who wants to begin?" Martin asked as always.

Carl was having trouble at work—he was a shipping clerk for a large department store. He couldn't focus, dreaded work, made too many mistakes, hated the truck drivers who made him feel stupid and small and inadequate. Terrence still wasn't working, but his mother was okay with that and was carrying him financially. People were on him at once—had he been to the employment office at all? Did it make him feel right to live off his mother? Was he exercising or altering his diet to combat depression? Had he changed any of his patterns?

"Jesus, I wish you'd cut him some slack!" Sonja said in a sudden outburst. "He's doing this without any slick drugs like the rest of us have!"

"Well," Janelle said, smirking. "Look who came to the party. Make you uncomfortable when Terrence gets asked questions like that?"

"You bet your big ass it does," Sonja shot back. "I didn't stand a chance without drugs. I was so far gone, I didn't know what planet I was on! I can't imagine what it must feel like to be Terrence!" Then she gave Terrence a weak half smile. "Sorry, Terrence. Didn't mean to get in your business."

"I'd like to hear more about that," Martin said. "If you're ready, of course."

"Well, I'm not," she said stubbornly.

"Come on, Sonja," Paul said. "Everyone else spills their guts. It's not going anywhere—we have a pact. It's not like we're going to call George…"

She drew her hair up in a ponytail and let it fall. "Shit, I never should've mentioned his name!"

"Um, the idea is to talk," Blythe reminded her, gently, not in her usual caustic, biting tone.

"Look, I'm not trying to be uncooperative," Sonja said with the far-fetched hope that maybe their teenage leader would report to Dr. Kalay that she was responding as instructed. "I can't remember much of it, honestly. It seemed like I was down in the dumps for a couple of days when, in fact, it was a couple of weeks and I was completely out of it. A total nutcase. I slept or sat on the couch and watched the shopping channel, something I didn't know existed before. My neighbor is a psychologist and she noticed something was wrong, took me to the doctor, and—"

"But what do *you* know about it? What did you piece together?" Janelle asked.

"That I lost track of time! That I slept or watched the shopping channel!"

"And that's all?" Martin asked. He rarely stepped in. He was the man with the chart, the pen. He was the one she had to please to put an end to this.

"I learned some things after," she said quietly. "But I don't exactly remember."

"What did you learn? How did you react?" Martin again. Oh, she shouldn't have defended Terrence. It had Martin all turned on. He was after her now. No escape. She knew how this worked, she wasn't stupid. She had to participate to get her free pass. She couldn't let him tell the doctor she was withholding. It would look bad on her report card.

She took a deep breath. "I learned that I packed up all the stuff that had once given me peace of mind. I must have realized it was all a big joke. The stuff that balanced my life—little fountains and aromatic candles and books on…" She paused. She felt her eyes begin to tear and she'd be goddamned if she snivel in front of this batch of sick vipers. She took another deep breath. "Books on feng shui, meditation, auras, serenity. Nutrition, herbs, natural holistic medicinal curatives. I had relaxing CDs. All that shit," she said in a derisive tone.

Blythe turned in her chair, looking directly at Sonja. "Sounds like healthy shit," she said. "I know I could do with a little herb."

"Not that kind," Sonja snapped. "I never did that. And I was conservative. Careful. I'm not an idiot—lots of things in nature are dangerous." She narrowed her eyes. "Cocaine, being one."

"Whoa." Blythe laughed. "Got me, girlfriend."

"I am not your girlfriend!"

"But you do have friends here, Sonja," Susan said. "Did that piss you off a little? What Blythe said?"

"No. But I wasn't radical. I was probably more consumed than the average person because I found it all fascinating—and I did lead meditation groups, teach yoga, but I *wasn't* radical. I was just trying to cover all the bases."

"What bases?" Paul asked, sitting forward, an earnest wrinkle to his brow.

"Body, soul, mind," she answered automatically. "My health, my environment, my relationships, my spirit. I was really just trying my best." Someone started to say something and she lifted a small hand. "I know, I know—already got this in the booby hatch—I was seeking control. So I didn't get it. I understand that now."

"Still, it seems like you were trying to do it with healthy stuff," Carl said gently. "Nontoxic, noninvasive, healthy stuff. What went wrong? How'd that turn out bad for you? I don't get it."

"I was trying to do all the *right* things," she said, sniffing suddenly. "Nothing to hurt the body or the mind or the spirit! What can be harmful about the soothing sound of trickling water? Or a healthy meal? Or regular exercise and a pleasant aroma in the home? I was so careful. Moderation! I wasn't opposed to George having a chicken breast or the occasional Scotch, but his cholesterol was up, his blood pressure was climbing— his job is so high stress!" She gasped in frustration. She didn't want to be doing this, but somehow they'd manipulated her—they were pulling it out of her. "Oh, God," she said. She collected herself. "Nontoxic, non-invasive, healthy stuff," she said, echoing Carl.

"So," Martin said. "What went wrong? Why did you pack it all up?"

"He left me because of that! He'd had it with the meals he said were bland, the stuff around the house meant to soothe him, relax him. Bring him comfort and peace of mind!"

There was quiet for a moment. Then Blythe said, "Whoa. He cut you deep."

Sonja turned her watering eyes to Blythe and, pursing her lips together so tightly they turned white, she nodded.

"What happened, Sonja?" Paul asked. "What did he do? Say? What are you fighting now? What did George do?"

She wanted to say, Please, could you not confront me like that? It's not your business! But knowing how the group-therapy game was played, she answered. "He said he couldn't take living in a loony bin anymore. That he felt like a Chia Pet…."

"What?" three people said at once.

"We couldn't hear you, Sonja," Martin said. "Your voice was too soft."

"He said he felt like a *fucking* Chia Pet! That he didn't want me in charge of his *fucking* cholesterol—he takes pills for that! That he didn't want me watching his sleep patterns or his blood pressure! That he'd like to come home, turn on football, eat bloody red meat, spill on his clothes, drink too much Scotch sometimes, fall asleep on the couch and wake up hung over once in a while and…" She crumbled. She rested her elbows on her knees, covered her face with her hands and sobbed in loud, angry cries. Certainly they could hear her *now*.

"Whoa," Blythe said. "Breakthrough."

"Big-time," someone else said.

Sonja sobbed for a moment and they let her. They *watched* her. When she couldn't stand their silence any longer, she lifted her head. Tears ran down her face and she had snot running into her mouth. "I hate you," she said breathlessly, gasping. "I hate you so much! Why would you do that to a person?" she choked out.

There was quiet for a moment. Terrence couldn't answer, Carl looked afraid to answer, Blythe had said enough. "Well, we care about you, in spite of the fact that you're very private and untrusting," Paul said. "And we do that to get it out where you can look at it. Because that's how you get well. It actually works."

One at a time she heard their voices saying, "We care." She cried harder. She didn't want their caring. *The assholes.* Someone pressed a box of tissues on her. She mopped up the mess on her face, but it was minutes before she came under any semblance of control. When she finally lifted her head, they were all watching her, but their faces were a blur.

"What happened, Sonja?" Martin asked.

"I *told* you! He *left!* He made total fun of me like I was crazy and took his suitcase to the car and left!"

"After that," Martin pushed. "When you kind of lost touch with reality. What happened to you?"

It took a couple of moments. She knew where this was going. She was tired of hearing about the episode from her doctor and hearing it from her own lips only made it harder, worse. But everyone in the group just waited, not giving up, probably so happy it was her falling apart and not them. She blinked, looked at each one of them individually and spoke. "At first, I slept. I couldn't get food down, couldn't swallow. I pulled out my hair in big clumps or bit my nails until they bled. Then I couldn't sleep because I saw monsters. I wanted to kill myself, but I couldn't figure out how—I don't like messes. I used to be very neat. I didn't have stuff in the house that could kill you and I knew overdoses of some things just landed you on dialysis for life." She laughed hollowly. "I didn't know how to rig the car for carbon monoxide, and I was afraid I wouldn't make it and George would keep me alive on a respirator even if I were brain-dead. So I struggled. It was horrible. But it didn't feel like as long as it was. Or maybe it felt longer than it was, I don't know…it was like suspended animation."

There was a moment of silence. Then Terrence, the sickest one in the group spoke up. "Wait a minute—you thought George would keep you alive?"

She shrugged and wiped her nose. "He's very responsible."

"That the only reason you think that?" Paul asked.

"What else?" Sonja asked, blowing into a tissue.

"Well, is it possible he cares about you, but he wants red meat and too many Scotches?"

"Blech," she said with disgust. "How can he imagine that's good for his body?"

Someone laughed softly. "Well, it's his body," someone said.

"Yeah, but—"

"All buts aside, it stays his body." She looked up. It was fat Janelle. Sonja had a sudden attack of remorse.

"Oh, God—what I said to you! I'm sorry! I'm not a mean person!" Sonja said.

"I'm not sorry," Janelle said with a rare grin that appeared wholly genuine. "I thought you were a double agent—here to see if we were playing the game. Shit, honey, you finally came out. Gonna tell us the rest of it?"

"Huh?" Sonja asked. "What rest of it? That's when I went nuts. What more could you possibly want?"

"Well," Paul said, "you were faced with some choices. You could've concentrated on taking his money or his kids, or finding yourself a better man—I mean, you're young and beautiful. Or you could've shot him or poisoned him or something, but you turned all that rage on yourself. So, what else went down?"

"Nothing else, and he doesn't have kids," she said. "I mean, there were little things—George said he was peeing so much he thought he had prostatitis. It turned out to be all the little fountains in the house. All that trickling water made him want to pee all the time. When I'd ask him what he had for lunch he'd always say he had a plate of grass. He said he wanted less candlelight, more flavor, loud annoying, aggressive sports on TV instead of all that relaxing in serenity…" She hiccuped. "I don't like to admit that I wasn't listening to those things. I thought I knew what was best."

"For you," Paul said.

"No. No."

"For you," he repeated. "You were clear on what worked for you. But it made him think he had prostatitis. Did you ever think he might be okay eating and drinking what he wants to?"

"But everyone knows that's unhealthy." Sonja turned to Blythe pleadingly. "Doesn't everyone know that's unhealthy?" she asked. She didn't allow herself to say what she really thought. *Even you?*

"Well, sometimes it's just as unhealthy to live rigidly, in denial, in deprivation. I mean, I don't make any argument for cocaine—so don't work me over here. But really, if I'd stuck to red meat and Scotch, I wouldn't be here in group."

"Sonja—is there anything you can tell us about before you were married that might factor in?" Martin asked. "What about your parents? Your home life?"

"It was just average," she said with a shrug. "I mean, they weren't ever into this health regimen of mine, but they were just ordinary people."

"You have brothers and sisters?"

"I had an older brother," she said, tearing up again. "He died in a car crash when he was seventeen. My parents never got over it. It was so hard on them. I was four years younger. They kind of locked down the house for a few years."

"And you stayed there until you were thirty? Did you talk about his death much?" Martin asked.

"That has nothing to do with—"

"Could we just look at that a minute?" Martin interrupted. "Did you? Talk about his death much?"

She was too exhausted to fight it. So it came out. Todd was killed in a freak accident when he was seventeen and she was thirteen. Her parents tightened the leash on her to keep her alive through her high school years, removing her from the mainstream of a typical adolescent social life, but they never talked about their pain, their grief. She didn't go to college, never—unremarkably—had a normal social life. By the time she was twenty-four, undereducated for a young woman in her age-group or economic status, her father was starting to treat her as if she were some kind of weirdo living in her strange world of spiritual balance and inner peace. When she met and married George, her parents were relieved someone responsible and capable was taking her off their hands.

"When did the dependence on these tools appear?" Martin asked. "How old were you when you started meditating, or whatever came first?"

Sonja shrugged. "I stopped eating meat at fourteen or so. I'm not sure I was meditating, but I taught myself how to rest my body and get in a trancelike place, thinking nice thoughts. It kind of started there and grew. They were just things that felt better than what was happening in my life."

"And did your parents get any kind of help for their pain?" Paul asked.

She shook her head and explained. The minister suggested a grief group, but instead, they stopped going to church. They were like a couple of zombies for at least four years, growing old fast, so worn-out and tired all the time. So silent. They didn't talk to her or each other. They looked like they were dying. She didn't want to be like that. She knew her brother wouldn't have wanted that. She missed him horribly but found a way to feel at peace. If there was anything as difficult as watching her parents wither in their pain, it was feeling fine in the midst of it. Or at least insisting to herself that she had to be fine and not crazy like them.

By the time she got to the end of the brief synopsis of her life, she was sobbing again; snot was running again. It was as if she had never spent any emotion on her brother before.

"He shouldn't have died, you know," she whimpered.

"Sonja," Susan said. "If your parents hadn't fallen apart like that, would it have given you permission to be less stoic? Less strong in the face of the greatest loss of your young life? You were only thirteen."

All Sonja could do was nod wearily. She didn't even look up.

"Whoa," Blythe said. "More breakthrough."

"Kind of sounds like the conflict for you goes back further than a couple of months ago with George," someone said.

"Maybe," Sonja said. She felt weak, worn down to a nub. "But back then, way back then, I never hurt myself. I wasn't crazy. I didn't tear my hair out or bite my nails."

"Or want to kill yourself?" Paul asked.

She shook her head.

"Sonja," someone said. "Sonja, way back then—were you hanging on for dear life? Holding back the pain?"

"Maybe," she said in a voice so soft she could hardly be heard. "But if I was, I never knew it…."

"Right below the surface," Paul said in a voice that was uncharacteristically gentle for him. "All those years. Right below the surface."

It was quiet for a moment. Sonja could barely lift her head. Then Martin spoke. "Well, folks, this has been an emotional session. I think we'll call it a night. We can't do all our work in one session. How about an early out?"

Several people voiced their agreement. Blythe put her hand over Sonja's. "You okay, girlfriend?"

"Okay," Sonja said weakly. She felt as if she should lie down right away and sleep for a year or so.

Everyone rose to file out, but several of them brushed by her to give her a pat on the shoulder or a word of encouragement or praise before leaving. Paul paused while she was collecting herself. "Let me give you a lift home," he said.

"No. I'm fine."

"Actually, I think you might be emotionally exhausted. You worked very hard tonight. I'd be happy to drive you."

"No," she said again, rising. But then she wavered on her feet and he caught her elbow.

"Listen, if you're worried about leaving your car here, I could pick you up in the morning to ferry it home again. Unless you can arrange that easily, but it's no trouble for me. I don't go to work all that early. By morning, you'll feel rested." He cracked a smile. "You're going to sleep pretty well tonight."

"I don't know...I don't trust you so much...."

He surprised her with a laugh. "I know. It's perfectly safe, though. They check us nutjobs out pretty thoroughly before letting us in a group like this. Even Blythe. Besides, we'll let Martin know I'm driving you tonight."

"I really am kind of worn-out..."

"Yeah, of course. I went through a similar thing in this group. I thought I'd been filleted. It was like there were no bones left in my body. Like my brain had been sucked out through my ear."

"Really? When was that? What was that about?"

"Sorry," he said, smiling kindly. "No inside stuff outside of group. You want to ask me about that, it happens when everyone is around. Right now, it's just a ride. That's all. No ulterior motives."

Sonja was a little shocked. "That's very nice of you."

"We usually look out for each other when we can," he said with a shrug. "Helping gets you helped sometimes."

"You weren't all that helpful," she said with a scowl. "I wanted you to leave me alone. You especially."

He chuckled. "I know. It's a dirty job."

eleven

Bob didn't want to get in the way of mother-son business, so he made himself pretty scarce in case Noel showed up at Andy's. He checked in by phone to be sure she was holding up all right, to see if Noel had come out of hiding, if they had talked, if there was anything he could do. Then, thanks to her neighbor's son, they finally made phone contact and met at her house later the same night. According to Andy, Noel was pretty upset by his dad's reaction but had known all along it would be like that. At least mother and son had talked it out, were back in touch.

And then Andy did something that thrilled Bob. She called him and said, "Are you available tonight? Because I really need to be with you. I've missed you so much!" Nothing in the world could have given Bob more pleasure, more deep down joy. So he took her out to her favorite Mexican restaurant, bought her a very large margarita, held her hand on the patio under the starlight for a long time while she talked about it and then they went back to Andy's house, to the bedroom. She was feeling a lot of distress, worried about what

Noel was going through, how difficult it would be coming out, facing people like Rick who could judge him so harshly, with such blistering rage. Bob had known from his sisters, it doesn't matter how old your kids are, when they hurt, you hurt. And this had to be so rough on the kid, to be disowned like that, separated from not only his dad, but from his younger brothers, as though he'd give them some kind of disease. So Bob held Andy until she fell asleep. He cradled her against him as gently as he could.

That same night, late, after they had fallen asleep, the phone rang. It was Noel asking if it would be all right if he slept there that night. He heard Andy say, "Of course, honey. Bob is here. Will you have a problem with that?" And then she said, "Good, because I want him to be here. I don't want to send him home."

When the key slipped in the lock at eleven-thirty, Andy rose, put on her robe and left the bedroom. It was only about ten minutes before she was back, crawling in bed, curling up next to Bob. "He looks all right," she whispered. "Maybe we'll get through this."

"Sure you will," he said, pulling her to him, giving her the comfort of his arms.

In the morning, Bob rose quietly at dawn—some habits were hard to break. He dressed, let Beau out and set up the coffeemaker. He fed Beau while it perked. Andy had purchased a couple of bowls and a bag of dog food for Beau, something that made Bob feel so welcome in her home. He took Beau and a cup of coffee onto the patio and watched the sun rising. He wondered if Andy fully appreciated the value of her lifestyle, the solid, pretty little house in a nice neighborhood, so quiet all the time. His sister and brother-in-law lived in a much grander house with a guard at the gate in their neighborhood, but he preferred this.

He'd been out there about fifteen minutes when Noel appeared at the back door. He looked scruffy, his curly black hair all crazy. He was wearing last night's clothes, hadn't showered or shaved. The kid had a rugged beard; all that black Greek hair from Andy's side. "Morning," he said. "I'm going to shove off."

"Aw, don't be in such a rush," Bob said. "I've never known a nineteen-year-old with plans this early. Grab a cup. Come outside and take a look at this morning."

"Naw, I'll just—"

"I don't bite, Noel. Give yourself a break. At least stay till your mom gets up."

He shook his curly mop of hair, but in a minute he was back with coffee and he grabbed a chair. Beau lumbered up and put his head in Noel's lap and Noel stroked it, almost unconsciously. "So, you want to ask me questions or something?"

Bob shot him a surprised look. "Questions? Me? I don't have any questions, son. Maybe you want to ask a few?"

"Well, how about— How'd you get hooked up with my mom?"

"Well, you know I was here working when she split up with her husband. I think she was upset, maybe lonely, maybe worried about things—I gather it had been rough for them for a while. I think because of that we did a lot of talking while I worked and she ate her dinner. For about a month we talked, got into some real serious and personal issues as well as some just plain old ordinary stuff. I guess you could say we became good friends. Then the kitchen was done," he said with a shrug. "But we weren't done with the friendship. We'd gotten pretty close by then."

Noel leaned back in his chair, holding his cup of coffee in both hands. "Don't you think it's a little strange? You and my mom?"

"Oh, yeah," he said with a laugh, shaking his head. "Pretty strange. Sure nothing I thought would ever come my way, but I have to say—I'm grateful. Your mom is awful special. What a great person. What a beautiful lady."

"Little too young for you, wouldn't you say?" Noel asked.

"I little too much of everything for me, son. She's too beautiful, too smart, too compassionate and honest and funny—just the best of everything. Too young? Probably. She keeps claiming to be forty-seven, but doesn't she just look more like twenty-seven to you?"

"I don't know about that," Noel said, scoffing. He snapped his fingers to bring the dog back and Beau obliged, laying his head in Noel's lap. "So. This is serious?"

"You might have to be more specific," Bob said.

"You have serious intentions?"

Bob laughed. It was kind of a kick being asked questions like this by a nineteen-year-old. "Well, Noel, to tell the truth, I'm trying my hardest not to have any intentions at all. Intentions or expectations. I figure your mom is way more than I deserve. I'm not going to take that for granted, believe me. But it sure is nice, spending time with her. As long as it makes her happy, I'm more than willing to go along with that."

"Sounds like you don't expect it to last long. Huh?"

Bob thought for a second, then sat forward, placing

his coffee cup on the ground beside his chair. "There's that word again. Expect. The thing is, Andy's young and beautiful. There's no telling how long she might be happy with someone like me. That's why I want to be real flexible with her—you know? If it turns out this isn't exactly right for her, I'd never make her feel bad about that. You understand, Noel?"

Noel was quiet a moment. "I'm not sure I do," he said.

"Okay, let me put it another way. I love Andy. There's no question about that. Oh, damn." He laughed. "I'm afraid I just told you before I told her—I should've been more careful about that. But I can understand if you have concerns about her feelings, so you need to know mine. I love her. Really, this is kind of new for me. I loved a woman before. I was married about ten years ago and I still love that girl—real special woman. But it was nothing like this. I love Andy in a way I never thought I'd get to experience. I want to give Andy everything I have. I want to be the best partner she could imagine. Just thinking that way, I realized the most important thing I can give her is my complete love and commitment for as long as she wants it. But I'll never make your mom feel boxed in by anything, by anyone. All I want is for her to be happy every day of her life."

"No strings? Is that it?"

"Not exactly," Bob said, shaking his head. "That would sound like I don't care all that much, that I don't want to be tied down. I couldn't care more, that's the truth. But I want the way I love her to be unconditional. I accept her, admire her, exactly the way she is. Not like she belongs to me—she'll never be property. Not like I have some claim on her—although," he chuckled, "she sure has a solid claim on me. No, son, I love her too much to make demands on her, to tie her up. With me, without me, it doesn't matter—I'll love her just the same." Then he smiled broadly. "If it's with me, that's twice as good, of course. Because I haven't been this happy in my life."

"You're saying it wouldn't bother you if she, like, dumped you?" Noel asked.

Bob shook his head. "I'm not a hero, boy. Just an ordinary guy. It would bother me, you bet. I'd miss her so much. But Andy deserves to have everything she wants, everything that makes her happy. When you really love someone, Noel, you don't concentrate on whether or not they're perfect or meet your expectations or behave in exactly the way *you'd* like. You just think about how lucky you are to have them in your life, and want them to have whatever is good for *them*. You hold them in an open hand, Noel. It's kind of like the way your mom feels about you—but more romantic."

"Feels…about…me?"

"You know. You're clear on that. There's nothing you could do to make her not love you, not stick by you. Nothing in the world. I know a fellow like you, going through a rough patch right now—you can appreciate that kind of commitment. That kind of love. It's deep and real."

Noel sat up straight. Shock registered on his face.

"I guess you haven't been thinking that way too much," Bob said. "I'm not surprised. When someone feels that way about you, one of the first things you do is get used to it, expect it to always be there because it always was. You can depend on it. But every so often something will come up to make you just a little afraid that person might stop loving you that way, accepting you that way, and it's a reminder about how good it is. You know what I mean."

"You mean my dad," he said.

"It's not an easy thing, Noel. To love someone without any selfishness, without a personal agenda. It takes thought and heart. Sacrifice and courage, sometimes. People can get mixed up about what's the most important thing—their own personal needs or the needs of the person they love. I think that must be what happened to your dad. He's mixed up. We're not perfect, you know. Human beings—so fallible."

"Yeah, right," Noel snorted. "Mixed up, my ass."

"Well, maybe I give the man too much credit," Bob admitted. "I don't know him, after all. And I never had kids so I could be talking out of turn, but my grandmother used to say, 'Your kids don't belong to you—they're only on loan for you to raise. They have their own lives, their own destinies. So you better get out of the way.' She was a real hot chick, my grandma."

"You shocked?" he asked. "About my *rough patch,* as you call it?" Noel asked, a note of challenge in his voice.

"When I said rough patch, I didn't mean you being gay. I meant having a standoff with your dad, who I'm sure you love a lot. That's tough. I'm real sorry you're going through that. And I can't think what you can do about it. You can't change him any more than he can change you."

"But me being gay? That doesn't *bother* you?"

Bob shrugged. "It's no different than if you showed up blond, or black or Chinese. Listen, you're not like everyone else, all right? Me, either. And so the fuck what?" Noel's eyes grew large at the curse. "Life—

it's a kaleidoscope. Your mom might've contributed the green, your dad the red, but you've got colors in there that come from just anywhere—even from old second cousins twice removed. You're not sick, you're gay. With black curly hair. Every turn of the wheel is its own creation."

"And you get along with gay guys?" Noel asked.

"Just fine," Bob said.

"You bi or something?"

He laughed. "No, whenever I felt an attraction, it was always to a female. I didn't have a choice. You're not going to change that about me and I'm not going to change that about you."

Noel laughed and shook his head. "Most guys your age aren't like that," he said. "Most guys your age hate anything that doesn't fit into their idea of what's okay."

"Yeah? I learned a little patience. Sad truth is, you get to learn that by the hard times. It's too bad. If I was in charge, we'd get insight from the fun stuff."

Noel took a sip from his cup. "My coffee went cold."

"Go pitch it and pour some fresh. There's plenty of coffee in the house."

"So—you learned a little patience. Got any advice?"

"I might," Bob said. "Doesn't usually appeal to men under forty, though."

"Try me."

"Well," Bob said, leaning forward. "I'd say, you stay as true to yourself as you can, try to be a good man, and go easy on the people who just can't seem to make it in the world without being mad about something. I figure, they have it a lot tougher. Being angry—that's hard work. Hard on the heart."

Noel relaxed in his chair. He scratched Beau's ears.

It made Bob smile. A good old dog who appreciated a little stroking was so good for a mood, a perspective.

"My mom's worried about me being gay," Noel said.

"Nah," Bob said.

"Yeah, she is. She told me some of her worries."

"I shouldn't speak for Andy, but if I heard her right, she's worried about it being hard on you to be just who you are. And she's worried about people filled with hate, hoping that doesn't get turned on you in any way. Anyone would worry about that. I have a sister with a son in the army. He went to Afghanistan. Her worries are pretty much the same. Of course, it won't help to worry—but sometimes when it's your boy, your pride and joy, you just can't help it—you want only good things for him. You hate to think he'd ever have to suffer in any way."

Noel looked at Bob and grinned. "So," he said. "You love my mother, huh?"

"Oh, kid." Bob laughed. "I do. I think she's the most wonderful person I've ever met. I love listening to her talk, laugh. She tells great stories. Brings great stories out of me. And you know what? I look in the mirror or get down on my knees to do tile or heft up some big heavy shelf, I know I'm getting old—full of creaks, all gray and bald, a little more flesh than I need...but when I'm with Andy, just out to dinner or sitting right here in this beautiful weather, talking, laughing—I swear to God I feel twenty-one."

Noel laughed. "Well, you're not."

"But isn't it terrific when you're with someone who can bring out your best self? I think that's the sign of a true friend, when they make you feel better when you're with them than you ever had a chance of feeling without them."

"Think she loves you back?" Noel asked, grinning.

"We haven't said those words yet—you got it first. I might get in trouble for that. I'm not good at this stuff. I'm *very* inexperienced. But the way she is with me, if it isn't love, it's damn sure close enough for me. Your mom, she's one of the best people in the world. But you already know that."

Noel dropped his chin. "She always put me first," he said without looking up. "Even when it meant she was alone, stuck with some little kid, she really always put me first…."

"It wasn't a sacrifice for her, Noel," Bob said earnestly. "I'm sure it came naturally. I think that's how it is with most mothers, at least my sisters say so. Once you have that child, those children, it would be very hard to do anything else. You don't have anything to pay back for that."

"Kind of lets me off the hook."

"I didn't say you couldn't tell her you appreciate it. Also, you could let her know that except for this bad spot you have going on with your dad, you're okay. Happy. You are happy, aren't you?"

"Most of the time," he said. "I have some good friends. No one special, but that doesn't mean there won't be. I'd hate to wait as long as you…."

"You won't." Bob laughed. "Hardly anyone is as introverted as me. You know, I was planning to be a teacher once. Professor. That was my goal. Then I started building things and it suited me—I think because I wasn't intimidated by the wood, the cement, and I was confident there. But you're not like that. You have all that personality, and guts. Son, it takes guts to face up to things the way you have. Lift your chin and be yourself. People will like you for who you are."

"You sure don't seem like an introvert. You're kind of, I don't know, up-front."

"With you," Bob said. "I'm better one-on-one. And you're Andy's boy. You're good stock. It's pretty easy for me to feel comfortable with you. Safe."

Noel was quiet for a second. "I think I'll pitch this coffee, get some hot."

"Good idea," Bob said. "I could use a fresher, too. And I think Beau looks like he's in the mood for a biscuit. You know where Andy keeps 'em?"

"No."

"Then I better show you. I think he might start counting on you for a treat."

"That'd be okay."

Bob draped an arm around Noel's shoulders and walked with him into the house. "Beau's a real good judge of character, you know. Dogs are like that. It doesn't matter what people say, how they act or look, dogs can see into a person's soul. They growl at a perfectly civil-looking person and it should serve as a warning—dogs know. But Beau, he took to you immediately. I guess that stands for something."

"You're full of so much shit, Bob," Noel said.

Bob laughed. "But don't I talk a good game?"

"I just hope you're telling the truth about how you feel about my mom, because I can't stand to think of her with some loser."

"One thing about me, I have a hard time making up lies. You'll get that after you know me awhile. I've always been like that. I just spit it out, the truth about anything. I got arrested that way once—when I was about your age, in college. A cop asked me, 'Is that marijuana you got there, boy?' and I answered, 'Yes, sir. I'm sure sorry, sir.'"

"No shit? You?"

"Unfortunately that's no shit…" He laughed. "But I really believe that stuff about dogs. Don't you?"

Noel laughed and headed for the coffeepot. "Whatever you say, Bob."

There was one nice thing about summer—Gerri didn't have to race around, getting kids out of bed, prodding them into the car for school, breaking up fights, trying to block snipes and arguments in the car. She enjoyed having the house quiet first thing in the morning.

And that was where the nice thing about summer ended as far as she was concerned.

Gerri had the kids programmed to check in before leaving the house, reporting their activities and locations. And they had additional reasons to talk to their mother—questions like how much detergent goes in the washer, why isn't there any lunch meat, where are the extra rolls of toilet paper, can you stop on the way home and get any number of unnecessary items. Her phone rang all day long or bleeped at incoming texts. It was all she could do to keep from losing her temper and demand they stop calling. But when they stopped, it signaled worse trouble.

She left them lists of chores every morning—with kids around the house all day, the place was crumbling in no time. Jed had a summer job at a local restaurant, working evenings, so he slept late and did little or nothing all day long, then ate almost everything in sight before heading off to work.

The phone rang and she glanced at her watch, hoping it was some charity or political tape she could hang up on. When she answered, she heard her mother-in-law's chipper voice. "Darling! I caught you before work!"

"Minutes before, but for you I'd even be late. How are you, Muriel?"

"Torn, that's how I am. We're all packed up in San Miguel, heading for two months in Maui, but I just don't feel right about it. I think I should come there—help out for the summer."

Gerri laughed. "That's very tempting. A live-in drill master sounds like just the thing, but—"

"Settled! I'll send Stan to Maui and get on the next flight!"

"You can't, Muriel," Gerri said. "It wouldn't work. Please, don't take this personally—if my own mother was still alive, I wouldn't let her come now, either. Really, Phil and I need the time—we're just starting to really talk about things. I have to know where it's going." She took a breath. "Although I admit, it would be fun to watch you glare at him for a couple of months."

"I don't have to harangue him, darling. I could manage to be civil. At least when the children are present."

"If I didn't know better, I'd think you were enjoying this…."

"Gerri, dearest, are you and my wayward son making any progress?"

"What has Phil told you?"

She laughed. "You're kidding! He won't give me a thing! The last time I asked him why he wouldn't talk about it, he said he didn't want me to screw up his lame attempts to get his wife back. As if I would!"

Gerri laughed. The idea of Phil's mother torturing him with her disapproval was not hurting her mood. "Did you and Stan ever have marital problems?" she asked.

"Of *course* not!" Then she cackled at her own joke. "Geraldine, everyone has marital problems, of one stripe or another."

"Did either of you ever have…" She couldn't go on.

"An affair?" Muriel asked. "Gerri, we never went through a situation like yours—interpret that any way you like. We limped along like every married couple. Some of our troubles seemed insurmountable, some stupid and piddling, but I think in the end I'd have to call it a very satisfactory marriage. Gerri, is there hope? It will be difficult to put him up for adoption at his age."

"There is," she said. "But until I know what kind, Phil's staying right where he is, and I'm staying right here. And we're not having any friends or relatives in this mix. I hope you understand."

Muriel sighed. "My other daughters-in-law don't take as firm a hand with me, you know. Though that doesn't mean I actually like them better, but that's irrelevant. Gerri—if you needed my help, would you call?"

"Of course. Muriel, I can't stop thinking about something my mother always used to say. If the rope gets cut, you can tie it back together, but there will always be a knot in it."

Muriel didn't respond immediately. After a long pause she finally spoke. "Darling, when I look at the rope that belongs to Stan and me, so imperfect, so often broken and reconnected, I just assumed all those knots were there to give us something to hang on to."

The June sun shone brightly, burning off the morning fog that tended to roll in from the coast and settle in the valley. Sonja had been digging in her yard for hours. The June sun on the fertile California land was like magic—stick something in the ground and it would grow and grow and grow. The air was moist and warm, nurturing the flowers. She'd already lined the border of her backyard with colorful blooms. Though she'd gotten them in the ground a little late, they flourished. She'd made a habit of returning to the nursery almost every afternoon so she'd have fresh plants ready to go in the ground, first thing each morning.

When she started the project, she'd worn gardening gloves, but that hadn't lasted long. She'd come to love the feel of the rich, dark soil on her hands, caught in the crevices, stuck under her nails. As her flower beds grew deeper, she began placing patio stones in little pathways through the garden so she could get around without trampling her new babies.

While she gardened, she could think. Much of her time was spent remembering Todd, sometimes talking to him just under her breath. It would have been so sweet to grow into adulthood with her brother, see where their lives intertwined, merged. She would likely be Aunt Sonja now if he had lived.

After the group session that everyone referred to as her breakthrough Sonja cried for almost two full days. Panicked that she was retreating into madness again, she had called Dr. Kalay, who asked if anything new or significant had happened right before the crying began. Sonja told her about the upsetting group session.

"Ah, more grieving. Long overdue, it would seem. Will you be all right? Or do you need some extra help getting through this?" Dr. Kalay asked.

"Will I be all right? Tear my hair out of my head?"

"Is anything like that happening, Sonja?" she asked gently.

"No, I'm digging in the garden, planting, crying on the flowers…."

The psychiatrist laughed softly, tenderly. "I can't think of a better place for your tears to fall. Please, call me in two days and tell me how you're feeling."

Two days later, there was less crying. Two more days, she was much better. After another two group sessions she could talk about her family, her brother's death and her failed marriage without succumbing to wrenching sobs. The tears still popped into her eyes sometimes, unexpectedly, when a particularly sentimental memory came to mind. Good tears, the people in group called them. The kind of tears that got you well.

She left the back patio doors open while she worked and it was just before noon when she heard the doorbell. Since school was out, Andy sometimes popped over in the middle of the day, just for something to do. Sonja sat back on her heels, then got to her feet, brushing the dirt off her knees. She kicked off her shoes by the back door. It was a good time to take a break, anyway. When she opened the door, it wasn't Andy, but George. He was dressed in an impeccable blue-gray pinstriped suit, his steel-gray hair perfectly combed for a day of business. She was thunderstruck for a second. Then she slammed the door in his face.

He knocked. Then he knocked again. "Go away, George," she yelled at the door. And then she turned her back on the door and under her breath muttered, "Asshole."

She hadn't even made it out of the foyer when she heard a key in the lock. She whirled to face the door as it opened.

"What are you *doing?*" she demanded, aghast.

"Letting myself into my house," he said. "I am still part owner, you know."

"What the hell do you want?"

"I want to see you, to ask how you are," he said simply. "You won't talk to me or return my calls. I hear from your doctor that you're making great progress and are feeling much better. I'd like to hear from you how much better you're feeling."

"She shouldn't be telling you anything," Sonja said angrily. "Doctor-patient privilege." She crossed her arms over her chest.

"She has to respond to me, Sonja—I'm the insurer and the one who's paying the bills. Now, why don't we just make things simple. Can you tell me how you're doing without all the profanity?"

She ground her teeth for a moment. "I'm crazy. Now you can go."

"You're not crazy," he said. "But you are muddy. What's going on?"

She took a deep breath. "I've been planting flowers. Really, I'm not ready to talk to you. Especially about how I am."

"It doesn't have to be a long conversation," he said, walking past her into the kitchen. He sat down at the nook table and waited patiently.

She followed him. "Aren't you just a little afraid you'll put me right back over the edge?"

He shook his head. "I checked with the doctor. She assures me you've become very resilient. You look a lot better than you did the last time I saw you," he said.

"Duh," she said. She yanked out the chair opposite George and plopped down. "I was on another planet the last time you saw me. Now I only visit—much too nuts for you to have to deal with."

He smiled at her. "Do you know what today is?" he asked.

"Friday," she said in a snotty tone.

"It's our tenth anniversary," he said. "It's okay, I didn't expect you to remember it."

For a second the shock registered on her face. She really hadn't spent a lot of mental energy on George and the marriage or its destruction in the past couple of weeks. She'd gone a lot further back in time. She realized her mouth was open and closed it. Then she pursed her lips. "I can't remember things like that. I'm nuts."

He laughed at her. "You don't have to play the nuts game with me, Sonja. I thought I'd stop by, force my presence on you to see how you're doing, invite you out to lunch."

"Lunch?" she shrieked, insulted to her core. "You want me to go to *lunch?*"

"I guess that's a no," he said pleasantly.

"You're damn right it's a no! You've got some nerve, you know that? You drive me insane and then you pop over to check on my health and ask me out to lunch? Fuck you, George!"

He merely smiled. "Sonja, give me a little credit. Don't you think it was important to me to understand whether I did this to you? Come on now. I talked to some professionals—I'm pretty clear on what happened. You can blame me all you want, but we both know this whole episode is no one's fault and you're going to be fine."

"No thanks to *you*. I was fine before!"

"Actually, no," he said, drumming his fingers on the table. "You had a little grenade inside you that was ready to blow. God, I wish someone else had pulled the pin—but you couldn't have moved on until that was taken care of. I had no idea, of course. But then, neither did you."

She clenched her teeth while she stared at him. She hated that he spoke the truth because she hated him. She would die before she ever thanked him for being the catalyst that set her free. "So," she said, lifting her chin. "You bring papers for me to sign or something? Get your prenup in under the wire?"

He looked surprised, but just shook his head. "You still have a copy of that? I tore mine up years ago when I was cleaning out files. By the time a couple spends a few years together, either it's no longer relevant or the relationship's in serious trouble. Don't you think?"

"Then why have it in the first place?" she asked, uncrossing her arms. She was astonished, and most curious.

"I had a lot of investments when we got married," he said with a shrug. "But I knew in two or three years you had no interest in taking my money. You're a lot of things, but you're no gold digger."

"Well, I want it now," she said meanly.

"Now it's a done deal." He laughed.

"You're taking it pretty well," she said quietly, wondering what nasty trick he had up his sleeve. "You've always been awfully proud of your balance sheet."

"Yes, we all have our shortcomings, I guess." He clasped his hands together on the tabletop and leaned toward her. "Listen, when we got married, there were a lot of good reasons. Neither of us wanted children, we were almost always compatible even if we weren't real exciting. You wanted nothing so much as to keep everything spotless and get the stains out of my shirts and all I wanted was someone as nice and beautiful as you beside me, supporting me while I worked to keep building retirement money for my clients, and my own portfolio at the same time. I didn't want a lot. Maybe I was wrong but it seemed like you didn't want that much. I'm not an exciting guy, Sonja, I know that. I don't have family. Your parents are old and kind of feeble now. We were two people who really didn't have other people—and I thought all your candles and fountains and stuff were kind of cute. And harmless." He shrugged and smiled.

She narrowed her eyes as he spoke. "I *loved* you, you sorry son of a bitch!"

"Oh, Sonja," he said sadly. "I loved you, too. I mean, I love you. Still. It's just that the kind of love you get from a guy like me doesn't have much sparkle to it. I'm dull and serious. They make jokes around the office about how I actually have a personality when I come out of my shell a little at those company functions. And I'm sorry—I never knew the whole health-spa atmosphere would get to me like it did. I kind of went over the edge, too."

She braced her hands on the seat of her chair and looked at him suspiciously. "You don't have some secret plan or something, do you? Some fancy lawyer behind the scenes, ready to cream me the second I let down my guard?"

"No, nothing like that. I haven't even talked to any-one about divorce—it seemed pretty inappropriate while you were trying to recover. This whole business just scared the crap out of me. Jesus, if something re-ally horrible had happened… If we can both get through this with our sanity, I won't ask for more than that."

"You want a divorce as soon as possible?"

"I don't care about that. It really doesn't matter," he said, shaking his head. "If you do…"

"But you're paying the bills! And they've been huge, considering Glendale!"

"You never spent any money during our marriage," he said. "Growing herbs doesn't cost anything. You never put actual meat in my food. If I added up the cost of all those fountains, chimes and candles, it wouldn't be two thousand bucks over ten years and I'm sure you earned way more than that with your classes and clients. Sonja—" He laughed. "Honey, you're a real cheap date."

She couldn't remember the last time he'd called her honey. She wasn't sure what to think about the cheap date comment. "Always so fiduciarily responsible," she said, crossing her arms over her chest again.

"Well, now you've traded all that for the nursery, it seems. Want to show me what you've been doing?"

"No," she said stubbornly.

"Okay," he said, pushing his chair back. He walked to the patio doors while she remained seated. He looked out into the backyard. "Wow," he said.

She chewed her lip. "It's possible I have a little OCD. Obsessive Compulsive Disorder," she said. "Kind of goes along with all the other stuff. When I get into something, I go all the way."

George looked over his shoulder at her. "Really?" he asked. "You might not want to cure that until you finish the yard. It's stunning. Amazing."

"You *really* like it?"

"It's beautiful. I wouldn't want to eat and sleep in a house that looked like a funeral parlor, but what you've done so far looks fantastic. You really do have a lot of talents. Seems like you just need to learn when to stop."

"Except I'm no good at making money," she muttered.

"Don't sweat it, Sonja. That's my talent. Fortunately I'm so good at it, you shouldn't have to worry. Unless your OCD extends to shopping—in which case we'll be tapped out pretty quick." He turned away from the patio doors and headed for the foyer. "I don't want to keep you, and I didn't come here to pressure you. I just wanted to see for myself that you're getting better. Happy anniversary. Sorry it wasn't a good one for you. Ten should be something special, though I have no idea what kind of special."

It was kind of special, she found herself thinking. It was actually the first time she felt George had accepted her as she was. Exactly as she was. And she had to be crazy for that to happen.

"George?" she said when he got to the door.

He turned. "Yes?"

"If you call, I'll talk to you. For five minutes. And not too often."

He grinned at her. "Okay, Sonja. Glad you're feeling better."

And then he was gone.

twelve

Gerri did a little further local research on BJ and found a guy with the last name of Smith who had a small but lucrative electronics repair firm in Mill Valley. On her lunch hour, she dropped by. BJ was behind a counter, staring at a computer screen when Gerri walked in. When BJ looked up, she looked stunned.

"Hey," Gerri said. "I was in the area. I thought maybe I could take you to lunch."

"How did you find me?" BJ asked, standing from behind her desk.

"It wasn't hard," Gerri said with a shrug. "I looked it up on the computer. So, can you take lunch? If not, we can do it some other time."

It was almost as if BJ knew. She said she'd find someone from the shop to cover her desk, but she was tense, on guard, as she did so. When they were walking out of the office she said, "I only have a little time. Half hour, forty-five minutes tops."

"I'm sure you know some places nearby," Gerri replied.

"I usually bring something," she said. "When I don't, we hit Taco Bell or Wendy's for a salad."

"Either of those works for me. Or, I saw this sushi place down the road. You eat sushi?"

"I haven't," BJ said.

"We could get some non-fish rolls. Break you in slowly," Gerri said with a smile.

"Okay," BJ said, cautiously.

"Come on, you're not leaving the kids alone or anything. Relax. Try to enjoy a little break."

"Yeah," she said, clearly not enjoying it a bit.

"By the way, where are the kids over summer?" Gerri asked.

"At my brother's house. They've been really great about helping me out while I'm working."

"They must like it there. With their aunt?"

"Yeah," she said. "Her kids are grown, but she's good to my kids. My brother has done pretty well here. The business is doing okay. I lucked out."

"Nah, you didn't luck out—you must have a good family, BJ. That's how we get through the hard times."

"Yeah," she said, glum. She got in Gerri's car.

Gerri made a little small talk, telling her about Matt's obsession with baseball and video games, Andy's ongoing thing with Bob, Sonja's new hobby of planting up the entire yard. When they were settled in a very sparsely populated restaurant and each had an iced tea, Gerri explained why she was there. "Let's not drag this out. You're clearly onto me. I just want you to know, I know."

"I guessed," BJ said.

"How?" Gerri asked.

"You said you could find things out. And I freaked out that night, with the thing in the parking lot."

"I wish you wouldn't freak out now—I'm on your side."

"How can you be?"

"I read the newspapers, got my hands on a couple of reports," Gerri said. "Look, I'm not going to say anything to anyone, not even Andy. The only other person who knows is Phil, who looked it up for me. And by the way, that's not really allowed. But right now Phil would kill Caesar for me, you know? We don't make a habit of doing background checks on neighbors." She sipped her tea. "Besides, hardly anyone has more shit going on than us."

"I do," BJ said solemnly.

"Yeah, you do win the prize, my girl. I have a million questions, but I'm not going to overwhelm you. Right now all I want is to be straight with you. I want you to know I know—and that I'm not going to run scared or gossip about you or judge you."

"Your husband prosecutes people like me," BJ said. "I look things up, too. I don't have a computer, but I can get on the internet at my brother's shop."

Gerri smiled. "He does," she admitted. "He doesn't like it, he sees the flaws, he goes with the patriarchal laws, we fight about it, he tries to plea down the sentence when he understands the defendant was helpless, and when he's prosecuting a case like yours, he suffers. Plus, I kick him every time I turn over in bed, every night." She reached across the table and squeezed BJ's hand. "Really, he hates it. And he understands. He won't fight the system, but he gets it. You were right about him—he's decent."

BJ looked down. "You could've played it a lot closer to your chest," she said. "I sure wouldn't have pressed you."

Gerri shook her head. "That wouldn't have worked," she said. "Besides, it would have kept you back. You would have distanced yourself."

"I would have," she admitted.

"Also, I'm not great at that. Pretending I know nothing."

"I bet you are at work."

"Work is different," Gerri said. "The people I'm there to serve are…well, most of them will plod along through completely dysfunctional lives forever, through generations, in fact. Those are easy to spot and I have to keep them at arm's length or it'll eat me alive. Then there are cases where if I don't play it coy, someone might get hurt. And of course, we help a lot at CPS. It doesn't look like it on paper all the time, but if you're right there in the middle of it, if you can see the eyes of a child you're working with, you can just tell. I'm not really good at that kind of thing where my intimates are concerned— you saw that with Sonja. With Phil."

"With Phil?"

She shrugged. "I never sensed it—the affair. I was too close to him. When I found out, it occurred to me to use some of my skills to get to the bottom of the whole thing before confronting him, but honesty has always been a priority in our house."

"I guess not with him, though. Huh?"

"With him, as well, which is why he made that stupid pact with himself to admit the truth if I ever found out." She lifted the tea to her lips. "I wish he'd used all that time to think of a good lie. It might've been better for us."

"It might've been better for me if I never knew you knew," BJ said.

"No, it wouldn't." Gerri smiled. "Oh, if my knowing was going to hurt you or your kids, you'd be right—but it won't. BJ, you've been through a lot. There isn't any reason for you not to have friends. I understand, you have to be careful. But…"

The waiter brought them sushi rolls and plates. Gerri set about the task of putting out the little dishes. "Watch. This is what you do." She demonstrated—some soy, some wasabi—then showed BJ how to hold the chopsticks. Gerri plucked a spicy tuna roll off the plate in the middle, dipped it, ate it. "Spicy tuna, shrimp and crab," she said, pointing. "This is a California roll—no raw fish. But take a chance, try the tuna roll. It's delicious."

BJ struggled with her chopsticks for a moment, then clumsily picked up a tuna roll, gently placed it in her soy and wasabi, lifted it and plunk, it splashed back into the soy. Gerri laughed. "It doesn't get much easier, either."

"No wonder they never gain weight," BJ muttered, attempting it again. She maneuvered the bite-size piece into her mouth and chewed it thoughtfully. "Not too bad."

"See. Trust me," Gerri said.

"I never thought I'd see this day," BJ said, going after another piece. "A chichi lunch in Mill Valley."

"Please." Gerri laughed. "Aim higher than this."

"So tell me something," BJ said. "How do you think the others would take the news? Andy and Sonja?"

"Andy, no question. I'm an advocate for children, but she's their champion. It's her life's work. Sonja, hard to tell. I haven't been able to read her for a while. She's between worlds right now. The old Sonja might've freaked out. But this new person is almost the opposite. Don't do anything until you're sure you are comfortable. And it's okay to never tell, you know. No one would blame you. I'm sure no one suspects anything." Gerri plucked another piece of sushi off the plate. "What are your plans?" she asked.

"I've been able to save some money," BJ said. "I think I'm good in that house until the end of summer, maybe through the fall. I'll get plenty of notice and time. The house is designed for women like me. In fact, it's pretty hard to be considered. I'm going to have to free it up and give someone else a chance. It's only right."

"Of course," Gerri said, but with disappointment. "I'm really glad it was you for a year, BJ. I like you."

"Thanks," BJ said. "I like you, too."

"If you could do anything? Absolutely anything?"

"School," she said. "I didn't finish high school. Got my GED in prison. And then a couple of college courses, but whether the credits transfer is questionable. I once thought I'd like to be a teacher, but I couldn't pass the background check. That doesn't matter—I'm interested in a million things. I'd love to do what you do—I can smell a family in crisis a hundred miles away. But for right now if I can just keep a roof over my head and take care of the kids, I'll be grateful. We're safe now, that's what matters."

"Do they need counseling?" Gerri asked.

"They're getting it. There's a very strong network for battered women, even the ones who crossed the line, like me. I had amazing support through the whole thing. They even helped me keep my kids, in a way."

"In a way?"

"They helped me find a good lawyer. His parents wanted the kids, and they're as crazy and mean as he was. Most of the people in the family had criminal records, but just to be sure, I traded the insurance money—which would have gone to the kids—for their signed promise never to seek custody of my children." She studied her chopsticks, maneuvering them. "Thirty thousand dollars. His parents didn't even have to think about it. They wanted the money more than they wanted their grandchildren."

"And the kids were with your brother?"

"No," she said, shaking her head. "My mom and dad. But I can't go back to Fresno to live, not ever. He had a big family, a lot of buddies as nasty as he was. A quick visit, in and out, that's all I dare, and I don't dare often. They're all big and mean, but they're not that smart. They won't try to find me, but if any of them stumbles into my path, they might want revenge, but they don't want the kids."

"Jeez, you've really been through it. So, the kids are getting counseling. Are you getting any support?"

"Some," BJ said. "There are groups available and I've dropped in a few times, but the best thing for me right now is to feel I'm taking care of my kids on my own. That really works for me. I got a lot of support in prison. In fact, I was kind of an orange jumpsuit celebrity—there are a lot of women in there who fantasized about doing what I did, whether they were justified or not." She smiled contritely.

"I'm sorry," Gerri said. "I wasn't going to ask a lot of questions. We have so much time to talk. About both our lives. Because no matter where you go next, I'm not giving you up."

"It's not going to be Mill Valley, Gerri. This place is too expensive. I'm thinking of leaving the state. Going someplace with a lower cost of living, but I want to be close to family if I can. I haven't figured anything out yet—but I should. If you have any suggestions, I'm open."

"I'll work on that. Selfishly, I'd like you to stay close. I'll use my connections, look into options."

BJ tilted her head and her eyes glistened. "One more," she said, her voice a little raspy. "One more question, then we eat this sushi and I have to go back to work."

"How'd you have the courage?"

BJ had to purse her lips tight and her nose turned a little pink. She glanced away for a second to gather her composure. Then she looked back at Gerri. "It wasn't courage," she said in a whisper. "All I had was fear and desperation. It was him or us. We were absolutely and truly down to that, I swear."

Gerri was quiet for a second. Then she said, "God bless you, sister."

BJ knocked on Sonja's door that same afternoon, after work. "Hi," she said when Sonja answered. "Still digging?"

"Can't stop myself," she said, but she smiled when she said it. "Wanna see?"

"I'd love to." She stepped inside. BJ didn't drop in on the women in her neighborhood. She mainly saw them in passing, outside. She rarely saw Sonja at all these days.

"How about a glass of wine?" Sonja offered.

"Gee, you can't drink wine, can you?" she asked. "I mean, with all you have going on?"

"You mean medication, lunacy, depression and marital disharmony?" she asked with a laugh. "I'm not exactly cleared for alcohol yet—and besides, being the health nut of the neighborhood, I've always been a spare sipper. But I keep a bottle of chilled white in the fridge for Andy and Gerri and I admit, I'm really looking forward to when I can join them. I might chug it."

"When do you suppose that's going to happen?" BJ asked, watching somewhat distractedly while Sonja breezed into her cheerful kitchen and poured a small glass of wine.

"I'm thinking about a year," she said. "Dr. Kalay says the antidepressant and antianxiety drugs are probably temporary for me. We'll see. I like having a full head of hair so I'm not going to argue about it." She handed BJ the glass.

"Thanks. I hadn't had a drop of alcohol in years, till I met you girls. I wonder if you're all a bad influence."

"I figure if Jesus could turn water into wine at a wedding, it's probably not the worst thing. Come out back," Sonja invited, leading the way.

BJ stepped out onto the patio and felt almost assaulted by the depth and color that surrounded the yard. On all four sides, against the house and three surrounding fences, were beautiful plants and flowers. She saw plants, six feet deep. Roses, lilies, gladiolas, daisies, bougainvillea, ferns, snapdragons and a multitude of unidentifiable blooms and stalks in every color. "Good God," BJ said, shocked.

Sonja laughed and went to sit down in a patio chair.

She had a couple of chairs turned toward the yard, a small redwood table separating them. BJ noticed there was a water glass there. Sonja had been enjoying the view of her hard work in the early evening sun.

BJ sat down next to her. "You did this all by yourself?" she asked.

"When I get going, I can't seem to stop," Sonja said. "It's probably going to require another pill of some kind."

"Sonja, landscaping companies can't pull this off in a couple of months," BJ said. "And there's no mess! Like it was all just dropped down from heaven!"

"Oh, there's a mess on the side of the house. I have a routine. First thing in the morning I throw away the empty containers—rocks, weeds, sod, junk—and start digging, planting and cultivating. Then at the end of the day I rinse off my tools and wheelbarrow and go to the nursery to get plants and supplies for the next day so I can start again. I finally had to buy patio stones to weave through the gardens because it all got so thick. But I never get rid of plants unless they're doomed and dying—I just relocate them very carefully. They're kind of like babies."

"How can you do this?" BJ asked. "It's just amazing."

Sonja shrugged. "No family, no husband, no job, no children…"

BJ was quiet. She finally asked, "Sonja, are you ever lonely?"

"Hardly ever, anymore. I just found out something so bizarre—I was lonelier before, when I had all those things and people in my life—the classes, the co-op, the little consulting business I did, George…not to mention all the meditating and endless work at keeping things perfectly balanced and serene. Like a cocoon. I could hear each twinge in my body and knew exactly what herb or vitamin would soothe or strengthen it. It was like I was insulating myself against feeling things, because if you let the feelings in you risk one that hurts sneaking up on you."

"And now?" BJ asked.

"Well, now I'm forced to take a look at all the scary feelings I worked so hard to keep out. Blech." She grinned at BJ. "They're every bit as bad as I thought they might be."

BJ smiled back. "Then why are you smiling?"

"Because. It had to happen. Keeping it all in makes you sick and nuts. It turns out to be correct—the truth sets you free."

"Just let it out, huh? Is that the prescription?" BJ asked, sipping her wine.

Sonja laughed at her. "It's not that simple. First you have to have a major meltdown, then lockdown, then the drugs they give you loosen up all the dams you'd worked for over twenty years to put in place and under the right god-awful confrontational circumstances, you're a sitting duck. First it's a trickle, then it's a stream, then it's a goddamn flood, pouring out of you—and there's just no stopping it. And then you have to *suffer!* Because once the secrets are out, you have to live with them. Probably the place most of the depression started was almost thirty years ago when my seventeen-year-old brother, Todd, was killed and my parents shut down. They were lost in such a horrible black hole, I couldn't express my own grief. It was like I lost my entire family on one rainy night. I was thirteen. So, when I got to that little gem of knowledge, revisiting that time of my life, I sobbed for days. Cried and dug in the yard and cried some more. My shrink said, "I can't think of a better place for your tears to fall than on the flowers." And then she turned slightly glistening eyes toward BJ.

BJ was speechless. Entranced. This was the most intimate conversation she'd had with another woman since leaving Chowchilla. She swallowed, trying to keep back her own tears. "You've really gotten good at it," she said, her voice catching. "You got this from therapy?"

"Group therapy, the bastards. They're relentless. And now, as revenge, they're programming me to do it to other people. We have a new woman in our group—a real nutball from the state hospital who probably needs to unload. Damn, I hate to do it to her—I know what's coming."

"Sounds kind of like you're in all the way now," BJ said, taking a sip of her wine.

"Yeah, how about that? Well, the upside is, you get some of the good feelings back, too. I guess what happens when you block out the bad feelings is your subconscious can't tell the difference—it just blocks all feelings automatically. You turn into a living corpse."

It occurred to BJ that there wasn't a human being on earth who didn't have deeply complex and emotional issues just under the skin. "You always seemed so prissy and high-strung—kind of like a thoroughbred. Physically perfect, with a whole bunch of reined-in energy."

Sonja held out her hands toward BJ, palms down. Her nails were broken, split, with dirt stuck under them and ground into the cuticles. "I guess that's changing."

"That's not all that's changed. You're so relaxed."

Sonja shrugged. "Could be the drugs," she said.

"Could be I had a lot of tension keeping stuff buried. I used to be afraid if I opened that closet door, unbelievable shit would fall on me and kill me. I never realized how much energy it took to keep the door *closed*."

"And out of it comes this," BJ said, sweeping her hand in the direction of the flowers.

"I'm going to have to figure out how to take control without being too controlling," Sonja said. "I can't let it overrun me, like all the other stuff did. When George saw it, he said I just need to learn how to stop. I hate to admit it, but it kind of put me on notice—he was right. That's what I did with the fountains, candles, chimes, music, bland food.... Shit, he didn't stand a chance!"

"George? George saw the garden?"

"Uh-huh. He stopped by a few days ago. He wanted to wish me happy anniversary—number ten."

"You're kidding me! You saw George?"

"I've talked to him a couple of times, too."

"Sonja! You're talking to George?"

"Uh-huh. Amazing, huh? We're not getting back together or anything. We're not getting divorced right now, either—at least not until all this other stuff is taken care of. It's pointless, he says. We might stay friends, though. We always liked each other a lot, but we got married for reasons that seemed to make sense at the time but were probably all wrong—a couple of lonely people with no attachments who could be alone together and feel a little bit less alone. It was supposed to be a simple marriage that didn't require too much and could meet a few mutual needs. But then I tried to take care of George so I'd never have to lose another person—and I lost him."

"What about the prenup?" BJ asked.

"He said he got rid of it years ago—he knew I didn't really care about his money. George is good at what he does. If you ever need a financial planner..."

"I'll keep him in mind," BJ said with good humor. "Sonja, I have to say, you took me completely by surprise. I didn't expect this from you. All this honesty, all these flowers. You're so different from the person I thought you were. And I'm really flattered that you trusted me enough to talk about all that personal stuff."

"Why wouldn't I trust you, BJ?" Sonja asked. "You saved my life. No one else could tell anything was wrong. And you—the one who knows me least—saw the most."

"Nah, it wasn't like that," she said. "Just dumb luck, that's all."

"Not the way Gerri tells it. It was you who insisted on breaking into the house and taking me to the hospital—and you who noticed the house was starting to smell bad. It's like we were sisters of the heart before we knew anything about each other. I owe you, BJ. I'll never be able to repay you, but I know I owe you."

"You don't owe me," she said, smiling, shaking her head. "But I did come over for a reason. You don't seem to be walking anymore in the mornings."

"I've been slacking on that," Sonja admitted.

"What are you doing for exercise?" BJ asked.

"Besides gardening eight hours a day?" She laughed.

"Are you stiff? Sore?"

"If I stay on my knees too long I can stiffen up—not too bad. But I know it's exercise. I use every muscle in my body."

"I'll bet. How'd you like to try something different?"

"Like what?"

"Run with me," BJ said.

"I don't run," Sonja said, shaking her head. "I'd never keep up with you for one thing."

BJ turned in her chair to face Sonja. "I'll go easy on you while you give it a chance, see if you can do it. A few years ago I was in a spot where I really needed some exercise bad or I was going to go all limp—but I had no real resources and very little time, so I started running. I got hooked. It changed my mood and helped me think more clearly. You can't imagine. Now I *have* to run, just to keep my thoughts and emotions from going berserk. I think it's the endorphins. And you know—if you're worried about the flowers taking over, you could try a couple of other things along with the gardening. Not everything about balance is cursed."

"Wouldn't that be like going back to the candles and fountains?" Sonja asked.

"Not while you're still in your group, I don't think," she said, shaking her head. "Try it. I get tired of running alone all the time. It might work for you like it worked for me." She shrugged. "If it doesn't, it doesn't. But what do you have to lose?"

"When?" Sonja asked warily.

"Tomorrow morning. Six."

"Aww, I don't know…I haven't been getting up that early lately. I'm drugged, you know!"

BJ grinned. "You're not that drugged. In fact, I think the drugs make you kind of even, if you get my drift. Besides, you *owe* me!"

Sonja made a face. "Pretty smart of me to give you a weapon to use on me."

"Come on," BJ said, standing. "I have to get back to the kids—they're supposed to be cleaning up their rooms. I'll see you at 6:00 a.m." She handed Sonja her wineglass. "Thanks, that was great. Try to keep me from getting in the habit, will you?"

"Six?" Sonja said weakly, furrowing her brows.

"With a smile on your face!" BJ said.

At six the next morning BJ had to knock on Sonja's door. She wondered if she was going to do it, get up and run. When the door opened BJ had to keep from laughing out loud. Sonja stood in the frame holding a steaming cup, her hair all ratty from bed, mud stains on the knees of her sweats, narrowed eyes and a scowl on her face. "Sonja, is that *coffee?*"

"Tea," she grumbled.

"Man, you look a lot like Gerri used to look when you rousted her out to walk," BJ said, laughing.

"I'm going to buy her something nice," Sonja muttered. "I should make amends for that."

"Come on," BJ coaxed. "Let's stretch."

Sonja put her cup down on the foyer table and pulled the door closed behind her. "Let's get this over with," she said, not realizing how much she sounded like Gerri, as well.

They stretched out legs, joints, backs, arms, loosening everything up. Then BJ suggested they start with a brisk walk. After a block, Sonja was moving along pretty well. "How do you feel about a nice, gentle trot?" BJ asked.

"I'm not sure," Sonja said. "I'll let you know."

"Come on," BJ said, setting an easy pace. Once they were moving along, BJ started explaining how things would work. "I've plotted my entire course a hundred times—I know all the exact measurements and distances. If you can jog a half mile, we'll walk again and see how you feel."

"I might not make a half mile," Sonja said, panting.

"You're doing great! How's it feel?"

"Like I need a hip replacement."

"Anything hurt?"

"Everything hurts! I'm weak and sick and *crazy!*"

BJ laughed at her. They cantered along for a couple of blocks and BJ said, "Let's pick it up just a little bit. How you doing?"

"Really sorry I made friends with you."

"Here we go, Sonja—nice and easy. Even out your breathing, don't come down too hard—just roll off your feet, heel to toe, swing your arms gently to give yourself a little help. You're doing great!" They ran a few blocks then BJ said, "Okay, we're going to pick it up just a little more. Not too fast, nice and easy. That's a girl. Hey, you're in very good shape."

"Ugh," Sonja said.

"Tell me when you run out of steam, but try to push yourself a little bit. It's always hard work at first, but then the endorphins kick in and it feels like you could go forever."

"Why…aren't…you…breathing…hard?" Sonja asked.

"Because I do this every day, that's why. I'm panting by the last couple of miles. Just go with it. Try to breathe evenly, nice and deep." They ran on and every few blocks BJ increased their pace just slightly. They went around another bend, down a long block. Sonja was panting beside her, but she was running. They didn't talk, just moved slick and easy down the road.

BJ could've gone faster, but she was happy with

Sonja beside her. She thought about the first time she saw her with Gerri and Andy, so prim in her pastel sweat combinations, her shoes so white and new-looking every day. At the end of their walk when the women converged again, Sonja would have a glistening of perspiration on her face and neck, but otherwise looked as pristine as ever. Now she had great rivers of sweat running down her neck, soaking her shirt from the collar to the middle of her back, sweat stains under each arm, her hair stringy and damp from exertion.

She thought about seeing Sonja sitting against her bedroom wall between her bed and bureau, her eyes wide and spaced out with the fear of not knowing what was happening to her, her face as white as bleached marble, gonzo. She glanced over at her—this was so much better. Running was a thing that required a certain amount of control and yielded a tremendous feeling of freedom.

"Have we…gone our…half mile?" Sonja said, gasping for air.

"Mile and a half," BJ said.

Sonja stopped dead in her tracks and turned wide eyes on BJ. "Mile and a half?"

"Yep. Keep moving. How do you feel?"

"Holy shit," Sonja said, stunned. Then she took off jogging almost effortlessly. "Holy…shit!" she said again.

Laughing almost too hard to run, BJ caught up. "Feels pretty good, doesn't it?"

"Not…sure…" she rasped. "But holy shit!"

"Didn't know you had it in you, did you, girlfriend? I think maybe you're a runner and never knew it."

"Wow" was all she could say.

Yeah, BJ thought. *This is better.* Flowers, running, cursing like a sailor—letting down the barriers so the sun could shine where the darkness had lived. BJ knew all about that. She felt her eyes fill with tears. This is better.

Andy was very much looking forward to meeting Bob's family. He confessed to her that Connie and Frank were so excited to meet Bob's new girlfriend, they wanted all four grown children, their spouses and nine grandkids to come over for a big family gathering, but Bob slammed the lid on that. At his insistence, it would be a cozy little backyard barbeque that would give the two couples a chance to get to know each other. There was plenty of time to bring in the entire supporting cast.

He explained that Frank and Connie were rich and their house was probably more of a small mansion. He didn't want Andy to think that had anything to do with him—he was just a poor relative.

"Bob, I figured if it had a guesthouse, it was pretty substantial, and that Connie and Frank weren't simple folks if they had all that," she said.

"But they are," he said earnestly. "Maybe I just kid myself about that—but they seem just ordinary to me. My other sisters and their families live in regular little houses, always worked hard and had to worry about things like paying for college and weddings. I know Connie and Frank are kind of different in that way—though they're hard workers, too. I can't explain it."

"Well," Andy said. "Maybe you just did. You're saying Connie and Frank are very wealthy, but down to earth."

"Frank started with nothing, just like anyone else. He

had aspirations to be a developer. He was a contractor who got small jobs. He had his own little company that Connie managed and kept the books for while she was having the kids. They moved into that house to renovate it and sell it at a profit to fund larger investments that could be used to develop condos, apartment complexes, small housing tracts—but he got his break before the big house was finished, so they never sold it. Frank was my first boss out of college, when I started custom carpentry." He whistled. "Tell you what, if Frank touches it, it turns straight to gold."

"Bob," she said, laughing, "are you nervous?"

"I think I need you to like them," he said weakly.

She put a hand along his cheek. "I'm sure I'll like them, but try to remember—it really doesn't matter. What matters is that I like *you*."

He put his arms around her and held her tight.

Andy wasn't overwhelmed by the house, which was indeed huge and beautiful, nearly ten thousand square feet of it. Given her work, she'd been to many a fundraiser and political rally in ostentatious settings and was well acquainted with the wealth of Marin County. The house sat within a small, exclusive neighborhood with a guard at the gate. It was set back on a beautifully manicured lawn with a circular brick drive. Although Bob pulled his truck around back, he insisted they go to the front door. They were drawn into a large, marble foyer by Connie, a woman in her sixties who wore a wide grin and pulled Andy immediately into her welcoming arms for a big hug.

"I am so glad to finally meet you," she said to Andy. "I thought Bob made you up!"

"Completely real." Andy laughed. "I never worried

that he made you up—I know every detail of your child-hood, and the childhoods of each of your kids!"

"Doesn't he just talk too much?" Connie asked. "Come in, come in. I'm not used to this at all—Bob coming to the front door like this. He usually just lets himself in the kitchen door." She bent to say hello to Beau, giving him an affectionate rub on the head.

"That would have suited me just fine," Andy said.

"Come on back—Frank's on the patio. You can relax and have something to drink."

"I'd be happy to help you," Andy offered.

"Even better," Connie said. "I could use a hand."

Andy glanced at Bob and saw that he seemed to breathe a sigh of relief that the preliminaries were going well. She tried giving him a smile of reassurance, but he appeared to be too tense to notice. Connie had already turned away from the front door and was leading them through the house toward the back. Andy chuckled, turned and followed. When she arrived in the kitchen—a kitchen clearly designed to play host to very large parties—she found Connie at the central workstation with food spread all over the place. Tons of food.

"Bob, please get Andy whatever she'd like and grab yourself a cold beer so you can relax a little bit. We like each other just fine."

While Bob busied himself fixing drinks, Andy and Connie exchanged amused glances. Bob handed Andy a glass of wine. "Would you like to meet Frank before you get involved in this mess?" he asked.

"I think maybe I better," she said with a laugh.

When they arrived on the patio, Andy barely no-ticed the man sleeping, openmouthed, his glasses slip-ping off his generous nose, a newspaper sliding off his lap. She was taken by her surroundings—a backyard showplace. The grounds were massive. The landscaping surrounding the patio and pool was lush, green and flowering. The patio and pool deck was large enough to hold at least two hundred people. There were tables and chairs placed strategically around the yard and two gazebos. Right beside the French doors that led back into the kitchen was a small table and chairs, a couple of matching chaise lounges and a large grill built into a brick console with what looked like a warming oven and small refrigerator. And there, across the yard with a driveway that led to the door, was the guesthouse. And it was not a tiny guesthouse, it looked big enough for a couple or small family, with a second floor dormer window indicating a loft or upstairs bedroom.

"Um, Frank?" Bob said.

Frank roused slowly, adjusted his glasses and looked at Bob. "Oh!" he said, sitting up as though shocked he'd fallen asleep. Then he stood.

"Frank, I'd like you to meet Andy Jamison—Andy, meet my brother-in-law Frank Sepelman."

"Well, it's about time." Frank chortled. "I wondered if he was ever going to share you!" He took one of her hands in both of his. "I'm so happy you came today, so happy! Good to meet you, Andy. Short for Andrea?"

"Anastasia," Bob said. "She'll rise again—that's what it means."

"Nice to meet you, too, Frank," Andy said. "If it's okay with you, I'll just let you men catch up while I help Connie in the kitchen. Then we can all visit together."

"Super," Frank said. "She probably needs some help. Did you see how much food she's got spread around?"

"I did." Andy laughed. "So—you're having the 49ers to dinner tonight?"

Frank grinned. "If there's anything you're allergic to, any special dietary quirks like you're a vegetarian or whatever—Connie's got you covered."

"I eat absolutely everything. And lots more of it since I've been seeing Bob, who likes food as much as I do."

"Well, that's a relief. Don't worry—we don't force people to clean their plates."

"I'm glad to hear that," she said. "Relax, you guys. I'll visit with Connie and see if I can give her a hand."

Andy was smiling when she entered the huge kitchen. She stood at the opposite side of the workstation from Connie. "I've never seen Bob so nervous," she said.

"I'm flattered," Connie said. "I thought he took me for granted." She pushed ears of corn toward Andy. "Shuck these, will you, dear? Into the trash there."

"Connie, you're going to make me eat corn on the cob at my debut?"

"Bob will probably shear it off the cob for you," Connie said with a laugh. "If you act pitiful, he might even feed it to you. Do you imagine there's anything we don't already know about each other?"

"Doubtful," Andy said, tearing the green husks away from the cob.

"Well, I've heard Bob's version of how you two got together. I'd love to hear yours," Connie said.

"Very simple, and yet the most amazing experience of my life," Andy said. "I was going through my second divorce while Bob was working on remodeling my kitchen. It's pretty embarrassing, going through two divorces in less than ten years. You start to feel like the biggest dope on earth. But Bob was there almost every day and we'd talk for least an hour, sometimes longer. He had this way of making me feel like I hadn't made two giant mistakes. He's just so kind, so supportive. I mean, no reason he should have to prop up my sagging ego in addition to all that hard renovating work—but it seemed to come from him naturally. It didn't take long, Connie. He won me over in no time—he's the most beautiful man I know. When the kitchen was done, I couldn't let him get away."

Connie stopped working and looked at Andy with that same precious, somewhat melancholy expression her brother wore so well. In fact, she was a lot like her brother—thickset and unfussy. She didn't color her hair. She had a short cropped salt-and-pepper coiffure and tanned skin, as though she spent lots of time in the sun. Plenty of wrinkles, too. She didn't seem at all the face-lift type. When she smiled, the lines around her mouth and eyes crinkled. If she was wearing makeup, it was lightly applied—all that was obvious was a bit of pink lip gloss. And she had that wonderful twinkle in her eyes.

"He tells it almost exactly the same way, except he didn't mention you until his truck started going missing from the driveway and I asked him about it. I'll admit something to you," she said. "I warned him to be careful, that you might be lonely because you were suddenly without a partner, maybe needing someone as giving as Bob, someone to lean on, but not ready for a replacement."

"You might've been right at the very beginning," Andy said. "But not now. I adore Bob. I can't imagine not having him in my life. He's so remarkable. I don't know how he hasn't been married for thirty years."

"Too solitary, I guess," Connie said. "He's terribly shy. Except around family—with us he's loud, hysterically funny and always full of mischief. He's everyone's favorite Uncle Bob."

"Connie, I know how close you are—he's safe with me, I promise. I've never been so happy, never felt so secure."

"And you have a son, Bob tells me."

From there the conversation went to Noel, then to Connie's kids, then to other family members. Eventually some things came out that Bob hadn't mentioned. For one thing, Connie and Frank were extremely busy people and were seldom around that great big house. Frank continued to run his company and Connie sat on several boards all over Marin County and San Francisco, from charity to political to community-service work. It was very important to them to give back to their community. In addition, now that she and Frank were in their sixties and had raised their family, they liked to do some traveling together, finally catching up on the trips there had never been the time or money to indulge in when they were younger. Between their many trips, committee and board meetings and obligations, they averaged a couple of dinner hours a week at home and counted on Bob to look after things for them when they were away, which was more and more often.

"When Bob moved into the guesthouse, it was one room with a large bathroom and a few kitchen items—bar-size refrigerator, microwave, hot plate—more for convenience than actual cooking. He had access to the house whenever it suited him. He could live here if he wanted to. But he preferred that little place, his own place, even when we're out of town. So he enlarged it—added a bedroom, put in a proper living room, dining area and small but more than adequate kitchen with full-size appliances so he could cook himself a real meal. He finished off the attic for good measure, making it an L-shaped loft up there. It's fourteen hundred square feet of living space now!"

Bob had mentioned to Andy that he helped out when he could, but he hadn't said he looked after things for Connie and Frank. "Has it been a problem that Bob's been spending so much time at my house?" Andy asked.

"Of course not." Connie laughed. "There are things to do around here every day, but not huge things. Check the place over, make sure the plants aren't dying, food isn't rotting, bring in the mail, be on call if something malfunctions—from the pool pump to the alarm system. There's a cleaning crew that comes in to clean this monster. It's so damn big, they have to come twice a week just to keep it decent. We have outside maintenance regularly. But if Bob ever leaves us, I have kids that can help with some things. Lord knows, we've helped them enough!"

Andy loved Connie and Frank immediately, and if she was any judge, they liked her just fine. Once Bob settled down, dinner with his family was just what she imagined it would be—full of poking fun, wisecracks, laughing, telling tales. Andy got a tour of the house while the men cleaned up, but the thing that intrigued her more was the guesthouse, which was charming and spacious—all work Bob had done himself.

Finally it was time to go back to Andy's. She rode alongside Bob in his work truck, feeling the lighthearted joy that comes from enchantment—from everything being, for the very first time, exactly how it should be. When they got home and she opened the door for them, she turned to Bob. "Are you calmed down now?"

"Uh-huh. Sorry. I guess I froze up a little, like I was around a bunch of strangers. Because…aw, because so many things," he said, putting his arms around her.

"Give me one reason," she said.

"It was a challenge for me, Andy. Putting the two women who are most important to me together and hoping they'd like each other. I didn't know what I'd do if it didn't work out."

"But that's so paranoid—and so not like you."

"I know. But I was never in that spot before. And I was afraid they'd take one look at you and figure you couldn't possibly have real, honest feelings for me."

"Bob," she said, running a finger over his lips. "You have to stop this. I can't prove my love to you every second of every day—you'll wear me out. Sooner or later it would be nice if you trusted me as much as I trust you."

He held her in silence for a moment and then said, "Love?"

"Of course, love. I love you as much as you love me. Maybe even more."

"You do?"

She nodded. "I heard you, you know. That morning with Noel. I heard you tell him you loved me, then apologize because you hadn't told me first. In fact, I heard everything you said to him. There's a little window in the bathroom that was cracked open. I listened. I was so touched, I cried for an hour, but you didn't even notice."

"I'm sorry, honey. I was busy with Noel. He needed

someone on his side real bad. I mean a man—he needed a man on his side. I promise, I'll never not notice again."

She laughed. "I loved you even more for giving all that to Noel because you're right—he needed you a lot more than I did. But I was so in love with you right then, when you took my troubled son into your great big arms."

"I never did…"

"I meant figuratively." She laughed. "You've had a very rough day. You're usually much quicker than that."

"I love you, Andy," he said.

"I know. You love me in a way you thought you'd never experience."

"That's right." He smiled.

"I like that very much. So could we get down to our skivvies now? And maybe do that thing where you concentrate on baseball stats?" He laughed at her. "That's so much fun," she said.

thirteen

After two weeks, Sonja was jogging four miles at a ten-minute-mile pace, itching to take it to the nine minute mile, then eight. She could talk to BJ for the first mile and a half, then the conversation had to stop so the breathing and running could be smooth. She loved it. BJ would come for her at six and she was raring to go. After forty minutes on the route BJ had carefully plotted, they'd end up at the park.

"This might be one of the best things I've ever done," Sonja said a little breathlessly. "And it never once occurred to me. Never once."

BJ walked around in circles, cooling down from the run, her hands on her hips, her head down. "You're still gardening, aren't you?"

"Yep. Just three to four hours a day, though. This was a great idea. I have to remember—not all things about my need for balance were stupid. I'm not enlarging my gardens anymore. I don't think the whole yard will be used for flowers. However, I am considering putting in a reflecting pool. Maybe a little waterfall. And goldfish. Right in the northeast corner, so it will be warmed by the afternoon sun. There's not a lot of morning sun there because of the fog, but the afternoon sun can be very nice for little fish."

BJ smiled. She sat on the ground, raised her knees and circled them with her arms. "That sounds very pretty."

"George thinks so, too."

"You're getting more involved with George?" BJ asked.

"No. I see him about once a week for just a little while. He appreciates that I keep the house so nice, that the landscaping is getting better. You have to understand George—he still thinks of it as an asset."

"What are the chances you'll let him move back in?"

"Zero," Sonja said. "I should probably never say never—the absolutes have always been my fatal flaw. But I've been encouraging him to buy himself something long-term instead of that apartment he's renting. Something a bachelor can manage—a town house or condo. But I do like finding George not to be the cocksucker I thought he was." She furrowed her brow. "Don't expect me to thank him for pulling the pin out of my grenade, however. That might be asking too much."

"Okay." BJ laughed.

Sonja knelt on the ground. "Thanks," she said. "For everything. You might be the first real friend I've ever had. At least since I was about twelve."

BJ was stunned speechless for a second. "That can't be right," she said. "You were tight with Gerri and Andy long before I moved in."

"I know, and I love them. But it's different with them. They're a little older, they have families, they have each other. And it's not a real big secret they always thought

I was close to a nutcase before I was an official nutcase. Plus, they've been best friends for a long, long time. But I don't mean to diminish the quality of their friendships," she said, putting up a hand as if to ward off the very idea. "Really, they've been awfully nice to me, including me all the time even when they thought I was an eccentric whack job. And I do love them, I do."

"Well, I hope so," BJ said. "Because they'd do anything for you."

"Yeah," she said, smiling. "All of a sudden I have a lot of good people around. But really, BJ, you've been there for me so much. I already thanked you for all that stuff—finding me bottomed out twice. But the running—thinking of something that could be good for me, then doing it with me every morning. I just love you for that!"

"Sonja, don't get melodramatic," she said. "I run every day. You know that."

"I think we could run a 10K. In fact, I think in time we could actually run a marathon."

BJ frowned. "Is your OCD kicking in? Because I'd feel terrible if I brought out a new avenue for your OCD."

"Dr. Kalay said she thinks running is a wonderful idea—she wishes more of her patients took to exercise. She also said if I find myself running through injuries or weakening and painful joints, I'm not running for exercise anymore and that's a signal I had to promise to tell her about."

"Well, that makes sense…."

"So what do you think? In a year or so could we actually run in some kind of race? I mean, not to win or anything, but to do it?"

"Sonja, I don't think I'll be living in the neighborhood that much longer. I think the owners of my house have other plans for it. I'll probably be moving in the next few months."

"You won't be moving to New Zealand, will you? Because we both have cars. And phones. There are a million places to meet and have a run."

"But with work and the kids…"

"I know, you're on a much tighter schedule and budget than I am—we can work with that. If you do have to move, I hope it's not too far. But I'm very flexible." She shrugged and smiled. "I doubt I'll find another running mate with as much patience as you have."

BJ was touched, but she didn't smile. "Listen, can I ask you something personal and very specific?"

"You can ask me anything. There are only a few things I can't tell you—and believe me, you wouldn't want to know."

BJ frowned. "What kinds of things? Just out of curiosity."

"I have a very serious pact with my therapy group," she said. "Their business is no one's business, and mine only during group. We don't tell each other's stories. We just can't run the risk of having someone who's very vulnerable recognized or identified outside the group. You know—we never say names, we never give descriptions, we never repeat confidences."

"And you guys don't ever slip up? Not even accidentally? Because there are drugs involved, you know. I mean, face it, Sonja—you've gotten a lot freer. Loose, if you don't mind me saying so."

She laughed. "I don't mind. I've loosened up a lot—

but I haven't lost my ability to be rational or logical. I know what's going on."

"Uh-huh," BJ said. "Well, listen, before you start planning our marathon, I should probably tell you some things about my past. But because I don't ever want my kids hurt by the things I've done, it would have to be confidential. I mean, even if you completely hate me after I tell you, it would *still* have to be confidential. Like the pact you have with your group—nothing said. Ever. Are you up to that? Or would you rather just not know?"

"What's the matter?" Sonja asked, concerned. "Is everything all right?"

"That depends on your point of view. But you have to make a promise—a pact of silence. And then the hard part—I have to trust you. Trust doesn't come easy for me."

"We're not going to draw blood or anything, are we?"

"No. Pact of silence?"

"Pact!" Sonja promised.

"Okay," BJ said, drawing a deep breath. "God, I hope you can do it—keep your mouth shut." She took another deep breath. "I'm an ex-con. I did time in prison. I killed my husband. I got out almost a year ago and I'm on parole, working for my brother."

Sonja went a little pale. She sat back on her heels, her mouth slightly open.

"Prison is where I picked up running. We had very little time for exercise and I needed it fast and hard. At first I did it to burn off tension and fear, but I figured out almost right away that it changed everything—my thinking, my ability to manage my emotions, my sleep, my energy. There was a small track we could use, a quarter-mile track, and we had an hour if the guards were patient and felt generous. I'd hit that track running and go as fast as I could for as long as I could, rain or shine. The others spent their hour gossiping or smoking or maybe lifting weights. I tried weight lifting, but it didn't give me the same high running did, so I stuck to running. I'm addicted to it, really. I need that daily run. You really shouldn't run six or seven days a week—it's not that good for the joints, the back. But I need it. It brings my crazy world back into place."

Sonja was quiet, her mouth still hanging open slightly. She closed her mouth, swallowed. "You *killed* your husband?" she asked quietly.

"I did. Let's start way back before that happened. I was a bad kid in junior high and high school. I was in trouble a lot. It made no sense because no one else in my family was like that. But I started smoking pot and drinking at thirteen with my friends, who were also bad kids. I got myself messed up with all the wrong people over and over, got in trouble with the police, had a juvie record and dropped out of school. And then I got hooked up with the worst one of all—my husband. He was a few years older and I was a wild child. We ran off and got married when I was eighteen—probably because my parents were constantly on me about working or going to school. In no time at all, he was knocking me around. Beating me senseless, even in front of his family and friends, who seemed to enjoy it as much as he did."

"Oh…" Sonja said weakly.

BJ swallowed hard. "Okay, here's what happened. He got worse. He drank and used more drugs, though he seemed to always manage some kind of job. I know he did crimes, but I never got the details. I know he sold dope when he had the chance. But there were other schemes and cons and burglaries that he and his friends pulled off. A lot of the time we lived with his parents and siblings. On and off we'd have a cheap, nasty place of our own, but the money would dry up or he'd be in jail for a while and we'd be back with his family—and they were all like that. They never questioned him beating his wife because they all beat on each other. My mom and dad were heartbroken, but they couldn't have him in their house, so they couldn't offer the two of us a place—only me, if I'd come home, alone."

"You wouldn't leave him?" Sonja asked.

"I couldn't. He threatened to kill me, my parents, my brothers, their wives, their kids. I don't know if he ever actually killed anyone, but his threats were real to me. I wasn't going to have kids but I ran out of pills and got pregnant. Then I got pregnant again. He put me in the hospital three times. I was in the emergency room a bunch of times. He actually did time for felony battery twice. His father did time for felony battery. My kids were so little when he started whacking them around—and I knew it was coming to a head.

"I had these precious little kids—they were two and four years old and he'd actually hit them—it was impossible to imagine. They were adorable little towheaded, freckle-faced kids—and when he'd let me see my folks, we'd show up with bruises where he'd knocked someone in the head or grabbed our arms so hard there were thumb and finger prints." She looked down. "I have three brothers. Three brothers who always acted like they'd like to beat the crap out of me themselves. But I heard them one night at my mom and dad's before I was picked up by my husband—heard them talking about how they could take him out, get us home where we'd be safe. They were trying to figure out how they could do it without being caught, but if anyone got caught it would be worth it if I could get free with the kids. They were going to draw straws to see who'd take a chance on prison to get me out of there. And God, they were all good men, all married with kids...."

BJ sniffed, wiped at her eyes and shook off the emotion. "You know, I didn't deserve that from them. I wasn't ever that nice to them, my brothers. Growing up, they were ruthless to me—I hated them. But they never hit me and they tried to keep me safe, warn me, get me to behave and I just blew them off like the idiots I thought they were. Then I heard them talking about killing my husband to save my life, to get my kids out of that hellhole."

"You must have been scared to death."

BJ cracked a half smile. "I was beyond scared. I'd tried everything. I went to counselors, went to shelters, called the police, ran home to my parents—I always ended up back in the same place. And then I began to worry about what would happen to my kids when he finally did kill me. Would his parents get them even if he went to prison? I was pretty desperate."

"I can't even imagine this," Sonja said, shaking her head.

"Yeah, I know. You ready for me to stop talking now? I mean, you don't have to hear the rest of this. You already know how the story ends."

"Are you kidding? Keep going. Finish it," Sonja said.

"You still up to the pact? Because if you're not..."

"Believe me, I'm not just a boring mental case. I

actually heard things in the nuthouse that would burn your little ears. Finish it."

"Well, there's not much more. He beat me mostly, but he hurt the kids, scared them to death. We were in our own place for a little while—he liked his own place so he could have his friends over without family around—and I decided that I wasn't going to let my family get in trouble for doing something to him. Not when he was my problem. I knew what was going to happen. I knew the laws. I'd have to finish him off when he was defenseless or I wouldn't be able to win against him, and that is not self-defense, not legally. I knew I'd end up going to jail. But that wasn't the most important thing. So one night when all his friends were over, I helped serve the shots. I kept adding some of his precious cocaine into his. Most of his buddies left, a couple of them passed out."

"What about your kids? Weren't you afraid of what would happen to the kids?"

"Only a little bit. My family was squeaky clean and his was full of priors, including prison time for battery domestic. I was betting on the system that had failed to help me. I couldn't imagine the courts giving the kids to his family. And I was careful—I never told anyone in my family I had a plan. That way they weren't a part of it."

"What happened?" Sonja asked.

"I put the kids to bed and told them to stay there. I added what I thought would be a fatal dose of coke to his last drink. I never did drugs. I even gave up alcohol after seeing firsthand what it had turned him into. I watched him throw back that shot full of cocaine. Tequila. And he crashed. I knew he might survive it even though I'd been poisoning him all night and I was scared to death. I woke the kids, put them in the car, drove them to my parents' house and waited. I didn't have the stomach to stab him or anything that awful. That's why he had to be stoned or drunk. That's why I OD'd him. And when the police came to find me and said someone killed him I was so afraid they might blame the wrong person, I admitted it was me."

"Wow," Sonja said.

"I murdered him," BJ said. "I didn't know what else to do."

Sonja was quiet for a long moment. BJ could see her trying to think it through, process it. Finally their eyes met. "Well. Damn. Good for you!" Sonja said.

Gerri forced herself out of bed at seven on Sunday morning and headed for the kitchen. She had to make her own coffee, get her own paper. Not for the first time she missed her partner and their routine. She decided that later she'd hit the grocery store, maybe make a nice dinner if everyone was going to be around. Including Phil.

She poured herself a cup of coffee and began leafing through the paper, beginning with the front page. On to local news. A quick run through the Life section and finally, the editorial pages where most of the political banter took place, especially with the op-ed columns. Suddenly she was looking at the face of her husband beside that of a well-known criminal defense attorney. The headline leaped out at her. Gilbert to Run in District Attorney Race against Archrival.

She stopped breathing. It was difficult to concentrate long enough to read the article, to get past the headline;

she had to remember to breathe again. Apparently the chief contenders for the position being vacated by Clay Sturgess were Phil and a criminal defense attorney he'd been up against in court many times, Byron Carter. Carter's campaign would revolve around his ability to put away criminals because of his vast experience in defending them. There was no comment from Phil.

He's running? Now? How could he do this to us?

Gerri left the kitchen. In her bedroom she exchanged her robe and nightgown for jeans and a sweatshirt, slipped on some flip-flops. She went back to the kitchen, scribbled a note for the kids, who probably wouldn't be up for another three hours. She grabbed her purse and the editorial section of the paper.

Gerri got in her car. She caught a glimpse of herself in the rearview mirror, then took a closer look. She hadn't even glanced at herself before leaving the house. Her hair was spiking every which way and she had a crease down the side of her face from her pillow. *What the hell,* she thought. This was hardly a social call.

She parked right behind Phil's car and went straight to his door. She tried just opening it, but found it locked, so she pounded. It was not yet seven-thirty, but she knew he wouldn't be asleep. When the door opened, she was met with his frown. He was freshly showered and shaved, his pants barely pulled on, zipped but not buttoned, his chest and feet were bare, a towel was draped around his neck. This was not his usual Sunday–morning routine or attire, to shower right off and wear decent pants, Gerri thought. In fact, he could usually manage to look like a vagrant till late afternoon. She said nothing, holding the newspaper toward him, her expression dark, her voice unreliable.

He didn't take the paper. He stepped aside so she could enter, then pushed the door closed. The coverlet was pulled over the sheets on his lumpy bed and the newspaper was scattered there. "It's a leak," he said as she came toward him. "I haven't announced anything. I'm as surprised by the editorial as you are. I was on my way over to the house to explain."

"*Someone* thinks you're running," she said angrily. "Without even mentioning it, much less talking to me about it."

"Because I made it clear that until you and I get our issues resolved, I can't make a firm commitment."

"So—you've been talking to *someone,*" she said hotly.

"I was approached, of course. Who else are they going to approach when Sturgess moves on? I didn't think it would be this soon, but I wasn't exactly shocked. He has bigger fish to fry."

"Who approached you?"

"First it was Sturgess. Then it was his election committee. They're trying to be patient, but if you read the article, you can see—they need a candidate right now. A strong one. They can't let that yahoo gather votes while they shop around."

"Why in God's name didn't you tell me you'd been approached?" she railed. "I didn't even know Sturgess was leaving!"

"Because I didn't want it to get in the way of the stuff we're trying to sort out," he said, raising his voice to match hers. "This isn't a reason to work things out! This is a possibility that comes *after* we've worked things out!"

"But you want it! Admit it, you *want* it!"

"Of course I want it! It's what I've worked toward for more than twenty-five years! There was a time we both wanted it! I want it almost as bad as I want you, but I'm not going to make that kind of choice. Not now. Not yet!"

"Have you told them we're separated? That you had an affair?"

"What do you think? I *had* to tell them. You don't let people put in their time and go looking for money if you're hiding things."

"And they still want you? With this shit going on in your life?"

"A consensual relationship years ago, brief separation and counseling—not even interesting these days. Certainly not front-page news. That bastard Carter is going to go after my prosecutorial record and try to make me look like a wimp who won't be able to put away bad guys and we're going to make him look like a defender of bad guys for over twenty years and therefore unable to make the transition. That's what the real fight's going to be about—not about our marriage. Besides, Carter has way more dirty linen than I do. If he draws first blood, he'll be up to his eyeballs in mistresses...."

"God," Gerri said, tossing her paper on his bed. "You already talk like a candidate. You can't reel this back in, can you?"

He stepped toward her. "This isn't how I wanted to do this. I wanted to get us back together, healthy and on track, then make a final, official decision, *together*. If this hadn't been something you'd always wanted to do *with* me, I wouldn't even have listened to the proposal. But you wanted it, too!"

"You're doing it again! Keeping secrets!"

"No! It's not a secret! I didn't agree to anything— aren't you listening?"

"Have you thought about what it will be like if it comes up—the other woman? Humiliating your family publicly?"

"I haven't told anyone but Kelly the reason for our separation!" he stormed. "You're not humiliated, goddamn it! You're self-righteous!"

She took another step toward him. "What makes you so sure she isn't going to come out of the woodwork and claim some kind of abuse or harassment? Making your situation *interesting?*"

"Because I may be an idiot, but I'm still an idiot who's a pretty goddamn good judge of character! She won't do that!"

"Did you give *them* a name?"

"No! I told them if I become a candidate and they have to investigate all the angles, they'll get a name!"

"Then *I'll* get a name," she shouted.

"Don't you think you'd look a lot better if you didn't know? Then it's about us, no one else! What's the difference, Gerri? You wanna go beat her up?"

"You bastard, you're going to do this. You're going to run! And I'm going to look like the bad guy again!"

He ran a hand through his damp hair. "I don't see how the hell this makes you look like *anything!* What more can I do to show you my family comes first? If this isn't good for us, we don't do it. Period!"

She took a deep breath and lowered her voice. "And give up something you've wanted your entire career? It wasn't easy staying in the prosecutor's office, doing the people's work, when private practice would've gotten you that stupid sailboat you've always wanted—don't you think that's been clear for decades?" Tears gathered in her eyes. "I can't ask you to give up the most important career move of your life! The kids would *hate* me! Your mother would never forgive me!"

"It's not about them," he said. They were nose to nose. He put a hand on her waist. "It's about us. You and me. I want *us* back."

"Broadsided," she said, a tear spilling over. "This was the last thing I expected. Jesus, I've wanted it, too! It's been almost as important to me as to you! You deserve to be the D.A. You should probably be the governor, but they're not smart enough to run you!" She leaned toward him, crying. "Goddamn you! You should've told me! Prepared me. You shouldn't have handled it like this, risking shocking me like this."

He slipped his hand under her shirt and gently stroked her bare back. "Yeah, guilty," he said. He put his lips against her forehead. "I couldn't do it. I couldn't tell you, not yet. I was afraid you'd think it was an excuse to get you back. And I don't want you back that way."

"But it's working out that way, anyway!" she cried. "Because if you don't step up now, whoever they put on the ballot is going to win against Carter and hold that D.A. spot for another ten or twelve years. And by then…"

"Whatever is best for us, Gerri," he said. "If one of your conditions was that I leave the prosecutor's office, I'd do it. Don't you get it? My marriage is more important than anything else."

"It's so unfair! I can't say go for it, I can't say don't!"

"Then don't do anything," he whispered. "Can't you

give yourself time to think? The kids aren't going to read the paper."

"They'll hear," she said. "Their friends' parents pay attention to these things."

He kissed her temple, her cheek. "We'll tell the kids we're still working on us—we haven't made a decision."

"That's when the pressure will start," she said. She cried and he soothed her. He pressed his lips to hers. And before long the crying stopped and the kissing intensified. There had been kisses good-night as he left the house lately, kisses that had grown long, deep, hot and tempting, so this wasn't new. He let his lips linger, touching hers carefully. Then he pressed his mouth against hers, tasting tears, her morning coffee, her sweet flesh. He pressed harder, forcing her lips open with his, breathing shallowly. His hand slipped around from her back to her bare breast and he heard her groan low in her throat. She put her arms around him to hold him closer.

"Don't you dare," she whispered.

"I want you back," Phil murmured.

"How dare you try to get me turned on in the middle of one of the best fights we've had in years!"

"Sorry," he muttered, going after her mouth again. He thumbed her nipple into prominence, tasted the inside of her mouth and pulled her very willing tongue into his mouth, crushing her against him hard enough to leave her breathing labored. His lips slipped from her mouth to her neck. "I'm not sorry," he whispered. "God, Gerri, I miss you."

"I hate you," she said.

"Fine," he said, going back to her mouth, his hand slipping from her breast to her butt to pull her hard against him. He was erect and ready and for a split second, knowing he was out of his mind, he hoped it wasn't just another erection that would prove meaningless. "Go ahead and hate me," he said still kissing her. She bit his lip. "Ah!" he shouted, pulling back, two fingers going straight to his lip.

He stared down into her eyes, now tearless but bright. They were glittering with rage or maybe something else. He felt her hands at his waistband and she gave a powerful tear, ripping the zipper open, possibly breaking it.

"Okay, then," he said, going after her mouth again, covering it in a passionate kiss that left little doubt where they were headed. He felt her hand snake down the waist of his shorts and grab hold of him. "Be very careful, Gerri," he whispered in warning, and for a breathless moment, he was afraid of what she might do with that special member in her hand. There had been a constant subtext to all her bitching that she'd like to see it yanked off. But she stroked him firmly, lovingly and he couldn't suppress a deep groan of pleasure. Her other hand slipped up his chest, running over his pecs, finding a nipple and stimulating it into a hard little pebble.

"You make me furious," she said against his open mouth. He couldn't make any fast moves. She had him at a disadvantage; she was in control of his favorite organ.

With great care, he pulled her hand out of his pants and once he was free, he whirled her around and pressed her up against the door. "You're really full of the devil this morning, aren't you?" he asked. Holding her against the door with the full length of his body, he slipped his hands under her shirt and captured her breasts, one in each hand. He kissed her again, feeling her hands run up and down his back, her breathing fast, response, sweet response in her kiss. He locked his hands onto the hem of her shirt and pulled it up in one fast motion, bringing it over her head and off her arms, leaving her bare. He bent his head to her breast.

"Don't hurt me," she whispered.

He lifted his head and looked down into her eyes. "I've never hurt you," he said. "You've never once been afraid of me." Then he continued, bending to her breast, teasing a nipple with his tongue, sucking gently. He heard the sound of her head dropping back against the guesthouse door, then the sound of her desire, a low, delicious moan. Her fingers were running through his hair, holding his head against her breast.

He found the snap on her jeans with his hands and opened them, quickly but much more gently than her performance on his pants. He put his hands on her hips under the jeans and began to slide them down, but she had her legs locked together tight and the jeans wouldn't move. He pushed down again—nothing. He rose to her lips, kissed her lightly once, twice, then said, "Give 'em up, Gerri."

"This is a bad idea," she said. "I'm mad at you. Very, very mad."

"So what? I'm a little pissed off myself. Give 'em up, come on."

The tension came out of her thighs and she relaxed her legs just enough so he could push her jeans down. When they were around her ankles she kicked them off and her hands went to his hips. She pushed his trousers down and he stepped out of them easily. They were both naked, pressed up against the door, the first time anything like this had happened in months. Maybe years…

"This isn't going to change anything," she said.

"It could change two things," he said, his voice husky and low. "One for you. One for me."

"I don't feel like it," she said sullenly.

And he laughed. "Cooperate and you just might."

"You're about the last person I feel like cooperating with," she said, but she held him close just the same.

"Maybe, but I'm the only one standing here naked with you, jabbing you with the best of intentions." He tongued her lips, she nibbled at his. "I think rage is an aphrodisiac for you, Gerri. Oh, God, you feel so good." His hand crept lower, slipped down over her pubis, probing. She tensed, but he pushed gently onward until she relaxed. He covered her lips hungrily while slipping his hand into that dark, secret place—no secret to him. He'd been here before, but it had been a long time. He met with slick folds. She could fool herself, but not him. This woman was his woman, and although the past ten years had been too void of this intimacy, it wasn't as though he'd forgotten the passion they were capable of sharing. He stroked, gently at first, then harder, his mouth on her mouth, her groans of pleasure echoing inside him, her knees buckling from time to time. He ran a hand down over her hip, down the back of her thigh to the back of her knee and brought it up again.

"God, oh, God," she whispered hoarsely. She'd never been quiet—never quiet, not in general or during sex. It made him smile. "God," she said again, her pelvis rocking toward him.

"You going to let me in?" he asked in a whisper.

"I don't know," she said. But she did know. She devoured his mouth wildly, hanging on to him as if she feared losing him.

With both hands on her butt, he lifted her just enough

to make entry, slowly, carefully. They might as well have been back fifteen years in time. She guided him in easily and he pulled her other leg up. And then he rocked his hips against her, pushing her against the door, making her moan and grab him even more desperately. She held on around his neck while he held her clear of the floor. And with each thrust she moaned and clung to him.

Phil thought the beauty of a long marriage was knowing what your woman likes. He held her against him, legs around his hips, and backed toward the bed, falling with her onto the rumpled coverlet and scattered newspapers, leaving her on top. She liked being on top; she liked the control. Gerri immediately pushed him back onto the mess of papers and leaned down to his mouth, which he took hungrily, his hands all over her. "I love you," he whispered. "I love you so much."

"Sometimes you make me so mad," she whispered back, kissing him deeply, passionately.

He laughed low in his throat, not giving up her lips. His hands ran down to her butt, grabbing her, hanging on while she moved on him. "Do your worst. You hate me as hard as you want," he said. She moaned, grabbed his lower lip between hers and rocked on him with a vengeance. She held his head in both hands, holding his mouth against hers and then it happened fast. She felt as if she'd burst into flames, exploded from within, drowning him with wet spasms so hot and powerful he gasped and just held on for dear life. She put her hands on his shoulders and arched her back, making a noise that was at once sheer pleasure and profound relief.

Phil seized the moment, pumped his hips a few times and joined her, pulsing into physical exhaustion. And

when she crumpled against him, he put his arms around
her and held her close, tenderly, gratefully, waiting for
their rapid breathing to slow, their heart rates to return to normal. Her head rested against his shoulder.
His hands gently stroked her back. He had only one
thought. *That was so sweet—please, God, no more
fighting, please.*

Gerri was spent. It was as though her bones had
turned fluid. She was limp, satisfied, completely subdued. After a few moments of recovery, she gently
rolled away from him, lying atop the collection of
newspapers. She put the back of her hand against her
forehead. "Phew. I wasn't prepared for that! That was
bizarre."

"That's not the word I would have used," Phil said,
his voice reflecting the weakness of postcoital bliss.

She laughed. "Just out of curiosity, give me a word."

"How about *awesome?* Can we go with *awesome?*"

She turned onto her side, propped herself up on an
elbow, and looked at him. "Did you have that kind of
sex with *her?*"

"Gerri, I haven't had that kind of sex with anyone.
Including *you!* You bit me, you used me, you screwed
my brains out. I was terrified of what you were going
to do when you had your hand around me. You went
completely wild. Out of your mind."

"Aw," she said, smiling at him. "I'm so sorry. I won't
let that happen again."

He stroked her arm. "It's okay, baby. You want to
hate me some more? I can live with that."

"You really screwed up, Phil. Even your mother
thinks so."

He shook his head. "My mother. Why did you have

to tell her? I've never before wished for a fatal heart attack."

"Do you really love me?"

"Baby, I love you so much. I've missed you so much. It's been torture, having you hate me. Except of course, today." He grinned at her. Then he became serious. "Gerri, I want to come home. I'll do whatever you want. I won't run for D.A. I'll tell everyone it's my decision and has nothing to do with you."

"Of course you'll run," she said. "I've been working toward this for as long as you have. I've listened to a million closing arguments. We've worked for this together, we'll run together."

"I don't want you to feel pushed into this."

"Just how expensive is this guesthouse?" she asked.

"Too expensive. Why?"

She shrugged. "Maybe we should keep it." Then she grinned. "Nice little hideaway for Sunday mornings. And other times."

"We could get a sailboat for about the same price."

"Can you do other things on a sailboat besides… sail?"

"Oh, yeah. Are you letting me come home?"

"I need time to think clearly. I think I should see my gynecologist. I think she might've given me an overdose."

"The hormones? Could your health be compromised?" he asked.

"I think I should at least ask— I haven't acted like that since I was thirty-five. God, how awful." She flopped on her back.

"Not awful," he said. "If there's no danger to your

health, don't be hasty. We can work with this," he said with a grin.

"Here I am, barely out of bed, looking like the wrath of God, and—"

"You're beautiful." He turned on his side and raised himself up, looking down at her. "You've never known that about yourself. You're beautiful. And you weren't wearing underwear."

"Um…I was in a hurry. I read that op-ed piece and just saw red—it took me completely by surprise. How the heck did this happen?"

"Who cares?" Phil said. Then he sobered. "But I'm not having any more affairs. I hope to God that didn't light a fire under you. Because I'm not…"

"Okay, give it a rest. I believe you. I'm going to watch you, though."

"Fine. Watch." He ran a finger around her hairline. "Your hair is all goofy."

"That's very complimentary, Phil."

"I love it goofy." His hand dropped and fell to her naked breast. "Let me come home. Please."

Gerri took a deep breath. "It's Sunday. How about Friday night? Then we'll have the weekend to talk to the kids, give them a chance to absorb another change, let them ask questions, you know. We're going to have to explain the election. Tell your committee that we'll announce in a week, once your family is on board."

"Are we back together? Are we okay now?" he asked.

"Almost, Phil," she said, getting off the bed. "We're going to have to make some adjustments—but I think we can work on things under the same roof. At least I believe we can make it now. And I started thinking that before this morning, but…" She stopped talking and started to laugh. She picked up a section of newspaper and showed it to him. "Oh, dear. Look at this. I left a little mess on Carter's face. Do you think that's an omen?"

fourteen

Gerri took a sick day from work—something she did as rarely as possible. It was more than just her work ethic, though no one worked harder. It was about her clients, those she was charged to serve. If she was using a work day for her own personal needs, it could mean someone wasn't getting all she had to give.

But today she had no choice. She couldn't allow Phil to come back home until she took care of a few things. She knew she wouldn't be able to look him in the eye and lie. She had to keep a secret from him, and she was achingly aware of the hypocrisy, since she'd been so angry that he'd withheld something important from her. But this was about saving her marriage and protecting her family. Elections were brutal. If her marriage was going to survive it, if her children were going to be safe through it, she had some behind-the-scenes work to do. Work that Phil wouldn't approve of.

The first task involved Kelly, Phil's administrative assistant and the woman who had delivered the news that had separated them for over three months.

When she entered Phil's office building in San

Francisco for the first time since that fateful day, she suddenly felt her chest swell with pride. She hadn't expected that—but there it was. Her husband was going to be the new D.A. And she had helped him all along the way. Oh, she was hardly the woman behind the man— she was the woman beside the man. She had listened to almost every opening and closing argument he'd ever prepared. She critiqued him ruthlessly, and he listened raptly, taking her advice. She counseled him on dealing with juvenile victims and defendants, and he'd have been lost without her. She was as much his professional partner as his marital partner.

She rode the elevator up to the eleventh floor to Phil's office, but she glanced at the button for the sixteenth. She knew it had a view of the bay, Alcatraz and the Golden Gate Bridge—it would be Phil's office soon. She was certain.

When she got off the elevator, there was the usual bustle of people scurrying around. A young associate glanced up and recognized her. "Morning, Mrs. Gilbert," he said very quickly before moving down the hall.

When she approached Phil's office, the receptionist perked up. "Morning, Mrs. Gilbert. Mr. Gilbert is in court this morning."

"I know, Cathy. I thought I'd say hello to Kelly since I'm in the building," Gerri said with a smile.

"Oh. Sure," Cathy said.

Gerri pushed open the door and entered an austere but elegant outer office. Kelly was facing her computer screen and glanced up at Gerri. She actually jumped in surprise. Then she quickly collected herself. "Gerri," she said cheerfully. "What a surprise. Phil's in court this morning…"

"I know," Gerri said. "I thought maybe you and I could have a minute. Or ten," she amended. Then she shrugged, smiled. "Maybe fifteen?"

"Sure," Kelly said a little nervously. "Of course. How have you been?"

"Separated," Gerri said. "And angry! Oh, you have no idea how angry I was with Phil. But I think I've moved past most of that now."

"Gerri, I…"

"You and I—we might have one or two little shit piles to clean up. But let me start by saying you didn't do anything wrong so I won't accept your guilt or remorse. Are we clear on that?"

"Yes, ma'am." Kelly nearly whimpered, dropping her gaze.

"Ma'am? Oh, Jesus, this might take longer than fifteen minutes if you're going to play the subordinate here," Gerri said. Kelly looked up and saw that Gerri had a smile on her face and looked at her with kind eyes.

"So," Kelly said. "You've been angry, huh?"

"It's been a rocky ride, Kelly. But we're getting back together."

Gerri watched as Kelly let out her breath in obvious relief. "I wanted to call you," Kelly said. "I wanted to call you so badly to apologize. I feel like I did this to you! But Phil said it would be a mistake."

"It would've been a mistake," Gerri agreed with a nod. "There was a lot of information to process, and before you get all paranoid—it wasn't information about your role. In fact, your part in all of it was minor and not even relevant in the big picture."

"Still…I'm so sorry. I got all the wrong signals."

"I can see how that could happen. I'm so flip sometimes. I make smart-ass comments, shoot for humor and miss, try to seem like one of the girls, a regular person with all the typical marital stuff going on—because I *am*. But you had no way to know what I really meant. You weren't in a good spot to understand."

"That's really generous of you to say."

"Kelly, are you and John okay? Did you get anything resolved?"

"Yes, ma—" She stopped herself. "Yes. He thought he was going to get laid off, but didn't want to tell me. He was busy putting out feelers for jobs, thus the dressing up for work. When I pushed him to go to counseling, he told me everything. The layoff didn't come—it was an unfortunate number of other people."

"Phew," Gerri said. "I'm sorry about the other people, glad John's okay. Things are better now?"

"Well, it's been stressful during the downsizing, but he's talking to me again and relying on me like he used to. I'm not worried anymore, just sorry for him that he has to go through it. But—we have my job, my benefits. We sat down and figured out how things would be all right even in the worst case. And we don't have to deal with the worst-case scenario right now, so we're better than we were."

"I'm glad to hear that."

"So, you and Phil?" she asked.

"It's been a revelation," Gerri said. "Things have been coming out that we put on the back burner for years, thinking they were unimportant concerns or we'd figure them out later. We both had our issues. But there's one thing that seems to supersede all the crap—we're a very good team. In all ways. That's very nice to know. Comforting."

Kelly smiled. "You are a great team."

"He's going to move home this weekend. Has he said anything to you?"

She shook her head. "He's very private. I didn't know you were separated for about a month."

"That doesn't surprise me." Gerri laughed. "Well, are we okay? You and me? Because I don't want you worrying about it. And for God's sake, I can't have you calling me ma'am! I feel old enough!"

"You're not old," Kelly said. "You're perfect. I think everyone wants to be like you."

"Please," Gerri said. "No sucking up. You're completely free and clear."

"I'm not sucking up! I'm telling the truth! You're one of the most admired women I know!"

"Okay," Gerri said, waving her off. "Thanks for that. But there's one thing I need your help with. The future of my marriage depends on it. I'm counting on you, Kelly. As my friend, as a woman, as my husband's closest confidant."

Kelly leaned toward her. "What?" she asked with a posture and expression that said she'd do anything.

"I need to know who she is and where she is."

Kelly sat back looking paralyzed with terror. It took her a long time to find her voice. Then she shook her head. "You realize that he never told anyone? That people suspected because they got along so well, but no one knew for sure? Even I didn't know! I guessed!"

"Yes, you did *know*," Gerri said with a smile. "Maybe you didn't know because of Phil—but you knew because of her."

"How can you say that?"

"Because I'm a genius." Gerri laughed. "Because I

read *Cosmopolitan* in the bathroom. She would need an ally. Who else would she choose? You take care of his professional life and she was a professional acquaintance. Oh, God," Gerri said, feigning shock. "She wasn't a hooker was she?"

"No!" Kelly shot back, coming out of her chair a little.

Gerri sat back and smiled. "Kelly, help me. I'm not going to do anything bad. I won't be visiting my wrath on her—it's Phil who pissed me off, not her. I just can't move on until I know the woman my husband would choose over me."

"But are you so sure he did that? I mean, maybe it wasn't a choice at all, but just some stupid…man thing! Because it was there!"

"I have to see her. You know her name, I know you do. You know where she is, I bet. You take care of things Phil wouldn't even think to ask you to take care of—because you're the best thing that ever happened to him. After me, of course," she added, grinning. Then the grin faded. "Tell me what you know, please. Woman to woman. I swear to God, he will never know. This isn't about Phil, not really. It's about protecting my family."

"I can't," she said, shaking her head miserably. "It would be such a breach…."

"Well, weigh this in your decision—the election committee is going to get the name so they can interview her and check her out to make sure she isn't going to disrupt his campaign. Now, does that seem fair? I just want to know who I was up against before something like that goes public."

Kelly's eyes flashed for a second. "I really can't see what good—"

"Oh, yes, you can," Gerri said. "I'm going to campaign with Phil, for him. I'm going to be standing in front of political support groups, probably women, and someone is going to ask me about her. You wouldn't want me to explain his affair is in the past when the Madam X being referred to is his dry cleaner. Or—maybe when I say I don't know who they're talking about, they'll tell me. Publicly. And then the newspapers will get it…"

"No," Kelly said, shaking her head. "No one knows anything. There was conjecture, but no one——"

"What do you think campaigns work on besides conjecture? Besides, someone knows, Kelly. I'll tell you why—she loved him, that's why. And he didn't love her back enough to make a life with her. It was two years, did you know that? It was on and off for two years—an eternity in a single woman's life. She cried to someone—an old college girlfriend, a sister, a neighbor. She cried about how much he meant to her, about the times they were together…"

"I can't imagine that Phil would mislead anyone, Gerri."

"You're right," she agreed. "He wouldn't. He's honest and he's decent and because of that he needs to be the new D.A. But he's also kind and tender, and even if he didn't make promises, I'm sure he would have treated her with care, dignity and chivalry so that she felt she just couldn't live without him. It's the way he is, Kelly. He's a gentleman. And a thinking woman would risk almost anything to have a man like him."

A funny, irreverent, brilliant gentleman, Gerri thought. A powerful lover, even at fifty-three. What woman wouldn't want him? She shook her head and laughed to herself. "And that's why he won't tell me who she is. In a way he's still taking care of her in the only way he can."

"Listen," Kelly said pleadingly. "I never knew anything, all right? I liked her—she's a nice person, but I don't think I was an ally. She was friendly to me—but they all are. I have the boss's ear; only a fool would be distant or rude. But with her—they got along, they worked well together. I heard some gossip and I blew it off as ridiculous because of the way you two are, the way he was about his marriage, his family. It wasn't until about six months before she left the prosecutor's office that I began to wonder because…" She took a breath. "Because he seemed to suddenly not notice she was around. He avoided her. As though they'd had a falling out of some kind, and you can't have a falling out unless…"

"Unless you were lovers," Gerri finished for her.

"She never confided in me. Never. And of course, Phil wouldn't say anything. But she left and then…"

"Then what, Kelly?" Gerri pushed.

"She tried to reach him. Okay—you have to believe this because it's true. I have to clean up after Phil a lot—he's too busy to keep track of every detail. Important papers get overlooked, emails get deleted by accident, stuff goes out that isn't ready. I screen his mail, I proof, I shred, I file and sort."

Just lay it on me, Gerri thought. *Hurry up and give it to me.*

"She sent him cards. They were thrown away unopened. I was looking through deleted emails and there were several from her, deleted unread. I finally braved asking him if that was a mistake and he barked at me that if he put it in the trash or deleted it, it was something he didn't want—so I never asked again. A few years ago she got in touch with me and said she wanted the office to know her current address and phone number. The *office,* she said—not Phil. I passed that along to Phil—just as an aside to regular business—and he very pleasantly said he had a detective unit assigned to this office and if there was ever anyone he wanted to find, he couldn't foresee a problem." Kelly's expression was pleading. "She sent a few emails to me, asking about the office and staff, never mentioning Phil—but I suspected it was meant to keep a connection alive, at least for a while. I responded that everyone was well, also without mentioning Phil."

He couldn't let a woman get that close and then dismiss her cruelly. Gerri knew her husband too well, she'd seen him in action—when he was pestered or pursued, he made polite excuses, avoided with finesse. It took a lot for him to lose patience, to harden up, to say, 'Stop bothering me!' The cards and emails suggested he'd had to say *it's over* more than once. Finally, he simply stopped responding.

"I'll need that last updated address and phone number," Gerri said firmly.

"I don't know if I can let myself do it, Gerri," Kelly said, shaking her head.

"It won't be better for her to have her first confrontation with the election committee—they're brutal. Half the time I suspect they so anger and terrorize the subject, she's pushed into making a stir. No, it would be better to come from me."

"What are you planning to tell her?" she asked nervously.

Gerri shrugged. "That I know about her. That he's running for office. Beyond that, I'm not really sure. But I'm not angry with her, Kelly."

"I don't think she's the enemy," Kelly said. "And I'm pretty sure Phil is going to fire me for this."

Gerri shook her head. "I'm certainly not going to tell anyone how I found her. And if he's not opening mail from her or taking her calls, he'll never know even if she wants to tell him. I can get what I want, Kelly. I can hold the election committee's feet to the fire—one little threat and they'll tell me anything. But we shouldn't do it that way. The fewer people brought into this, the better. I just want the facts. Not for the election. For my relationship with Phil, which is more important. And before the mystery woman is revealed publicly and my children are hurt. I have to protect Phil, my marriage and my family. Honey, I have to get this fixed. Trust me. Please."

Kelly sat stone still for a long moment. Then she turned to her computer, pulled up a file, scrolled through it until she highlighted a name. She pressed print and a page came out of the printer. She handed it to Gerri. It held the name of a law firm with address, phone number and a woman's name. *Elizabeth Hensley.*

Gerri didn't recognize the name, but that didn't surprise her. "What does she do?" Gerri asked.

"I'm done talking about her," Kelly said. "Please don't do anything that will…" Her sentence trailed off, unfinished.

"That will hurt her? Hurt Phil?" Gerri asked.

"Hurt anyone," Kelly said. "It was too bad, that anything happened. Nothing more should happen."

Gerri nodded. "Nothing more will. If you feel some

kind of bond with her, you can warn her—I really don't care."

"I feel the bond with you and Phil," Kelly said. "If I'd treated it more carefully, we'd still have it."

"We still have it, Kelly. It's all over now. You can consider this matter closed."

Gerri stood in the foyer of the government building, staring at the piece of paper that bore the woman's name and a San Francisco business address. *Right here in the city.* The very first thing she wondered was whether they ever ran into each other. This woman would know where employees from the prosecutor's office liked to take lunch, meet for a drink after work. All connected groups in big cities had their favorite haunts.

She took the trolley to the other side of the city and once she was in the general vicinity, hailed a cab to find the exact address. She ended up in front of a rather run-down office building and her immediate thought was, *that brute!* It was easy for Gerri to identify with the psyche of a woman wronged—a mistress, run out of the prosecutor's office, left to find a job anywhere she could.

But she knew Phil would never, under any circumstances, run off an innocent woman. He'd liked her. He became involved.

Gerri asked the cabdriver to wait. If Elizabeth Hensley wasn't there, she'd leave the area and contact her by phone, try to persuade her to meet. Gerri went into the building and studied a wall-mounted marquee, finding the name of the law firm. She walked up the stairs to the second floor, let herself into a crowded waiting room and the recognition was instant. A woman in her forties stood behind the glass-enclosed receptionist's area reading from a large sheaf of papers. Gerri looked at her just as she lifted her head and looked at Gerri.

Gerri remembered her, though vaguely. She'd seen her around the prosecutor's office, but couldn't remember ever being introduced, and she had no idea in what capacity the woman had worked.

The expression on Elizabeth's face was one of pure shock. Gerri watched as she slowly closed her mouth. Gerri tried out a smile she wasn't quite feeling, then stepped toward the reception window just as Elizabeth came forward to meet her there. Elizabeth slid the glass open.

"I hope you can take a break," Gerri said. "I really want to talk to you."

"I have a full schedule," she said somewhat nervously. "Can I ask what this is about?"

"It's about Phil, and it's very important. I can see you're busy. Cancel for an emergency. This one time only."

After only a brief consideration, Elizabeth gave a nod and slid the window closed. While she turned and spoke to some people, passing off paperwork, Gerri stepped out of the waiting room into the hall outside the office.

Gerri had been completely unprepared for this. Where was the fluffy, big-breasted blonde she had envisioned? Elizabeth Hensley was attractive in an unremarkable way. Tall, slender, somewhere around Gerri's age. Her short dark hair was threaded with some very flattering silver. She was dressed conservatively, wearing stylish glasses that gave her arched brows and dark eyes prominence. Gerri's first impression was that she looked smart and poised.

Gerri realized she wasn't quite prepared to deal with a real human being. She had expected a much younger woman, no more than thirty-five. In her original rage, she'd assumed she was twenty-five and an idiot. Perhaps a lawyer, but still an airhead. Someone who had the total effect of setting Phil's hormones on fire, leaving him helpless because of testosterone poisoning. After all, men were only men. And everyone knew where their brains were stored.

The office door opened and Elizabeth stepped into the hall. "Is Phil all right?" she asked.

"He's fine," Gerri said. Then she stuck out her hand. "Gerri Gilbert."

Elizabeth shook her hand. "Actually, we met. Quite a long time ago."

"I wondered. I recognized you, but not the name. Listen, you have nothing to worry about. I'm not some crazy woman. Well, I am crazy most of the time, but today I'm feeling very stable and in control. There's a lot going on with Phil's career right now and you're eventually going to become a part of it all. Let's you and I sit down and talk. Please?"

"I saw the paper. It says he's running."

"So it says. I have a cab waiting. Let me buy you lunch."

Elizabeth laughed nervously. "Under the circumstances, shouldn't I pay for lunch and the cab?"

Gerri smiled. *This isn't going to be easy,* she thought. *I already like her!* "It's my pleasure," Gerri said. "I think I'm going to regret we'll only do this once."

Elizabeth laughed again, cutting the tension. "I would have expected something like that from you," she said. "You've already out-classed me."

"Let's take the stairs," Gerri said, moving in that direction. "You have me at a disadvantage, I see. I know nothing about you. Absolutely nothing."

"Yet you found me."

"I can play hard ball when I have to—but I didn't find you through Phil. In fact, I have no plans to tell him about this." When they reached the cab Gerri said, "Recommend the closest place that's fairly quiet and has good wine. Consider this a special occasion, the cost doesn't matter."

Elizabeth directed the cabdriver to a small Italian bistro. It was only a matter of six or seven blocks and while it didn't take them out of that poor section of town, it was charming and comfortable. There were quite a few people already dining who were far better dressed than the clientele in Elizabeth's office, but it was quiet enough that they could talk freely without being overheard. The waiter was at their table when they were barely settled and Gerri quickly ordered wine, hoping she wouldn't guzzle it desperately.

"So," Gerri opened. "Did you have any warning I was coming?"

Elizabeth shook her head. "I wouldn't have looked so shocked had I known. You took me by surprise. Well—it's finally happening. He's running?"

"He is. And I'm afraid the election committee has some nerves about you and your…relationship. They'll probably be in touch. They might be invasive and rude. I'm sorry—I can't do anything about that."

"I know. I always knew," she said. "It was an issue."

"It was?"

"Of course. Your husband has a public life. It comes with the territory."

"Right," Gerri said. "I thought it best, the warning coming from me. At some point I'm going to be asked about you."

She shook her head. "There shouldn't be any panic there. I can honestly say he was my boss for a while and we eventually became friends, but I haven't spoken to him in years."

"He told me everything," Gerri said.

The wine arrived, as if it had been an emergency order. Gerri quickly and perfunctorily ordered an Italian salad without even glancing at a menu and Elizabeth did the same. This meeting wasn't about food. And then, cautiously Elizabeth said, "I think you'd better be more specific."

Gerri took a calming breath. "I'm not trying to trick you into telling me secret things. I heard about it accidentally. I confronted him and he told me he'd had an affair, on and off for two years. That it had been over for five. Does that mesh with your memory?"

Elizabeth sipped her wine. "Perfectly," she said. "He said he'd do that. That if it got out, he wouldn't lie to you. He's a terrible liar. Oh, he can evade and hedge and redirect, he's brilliant at it in court, but when confronted with an absolute, he just can't lie. He's been pursuing the truth for too long. I guess it's his destiny." She put the glass down. "How'd it get out? I never told anyone. And I can't believe he did."

"Someone in the office made an assumption, not based on actual knowledge," Gerri said. "Really, if he'd exerted the slightest effort, he could have talked his way out of it." She took a big gulp of wine. "Listen," she said. "I was unprepared for you. I was looking for a young, sexy, big-breasted nymphomaniac who held the delusion that prosecutors actually made money...."

This time the laugh that escaped through Elizabeth's bright smile was spontaneous. "Are you saying I'm a disappointment?"

Gerri thought this might be a two-glass lunch. "Yes, actually. You're much too real. Much too competitive."

"There was never any competition," Elizabeth said, shaking her head. "I had an affair with a tortured man. He hated himself the whole time. That's not exactly flattering."

"Are you making excuses? Lying to make me feel better?"

She picked up her glass and looked into it. "I wish," she said, without lifting her gaze.

"You must have been drawn to him for a reason."

"Wait a minute," Elizabeth said. "I was drawn to him for many reasons, but I don't care what he might've said, I didn't make a move. I swear to you. I probably sent out signals because I couldn't help it, but I never..."

"Relax," Gerri said. "He said that, too. He made the pass."

"And I apologize," Elizabeth said. "I was so enamored of him. I admired him. And it doesn't hurt that he's handsome and very, very smart. He has that power aura, yet he's kind and humble. It was lethal for me. But I never thought I would get in another woman's territory."

"Then why?" Gerri asked, leaning forward.

"Put simply, I hadn't had a man in my life for years. Literally, years. I married young, had children young, got a divorce young and my degree came late. My kids are now twenty-four and twenty-six. I was alone—the kids were with their dad or in college while I was finishing school—I'd been completely uninvolved for a long time. And Phil is a wonderful guy. Surely you know that—you're still together."

"We're barely back together. Both still trying to understand what happened"

"There's not much to understand," Elizabeth said. "He loved you so much, I couldn't even put a dent in the armor around your marriage. I'm not proud of it, but I tried, believe me. I'd have taken him with all the baggage in a heartbeat. But he was committed, which put curious doubt on what was happening with us."

No, it doesn't, Gerri thought. And then she strangely found herself wearing this woman's shoes for a moment. She felt terrible knowing he'd have sex with her and talk about Gerri and how devoted he was. "How do you know all that? About his commitment? About me?"

"We did more talking than anything else," Elizabeth said with a shrug. She took a sip of her wine. "I asked him questions about you— You aren't the only one trying to understand. He'd answer superficially, giving very little information, but the real stuff came out when he was explaining, numerous times, why we could only be casual friends or not at all because he'd never leave you, he couldn't make it without you. He was in awe of you, your strength, how you managed your clientele, your family, your kids, him. He said that you could do your job without him but he could never keep up his position in the office without your support, without your input. He said you were the most amazing woman he'd ever known. I kept trying to get him to level with me—you couldn't be that perfect and have him fooling around with me. *Couldn't!* I kept searching for a crack in the porcelain. Instead, I had a man in my life—the first man in years—who loved someone else. It was a very lonely, hopeless time for me." She took another sip of wine. "I met you once in the office—I think one of the young A.D.A.'s introduced us and you were nice but—"

"Just a regular person?"

She sighed. "I hated you, but I was sorry I'd never get a chance to find out just how incredible you are."

"It's all bullshit," Gerri said. "The only thing incredible about me is that I hung in there with a man who worked horrible hours under ever worse pressure for miserable pay—and I was interested enough in his work to be his best audience. There was no discipline involved. I was really interested. His caseload mirrored mine in many ways."

With precision timing their salads arrived. Gerri took one small bite. "Where are you in your life now? With work? With men?" she asked.

Elizabeth smiled. "I'm seeing someone. I don't know where it's going, but he's a good man and I admire him. I'm happy with him. And as for work, I do what I love to do."

"And what do you do?"

"You don't know?"

"I know nothing but your phone number and business address. Trust me."

"I'm an attorney. I was doing an internship at the prosecutor's office while waiting to take the bar exam, then briefly after passing the bar. I specialize in guardian ad litem for children without representation. There's not much money in it, but it's my calling."

Children at risk, Gerri thought. Then she took another look at Elizabeth and thought, *Oh, my God, she's me!* Phil had an affair with a woman enough like Gerri to be her sister—same height, approximate weight, age, short hair, career field.

"We have a lot in common," Gerri said. She tried to sound casual.

"You're just getting that?"

"I'm just getting that," Gerri said a little weakly. "God." She concentrated on her salad for a moment, thinking. She looked up. "Do people call you Elizabeth?"

"No. Liz. My dad still calls me Lizzy. Only Phil called me Elizabeth."

Gerri smiled, took another bite of salad. "You're under no obligation to answer this," she said with great trepidation, "but if I'd come here to tell you we were divorcing, would you get back in touch with him?"

"No," Elizabeth said easily. "He made it pretty clear he doesn't want to hear from me. And if he did want to reach me, he could find a way. I think I've finally passed that place in my life. I realized I'd never be what he wanted, but was as close as he could get, and to my utter embarrassment, that was good enough for me. Listen," she said, "you're asking all the personal questions here. Do you have any idea why your husband had an affair?"

"I'm starting to, yes," Gerri said. She felt her eyes begin to mist and willed herself not to get emotional. "Neither of us is quite sure what changed or exactly when, but there are certain events, some markers that—" She took another sip of wine before continuing. "Well, nine years ago both my parents died in the same year. Long, slow, painful deaths ending with hospice care. I'm sure I was depressed for at least a year after that. It took a toll on our lives." Suddenly Gerri could see how their drifting apart started. Phil was exhausted from carrying almost the whole load for a couple of years. Gerri was whipped by personal tragedy, weak and dysfunctional.

"Oh, God, I'm so sorry," Elizabeth said. "I'd be lost without my mom and dad."

"Well, I think I came out of the depression, but I might not have come all the way back," Gerri said. *Life held less joy, less spontaneity, less sexual hunger.* "I had no idea, of course," she said, smiling at Elizabeth, who seemed oddly like a friend. "As Phil puts it—everything about us became keeping the boat afloat. We've always been a functional team—we could really get the job done. That's the beauty and the problem. So much about us has always worked. I had no idea there were gaping holes. I thought we were doing so well under the circumstances. Better than most couples. If I had no idea things were missing, I guess it's reasonable that he didn't understand it, either."

"I think you can rest easy on that," Elizabeth said. She reached across the table and covered Gerri's hand with hers. "I don't think Phil had the first idea why he was involved with me. And his involvement was not as physical as you might think. But, he was like a man who couldn't help himself, a man confused by his own actions. I loved him, but he loved you and only you. The whole time. And yet, he was searching for something."

Gerri could have explained it to her, but she demurred. Phil was looking for intimacy with someone to whom he'd been deeply bonded, his best friend for over twenty years. He wanted to reconnect, to be as one with his mate. *It wasn't just the sex,* she thought with some relief, some sadness. Gerri had been emotionally unavailable, not just sexually unavailable. She couldn't have gotten through those two years without him and she was unsure how much longer she'd been numbed by loneliness—she was an only child who missed her parents so much. Phil had been completely there for her, but the truth was, she hadn't been there for him at all. She couldn't because she was worn-out and empty inside. He might've wanted the sex at that time in his life, but what he *needed* was his partner back, all of her. He wanted to give her all of himself, but she just hadn't been present.

She wouldn't ask, but she was sure he couldn't stand in the bathroom naked with Elizabeth and talk about the stock market, or the carpool schedule, or the op-ed columns. You have to be best friends and lovers. He couldn't give up the friendship any more than she could. He thought he could fill the gap, but it didn't work for him.

"God, I'm almost sorry for you," Gerri said. "Shouldn't I hate you for taking advantage of our problems?"

"You should probably hate me for hoping he'd find what he was searching for with me. But I guess we were all subject to circumstances we didn't understand. In my defense, I knew so much about you, yet he never mentioned your parents' deaths. I don't think either you or Phil put all those things together, so how could I?" She was becoming a little emotional. "Oh, how I wished I could have what you had—a man that committed. I know," she said with a wave of her hand, "you could argue he wasn't that committed, given the events. But he *was*. Which is why I moved on and you're trying to put things together."

"But was he at least good to you?" Gerri asked.

"He's a remarkable man. I considered him good to me, and then he tried very hard to let me down easy." She smiled warmly. "In case you're concerned, he never bought me gifts or—"

"I'm not worried," Gerri said, suddenly feeling irrationally sorry that Phil hadn't done anything special for Elizabeth.

"And you're not going to tell him we met?" Elizabeth asked.

"I'm going to do exactly as Phil has done," Gerri said. "I'm going to be honest with him. If he asks me, I'll tell him the truth. But if I know Phil, he won't ask." She shook her head and laughed lightly. "This is very bad," she said. "I think you're a good person. I think we could be good friends. Of course, it can't happen. We have to move on, but—"

"But in my life," Elizabeth said, smiling almost shyly, "I've never been paid a higher compliment."

Gerri Gilbert always thought the worst thing that could happen to her marriage was an affair, because she and Phil were different from other couples. Their bond went so deep that when friends and acquaintances went through marital rifts, they couldn't relate. And they'd seen some ugly ones.

One of the first was Andy and Rick. Their split had been both difficult and mystifying. Suddenly, Rick was unhappy. The testy arguments escalated, grew vicious. Gerri and Phil got right in there, got their hands dirty, tried to mediate from positions of professional skills and a solid marriage of their own. It seemed to come down to Rick being unhappy as a married man. He cited Andy as controlling and demanding, which certainly hadn't been the case until Rick became absent, distant, irritable, uninterested in sex. Gerri and Phil counseled, argued, begged them to get professional help—but it was clearly over. Rick moved out. He filed for divorce. He got engaged to the school nurse.

The stunning clarity of what had really happened hit Gerri almost as hard as it hit Andy—Rick had been unhappy in his marriage because he'd found someone new, someone he liked better. He stopped making love to his wife because another woman had already become his partner. The fights were a ruse, the dissatisfactions and shortcomings were all a spin on the facts. At the end of the day it had all come down to infidelity. In Rick's case, the other woman won.

"That gutless wonder!" Phil had stormed when he learned the truth. "If he'd been honest for one goddamn second, Andy would have known what she was fighting for! You know—I always knew that whole thing about freedom and space was a crock of shit! Men don't want space—they want to get laid!"

Was that when Phil decided that if it ever happened to him, he'd tell the truth? Give his marriage a fighting chance?

Now that the facts were in, years later, Rick had no regrets. And Andy was shed of a cheating husband and father who would abandon his own son. The years after Rick had been hard for Andy, but in the end she was finally with a man who loved her unselfishly and embraced with genuine acceptance and affection the boy who was suddenly fatherless. *What would Andy say now about regrets?*

There had been quite a few other nasty splits. People did unconscionable things to each other. One of Gerri's coworkers had come home from a business trip to find her house bare and her bank accounts empty, spouse missing. There was a couple in the neighborhood who had thundering fights and frequent separations, having actually been divorced and remarried to each other twice. Phil worked with a couple of men who had cheated, one had a child with another woman.

Sonja came to Gerri's mind. Her meltdown brought out an entirely new human being, stronger and healthier than the one before. But it was BJ who tipped the scales to the side of the truly catastrophic. She was the poster child for the worst-case scenario. The best that small family could hope for was survival, coping in the face of tragedy.

Relationships floundered—it was the rule rather than the exception. Some kicked and squirmed and fought right up to the death, some recovered. It was all in what you did, whether you created a break in the rope or a knot to hang on to.

Gerri actually enjoyed her long and revealing lunch with Elizabeth. It was a pity they couldn't do it again, but they both knew they couldn't. It would be their one and only meeting. Though she couldn't think of anything else she wanted to know from Elizabeth, certainly something would come to mind later, and she'd have to let it go. That part of their lives was now complete. Gerri was certain that even if she dropped dead that very evening, Phil wasn't ever going back to Elizabeth. He'd tried to fill the festering hole inside him, but it hadn't worked. It hadn't made him happy. No, if Gerri suddenly fell off the planet, Phil would carry on. But the next woman in his life would not be Elizabeth. Gerri had suffered pretty dramatically for a few months, but she now knew Phil had been torn up about what he'd done for a few years. The meeting with Elizabeth verified it. *It wasn't exactly flattering.*

On her way home, Gerri stopped off to see Joyce Arnold in her clinic.

"What are you doing here?" Joyce asked.

"I'm not sure about the hormones," Gerri whispered. "Can we talk somewhere private?"

"Sure," Joyce said, leaving her scheduled patients for a quick consult, leading the way to her office. "What's up?" she asked, sitting behind her cluttered desk.

"I wonder—is it possible I'm getting too much?"

"Any symptoms? Are you feeling all right? Why are you so concerned?"

"I feel fine, actually. But last weekend I went to Phil's little rented guesthouse to have a big fight with him, and I almost killed him with the wildest sex I've had in twenty years."

"Oh, *really,*" Joyce said, smiling mischievously. "And you think I did that to you?"

Gerri scooted forward. "Just how powerful is all that cream?" she asked.

Joyce laughed and shook her head. "It can kick start a dead battery, but after that you have to do all the driving." She grinned. "Things going better at your house or were you just slumming?"

"Cute," Gerri said.

"It's only partly the hormones, Gerri. I told you, if

you don't use it, you lose it. That seems to be the rule of thumb for most body systems, from muscles to brains. Most women, once they get reacquainted with their sex drive, don't use the testosterone cream anymore. If you think Phil's life is in danger, you could use a small amount every other night, but chances are it'll be something you keep in the back of the drawer for emergencies. How was the vagina? Scratchy? Sore?"

"Like old times," Gerri said with a shrug.

"Ah. Nice." Joyce stood up. "Stick with the estrogen and progesterone—it's a low dose and no reason you should flash and whimper and wail. Medically speaking, we're dealing with menopause much more intelligently these days." She shook her head and laughed. "What did I tell you about women in their fifties? They can really get a second wind."

"I'm not fifty! Yet."

"Well, then, Phil better look out! I take it he's still functioning?"

"Oh, yes. He's always been good at that."

"Well, that's a relief. But when and if he hits that predictable slump, we can deal with that, too."

"Every other ad on TV is about helping men get it up. Why aren't there ads for women?"

"I can't answer that," she said. "A lot of women don't want help, they just want to be set free. But you're right—we should educate each other a little better than we do." She smiled. "Welcome back. Enjoy yourself. Now, if you have no other concerns besides wild sex, I have patients waiting."

"Sure. Thanks for squeezing me in."

"You know, you actually look better. Hmm. I think

it's a draw between vitamin B12 and orgasms, which one puts more color in your cheeks."

On her way home from the doctor's office, Gerri went to the mall and bought all new underwear. *All* new. Some of it on the provocative side.

Gerri had gone to her bedroom at about eight, leaving Matt in the family room, hooked on his favorite television show. She took a long soak in the tub, relaxing in a way she felt she hadn't in years. She thought about the honest conversation she'd had with Joyce. At her doctor's appointments for the past ten or more years Joyce had asked questions about everything, including, "Sex still okay?"

And Gerri's response had always been the same. "Fine." Because she was fine with it. But she had never added the rest of the information. "We hardly ever have sex anymore." That would have sent up a flag. *I guess I was one of the women who just wanted to be set free.*

It was after nine when Gerri came out of her room wearing nice slacks and a crisply pressed blouse. Jed wasn't home from work yet, Jessie had a girlfriend over and they were giggling in the bedroom behind closed doors.

Gerri knocked on the door and when she opened it, the two girls were a little wild eyed and stirred up—looking guilty of something. "Are you doing bad things?"

"No!" both girls exclaimed.

"Hmm. I don't think I believe you. But I have to go out on a work call," she said. "I could be back in fifteen minutes or four hours, so don't try anything. You are not to go out. Understand?"

"Sure, Mom," Jessie said.

"I have my cell phone."

Matt was in the family room devouring a bag of Cheetos. "I have a call. Business. You okay here by yourself?" she asked.

"Isn't Jessica upstairs?" he asked without looking away from the TV.

"She is, but you're too old for a babysitter, so that leaves you on your own. You going to behave?"

"Yeah," he said.

"Don't wipe your orange fingers on the couch. I have my phone. I'll leave a note for Jed."

"Why bother?" Matt asked. "He has nookie-nookie with Tracy till two in the morning."

"Gross," she said, mimicking his typical response to suggestions of romance.

Five minutes later she pulled up to the guesthouse. When Phil opened the door, she walked into his arms, planting her lips on his. A moment of shock passed before his arms went around her and he fell into her kiss like a man who wanted to be drowned. Consumed. Without letting her go, without breaking their kiss, he pulled her inside and slammed the door, immediately pinning her against it, pressing her so solidly against the hard wood he could feel every curve of her body. And then his lips slid to her neck, his hands to her hips, rocking her against him.

"How'd you get free of the kids?" he asked hoarsely.

"I said I had a work call. It kind of feels like an emergency."

"I'm good with emergencies," he said.

"You were taking a big chance, you know," she whispered. He lifted his head. "Telling me you didn't want us to be how it was, but how it should be."

He ran fingers through the hair at her temple, his hand cradling the back of her head, bringing her mouth against his again for a deeper taste. "This isn't like you," he said.

"I want it to be," she answered.

"This isn't because…." His question trailed off and when he couldn't finish, he just kissed her again.

"Because what?" she asked, tugging his shirt out of his jeans.

"Because I asked for more of you?"

She laughed. "No. I've never been a good fake."

He started to unbutton her blouse while she ran her hands up under his shirt, and they kissed again, hard and hot, pressed together so tightly she could feel his excitement against her. She could almost feel the thundering climax building inside her. He opened her blouse and put his lips against the top of her breast above the line of her bra. Then with a finger, he pulled down the bra. "Hmm," he said. "New bra."

"New panties, too," she said, nibbling his ear.

"You're not afraid I'll have a heart attack and drop like a stone?"

"No." She laughed, sucking on his ear, using her fingers to deftly open his pants. He had the bra unhooked and his mouth against an erect nipple. "We definitely have to keep the guesthouse," she whispered, easing his zipper down. She slipped a hand past the waist of his boxers. "Or, at least the door."

fifteen

Bob wanted to make Andy a nice dinner in his home, something special. He made sure she knew that his sister-and brother-in-law were out of town for a long weekend, so there was no pressure to go visiting. He told her they wouldn't be disturbed. In fact, if they wanted to go for a late-night swim, they'd have the pool to themselves.

When Andy arrived, he fixed her a glass of wine and put out a little plate of cheese. There were wonderful smells coming from his compact kitchen. "You've gone to a lot of trouble," she said.

"I have." He smiled. "Except, it's only a casserole. The famous Uncle Bob casserole. A little of everything—a combination of chicken pot pie, shepherd's pie and burritos."

"Whoa," she said, laughing. "It actually sounds—disgusting!"

"Doesn't it? The kids love it. And the kids' kids love it."

"Can I stay the night?" she asked.

"Yes, you can." He smiled. "Or, if you miss your

bed, that's okay. Or if you want both of us to miss your bed, that works, too."

"You are so sweet."

"I have something for you. I was going to wait till after dinner, but I can't. Now, I want you to know that I don't presume anything. This isn't about pushing you, Andy. This is just about peace of mind."

"What is it?"

"Sit tight." He went to his bedroom and came back with a fat envelope. He handed it to her.

Andy looked at him while she opened it. She pulled out a thick sheaf of papers. She read the bold print on the top line. *Dissolution of Marriage.* "Bob?" she asked. "You got a divorce?"

"I called Wendy and told her we needed to finalize things. I promised her we'd always be good friends."

"But…why?"

"I just wanted to make sure you understand. I don't have any unfinished business. It doesn't mean I expect anything from you, but—the way I feel about you, I didn't want any legal connection to another woman, even if it's just been friendship for years. This had to be taken care of."

"Bob…" She gripped the documents and tears came to her eyes. "Oh, Bob."

"Oh, Andy, I didn't want to get you upset. Honest." He got down on one of his bad knees and pulled the pages from her so he could hold her hands. "It doesn't mean anything, honey. It's not like I expect anything. It's just—"

"My divorce isn't final yet."

"But it will be," Bob said. "At least you're getting it

done. I don't mean for me, but because it's really finished. Have you even heard from him, Andy?"

"Bryce? No, nothing. That's fine with me—but I'm sad he didn't even get in touch to ask about Noel. I know they had their problems but still."

"See—that's in your past, and you're bringing it to closure. Noel doesn't need Bryce, so don't worry about that. I thought I should bring closure to my situation, too. So you know there isn't anything lingering. It's just you. But, Andy, I'm not doing this so you feel obligated to me in any way. I did it to have it cleared up. There isn't anything on my slate right now. Just you, for as long as—"

"But what if we decide to get married someday, down the road, after we're sure we'll stay as happy as we are? Are you opposed to that idea, after Wendy? After I've failed at marriage twice?"

"Andy, my relationship with you doesn't bear any resemblance to what I had with Wendy. But you've been through a couple of rough marriages, so I understand that—"

"Bob, it's taken all the willpower I have not to ask you to move in with me," she said. "I've been just gutting it out because I know we have to give this some time. Those nights you do contract work and just go home to your own house so you can sleep fast and get up early? I hate those nights."

"Really?" he asked, surprised. "Really, you mean that?"

"I do. And I think because of my bad track record, to keep you safe, we have to wait a while. But the way I feel right now—I don't think I could possibly change my mind."

He was a little stunned for a moment. Then he took her into his arms and held her close. "Oh, Andy," he said breathlessly. "You just have no idea how happy it makes me to hear you say something like that. I think you're just plain crazy, but I love you so much."

"Thank you for doing this for me. Just for my peace of mind. It means a great deal."

He pulled back and grinned at her. "Want to go skinny dipping with a chubby old man?"

"I'd love to," she said. "You're sure no one's around?"

"I kind of wish there was a chance of that," he said with a laugh. "Even a security guard or something. They'd never believe it."

"The only thing that matters is that you believe it. Tell me, Bob. Do you believe what I tell you is genuine? Do you believe I love you? That I expect to love you forever?"

"I do, honey," he said. "I'm not even sorry it took me this long. If I'd known twenty years ago I was saving up for you, I'd have been more patient."

Gerri couldn't believe how much things had changed over the course of a few months. Phil moved home and his candidacy was announced. BJ told Andy her secret so that Sonja and Gerri wouldn't have to guard it for her. Bob was doing even less contract work and sleeping a little later in the morning. George and Sonja were friendly, spending more time together and it appeared the neighborhood might be falling into some sort of new order. What started out in March as three marriages was now one and a half if you counted Sonja's as the half, and it looked like it was only a matter of time before Andy and Bob made it official.

June evaporated like so much summer fog, July came and went, August arrived and signaled the end of a perfect summer. Sonja had a small pond installed in her backyard with a trickling fountain and fish. She stopped there. She was running with BJ every morning and on some days they did five miles, on rare days they did eight, just to see if they could do it. Sonja had the lean but muscular body of a runner and had signed up for a 10k race in San Francisco without BJ because BJ didn't want to commit.

As the end-of-summer block party approached, Sonja got up for her run with BJ but was stopped at the edge of her walk by the sight of a truck in front of BJ's house. She stared openmouthed as she saw a couple of guys carry a piece of furniture out of the house, onto the truck. "Oh, God," she said. "Oh, God. Oh, God."

She ran to Gerri's house and pounded on the door. Phil was up, showered and in his pants and shirt, almost but not quite ready for work. "Phil," Sonja said in a near cry. "Oh, Phil. Oh, God! Get Gerri! Please get Gerri!"

Phil instantly grabbed hold of Sonja's upper arms. "What is it? Are you okay?"

"No," she said, shaking her head. "My best friend— look!" She pointed down the street to what was obviously a moving truck, or at least a truck being used for moving.

Gerri appeared in the doorway, pulling on a ratty plaid robe over some black pajama pants that came to just below the knee. "What's going on?"

"Look!" Sonja said. "Look!"

"Oh, God, she said she'd have notice. This doesn't look like notice. Sonja, go get Andy up, right away. I'll get some shoes and meet you across the street."

Sonja jogged off in the direction of Andy's house while Gerri went back inside to grab a pair of flip-flops. As she made to follow her friend, Phil grabbed her arm and pulled her back to him. He held her briefly and closely against him, smiling against her lips. "Thanks," he said. "Sleeping with you is better than I remember it."

"I agree. And I think I should apologize for costing us so much time. I didn't know, Phil. I thought that's what happened after so many years of marriage."

"I know, honey. And I was afraid you were right."

"I'm sorry," she said, giving him a quick kiss. "I should never have left you out in the cold like that. I shouldn't have left myself alone like that."

"Tell you what—we don't have to go over what you did with those years if we can just forget about what I did."

"I think we understand each other now."

"I have to get to the office. Kiss me."

She planted a quick and deep one on his lips. "I can't play with you now. I have a girlfriend crisis."

"Play with me later?"

"Absolutely. I better make sure they're okay."

"Sure," he said. And when she turned to go, he gave her a smack on the butt and she took off down the walk. She turned back to him, smiling. Then she hurried over to Andy's.

By the time Gerri got there, Andy was at the door in her pajamas, looking where Sonja was pointing. The three of them trudged down the block—Sonja in her running gear, Gerri in her flannel robe that had been rejected by Phil years ago, Andy in pink-and-yellow-striped pajamas and slippers, Bob's truck still parked in her driveway. As they approached, they passed a couple of guys carrying the TV. The women slipped into the house.

BJ was in the kitchen, standing at the counter, looking over a list of things to do. "Hey," Sonja said, surprising her. BJ turned, and when she saw them, tears came to her eyes.

"There's a woman," BJ said. "Nowhere to go. A couple of little kids. I don't know her story, so you don't, okay?"

"Okay," they said in unison.

"If I could do something quickly, she could have the house instead of some shelter..."

"But the shelters in Marin are so good!" Sonja objected.

"Sonja," BJ said, grabbing her hand. "Honey, she's not in Marin County. I don't know where she is, but I guarantee she's scared to death. Honest to God, I don't know anything about her. I don't know if she's on the run, if she's just getting out of prison. I don't know anything except it's down to a shelter or this house. So I can stay at my brother's for a while. I'll put my stuff in his garage and—" She stopped when a man came into the kitchen. "Oh, Tony," she said. "These are my friends, my neighbors—Gerri, Sonja, Andy. This is my brother Tony. My other two brothers are also helping me move."

"I'm going to take apart the bed," Tony said after giving the women a brief and serious nod. Then he turned and disappeared.

"I'll stay with Brian—he's the closest to Mill Valley. He has the business. But I'll try not to impose on him for too long. I know how bad that can turn. I'll be looking for my next job, my next town."

"I'll get right on that," Gerri said. "I'll see what I can find for you—maybe not too far away. There are some good little towns up the coast. I'll vouch for you, give you a recommendation for a job and a lease. Where are the kids?"

"At Brian's. When I heard about this yesterday, I took them over there and spent the night packing. Look, I'm sorry. I didn't mean to do it like this. I had a fantasy about us having a bottle of wine on your deck, Gerri, talking about the move, that kind of thing. Saying a proper goodbye. You guys…" She hiccupped and a tear spilled over. "You girls," she corrected. "Man, I never saw it coming. You were so good for me. In such a totally bizarre way!"

"You can live with me!" Sonja said. "Really! I have room! You can keep your job with your brother and stay in the neighborhood."

BJ took Sonja's hands and looked into her eyes. "Listen to me. I can't. I can't be on charity. I have to earn my way, take care of my family. It's important, Sonja. It's about building some self-esteem, letting my kids see me working hard and doing it the right way—on my own. They'll remember that. I appreciate your offer, but really, it would be more for you than for me. If I want free board, I can get that from any one of my brothers. I'm not going to let our friendship go that way. You have enough work to do, getting your life back."

"But—"

"You know I'm right," BJ said. "You know it. I'll be nearby for a while. I'll drive over and run with you. Until I have to—"

"We'll work on this," Andy said. "We'll find you

something good, something safe. Hopefully not too far away."

"I'm sorry," BJ said again. "I didn't mean for it to go like this. But it's important. I remember when I was the one with nowhere to go, scared to death."

The four friends stood there in silence for a second, then Gerri reached for BJ's hand and Sonja's. Sonja took Andy's, Andy took BJ's other hand. The four of them stood there holding hands in a small circle.

"I'm going to go home and get dressed," Gerri said. "Then I'm coming over here to help you pack and clean the place up."

"What about work?"

"I'll go in late, or not at all. Some things have to be done and done right."

"Me, too," Andy said. "I'll get dressed and be right back."

"I don't have to dress," Sonja said. "I'll get started right now."

BJ had been gone one week. It was only another week until the block party and she promised she'd come back for one last hurrah. Gerri met Andy in her open garage at 10:00 a.m. Sonja was just leaving her house, carrying a large platter covered with plastic wrap. She juggled the platter to lock up, then crossed the street to meet her friends.

"Whatcha got there?" Andy asked.

"Muffins. Chocolate chip muffins," she said. "I figured we could use all the ammunition we could get."

Andy ran a hand along Sonja's shiny mahogany hair. "Now, try not to say too much," she advised Sonja. "Try not to swear."

"I'm not a child, you know. Well, I mean, I am in a way—I have to go all the way back to thirteen years old and start growing up all over again, but even a thirteen-year-old can manage not to swear."

Gerri lifted the wrap and inhaled. "And apparently a thirteen-year-old can really bake up a storm."

"You want to follow us to Connie's?" Andy asked Gerri.

"Yes, and I'll go on to work from there. All set?"

"All set," Andy said, taking a deep breath.

"Now remember—no expectations. It's a shot in the dark."

"Gotcha."

"And I have some other ideas for BJ, so this isn't the only possibility," Andy said.

"Gotcha. Let's just do it," Gerri replied.

Less than fifteen minutes later, the three women were knocking on the front door of Connie's massive house. Sonja carried the muffins, Gerri held her briefcase. Connie opened the door with a bright smile. "Well, isn't this nice," she said. "I put coffee and some cups on the patio table, if that's all right."

"It's very nice of you, Connie," Andy said. "Please meet my best friends, Sonja and Gerri."

The women all shook hands, greeted each other. "I can't wait to hear about your special project, Andy."

"You're going to think we're crazy—but I'm the only one who's crazy," Sonja said. Andy glared at her and Sonja continued. "They asked me to try not to say too much, and not to swear," Sonja explained. "I made these," she said, presenting the platter.

"Well, now," Connie said. "Don't you worry. I know how it is—sometimes those little words just slip out. If you have to swear, I promise not to blush if you swear with passion!"

Sonja grinned and flashed her eyes at Andy. "I *like* her!"

"Come on." Connie laughed. "Let's get some coffee to go with these muffins."

As Connie led the way through the house, Sonja looked around and muttered, "Holy shit." Andy elbowed her while Connie looked over her shoulder and laughed.

When they got to the patio, Connie put Sonja's platter on the table. "Go ahead and pour the coffee. I'll be right back."

As they took seats around the table, Sonja saw the guesthouse. "There it is!" she exclaimed.

"Now listen. This is a very big thing we're suggesting. This is their home! Try to be a little—"

"Patient, I know," Sonja said. "I *know!*"

Gerri just shook her head. Years of experience had rendered her fearless when it came to asking for things—fund-raising was always a huge aspect of any public servant's way of life. Tax dollars just never got them up to speed.

Connie brought small plates and napkins to the patio. "Connie, do you ever get just plain intimidated by this house?" Sonja asked her.

"Not anymore." Connie laughed. "As hard as we had to work to get this place presentable, I feel like it's my blood, sweat and tears in here." She passed the plates and sat down, lifting her coffee cup. "We don't need this kind of room, of course. But we have four grown, married children and nine grandchildren right in the area. We're a formidable crowd when we're all together. Plus, I have Bob and two married sisters with families and Frank has a large extended family. Everyone visits. We're not likely to let this monster slip out of our family—I can't think of a better gathering place. When it's just Frank and I we kind of live in the master bedroom. We fix small, lazy dinners, take them on trays to the bedroom and watch TV. The house isn't for us," she said. "It's for everyone around us."

"Connie, I'd like to tell you something," Andy said. "Before this special project we'd like to share with you even came to mind, I asked Bob if he'd consider moving in with me sometime in the future. He said, whenever I was ready, he was ready. He also said he wouldn't have any trouble looking after your property—after all, I live so close."

"Well, this is getting serious," Connie said.

"Oh, Connie, it started serious. I'm so crazy about Bob, you just can't imagine. He's the best thing that ever happened to me. I wish I'd found him ten years ago. And he's been so good for Noel."

"Bob has a lot of experience with youngsters. He has a ton of nieces and nephews."

"So," Gerri said, directing the conversation where it needed to go. "Andy says you and your husband are very involved in community service."

"Partly true. Usually Frank gets involved, then can't keep up and I step in."

"Have any local pet projects of your own?" Gerri asked.

"I'm afraid not in Marin County," she said, plucking a muffin off the platter and transferring it to her plate. "In Marin I concentrate on the arts, in a small way. I support the library system and a couple of children's literacy programs. But Marin is rich in many ways—

there's lots of endowment money here. I find myself more often in the city where the needs are more immediate. Grittier. Primarily AIDS research, babies born addicted to drugs and the Gospel Mission. I've always thought, you've probably just about reached bottom if you're eating and sleeping at the mission. They need help constantly. And there's a food bank…"

"Any women's work?"

"Women's work?" she asked, biting her muffin. "The rape crisis center gets some money and I sit on the board, but I couldn't cut it as a counselor. I'm afraid that's about it—I keep thinking about the kids."

"Gerri's a counselor," Andy said. "Child Protective Services. And her husband is Phil Gilbert—running for D.A. in San Francisco."

"That's your husband?" Connie asked. "Congratulations. The press likes him."

"Today," Gerri said, laughing. "Listen—this is a wild card, Connie. We have a neighbor who's been the victim of domestic abuse and is having a hard time getting on her feet. She's a good woman with a couple of nice kids. Her past is very provocative. No, it's worse than that—it's downright shocking. But as we've gotten to know her, the three of us agree she's a stellar woman, a devoted mother, a loyal friend. Right now she's basically homeless. Some nameless philanthropist who tries to help women coming out of terrible ordeals like hers let her use a rental property for a year. That's how we got to know her. But that year is up and there's another woman with children who needs a hand and our friend BJ has to move on. She's staying with her brother while she looks for her next job, her next home."

"Really? Someone just gave her a house?" Connie said.

"It's a transition home, a stepping-stone," Gerri said. "I hope someday I get to meet this person."

"She was okay with that, but when I offered to have her move in with me, rent-free, she wouldn't do it," Sonja blurted. "She said she has to build self-esteem, support herself and her kids, that they'd remember that."

"She's right about that," Connie said. "Kids. They won't listen to a word you say, but they'll end up acting like you acted while they were growing up. As a result I have two sons who are buying dilapidated real estate and working themselves to death to fix everything up. You'd think they'd have looked at our years of labor on this house, our bitter fights over what to do and how to do it, and choose another path."

"Well, BJ is adamant," Gerri said. "She doesn't want any more charity. She has a decent job with her brother, who's an electrician with a small company in Mill Valley, but there's no way she can afford to rent here. I've been looking for another town somewhere around here where she can afford the rent and get a job."

"Do you need a donation?" Connie asked.

There was silence for a moment. Gerri knew there was no point dragging things out. "No, Connie—it's something much more personal. We wondered if you'd consider offering her a position as your property care-taker, with perhaps a break on the rental price of your guesthouse." She shrugged. "Andy's got her talons in Bob—she's going to snatch him away from you. I understand that wouldn't leave you without help, and I guess you've got lots of other family who could step in if you needed someone to look after the place—but that little house could take on BJ and her two kids for a good, long time. She could do it and keep her job with her brother—she could make sure your big house is tip-top, do whatever your caretaker routinely does. Any number of chores could be accomplished in the mornings, after work and school, on weekends. She could probably handle some housekeeping or errands or outside work, whatever is necessary. She's young—thirty-five—energetic and tenderhearted. A real find. She's doing a good job of turning her life around."

There was a long silence. "My," Connie said, clearly surprised, probably overwhelmed.

Gerri reached into her briefcase and withdrew a large envelope. "Don't look at this until we leave, please. I printed out some newspaper articles and miscellaneous information about her that you'll have to take into consideration. Her history is so shocking, we've all taken an oath not to share it—for the kids, of course. The kids should be free to have a normal life if they can. One thing that's not in there that I'd like to point out—she has no ties to dangerous or felonious persons from her past. She comes from a solid, stable family, the only girl with three older brothers, all decent, law-abiding, hardworking and very supportive of her."

"Her parents can't help her?"

Gerri shook her head. "She can't live in the same area as her abuser's family and friends. I think you'll understand when you graze through this stuff. One brother is here, the one with the business that employs her. The other two are still back in Fresno, but they come here often, whenever she needs a hand. It's very important to her to earn her own way. She even has a fantasy that one day, when the kids are older, she'll finish her education. Go to college."

"How old are the kids?"

"A nine-year-old daughter, an eleven-year-old son."

"But this is crazy. I shouldn't consider something this bold without talking to Bob. Bob does know this woman, right?" Connie asked.

"He's met BJ," Andy said. "But he doesn't know anything about her history. I honored the promise to keep it all quiet. But, Connie, Bob's the last person I'd hesitate to tell. I've never known anyone like him when it comes to understanding and acceptance."

"We shouldn't say anything more, except that there are also references in this packet, people you can call to discuss her. And we vouch for her. We'd be willing to help if she'd take our help and we realize this is a real long shot. I mean, that guesthouse isn't even empty yet!"

"Well, it is most nights," Connie said with a sly smile, peering at Andy. "That makes me very happy, by the way. But are you two really ready to live together so soon?"

"Didn't he tell you? He didn't say it was a secret, so I guess it's okay. He and Wendy have divorced now. He's so thoughtful—he didn't want me to feel he had any unfinished business. I swear, I didn't ask him to do that."

Connie's mouth hung open slightly. She filled it with a bite of muffin. After she chewed and swallowed she spoke again. "I've been asking him for ten years if he was ever going to take care of that!"

"I guess he didn't think it mattered. It was a complete surprise to me. But, he promised her they'd always be good friends. Isn't that just so *Bob*?"

Connie nodded. "It's so nice to have someone appreciate him as much as I do."

"Well," Gerri said, "I have to get to work. Listen, if you'd like a chance to meet BJ before you seriously consider this proposition, we're having a neighborhood party next weekend and she promised to come back for it. She doesn't know anything about this idea. We didn't run it by her." Gerri stood.

"Wait a minute? What about all these muffins?" Connie said.

"They freeze," Gerri said with a smile. "And hopefully, you'll have us back for coffee when we don't have such an alarming agenda." She put her hand out. "It was a real pleasure to meet you, Connie. Thanks for letting us knock you off your feet. No matter what comes of this, you're a very good sport to even listen to us."

A little reluctantly, Andy and Sonja also stood. Sonja reached across the table and tapped the envelope. "There's something that isn't in all those reports and articles. She saved my life twice. And she jogs with me every morning because it's good for me. She doesn't need me to go for a run—she's been doing it for years. She drags me along because it's good for *me*. She's one of the best people in the world."

"I'll remember that," Connie said, smiling.

"Listen, we understand it's just not possible to ask you to consider anything more personal," Andy said. "No matter what you decide, I'm going to try to take Bob off your hands, and I can't wait to meet the rest of the family. I just hope you understand when it comes to a good friend, we have to step outside boundaries sometimes, take a risk, ask the unaskable." She shrugged. "It's just what you have to do if you believe in someone."

Connie smiled gently. "I understand. Even if I can't invite your friend to my home, I might think of something."

"We're up a creek," Andy said. "She's so proud. But—I guess that's what got her through the worst of it."

"Aren't we all so lucky?" Connie said. "When you think about it? I mean, everyone has problems, but really we've all ended up being so lucky."

"Well," Sonja said, "square-footage-wise, I think you win."

The block party came together nicely, even though it had depended almost entirely on Gerri and Andy making phone calls. The neighbors did all the work, but at least it was their usual work, divided equitably. There was an enormous amount of food, activities were planned out, prizes for winners were displayed and the neighborhood children were kept busy and happy.

There was one new feature this year. A booth under a huge banner—Phil Gilbert for San Francisco County District Attorney. Although it was another county, many residents of Mill Valley commuted to San Francisco to work and word about him could spread. Plus, it was one of their own moving up in the world. Phil spent much of the day accepting congratulations and taking campaign donations from people he'd known for years.

BJ and her kids showed up, ate, played, ran a few races, hung out with Sonja, Andy and Bob most of the time. George—who really didn't enjoy gatherings with a lot of people—came around and stayed much longer than anyone expected. Sonja didn't seem in any way uncomfortable with him there. In fact, he had his arm casually draped over her shoulders or around her waist quite often. Noel attended, though he hadn't brought his good friends, apparently not quite ready for that. But he was very chummy with Bob. They ran an egg relay together and although they did miserably, they seemed to find it hilarious.

It was getting a little late in the afternoon, close to five, when Phil found Gerri and pulled her against him. "Sneaky," he said. "You found a way to keep me from drinking too much at the block party. Turn it into a campaign rally."

"I had nothing to do with that," she insisted. "It was them. God, I already hate them, your committee. They're so damned *bossy*."

"I know." He laughed. "But I don't have anyone better in mind and I guess they get the job done. After all, they got Clay elected and re-elected I don't know how many times. And we both know…what we know," he said.

"Are you going to put on the Velcro suit and let them throw you against the dartboard?" she asked, grinning. "You know that's my favorite part of the whole party."

"I was hoping to skip that this year. Since I'm not half-tanked and stupid."

"Aww. Would you do it for me? Because I really love that."

"You have a mean streak."

"I know, but I've tempered it a lot lately and now it's just for fun."

"We'll see," he said, because in point of fact, he'd let them hurl him off the Golden Gate Bridge if it made her laugh, tease and take her clothes off. He squeezed her and kissed her neck.

"I'm not sure this is normal," she said to him. "We're

having sex like teenagers. I honestly don't remember anything like this when we were much, much younger. When we were much less flabby and creaky."

He laughed. "It may not look as pretty as it used to, but it sure works for me."

"Look," she said, stiffening enough to pull away slightly.

Across the park, a big gold SUV had pulled up and double-parked. Connie and a man Gerri assumed was her husband walked into the park. Andy and Bob spied them and greeted them.

Phil and Gerri watched while they seemed to chat awhile. Andy ran off and returned with BJ and again there was chatting. Then Connie reached for BJ's hand. She held it while she talked to her.

"It's happening," Gerri whispered. "What I told you about. Connie's guesthouse."

"Don't get your hopes up," Phil cautioned, pulling her against his side.

But then BJ put two fingers in her mouth and let out a powerful whistle that brought her two children instantly to her side. BJ made introductions. Connie bent slightly to smile into their faces and say hello. Then they all went to the double-parked SUV—BJ and her kids, Andy and Bob.

"Oh, God," Gerri said. "It's really happening."

"Stay calm," Phil said. "Nothing has happened yet."

"But Connie is taking them to her house, to see it, to talk about it. If she'd decided against it, she wouldn't come to meet her, chat with her and then leave to think about it some more."

"There will still be negotiating," Phil reminded her.

"It might not be right for them. I mean, it could be, but…"

"No! Andy and Bob will help make this happen. Oh, by the way, I said I'd give any help that BJ would accept. If that means subsidizing rent, I'm committed." She turned to look into his eyes. "I feel strongly about that."

"That's okay," he said. "If we can beat this dickhead Carter, there will be a raise involved."

She laughed. "And I already spent it. That must make you very happy with me."

"You spent it on keeping our guesthouse. I don't know how long I can live with the idea of that little old lady who owns the place—who probably has a nanny cam or something in there—figuring out we have it just for sex. It's kind of kinky, don't you think? We could get a sailboat and hardly ever sail."

"I'd be willing to talk about that. After the election."

"The election is two years away!"

Gerri laughed wickedly.

"Listen, I have to come clean about something."

"Oh, Jesus!" she gasped. "What have you done *now?*"

"I called Elizabeth," he said. "I wanted to get to her before those political mongrels feasted on her. And she told me. How'd you find her?"

Gerri smiled and said nothing.

"You took her to lunch. You interviewed her?" he asked.

She nodded and smiled.

"You're scary," he said. "Whatever that was about, the affair, I'm cured."

"Good, because I'm on the alert now. And I'm watching. By the way, how did *you* find her?"

"I have detectives." He shrugged. "I have to find old employees all the time—to ask about cold-case files we're pursuing. It wasn't a big deal."

"So," Gerri said, "she told you everything?"

"I don't know. How long was your lunch?"

"Two hours."

"Then she didn't tell me everything—our conversation was ten minutes, tops. All she said was she was glad to know we'd worked out whatever kinks had us messed up and to tell you hello."

"I liked her," Gerri said. "You're not allowed to talk to her anymore…but I liked her. At least you have good taste. I thought I was going to meet some stupid bimbo in a nice package with no brains, no substance. That woman—she was pretty high quality." She gave him a kiss. "I was actually impressed."

"I love you, Geraldine. You're a pain in the ass, but you're a damn sexy pain in the ass. It turned out I couldn't settle for less. It turned out I couldn't settle at all. It has to be you."

"Lucky for you, it's going to be me. Only me. From now on."

"I can live with that," he said. "You're all I ever wanted."

"Phil," she said, her voice husky and serious, "you're the only man I've ever loved. I'm not about to give you up."

* * * * *

acknowledgments

This novel was a great joy and enormous fun to write. I wanted to look closely at extraordinary women facing ordinary problems, the kind that, if we haven't faced them ourselves, our sisters or neighbors or best friends have. I'm never really sure how things are going to work out until I've written about them. To that end, I had a lot of early readers. I asked them all, how can I make this story richer? More real? Closer to the heart?

And my early readers, my friends and experts and advisors, gave me wealth. My deepest gratitude for help in shaping this story goes to:

Kate Bandy, PhD, Sharon Lampert, WHMP, Beki Keene, Jamie Prosser, Denise Nicholl, Lori Sokovan and Dee Mazzanti. Thanks also to Nancy Berland and Sarah Burningham for your valuable insights.

Special thanks to my agent, Liza Dawson, to Harlequin's wonderful Margaret Marbury and my amazing editor, Nicole Brebner—your support and encouragement means everything to me.

And to my friend and colleague Kristan Higgins—
your instincts and brilliant assistance worked miracles
on the final draft. Thank you!

Questions for Discussion

1. The four friends in this book are four women juggling the responsibilities facing many women today—family, friends, careers—while trying to maintain their own identities. Who do you most identify with and why?

2. On the surface, Gerri has it all, yet something was missing in her marriage that she didn't want to or wasn't able to address. How difficult is it for men and women to have honest discussions about their sex lives and what they need to make them happy?

3. Does the fact that Phil's affair took place in the past lessen the impact on Gerri? Do you think she would have forgiven Phil if the affair was current?

4. Would you be able to forgive your spouse for an infidelity? Do the circumstances matter, or is cheating always unforgivable?

5. Is Gerri's reaction to Jessie's drunken situation reasonable? Does she overreact? Should she have been even more concerned, and perhaps called the police or taken her to the emergency room?

6. Are you able to have open conversations with your children about sex and the risks involved, or are you uncomfortable and just hope for the best?

7. Andy has a difficult situation to manage with her son being gay and his father rejecting him. How would you handle such a challenge?

8. Does Gerri have the right to meet Phil's mistress? Would you do it?

9. Does the support of their friends make the difference for these women in the choices they eventually make? Does it help you to know that other women are facing challenges in their lives and marriages and to see that even *perfect* marriages have flaws?

10. Are you able to discuss your sexual health with your doctor? Would it have made a difference to Gerri's marriage if she'd been able to have that conversation when her menopause symptoms first started?

11. Which one of the four friends would you want as your best friend?

Limited time offer!

$1.⁰⁰ OFF

#1 *New York Times* Bestselling Author

ROBYN CARR

Starting over is never easy, but in Thunder Point, where newcomers are welcome and friends become family, it's possible to find yourself again.

$8.99 U.S. / $9.99 CAN.

Available June 30, 2015, wherever books are sold!

MIRA®

$1.⁰⁰ OFF the purchase price of A NEW HOPE by Robyn Carr

Offer valid from June 30, 2015, to July 28, 2015. Redeemable at participating retail outlets. Limit one coupon per purchase. Valid in the U.S.A. and Canada only.

52612565

5 65373 00076 2 (8100)0 12047

MRC1787CPN

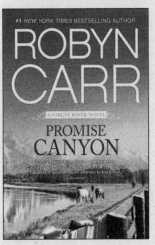

Get 2 Free Books,
Plus 2 Free Gifts –
just for trying the _Reader Service!_

ROM15CT

ROBYN CARR

32897	DEEP IN THE VALLEY	___ $7.99 U.S.	___ $9.99 CAN.
31772	ONE WISH	___ $8.99 U.S.	___ $9.99 CAN.
31733	MOONLIGHT ROAD	___ $7.99 U.S.	___ $8.99 CAN.
31728	A SUMMER IN SONOMA	___ $7.99 U.S.	___ $8.99 CAN.
31724	THE HOUSE ON OLIVE STREET	___ $7.99 U.S.	___ $8.99 CAN.
31702	ANGEL'S PEAK	___ $7.99 U.S.	___ $8.99 CAN.
31697	FORBIDDEN FALLS	___ $7.99 U.S.	___ $8.99 CAN.
31664	'TIS THE SEASON	___ $7.99 U.S.	___ $8.99 CAN.
31644	THE HOMECOMING	___ $7.99 U.S.	___ $8.99 CAN.
31620	THE PROMISE	___ $7.99 U.S.	___ $8.99 CAN.
31599	THE CHANCE	___ $7.99 U.S.	___ $8.99 CAN.
31590	PARADISE VALLEY	___ $7.99 U.S.	___ $8.99 CAN.
31582	TEMPTATION RIDGE	___ $7.99 U.S.	___ $8.99 CAN.
31571	SECOND CHANCE PASS	___ $7.99 U.S.	___ $8.99 CAN.
31513	A VIRGIN RIVER CHRISTMAS	___ $7.99 U.S.	___ $8.99 CAN.
31459	THE HERO	___ $7.99 U.S.	___ $8.99 CAN.
31452	THE NEWCOMER	___ $7.99 U.S.	___ $9.99 CAN.
31447	THE WANDERER	___ $7.99 U.S.	___ $9.99 CAN.
31428	WHISPERING ROCK	___ $7.99 U.S.	___ $9.99 CAN.
31419	SHELTER MOUNTAIN	___ $7.99 U.S.	___ $9.99 CAN.
31415	VIRGIN RIVER	___ $7.99 U.S.	___ $9.99 CAN.
31385	MY KIND OF CHRISTMAS	___ $7.99 U.S.	___ $9.99 CAN.
31317	SUNRISE POINT	___ $7.99 U.S.	___ $9.99 CAN.
31310	REDWOOD BEND	___ $7.99 U.S.	___ $9.99 CAN.
31300	HIDDEN SUMMIT	___ $7.99 U.S.	___ $9.99 CAN.

(limited quantities available)

TOTAL AMOUNT	$ _____
POSTAGE & HANDLING	$ _____
($1.00 for 1 book, 50¢ for each additional)	
APPLICABLE TAXES*	$ _____
TOTAL PAYABLE	$ _____

(check or money order—please do not send cash)

To order, complete this form and send it, along with a check or money order for the total above, payable to MIRA Books, to: **In the U.S.:** 3010 Walden Avenue, P.O. Box 9077, Buffalo, NY 14269-9077; **In Canada:** P.O. Box 636, Fort Erie, Ontario, L2A 5X3.

Name: _____
Address: _____ City: _____
State/Prov.: _____ Zip/Postal Code: _____
Account Number (if applicable): _____

075 CSAS

*New York residents remit applicable sales taxes.
*Canadian residents remit applicable GST and provincial taxes.

MIRA®

www.MIRABooks.com

MRC0515BL